Praise for
## *Kings, Queens, and In-Betweens*

A Winter/Spring 2019 Indies Introduce selection
A 2020 ALA Rainbow Book List selection
A Summer 2019 Top Ten Kids' Indie Next List Pick

"Poignant and important." —*Refinery29*

★ "A story filled with glitter, feather boas, lip-syncing and dancing, where gender identity is flexible and performance is the embodiment of joy." —*BookPage*, starred review

"A bright and sparkly celebration of love and self-acceptance."
—*Kirkus Reviews*

"[A] successful presentation of the highs, lows, and midways of a teen finding her place in queer culture." —*SLJ*

"Satisfying . . . Who doesn't need a glamorous drag queen fairy godmother?" —*Publishers Weekly*

Also by Tanya Boteju

*Bruised*

# KINGS, QUEENS, AND IN-BETWEENS

## TANYA BOTEJU

SIMON & SCHUSTER BFYR

NEW YORK LONDON TORONTO SYDNEY NEW DELHI

SIMON & SCHUSTER BFYR

An imprint of Simon & Schuster Children's Publishing Division
1230 Avenue of the Americas, New York, New York 10020

Text © 2019 by Tanya Boteju
Cover illustration © 2019 by Marina Esmeraldo
Cover design by Sarah Creech © 2019 by Simon & Schuster, Inc.
SIMON & SCHUSTER BOOKS FOR YOUNG READERS
and related marks are trademarks of Simon & Schuster, Inc.
For information about special discounts for bulk purchases, please contact Simon & Schuster Special Sales at 1-866-506-1949 or business@simonandschuster.com.
The Simon & Schuster Speakers Bureau can bring authors to your live event. For more information or to book an event, contact the Simon & Schuster Speakers Bureau at 1-866-248-3049 or visit our website at www.simonspeakers.com.
Also available in a hardcover edition
Interior design by Tom Daly
The text for this book was set in Adobe Caslon Pro.
Manufactured in the United States of America
First SIMON & SCHUSTER BFYR paperback edition February 2021
2  4  6  8  10  9  7  5  3  1
The Library of Congress has cataloged the hardcover edition as follows:
Names: Boteju, Tanya, author.
Title: Kings, queens, and in-betweens / Tanya Boteju.
Description: First Simon Pulse hardcover edition. | New York : Simon Pulse, 2019. |
Summary: After a bewildering encounter at her small town's annual summer festival, seventeen-year-old biracial, queer Nima plunges into the world of drag, where she has the chance to explore questions of identity, acceptance, self-expression, and love.
Identifiers: LCCN 2018031034 | ISBN 9781534430655 (hardcover)
Subjects: | CYAC: Male impersonators—Fiction. | Lesbians—Fiction. | Self-acceptance—Fiction. | Racially mixed people—Fiction.
Classification: LCC PZ7.1.B6755 Ki 2019 | DDC [Fic]—dc23
LC record available at https://lccn.loc.gov/2018031034
ISBN 9781534430662 (pbk)
ISBN 9781534430679 (ebook)

*To all those young people who live beyond the so-called "norm":*
*you're beautiful and magical and perfect.*
*This book is for you.*

WITHDRAWN

# CHAPTER 1

The first time Ginny Woodland spoke to me, I vomited all over her Reeboks.

At the time, I was a haphazard assortment of fourteen-year-old body parts—frizzy black hair sprouting from an unruly ponytail, bug eyes, wide nose, ashy dark skin, practically inverted breasts, and a variety of other genetic hilarities.

She, on the other hand, was a year older, and her body parts were decidedly better suited to one another. Fair skin, freckles, a cascade of fiery red hair—from the neck up alone she was a Botticelli to my Picasso.

Her artistic head bobbed along beside me now—even more beautiful three years later. She'd just finished her shift at Old Stuff, the thrift store where she worked part-time, and I'd biked over to meet her and walk her home—part of a petrifying plan I was no longer sure I could carry out.

Sneaking sideways glances at her as we walked, I could tell she was in a good mood. She was humming some tune I didn't know and tapping a pebble forward with her toe each step she took. I wished I was as at ease as she seemed. But as my bike rattled along beside me, my heart rattled even more inside my chest. I was trying to generate some magical source of courage to say what I came here to say, but all I seemed able to do was plod along beside her like a dolt, listening to her hum.

Though we'd known each other for three years, somehow that initial nausea had never fully disappeared, even though our relationship had managed to move past that early, revolting debacle.

When I'd first laid eyes on her in the ninth grade, Ginny had been playing basketball in the schoolyard, her lean arms and legs accentuated by a sporty top and knee-high socks, and my heart just about leaped out of my mouth.

Up to that point, my heart hadn't experienced much in the way of leaping, or thumping, or any similar exertions. Life had been crammed with more "existing" and "observing" than other, action-related verbs. In fact, that September, my best friend Charles and I had made a habit of sitting at the same table at lunch in the schoolyard, under a forlorn cottonwood tree, watching and waiting. We didn't mind the tree's patchy shade or despairing limbs—the heart-shaped leaves abandoning their branches and floating down around us felt like a shield against the pandemonium of more boisterous teenagers nearby.

Our tree also provided a great vantage point from which we could safely observe all the high school "flora and fauna," as Charles called the school's cliques. He'd fabricate scientific-sounding categorizations for them while I'd invent extended metaphors—two nerdy kids playing a lunchtime game to distract us from the fact that our only friends were heart-shaped leaves.

"Ah look, Nima, there's the *dividas et conquer-ass*," Charles would say, pointing to one of the popular kids in grade eleven who swept past the courts with a trio of minions tailing him. Charles's full lips would twist into grotesque shapes as he used an unidentifiable accent. "These trees are known to grow in tight clumps for protection, but will easily turn upon one another if forced to fight for the sun, scraping their way past each other's tough bark and branches and displacing their own flowering blossoms in the process." He'd curl his fingers into claws and force them upon one another in a simulated attack, his eyes going cross-eyed.

"Notice," I'd add, "one member has separated from the group—a single fallen petal from a tree of deceivingly delicate blossoms. What fate will follow for our forgotten friend? Will the damp ground seep into her fine features? Or will some romantic soul pass by, pluck her off the pavement, and savor her forever?"

Admittedly, I could get carried away. When I did, Charles would throw a Froot Loop at me—he always had Froot Loops in his lunch, sometimes *for* his lunch—and we'd dissolve into giggles.

This was less exciting than some high school experiences, I suppose.

However, it was from the sparse shade of our cottonwood tree that Ginny Woodland—with her athletic body and radiant smile—took hold of my heart and sent it spiraling into a whole host of action verbs.

I'd had crushes on girls before. I'd realized in sixth grade that girls did something to my body and brain that boys never seemed to when Cassidy Grims dared a bunch of us to touch the tips of our tongues with one another's. My tongue touched the tips of three girl tongues and four boy tongues that day, and let's just say I had zero interest in touching any more boy tongues, but the flutter in my heart and the warm surge in other parts of my body made me want a lot more girl touching of all kinds.

Unfortunately, no more touching had taken place by the time ninth grade rolled around, but those warm and fluttery feelings perked up considerably when I saw Ginny. It didn't even matter that she seemed, as I discovered, to prefer boy tongues.

But after barfing on her shoes, those feelings remained concealed, I remained an unfortunate assembly of features, and Ginny continued to be a distant desire.

Today I'd finally decided to bridge the gap.

In my mind, it'd been long enough since the Barf that I'd replenished whatever minor amount of self-respect I had in order to finally divulge my everlasting love for her. On top of that, she'd be graduating and leaving behind our small West Coast town for a university at the other end of the country when the summer ended. It had felt like a now-or-never situation.

But here, in the late afternoon light and with her smiling and laughing beside me, too many obstacles were presenting themselves.

For one, I'd apparently been rendered speechless.

As preparation, I'd envisioned the love scenes I read during my brief romance novel phase and practiced the conversation in my head over and over again.

*Ginny, it's time you knew: I've loved you for three years. Make me the happiest girl in the world?*

*Ginny, I know you haven't shown any interest in dating girls, but gender is a construct. Be my girlfriend?*

*Ginny, before you leave for university, you need to know I loved you even before I barfed on your shoes.*

*Ginny, you're perfect. I love you.*

Those all seemed preposterous now. How was it that I had all the words in the world to refashion life into metaphors, but still couldn't form a damn sentence around this girl?

Another obstacle was her current attire. It was June, and warm (and getting hotter by the second), so Ginny wore a spaghetti-strap tank top, revealing her adorable freckly shoulders. I swear, those freckles would be the death of me. They'd been part of my downfall from the beginning.

That woeful, pukey day in ninth grade, I'd been staring blissfully at them as she sat in front of me on the gymnasium bleachers. After watching her (in an innocent, non-stalkery way) play on the outdoor courts each lunch hour through-out September, I'd somehow convinced myself that attend-ing basketball tryouts would give me ample opportunity to win Ginny over with my wit and literary flair. If you ask me now to check my math on that particular equation, I might politely decline the request, but at the time, it all made per-fect sense in my pubescent brain.

So it was on a chilly fall day in October that I found my scrawny self in a group of mostly tenth-grade girls who looked like they had more justifiable reasons for being in that gym than I did.

I'd strategically situated myself just behind Ginny. Her hair soared from the top of her head in a high ponytail, the red, precisely trimmed tips reaching the nape of her neck. The light brown freckles that dotted her shoulders were perfectly visible because she was wearing an actual basketball jersey, not a cotton T-shirt that said SCREAMING WEENIES—NO MESSIN' AROUND! on the front and had a cartoon on the back of a serious-looking hot dog in a cowboy hat hollering and waving around a smaller hot dog like a gun.

This is what I was wearing, by the way.

I was busy counting each freckle on her right shoulder when Mrs. Nicholls, our PE teacher and coach, marched in bouncing a basketball and carrying a clipboard. Tossing the ball to one of the girls in the front row, she told us to call out our names one by one so she could write them down.

Just the sound of Ginny's voice on a normal day sent my

insides rolling, and at her enthusiastic "Ginny Woodland!" my stomach performed a full backflip. It was still trying to find its footing when my turn arrived, and my own name toppled from my mouth sounding like "Numatark" rather than "Nima Kumara-Clark," which is my actual name. A few girls snickered, but Ginny looked back at me, and the freckles on her cheeks lifted in a friendly smile. I almost threw up right then and there.

But "the Great Basketball Barf," as both Ginny and Charles so cleverly christened it later on, occurred about halfway through the tryouts, which were moving along fabulously.

And by fabulously, I mean I'd never been exposed to such torture in my life. One such agony occurred when Mrs. Nicholls forced each of us to shoot a free throw, the consequence of a missed shot resulting in a "suicide"—an inappropriately named procedure requiring you to run back and forth between each important line on the court.

Of course, I missed my free throw because, quite simply, I'd never shot one before. I hadn't even thought to practice or watch a couple of WNBA highlight reels. Let's face it—I was fourteen, crushing hard, and nowhere near clearheaded enough to think all this through. Was I the only one to miss my shot, resulting in a suicide? No. But was I the only one to shoot the ball over the backboard, hit the wall, and have it rebound into the back of Penny Dupuis's head?

Perhaps.

By the time each of us had our turn (of course, Ginny's shot

barely touched the net as it sailed precisely through the middle
of the hoop), most of us were already on the verge of throwing
up from the twelve suicides we'd run. So when Mrs. Nicholls
randomly placed us in pairs for our next activity/ordeal, and
Ginny got stuck with me, and she thrust out her hand to introduce herself and said, "Hey, my name is Ginny!" in the friendli-
est voice imaginable, I vomited all over her brand-spanking-new
Reeboks—flecks of ham sandwich from my lunch dappling
the white leather and laces along with much of the gym floor
around them.

Ginny stood frozen for what felt like thirty years, her
mouth agape and her eyes glued to her shoes. Bent over and
holding my stomach, I too shifted my eyes to her shoes, completely incapable of comprehending what I'd just done. The
gym remained silent. I could feel my eyes begin to water.

Mrs. Nicholls's whistle finally screeched across the quiet,
followed by, "Well, what're you all lookin' at? Somebody get a
mop, for Pete's sake!"

Despite the tight cramping in my stomach, I simply turned
and ran from the gym all the way home, determined never to
play basketball, talk to girls, or eat ham sandwiches ever again.

With a swift movement, Ginny punted the pebble in front of
me as we continued to walk.

"Kick it, Nima!"

The pebble tapped off the front wheel of my bike and
paused in front of me.

I gave Ginny a halfhearted laugh, but my body instantly tensed. Given my abysmal athletic abilities, even the smallest things that required coordination—like kicking this pebble, while walking, while holding my bike—gave me anxiety. But if I didn't play along, Ginny would think I was no fun. And I needed to prove to her that not only was I fun, but I was fun enough to spend the rest of her life with.

So, using my bike for stability, I focused hard on the pebble, performed an awkward shuffle-shuffle-step routine to negotiate the space between me and the pebble, and then tried to boot it as hard as I could.

Because not only was I fun, I was strong, too.

I guess I misjudged the amount of pressure I needed to hold on to my bike, though, because as my one leg kicked, the other leaned hard into my bike, and both bike and scrawny body began to tip dangerously over.

Ginny didn't miss a beat. Her hands shot out instantly and grabbed an arm and a bike handle, pulling us both back to a safe, standing position.

"Whoa! Close one," she said, an affectionate grin on her face.

More awkwardness followed when I couldn't find the words to address any of this mishap and just tittered uncomfortably.

The pebble, of course, remained in the exact same spot it had been, likely snickering at me from its cozy patch in the dirt. Ginny's grin also remained as she began to tell me a story from her workday—presumably to distract me from my utter failure as a pebble kicker.

That smile—though it just made me feel even worse now—had been a saving grace the day after my big barf. Ginny had approached me and Charles at our usual picnic table at recess. I'd conjured up images of brick walls and barbed wire to protect me from her impending ire, but to my amazement, her friendly grin greeted us and she'd simply asked how I was feeling. My mouth hadn't worked very well during our exchange, but I'd managed to stammer out an apology, and she'd managed to artfully ignore my general ineptitude at conversation.

Shockingly, I didn't make the basketball team, but I did become team manager. I think Mrs. Nicholls just felt sorry for me, but I had to take what I could get. I recorded stats and made sure water bottles remained full. I'd also rebound for Ginny at lunch sometimes whenever Charles had something science-y to catch up on, and she tried to teach me a few things about shooting and dribbling.

I kept waiting for her and her friends to play some prank on me or tell me how weird I looked in my hot dog T-shirt, but they never did either of those things. In fact, some of her friends would even say hi to us when they walked by our picnic table at lunch. They'd never sit with us, mind you, but we weren't entirely ignored either. Ginny seemed to have blown a cheerful, protective bubble around us, and we were grateful for it.

By the end of the season, I still couldn't dribble without bouncing the ball off my foot, nor could I seem to find the hoop when it was right in front of me, but Ginny Woodland and I had become friends. And despite my ongoing desire to kiss her and feel her hand in mine and call her my girlfriend, and her ongoing, unfortunate interest in boys, I saved all my emotional turmoil for Charles and told myself that friendship was better than nothing.

And that was the story I stuck to, for a while.

I blinked back the memories of barf and turbulence as I shuffled along beside Ginny now, my face still hot from my blunder. I focused hard on just moving one foot in front of the other, worried about tripping over myself again. But I was also willing myself forward, when all I really wanted to do was stop, get on my bike, and ride away from the impending exchange between us.

Ginny was chatting gleefully about one of her customers at Old Stuff—something about a retiree asking for "hipster pants"—and I quickly assessed the decision-making process that had led me to this moment in order to convince myself that my methodology was sound.

I'd done all the requisite research in the days leading up to my grand revelation.

First I'd asked my dad for his advice, since he'd somehow managed to nab my mother, who—and I'm not trying to be cruel—was definitely a lush bougainvillea to my dad's stout desert cactus. He had his charms, mind you—a strong chin, enormous but dexterous hands, soft curls that fell across his face. But to see him—looming, pale, slow—next to my mom, whose dark brown skin and compact frame seemed to be in constant, vibrant motion, startled one's sense of symmetry. So I thought he might have some insights for a skinny brown kid with her eyes on a perfect goddess.

The tricky part was this: my mom left us a year and a half ago, and we didn't talk much about her or her inexplicable departure. It was sensitive territory for both of us, but I'd figured if I could manage to ask about her, my dad could probably manage an answer, right?

I'd tried to keep it light as I made tea one morning last week and he read the newspaper at the kitchen table.

"So, Delford, tell me: How'd you manage to score Mom?"

He hadn't even looked up. "I got skills, that's how."

I hated when he tried to talk like a teenager. "Right. And which skills would those be?"

He snapped the paper to straighten out the creases and folded it closed. Leaning back and pushing his hair out of his face, he'd replied, "Mad skillz. And that's 'skillz' with a z."

I flared my nostrils at him and shook my head. "Cool . . . now, how about the truth?"

Placing a finger to his lips, he'd looked up as though the answer floated somewhere along the kitchen ceiling. Finally he said, "I have no idea. I still can't believe I *did* score her. That's the truth." He looked at me—a glint of wet in his eyes—then shrugged and went back to his paper.

*Okay, Nima,* I'd thought, *maybe not the smartest move.* Circling my arms around his neck from behind, I pecked his cheek and offered, "Well, you did, and she was lucky to have you."

He'd ruffled his paper in response.

Not much to go on there. Next I'd consulted Charles, who also turned out to be generally useless (his love life had remained a desolate wasteland throughout high school too).

He just launched into an indignant lecture, his eyes rolling behind the blue-tinted glasses he always wore: "Think carefully, Nima. Is it really worth the risk? Remember the pre-Ginny era? We were perfectly contented fourteen-year-olds until she walked into the picture!" He'd shoved his glasses up the bridge of his nose and crossed his bony arms.

His chagrin wasn't completely unreasonable. After all, he'd had to listen to three years' worth of woe over my perpetual, unreciprocated desire for Ginny. I guess it was also understandable, then, that his only advice when I asked him how I should finally display my love for her was "Don't."

Having exhausted my limited resources—Dad and Charles—I'd found myself lying on my bed last night, staring at my bookshelf and wondering why I couldn't just look like the typical, irresistible heroine, or why an enchanted fairy couldn't whisk me up in one of those magical makeover tornadoes. Then I found myself wishing my mom was there to give me advice, but that just plopped sadness on top of my anxiety over Ginny, so I'd turned to look at the photos taped above my desk instead.

Ginny and me with the basketball team. Ginny squishing

Charles into a selfie against his will. Ginny and me with straws up our noses.

I'd reminded myself that Ginny would be gone at the end of the summer, and if I didn't go through with this soon, I'd be left staring at old photos forever.

Now, sneaking another glance at her perfect face next to me, I wondered for the billionth time what Ginny saw when she looked at my face. When I saw her, I thought about whether her lips would feel soft or spongy against mine. I thought about how long I could stare into her clear green eyes without getting embarrassed and looking away. I thought about kissing each and every freckle on her face.

I couldn't imagine someone thinking any of those things about me. Whereas my features had been a befuddling mix as a fourteen-year-old, now they just seemed unremarkable. I had zero kissable freckles, plain brown eyes, and constantly chapped lips. People always seemed to think that having parents in different shades automatically made you exotic and beautiful. But I felt like my features might die from boredom.

I clicked my brakes in and out on my handlebars a few times. *Should she hit the brakes now, before careening into a cavernous heartache? Or does she shift into high gear and grind her way up the steep hill of romance?*

My jaw had grown so tight in the time we'd been walking, it felt like I'd need a crowbar to pry my mouth open. But her house was getting closer and closer, and somehow, the thought of making my declaration in her kitchen, or living room, or—God forbid—her bedroom, seemed infinitely more terrifying.

Staring hard into my handlebars and mustering up every ounce of daring I had in me—which was exactly half an ounce—I finally spit out, "Ginny, I consider you a good friend. You know that, right?"

"Yeah, silly, I know." She pushed my arm and I almost fell over my bike again—from the push mainly, but also because my feet felt like flippers.

"But do you also know that—"

She stopped walking and put her hand on my arm. I stopped too. "Nima. You know I love you, but I love you as a friend, and I don't want anything to get in the way of that. Okay?" She gave my arm a squeeze and then let go.

My eyes immediately found my shoes.

*She knew. All this time. And never said anything.*

*And I didn't even get to finish my sentence.*

My fingers, wrapped around both handlebars, gripped tighter and tighter until they hurt. Tears pricked, but I blinked them back. As I did, I willed a grin across my face and forced myself to meet her green eyes. "Oh, yeah, for sure. Keep it simple, right?" My voice echoed thinly between us.

The crack in my heart widened when her face settled into relief. "Exactly. Why ruin something as great as this?" She threw her arm around my shoulders and nattered on about my rebounding abilities.

I barely heard a word she said. I was too busy wishing

for the Giant Hand of God to squash me with its enormous thumb.

By the time we parted and I trudged up my patio steps, I'd thought about all the things I could have—*should have*—done differently before blurting out my feelings like an ass. Tell her a funny story. Reach for her hand. Gaze into her eyes. And I thought about the worst offense of all: *I couldn't even finish telling her I love her.*

As each missed opportunity emerged, my body slowly caved in on itself. I barely made it upstairs to my room before collapsing onto the bed, where I remained for hours torturously replaying each moment of my unfulfilled desire over the past three years in my head and wondering if I'd ever have those opportunities again. If I'd ever know what it was like to be wanted by someone else.

Sorrow was becoming an unrelenting companion. When my mom left, my heart experienced its first deep wound. Now that Ginny had stomped all over it, I guess you could say I was starting to develop some pretty solid calluses.

# CHAPTER 2

So here I was, finishing my junior year, my heart wizened by two major disappointments, and my brain further distressed by the fact that Ginny would be heading across the country for university at the end of the summer. Even though she'd drawn a clear boundary around our relationship, my emotions still wanted to color outside the lines. And pining away for her my senior year sounded about as fun as coloring with a box full of gray crayons.

Ginny, of course, instantly managed to move past my pathetic attempt to profess my love to her and acted as though nothing had changed as we finished out the last few days of the school year. I guess nothing really had changed for her. But having to sign Ginny's yearbook on the final day of school, a mere three days after my epic failure, just about broke my brain and I ended up writing, *Thanks for not making fun of my weenie T-shirt. Sorry about that whole barfing thing. Smiley face. Nima.*

When the final bell rang at noon, Charles and I left to get ice cream from the Fast Pick, our local convenience store.

Foggy with woe, I took a minute to register what was happening around me as we crossed the street in front of the school.

"Move, freak show!" A booming voice broke through my gloomy trance.

Charles's voice followed. "Nima, what are you doing?"

I blinked. Then shook my head and contemplated Charles, who was standing a couple of feet ahead of me, looking back. "What?"

"Hurry up!" he said, urgently waving his hand toward himself.

I realized I was in the middle of the crosswalk, paused for no good reason.

"ASSHOLE. MOVE."

I looked to my left. A massive blue truck bore down on me, grunting and puffing smoke out its backside. The driver was Gordon Grant. Talk about assholes.

I'd known Gordon longer than I'd known Charles. He and I had even been something like friends for a while during fourth and fifth grades, improbably bonded over produce. My dad used to take me to the community garden and teach me how to plant and grow vegetables. We'd hunker down in the soil and he'd show me how to dig little holes far enough apart for the roots to stretch, and where to sow which plants according to the sun's arc. Dad would bring me to the garden at least two or three times a week to help water or weed or check for pests.

As July drew our vegetables into full growth, one such pest we found—plucking young carrots and tearing leaves off the lettuce—was Gordon.

He was a year older than me but had already been kept back a grade by that point, so we'd been in the same class for a couple of years and it was clear why he'd been held back. He barely said a word or handed in any assignments, from what I could tell. He'd just slouch over his desk, pencil-drawing chaotic patterns across the laminate wood until our third-grade teacher, Mr. Chan, told him to "straighten up and start erasing."

The first time we'd come upon him in the garden, he'd been kneeling in the dirt, a bony ten-year-old with shaggy, dark brown hair and a surly forehead. A scattered pile of carrots and new potatoes lay beside him. When he heard us enter the squeaky garden gate, he grabbed whatever veggies he could and tried to hop the fence on the opposite side, but with handfuls of carrots and potatoes, this proved a challenge.

Sauntering over, his hands out in front of him, my dad asked with complete sincerity, "Want me to hold those while you climb over?"

After that, Dad, in his typical way, managed to coerce Gordon into helping to harvest, rather than attempting to steal from the veggie patch. Gordon didn't talk much at first, but it was easy to see he enjoyed the work—learning something useful, getting his hands dirty, tasting the fruits of our labor. Over the next year or so, he didn't change much at school, but the three of us worked diligently and consistently over the small plot of land, and by the end of grade five, Gordon and I had even worked a few times alone. We gardened mostly in silence, but from time to time, a conversation would spring up between us.

"What d'you do with this?" Gordon might ask about some vegetable—cauliflower or beets.

"Um, my mom bakes the cauliflower till it's crispy, usually. Sometimes she makes curry with it."

"Is it good? It looks weird." He'd sniff it or break off a piece to taste, his mouth and dark eyes displaying his disgust or surprise.

A few times, Dad invited him to dinner so he could try these dishes, but he never came. He'd show up in the garden at our designated times and trudge off afterward, and the only other time I'd see him was in class.

After fifth grade, though, Gordon stopped coming to the garden. He appeared less and less in class, too, and when I tried to ask him if he'd help harvest the new crop that summer, he walked right past me and grumbled, "That shit's for losers."

My dad said all we could do was keep inviting him back, but after a few more attempts and just as many unpleasant responses, I gave up.

All I really knew about him now was that he smoked a lot

of weed, hooked up with a lot of different girls, and skipped classes more than anyone else at school.

"Sorry," I mumbled, and shuffled forward past his truck.

The second I cleared his bumper, Gordon vroomed past me, yelling, "Get your head out of your ass, Clark."

*Watch as a rampaging rhino plows through innocent bystanders.*

"What were you doing?" Charles asked when I caught up to him.

"Got a little lost in my thoughts, I guess."

"Ginny?"

I'd told him about how successful I'd been with her. I shrugged, then changed the topic. "Why do you think Gordon's such a jerk?"

"Who knows. Maybe he's super disappointed school is over."

"Ha-ha, right," I said, shaking my head. "That must be it."

He smirked. "But also, maybe don't pause randomly in the middle of the road."

"Yeah, I guess that didn't help." I smirked too, even as I tried to ignore a stubborn anticipation in my stomach for the disappointing summer ahead.

After ice cream, Charles and I parted ways but agreed to meet up later. At home I celebrated the end of school rather extravagantly by first, mowing the lawn, and then, hanging the laundry.

Such was my thrilling life.

Laundry was always something I'd done with my mom. When I was really small, she'd turn it into a game. Once I'd created two separate piles of whites and colors, she'd make me place the colors in the best rainbow I could before adding them to the washer. If the rainbow lacked variety, it meant that our wardrobe hadn't been vibrant enough that week, and we had to step up our fashion sense. "Only boring people wear black and white all the time," Mom said. I don't think I ever saw her in just one or two tones.

After she left, I staged a quiet revolt by reverting to jeans and T-shirts as my standard uniform. My dad, however, retained some of her fashion sense. Even though he spent much of his day in fairly run-of-the-mill overalls for his work at the carshop, he always managed to embellish his outfits in some way. I was about to fasten a pair of his extremely purple underwear to the clothesline when I heard "Nima!"

"Charles!" I yelled back, not needing to look past my dad's gigantic briefs to see who it was.

"Hey," Charles said, breathless, as he bent over and rested his hands on his spindly knees.

"Lord love a lemur. You really need a little more fitness in your life, friend." Like I should talk.

He rose, pulling at his shirt like he always does. He had on his Einstein T-shirt and the same ratty jeans he always wore, rain or shine. His clothes and scrawny body, combined with what he liked to call his "loose and lush" Afro, always made him look younger than he was. "What are you doing after you're finished hanging your nasty underpants?" he asked, once he'd stopped huffing and puffing.

I threw my days-of-the-week undies at him. He caught them, realized he had my Sunday underpants in his hands, made an absurdly grotesque face, and threw them back up into the air. They floated to the uneven, dusty lawn.

"Great, you jerk. Now I have to wash them again," I said, prodding my toe beneath them and flipping them up into my hand—which finally worked after three tries. "You can make up for it by helping me. Then we can grab a snack and head down to Old Stuff to see what Ginny's up to. I need to buy some new old underpants."

What I really needed was to see Ginny. I was caught in that limbo between rejection and letting go, and my heart straddled a confusing line between wanting to see as much of Ginny as possible before she left in September, and wanting to avoid her for the sake of my sanity.

"You are *not* buying underpants from a thrift shop," Charles responded.

"What if I am?"

"You're hideous."

"You're insidious."

"Supercilious."

"Stupid penis."

That made him laugh, which made me feel lucky to have a friend who thought I was funny.

After we'd finished hanging clothes, we headed back into

the house and started rummaging around in the fridge for something to eat. I could hear the TV on in the living room, which meant Dad was having a nap. He liked to doze with TV shows in the background. Particularly soap operas. He said other people's drama made him feel peaceful and put him right to sleep.

Charles and I settled down at the Formica kitchen table with some tuna salad, crackers, and a couple of apples. As soon as we sat down, my year-and-a-half-old mutt, Gus, bounded into the kitchen from the living room, where he'd probably been napping with my dad.

Gus looked a little like a cross between a schnauzer and a skinny raccoon—gray fur; short, wiry beard; and black markings across his stubby tail and around his left eye. He was ugly-cute, and I adored him. Dad brought him home just after Mom left, some sort of consolation gift in his mind, I think.

As Gus huddled up against my feet, willing me to drop something from my plate, Charles contemplated a cracker and said, "Nima, in your expert opinion, what should I wear tomorrow?"

Tomorrow was the first night of Summer Lovin', the town's summer extravaganza. It was the biggest thing that happened in Bridgeton. People drove in from all the surrounding areas to experience everything you'd expect from a local festival: games, baked goods competition, pie eating, bouncy castle, Ferris wheel, small-town bands, variety shows . . . you name it.

But the festival enticed performances and attractions from elsewhere, too—terrifying rides and unusual acts that wouldn't otherwise reach us. Somehow, Summer Lovin' had acquired a kitschy, energetic following, and for four days, Bridgeton felt like double its regular size, with crowds of locals and out-of-towners descending daily upon our limited but well-used resources.

Despite our usual reservations about most large-group activities, Charles and I actually looked forward to the opportunity to people-watch and eat fried food. I liked the atmosphere: dim, dusky evenings all aglow with gleaming lights and every imaginable delicious smell in the air; people laughing and acting like fools; dogs snuffling the ground for threads of cotton candy or stray popcorn kernels. It was a nice way to begin the summer, anyway, and a break from the monotony of life in Bridgeton.

I began to wonder if this year, it might also give me a chance to liven things up in my own world. Even though Ginny hadn't said it, I could see what she saw—simple, awkward, humdrum Nima. Let her record your stats, watch her chase your rebounds, but what else is she good for? I needed more than paint-by-numbers. I needed van Gogh or Matisse. Maybe then I'd be worth framing and displaying on someone's wall.

"Helloooooo." Charles.

"Sorry, what?"

He rolled his eyes and tried to wipe his tuna fingers across my cheek, but my bob-and-weave was too quick for him. He slumped back into his seat, his arms falling limp to his sides and his head thumping against the back of the chair. "What should I *wear*, I said."

"Good God in a Gucci bag, I don't know. Why wouldn't you just wear what you always wear?"

He leaned his elbows on the table and rested his head in his upturned hands. Staring at me. Blinking deliberately.

I blinked back for a few moments. Then, "Oh. Right." The girl. He had a new, somewhat surprising crush on one of the girls in the grade below us, Tessa. I didn't mind her, I guess, but she giggled too much for my taste. I was a little protective of Charles. This was his first major crush and I was scared he'd get hurt. . . . I knew how it felt, after all. Instead of expressing that much warmer sentiment, though, I said, "Maybe don't wear that T-shirt. Or those jeans. Or anything in your closet."

"Such an a-hole." He got up, stacked my plate onto his, and took both to the sink.

"Want to borrow something?" Charles and I were lucky. We were about the same size—he was small for his age, and I had the smallest breasts known to man. Or woman. Or basically any human alive. I had very little going for me in the butt department also.

"Like what?" he asked.

"Ummmm . . . how about my gray cords and . . . a black T-shirt? Casual but classy? It's Summer Lovin', after all.

You'll look like a dinkus if you dress up too much."

"*You're* a dinkus. Come on, let's go to Old Stuff and see if we can find something super cheap. But please don't buy someone's dirty underpants," he pleaded.

"I do what I want, dinkus."

We grabbed my bike, then walked over to Charles's house to get his. Since everything in Bridgeton was a short distance from everything else, we rolled up to Old Stuff in about three minutes. We only had about half an hour before it closed, but Ginny would keep it open for us if we asked her to.

The bell attached to the door ding-a-linged as we entered. Instantly, the musty smell of old clothes met our nostrils.

Ginny crouched by the shoe section, lining up a selection of tattered army boots and sneakers. She looked up when she heard us come in. "Hey! What are you two punks doing here?" she said, bouncing up into standing position and flashing her stupidly cute smile. A piece of my heart splintered off and pierced my chest.

"Hey," I said, mentally reconstructing my upper torso. "Charles needs some snazzy pants. Somehow, we have to make him look presentable."

"Impossible," Ginny replied.

"That's what I think."

"A-holes," Charles mumbled, pulling at his shirt.

Ginny crossed the short distance between her and Charles in two graceful leaps, gave him a giant hug, and finished with several violent kisses to his cheek.

I wondered if she'd ever kiss my cheeks like that again after my fumbling attempt the other day. I'm sure I'd managed to shift our friendship into a more formal zone. I hated to think that everything I did now would be tainted with my choice to try to share my feelings with her. I watched helplessly as Charles squirmed in her arms.

"Get off me!" he grunted, but the corner of his mouth betrayed the beginnings of a smile.

"Come with me, monsieur. The 'Boys on the Verge of Manhood' section is right this way," Ginny said, grabbing his arm.

She led us to the back of the store, passing women's coats and children's wear. Old Stuff wasn't huge, but every inch of it was used to maximum capacity. The aisles between clothing racks were narrow, and beneath each of the racks were cardboard boxes of random bits and pieces that didn't fit anywhere else, like candleholders and unopened skin products. You really had to be in an excavating kind of mood to dig through those.

While Ginny rifled through several pairs of corduroy pants for Charles (great minds), I had a look at the meager hat selection. As I tipped a black trucker hat over my head, the entryway bell dingled.

"Trying to butch it up, Clark?"

Gordon Grant.

"Trying to jerk it up, Gordon?" I mumbled, keeping my

eyes on the smudged mirror leaning against the wall. The hat felt too tight across my forehead. I pulled it off and rubbed at the line it left above my eyebrows.

"What'd you say?" he asked, and I could see him in the mirror, coming closer.

"Now, now, kids." This was Davis McCain, Gordon's loathsome sidekick. Like Gordon, I'd known him since elementary school, and he hadn't always been awful. But I also knew his very wealthy parents were almost never here, given that Davis's house was the go-to spot for most weekend parties (not that I ever went). I guess being ignored can make you cruel.

Apart, Gordon and Davis each had an edge that made me uncomfortable. Together, they were a double-edged sword ready to slice you without warning.

At that inopportune moment, Charles and Ginny walked out of the curtained-off portion of the store that served as a changing room. Charles wore some sweet burgundy cords and an even sweeter gray shirt with several screen-printed crows across the chest.

Gordon and Davis would have a field day with how slim-fitting and colorful those cords were unless I did something, quick. Charles found these two even more unnerving than I did. His eyes flashed panic now as he noticed them.

Desperate times. My stomach flipping, I called out, "Here!" and flung the hat over to Gordon. It came close enough to Gordon's head that he flinched. My body tensed but I pushed through it, thinking too that I could show Ginny a brief moment of color among my usual gray tones. "Why don't you wear it? The black matches your mood."

As soon as I said it, I instinctively took a step back. Gordon could be unpredictable. He'd never done anything to me, but I know he'd been in plenty of fights before. I heard he'd whacked some guy with the guy's own textbook in class once—right in front of the teacher. But his eyes flickered something other than anger for a moment—something that momentarily put me off-balance.

Before I could figure out what it was, though, it shifted into an icy glare and I braced myself for whatever was coming. But then Davis wrapped his arm around Gordon's neck in a headlock and yanked him close, following with, "But I love Gordon's broody moods!" Gordon immediately started punching Davis in the gut. I turned away in disgust toward Ginny and Charles, who were staring—also in disgust—at the two jerks behind me.

"So? How'd you make out?" I asked.

Davis paused his assault on Gordon long enough to offer, "You guys were *making out* back there?"

Glancing at them nervously, Charles answered in a whisper. "I was gonna go with this. What do you think?"

"I think you look like a black version of my little sister!" Davis called out through a sleazy grin. At this, Gordon glanced sideways at Davis, then laughed—a loud, forced laugh, it seemed to me. That same unsteady feeling made me shift my feet a little wider. Gordon was giving off signals I couldn't quite get my head around.

While I tried not to tip over, Ginny snapped, "Shut your mouth, Davis, or I'll kick you out of here."

Luckily, Ginny was the prettiest angry girl you've ever seen. This had two simultaneous effects on people: they melted a little, and also looked as though they were going to pee their pants. I was never sure which reaction had to do with fear, and which with hormones.

Davis almost looked chastened, scratched his chin, then shoved Gordon off to the other side of the store.

I was relieved that Ginny had managed to defuse the moment, but also disappointed in my own predictable inability to offer anything of value to the situation. With great difficulty, I blinked back the burning in my eyes and looked at Charles. "I think that's basically the outfit I told you to wear from the beginning, but whatever."

Ginny, restored to her genial self, placated me. "Nima, sometimes it takes an expert to get through to someone in a truly meaningful way."

*Yup. And that expert is definitely not me.*

"Now let's ring these gems in so I can close up," she continued. "I don't want to have to deal with the two beasts behind you any longer than necessary."

While Gordon and Davis continued to pummel each other across the store, exploding the carefully arranged shoe section, Charles paid for his pants and shirt. Then we helped

Ginny count the receipts and tidy other parts of the store.

Ginny planted herself by the door, arms crossed. "That's it, everyone—we're closing up shop. Time to go," she announced.

"Too bad, we're not done," Gordon said, a pair of bowling shoes in his hands.

"Yeah, what kind of business is this, anyway?" Davis shouted over his shoulder.

"The kind that closes at five p.m. We're open tomorrow at ten, though. Feel free to come back then." Impressively, she kept her tone light and cheerful.

Davis picked up a child's toy tiara from the shelf next to him and placed it on Gordon's head. "Ooh, look, Gordo, you make such a pretty little queen!"

With an abruptness that startled even Davis, Gordon swiped the tiara from his head and flung it to the ground. The cheap plastic snapped in two and skidded across the floor.

At first everyone just stared at the broken pieces. Davis was the first to shift the moment out of silence with an uneasy and feigned bout of laughter. But Gordon merely stared at the segments of plastic for a moment longer before digging his hand into his pocket and pulling out some change. He slammed the coins on the shelf that had held the tiara and dared anyone with his eyes to say anything.

Ginny was the only one who actually did.

"Good grief. Can you two please just get your shit

together and go before you break anything else?" she ground out through her teeth.

Pretty, Angry Girl strikes again. Gordon and Davis slunk toward the entrance, Davis kicking at the tiara remnants along the way.

We let them pass by us, all in silence, until Davis offered a witty, "That's it! I'm leaving!"

I watched them go as Ginny locked the door, Gordon's long, lanky figure a stark contrast to Davis's stockier, block-like frame. Gordon turned and looked back at us in that moment, something both menacing and hesitant in his face.

"Shall we?" Ginny asked.

"Those guys freak me out," Charles muttered as we started walking away.

Ginny rubbed his hunched back. "Forget 'em. They're not worth the worry."

"Well, they're worth a *little* worry," I said. Ginny gave me a look. "Well, they are!"

"Maybe. But why waste any more breath on them?" She placed her arm around Charles's shoulders and guided him forward. I wished I was in his place. Maybe if I hadn't said anything, I would be. The same empty feeling that had consumed me three days earlier on this same pathway with Ginny crept into my belly again.

In an effort to fill the void, I asked, "What's for dinner, everyone?"

"I've gotta head home," Ginny replied. "I told my parents

I'd have dinner with them. See you guys tomorrow, though?" She gave Charles one last punch to the shoulder and split off toward her house.

"Okay, yeah—see you tomorrow," I said, with as much nonchalance as possible. Watching her go, I thought I'd feel a little relieved it was just going to be me and Charles for the night. But as my evening stretched out in front of me—dinner with Charles, on my patio, with our books, in silence—it seemed my entire summer might unfold in the same manner.

On our way back to the house, we stopped by the Fast Pick to buy some bread for Charles's and my go-to dinner: grilled cheese. Mr. Helms greeted us from behind the counter with a grimace and an armpit scratch. He'd owned the Fast Pick for as long as I could remember. Small white tufts of hair poked out of his ears, and a perpetual smattering of stubble grew along his jawline. He could give you the hardest stare with his glassy blue eyes, and his bulbous nose reminded me of three cherries—one large flanked by two smaller ones.

I asked Dad once why Mr. Helms was such a grump. Dad said he was probably lonely. That loneliness makes us grumpy sometimes. He seemed to know what he was talking about, and even though this conversation happened before Mom left, I often wondered if he already felt lonely at that point for some reason.

Strangely enough, as we paid for the bread—the same plain white bread we always bought—the idea of our usual grilled cheese sandwich imbued me with a similar feeling.

At home, I tried to override my gloom by ordering Charles around. I commanded him to grate the cheese, and I melted some butter in a pan. We ate on our own, since Dad had gone back to work while we were out. He did a lot of mechanical tinkering for Summer Lovin'—tightening bolts, safeguarding against malfunctions, and greasing mechanisms all week long before the festival began. I'd barely seen him that week, but the extra work was good for him, and I was glad he'd gone back to the festival job.

Last summer he'd declined to help and almost skipped the festival completely. Understandably, he couldn't seem to bear the thought of going without Mom. She adored Summer Lovin', and in years past, they'd stroll up and down the booths for hours, trying a bit of every food on offer and competing with one another at the games. I guess he didn't feel right wandering around without her. Eventually, I persuaded him to join me and Charles, and we spent the entire first night with him until he got tired of us hovering and told us amicably to "bugger off already."

I took it as an encouraging sign that he was back at it this year.

Despite the prospect of another Summer Lovin', though, and a belly full of cheese and bread, an emptiness spread through my heart. As Charles and I draped ourselves across my patio furniture after dinner, my surroundings seemed to reflect the general pallor of my life—the brittle grass, the slivers of graying paint peeling off the banister, the brown moths shuddering next to the porch light. *This is it. This is what I have to look forward to,* I thought. And in the dimming light of a summer just begun, the hollow already growing in my gut widened, like a deep, dark cavern.

# CHAPTER 3

The next day was the first morning of the festival, and despite my general melancholy, I woke up early, as usual. Gus was my primary alarm clock. I let him sleep in my bed, and in the morning, he'd plow his snout beneath my pillow to raise my head off the mattress, then pull out quickly so my head thumped back down onto the bed. Then he'd do it again and again until I'd had enough, which was about twice.

This morning, after his endearing ritual, I rolled out of bed, noticing that the sun was just rising. My night had been fitful—occupied by a very conscious panic over a looming life of mediocrity followed by unconscious dreams about everyone growing disinterested in me because of it.

Every part of me seemed to drag as if in slow motion. But as the glow of pink sunrise slipped through my sheer curtains, I closed my eyes and absorbed the warmth.

I needed to get outside. To find some color, some fresh air.

After I shook the sluggishness out of my body and put on

a light sweater, Gus and I marched with purpose to the community garden to start digging out squashes.

Dad and I still enjoyed tending to the shared plot of vegetables near the center of town. Today my contribution would be to collect all the summer squash I could for the festival veggie booth.

In a couple of hours, everyone in town would be scattering in different directions to prepare, darting into stores and back out again like bees to flowers. But this early, Gus and I had the streets to ourselves.

I drew open the gate and perched myself at one end of a line of ripe, long squash. Gus snuffled around, yelping at the tiny bugs flitting about. As I began to part squash from vine, I allowed myself to get lost in the morning quiet and my slow, methodical movements.

Shortly, however, a gravelly voice interrupted my Zen moment.

"Somebody shut that freaking dog up." I hadn't noticed it before, but a rusted, light blue truck was parked just outside the garden fence. The voice came from the open driver's-side window. I knew that truck.

As soon as he heard the voice, Gus went nuts and began barking in earnest, bouncing around next to the fence. A hand grasped the top of the truck door and heaved forward the rest of the body attached to it. Gordon's face appeared in the window, his hair greasy and disheveled and his face pale. When he saw me, he huffed a bitter laugh. "I should have known.

A yappy dog for a yappy chick." He rubbed his face with his hands.

I snapped my fingers for Gus to calm down and come sit by me, which he did, reluctantly. Frustrated to let go of the small oasis of peace I'd found, but also surprised to see Gordon looking more haggard than usual, I asked, with as much calm as possible, "What are you doing?"

"What the fuck are *you* doing? The sun's barely up. People are trying to sleep, for shit's sake."

Jeez. He made it hard to maintain any sense of composure. "Why are 'people' trying to sleep in their cars, next to public space?" I muttered.

He set his hands on the steering wheel and yawned forcefully. "None of your damn business," he said, staring through his front window. His jawline tensed. I wondered if it ever loosened. The memory of my dad standing near the fence, hands out, as Gordon fumbled with an armload of carrots and potatoes fluttered in front of me like a falling leaf.

"Well, since you're awake, I could use an extra hand." I scrunched my nose in anticipation of his derision.

Without turning his head, he stretched his arms out straight against the steering wheel, but I could see his eyes dart toward me and the garden. *He's actually thinking about it.* I unscrunched my nose.

Too soon.

He shook his head, laughing that bitter laugh again. "Fuck that." He dug in his pocket for a second, pulled out a key, and started the ignition. "Get a life, Clark." His awful truck growled like it was pissed off too and spat out a dark cloud of exhaust. Without another word, he roared off toward his house, which was way past the high school, as far as I knew. It wasn't like he'd ever invited me over for tea, after all.

Great. Tranquil morning ruined. Worse still, even Gordon seemed to know I needed a life.

I was committed to completing my task, though, and after a short while, I'd collected a small fortress of thick, hard squash in one corner of the garden. This would be picked up later for the festival. Good deed done, I brushed off the soil from my knees and called Gus after me as I passed back through the gate to head home.

As I crossed the square, hints of opening day were beginning to pop up—the owners of the Two Suns Café were setting up their outdoor seating area, a few vendors were already unloading vans, and I could smell barbecues beginning to smoke. The festival took up almost all of Bridgeton. It started in the square and ran down to the south end of town, where it opened up into a wide field most people referred to as the Weeds, due to the fact that it spent most of the year overgrown and unused. The Weeds' sole purpose seemed to be to accommodate this festival four days of the year.

By the time I arrived home, Dad was up and making a festival day specialty he'd picked up from my mom—pancakes and chicken curry.

He was wearing his ocean-themed muumuu, his thick, hairy legs and plump feet appearing out the bottom. I'd given him that muumuu eight years ago for his birthday, before I knew muumuus were for women, and he's worn it at least once a week ever since, even though it was wearing thin in places. I don't think he wore it just to make me feel good either. He actually seemed to appreciate its comfortable looseness, some-times wearing it for days at a time. He said Mom's dad wore a sarong all his life—why couldn't he wear a muumuu? Mom couldn't argue with that. When my mom and I realized how much he loved wearing it, we started buying him a new one for each birthday. He had a whole collection now, but this first ocean one with its fish and seaweed tangles remained his favorite.

I was ravenous, and I welcomed the mound of food he set in front of me as soon as I plunked myself down at the table.

"Squash?" he asked.

"Yep."

"Good yield?"

"Yep."

"Hungry?"

With my mouth full of pancakes and curry, I nodded my head. I'd done my best not to show too much of my heart-ache around him these past few days. He had enough of his own and certainly didn't need my pitiful mistakes added to his plate. Besides, as far as he knew, Ginny was just a good friend.

Maybe not even that anymore.

He got his food and sat down with me. Gus let out an eager whine from beneath the table, and I slipped him a piece of a pancake.

Dad took a sip of his coffee. "So what's the plan, Stan?"

I swallowed another mouthful. "Shower."

"I was going to say . . . ," he murmured, giving me a cheeky sideways glance.

I kicked him under the table. "Then probably head to Jill's and help out around there. Charles is coming over around five."

"Okay. I have to be at the fairgrounds in a bit to finish tuning up the machines. Meet you back here, then?" His curls sprang out haphazardly in wild, bed-head fashion. On him, the look was somehow artistic. On me, it was more like . . . undecided.

It was nice to see him looking forward to the festival, though, and I gave him a smile to make sure he knew I was looking forward to it too. "Yup. Meet you here."

After breakfast and a quick rinse, Gus and I headed back out to Jill's.

Jill was Mom and Dad's best friend, and she'd stepped in to help my dad and me after Mom left last year. She owned and operated one of the only artsy places in town—the Garden and Gifts Emporium. Her business mixed landscaping with garden decor. She made everything in the store, from clay gnomes, to birdhouses, to pots, to wooden trellises. She showed me how to work with wood and clay and shared all kinds of tips about gardening.

Dad said Jill was really sad after Mom left, but she didn't let it make her bitter. Instead she focused her attention on us. She used to be married but left her husband many years ago, before she moved here from Seattle. She'd never shared the specifics of that part of her life, though. All I did know from the plain evidence was that she'd never remarried and seemed content enough on her own.

I plopped my bike down on her front lawn, among several garden gnomes. These were not the "garden variety" garden gnomes one might expect, however. Instead Jill had cornered the market on oddball gnomes—old man gnomes in tutus, lady gnomes in butler uniforms serving up platters of snails and tulips, gnomes lying on their bellies in pink camouflage, looking through binoculars—one of Jill's goofy gnomes decorated almost every lawn around here. We had three of them in the backyard and six out front. They were her go-to birthday gifts, and we didn't mind a bit, since the ones she made us were always one-of-a-kind and bore some resemblance to the birthday person of honor. We had more than one sturdy gnome in a muumuu, and last year she gave me one with a curly ponytail that sat on top of a wrought-iron bicycle, its nose buried in a book.

"Hey! Anybody here?" I called out, entering through the front door.

Jill's shop was also her home, and it was close to the high school. She'd renovated a two-story house so that the second floor accommodated her primary living space, while the main floor contained the kitchen, a shop space, and storage.

I paused in the middle of the front room, a wide space with Jill's smaller goods, like clay plates, figurines, and such. The room was both workspace and display area, and while warm and welcoming, the floor remained under a perpetual layer of clay dust, and grit seemed to float in the air.

Hearing no reply, I went through the kitchen and out back to an enormous yard half-covered with plastic corrugated roofing. Most of Jill's stock tumbled out in every direction—giant plastic pots packed with dirt and trees, a crowd of garden gnomes in one corner, a trio of wheelbarrows that never seemed to sell, trellises in varied shapes and sizes, shovels, trowels, rakes, and more.

As I pushed open the screen door from the kitchen, I let out another shout.

"Who the hell's hollering at me this early in the morning?" Jill's gruff voice arose from somewhere behind a wheelbarrow full of potted plants. She could be a little rough around the edges, but Jill was as dependable as the clock tower standing in the town square, and about as sturdy, too.

She emerged, a wide-brimmed black hat hovering around her head like the fins of a stingray. "Well, well. If it isn't Nima Clark!"

I ignored the fact that she'd left the "Kumara" out of my last name. She'd taken to doing that after Mom left—an indication that some resentment had taken root. I couldn't blame her, so I let it slide.

She tipped her hat up and wiped her brow. "Just in time to help!"

I rolled my eyes, but with a smile. I knew she'd waste no time putting me to work. Soon I'd be starting my regular job with Jill anyway—a part-time gig I'd had since I was twelve. But today would be full of free favors, which I didn't mind a bit.

"All right. What can I do?" I asked, walking over to her. She was wearing overalls and a ratty T-shirt, both covered in dirt and dust and who knew what else.

"Wheel these out to the van and start loading them up. Then come get more." She went back to digging up plants from her garden bed. Typical Jill—straight to the point. Niceties weren't her strong suit when there was work to be done.

When we finished loading up the plants, Jill allowed us to enjoy some iced tea in the backyard.

"How's the summer lookin', doll?" she asked, resting her head against the back of the bench we shared and splaying her long legs out in front of her. She'd removed the floppy hat, and her short blond hair lay flat and damp against her scalp.

I measured my response. The only people who knew about my feelings for Ginny and the sad outcome of those feelings were Charles and Ginny, and that's how I wanted it to stay. It's not that I thought Jill or my dad would care about the object of my affections. I just couldn't bear the thought of my embarrassing attempt being revealed to the masses. It was bad enough that it'd happened at all.

"So far, so good," I lied, then followed with a bit of the truth. "Just some reading and putzing around with Charles." As I said it, I immediately felt a twinge of desire for something else poking in between my ribs, jabbing at the familiar emptiness. Like maybe, if I could change things up somehow, I might be able to fill some of that blank space. And maybe, if I weren't so blank, people would actually be drawn to me. To want me.

Unfortunately, change wasn't my strong point.

But staring at Jill's plant beds, those thoughts were quickly replaced by my irritating run-in at the community garden that morning. "Oh, except that a-hole, Gordon Grant, keeps ruining my summer buzz."

"Gordon Grant?" She twisted her mouth, thinking. "That Bill Grant's kid?"

I shrugged. "Yeah, I guess." I'd seen Gordon's dad plenty of times around town but had never spoken to him. He didn't seem like the kind of guy I'd want to talk to.

"What'd he do?" Jill asked.

I told her about that morning, the past couple of days, and his general crappy attitude.

"Hmm. Well, you know, I expect if he's sleeping in his truck, it's because something's keeping him from sleeping at home. And I bet that something is Bill."

"What do you mean?"

She rubbed her eyes and said nothing for a few moments. Then she sat up abruptly and dusted some dirt from her pants. "He's just not a nice man, is all." She took a few giant gulps of her tea, like she was trying to finish it quickly.

Ignoring the hint, I asked, "How do you know him?"

She wiped her mouth with her shoulder. "I just do. From around." And then, dismissively, "All I'm saying is there's usually more to the story than meets the eye. Sometimes assholes are just hurt souls."

Her poeticism surprised me a little. Jill wasn't usually one to fiddle around with words. But her tone signaled a clear end to the conversation, so I left it alone. I took a few sips of tea and changed the subject. "Anything else you need me to do before I go? Any gnomes going to market today?"

"Yep. But I've got plenty of time for that. You go on." She winked at me. "I'll see you tonight at the festival." She downed the rest of her tea and stood up, spreading her arms out wide in a stretch.

"All right. If you're sure." I quickly finished my tea too. Grabbing her glass and mine, I turned to leave them in the kitchen and go.

"See ya, kiddo."

"See ya."

Biking home, I thought about what Jill had said. I guess I'd never really considered Gordon's backstory. He didn't give you much chance to cut him any slack, after all. But now I wondered if his dad had anything to do with why he'd stopped coming to the garden, or with how he was in general. The more I thought about Jill's words, and about the fleeting moments of something other than anger or unpleasantness I'd seen in Gordon recently, the more curious I became.

# CHAPTER 4

Just after five, Charles appeared, all gussied up in his hip shirt and cords. I wore my usual summer wear—blue jean shorts, black tank top, backpack, hair in a ponytail. I was only his wingman, after all. We left the house together—me, Charles, and Dad. Eventually, Dad would do his own thing, but we liked to walk up together.

We turned a corner toward the center of town, and the festival opened up in front of us like some whirling, buzzing panorama. The square was in full swing. It housed the game booths, food tents, and main stage.

Ginny and Jill were both working booths just off the square, so we might see them later. I was simultaneously eager at and distressed by the prospect of seeing Ginny but tried not to let it get in the way of my enjoyment of the festival itself. In fact, the colors and textures of the festival could be the perfect antidote to my lackluster palette, and as we entered the square, a gnawing desperation for something—

anything—to invigorate this drab summer and my matching life pulled at my stomach and chest. I dragged Charles and Dad around with me, craning my neck to see what each booth offered, pushing them through the crowd to get to the next thing.

Charles kept foiling my attempts to find some excitement. He'd brought his big, fancy camera that his parents gave him a couple of years ago and was trying to snap photos of anything and everything, it seemed. It was obvious to me, though, that he was trying to spot Tessa without looking like he was trying to spot Tessa by using his camera as binoculars. I sighed emphatically every time he stopped to take a picture.

Dad just had his hands in his pockets and a wide, closed-mouth smile on his face, cheerfully taking in the sights wherever I led him. As Charlotte Bronson danced past us in clown makeup, she handed him a small happy-face sticker, and he gleefully pasted it to his cheek. The sight made me smile.

It also made me a little sad. I wondered if his smile was genuine or if he wore both smiles to cover his true feelings, like I'd been doing. Was he thinking about Mom? It was hard not to, surrounded by all these vibrant sights and sounds. I thought about all the times she tried to drag us to see the smaller, stranger acts at the south end of the festival and how both Dad and I looked at her skeptically before leading her back to the main tent for the usual circus antics.

Maybe she'd left us because we'd held her back. Maybe she needed to see something beyond our familiar, small world.

Maybe she'd grown as bored with me as I was becoming with myself.

I spun around, looking for something, anything to turn this sad clown existence into a death-defying trapeze act as soon as possible.

Unfortunately, my zeal ended abruptly when I saw Gordon and Davis standing close by at the shooting booth. It's a small town, but the frequency of my Gordon sightings was becoming ridiculous.

Gordon seemed to be taking this very seriously. He'd propped the toy shotgun against his shoulder and was peering over the barrel as though hunting deer. He waited patiently for the conveyer belt to change direction before shooting, using that small pause to make his move.

Davis leaned over the counter, talking incessantly, trying to throw Gordon off his game. The bored booth girl tugged at her cheeks as if to stay awake. Gordon pulled the trigger and wounded one poor, stuffed mouse. It fell to the tarp spread on the ground for gunshot victims. The girl went over to Gordon first to take away the gun (smart), then stooped to pick up the mouse. She threw it on the counter in front of him, but Davis swiped it off. Gordon didn't seem to care. He just threw the girl another couple of bucks and snatched the gun back. I tried to remind myself of Jill's words, but watching him intently maim small stuffed animals made it difficult.

Davis huffed and crossed his arms. "C'mon, man. I'm bored as fuck."

Gordon's sight line dropped for a split second before he relinquished the gun and shoved his hands into his pockets. "Yeah, whatever. Let's get out of this shithole." There was that tight jaw again.

As they turned to go, I was relieved to know I wouldn't have to see them again tonight, but also found myself wishing I could somehow understand what the hell was up with that guy. Then I found myself shocked at my wish.

Charles's voice cut into my observations. "What are you looking at those two for?" He pulled at his shirt and rubbed his nose. He was clearly agitated—nervous about the Girl.

"Just trying to figure out what makes people tick, is all."

"Yeah," he replied, barely listening. "Come on, let's keep looking."

"Looking for what, Charles?" I asked, eyebrows raised in mock curiosity.

"For . . . nothing. Whatever." He sniffed and looked away. I jabbed at his shoulder. He smacked my hand.

Dad took that moment to pat us both on the head and wander over toward the hardware stall. Charles and I began picking our way through the game booths to see how much we could win with five dollars each.

A little while later we headed over to the Old Stuff table with a bottle of pink cream soda and a bag of hard-earned candy in my backpack. By this point, the razzle-dazzle atmosphere had managed to creep its way into my bones and I was really starting to enjoy myself.

I'd resolved to at least browse the Old Stuff items and greet Ginny with a blasé "Hey," but when we got there, she seemed pretty busy chatting up a couple of guys I didn't recognize, which substantially reduced my resolve and my enjoyment.

I stared tactlessly at them as they flirted and teased each other. Their laughter was boisterous and unrestrained. I don't think I ever made Ginny laugh like that.

Charles bit his lip and shot me awkward glances. I squeezed all my disappointment and frustration into my fists and turned to go. Charles followed.

Since the square wasn't big enough for rides or circus tents, these were relegated to the Weeds. We hadn't seen Tessa yet, and Charles was getting a bit antsy, so we decided to try our luck down there.

The crowd tended to shift as you got farther south. More of the "oddball" kids gravitated toward this end of the festival, probably because there were fewer adults, but also because the attractions became somewhat less traditional. In general, Bridgeton didn't offer much in the way of avant-garde interpretive dance and such—but unusual things did drift here once in a while from surrounding areas, and many of those unconventional things tended to pop up during the festival.

At the moment, though, we had a minor emergency on our hands. Tessa had just burst out of the Fast Pick, talking up a windstorm with two girlfriends of hers. She held an open bag of chips and crashed into me, too busy chatting to look where she was going.

Since she was three inches shorter than my five foot six, I couldn't help but look down my nose at her.

"Oh! Sorry, Nima. Didn't see you there. Chips?" She held the bag out.

"Thanks, no." For Charles's sake, I fought hard against the part of me that just wanted to shield him from the heartache he'd inevitably suffer at the hands of this popular, confident girl. "Maybe Charles would like some, though," I said, yanking him in front of me.

Tessa smiled at him and held out the bag. He looked at her, looked at me, and without breathing, I don't think, managed to murmur, "Thanks." But then it got (more) awkward as he dug his hand into the chip bag and did that thing where his hand stays in a little too long and you just know he's touching every single chip in there. And then he pulls out just one and you're wondering, *What the hell took you so long?*

At least, I'm pretty sure that's what Tessa was thinking, given the look on her face.

I wrapped my fingers around his skinny bicep. "Come on, Charles. We were supposed to meet the others soon, remember?" I lied.

"What?" He was still holding the damn chip.

"Come *on*."

"Okay . . . bye, Tessa."

*Great galloping goddess, at least he got that out.* I kept a firm grip on him until we were safely out of earshot.

"Buddy," I said, swiping the chip out of his hand, "we gotta work on your reaction time."

"Gawwwwd, I knoooowwwwww." Charles's shoulders slumped forward. "What is *wrong* with me?"

Immediately feeling bad for him, not to mention hypocritical, I swung my arm around his shoulders and pulled him in close. "There isn't one thing wrong with you. It's not as terrible as you think." I wished I could take my own advice.

"Really?" His eyes thinned with skepticism as he adjusted his glasses.

"Really. You'll get another chance. Don't worry about it." But I only half believed myself.

By the time we made our way to the Weeds, it was already about seven o'clock. The light spread into a deep, rich orange—appropriate entrance lighting, it seemed, as large tents loomed over us and rickety rides clattered by at alarming speeds. The air became thicker with sweat, and a thin veil of amber coated every nook and cranny.

The two of us walked for a bit, not saying a whole lot. I supposed Charles was obsessing over his faux pas, and I was trying not to make him feel worse.

The tents dotted the far corner of the Weeds, and the rides occupied the rest of the space. Surprisingly, Charles loved rides. Unsurprisingly, I hated them. I couldn't see the point of scaring the crap out of myself. Life is terrifying enough as it is.

Charles, on the other hand, though he was petrified by

young female teenagers, couldn't fight his way out of a pile of kittens, and was about as courageous as my left baby toe, grew into a frenzied fanatic when it came to roller coasters. I could see it in his eyes right now. They darted back and forth, trying to figure out which ride to test out first.

Lucky for me, he knew how I felt about these things and understood that going on a ride meant that he was going by himself or making a new friend.

"All right, let's split up. You get the rides out of your system, and I'll go find interesting people to watch. We'll meet back here at eight o'clock. Okay?"

"Okay!" Charles said, already speed-walking across the Weeds toward the Hell's Gate roller coaster. Watching him go, my head shook as though acting independently of me—judging me for being even *less* adventurous than Charles. *Charles.*

I turned the other way and moved toward the southeast corner of the Weeds. As I passed between the bigger tents, applause and "Ooohhhs" floated out on the night breeze. I rubbed my eyes, willing the drowsiness of the day from them. A part of me would have gladly walked home and curled up in the hammock. But I couldn't go home. Not yet. Not without piercing my monotony with a sharp sword.

From my backpack, I pulled out the candy bag we'd won and yanked a gummy worm in half with my teeth. Determinedly working the jelly with my jaw, I advanced on the other tents.

Three smaller tents advertised a fire-eater, a magician,

and a snake charmer, none of which appealed to me.

I backtracked toward a group of tents clustered around an unlit bonfire. Later on, when it got dark enough, I supposed the woodpile would be set ablaze, and the party would carry on late into the night.

*What would that be like?* I wondered.

The first of the five tents held two figures—one was a bearded lady, as far as I could tell, and the other was a guy with tattoos over every inch of his body.

Not interested.

After dipping into two of the other tents, I found myself beginning to succumb to the tiredness creeping into my body. Pausing in the middle of the tent cluster, animated couples and groups brushing past me, I tightened the straps of my backpack and took a deep breath, recounting my options.

*One: boring and alone. Two: not that. Your choice, Nima.*

Twisting around, I focused on the fourth tent. It squatted lower to the ground than the first three and was much louder. Punk music clattered out through a slit in the front, and a guy in a studded leather jacket with a shock of unruly hair stood outside, calling out to anyone passing by.

Normally, loud noises and guys in leather would send me fleeing in the opposite direction. But I forced my feet forward and made direct eye contact with the dude just as he called out, "Pretty pixies performing poetic puzzles in pinafores to pretentious punk! Only two bucks!"

*Well, this is different.* I took his alliterative flair as a sign, pulled out two dollars, and handed the money to him. He gave me a high five and bowed extravagantly as he held open the tent flap.

Inside, twinkle lights and a few scattered candles provided the only illumination, apart from the gleam of what seemed like hundreds of silver studs and zippers decorating the guitarist to my left. From his fingers, a commotion of guitar chords pummeled my eardrums. The tent was mostly empty. In the flickering, dim light, I made out only two other people sitting on pillows near a large wooden crate a few feet away. They turned to look at me.

I almost took a step backward to retreat the way I'd entered, but from an opening in the tent behind the crate, an elfin figure stepped out, slathered in a leather body suit with a lime-green pinafore over top, a strap slipping off her left shoulder. Her legs bottomed out into thick, heavy boots while her jet-black hair rose into a twirling peak—reminding me even more of a forest sprite or some other mystical creature. Deep red eye shadow painted her eyelids, and the faintest hint of sparkles winked off her pale brow and cheekbones.

I imagined cement blocks around my feet, despite the sudden thumping in my chest. *Just see what happens, Nima.*

She stared right at me. I immediately looked at my shoes and used my tongue to dig a defiant piece of gummy worm out of my molar. After a few moments, a hand drifted into my vision. I raised my eyes to stare at the hand, which was attached to the nymphlike figure. Her fingers rippled invitingly. My jaw went slack. Her arm remained an invitation, hovering, and my hand acted of its own accord, rising to meet hers. Her skin was cool and sent a shiver through me.

She gently steered me to the collection of cushions scattered on the ground. The two other people—a couple, I gathered, since they were draped over one another—gazed at my enchanted guide as she led me to a bright blue pillow. Her hand slipped out of mine, and as she moved toward the crate-stage, she looked over her shoulder and gave me the slightest of smiles.

It's entirely possible I imagined that part, though.

I slipped my backpack off and sat down, hugging the bag to my chest, then folding my knees in after it as tightly as I could.

The guitar's remonstrations quieted down behind us, and the musician began plucking the strings in a slow, low cadence. Our "pretty pixie" stood onstage with her back to us, her pinafore parting like a tent entrance itself, revealing that the bodysuit was backless. A geisha tattoo stared out at us from the performer's skin—the inky figure bent low, hands meeting at an uptilted chin.

Just as I had convinced myself that this dark blue geisha was about to dance for us, the tattoo disappeared in a twirl and the crimson eye shadow drew my attention again.

"You can call me Winnow," she said, meeting each of the three of us with her eyes.

*I'll call you whatever you like.*

After a deep breath, she recited in a singsongy voice, in time with the guitar:

> "That girl feels like
> Poppin' wheelies on her trike
> Riding by dingin' her bell
> I wonder if she'll ever know
> She's dingin' my bell as well."

Her voice brought to mind fine dust, slipping over everyone and everything in the space. After a moment, she looked down at the couple to my left, who appeared to be as transfixed as I was.

"Body part."

The couple looked at each other, then back at her.

"Favorite body part," Winnow repeated, her fingers clasped in front of her and a faint smile on her lips.

The guy grinned. The girl placed her hand over his cheeky face before he could say what we all knew he wanted to say. She called back to Winnow, "Hands."

"Hands."

Then Winnow looked at me.

*Lord lick a lollipop. No one said there was audience participation.*

"Body part."

I stared at her mouth as she said it. I understood what she was asking, but my own mouth wouldn't work. I licked my lips. Bit my bottom lip. Hugged my backpack a little tighter. I glanced over at the couple, who waited with way-too-cheerful smiles on their faces. *God. What if I say the wrong thing? The predictable thing?*

"Uh . . ."

"Favorite . . . body . . . part."

I couldn't tell whether she was actually speaking more slowly or if time itself had begun to wind down.

Finally: "M-mouth?"

There was that barely-smile again. My cheeks flushed. I tried to generate some spit to wash away a mouthful of sand.

Winnow looked down and closed her eyes for a few moments. The guitar continued to plunk away in the background. She shook out her hands and looked up.

"That girl feels like
singeing her hands on burning sands
Her mouth is on fire too
She touches her lips with her fingertips
To feel the blaze run through."

She paused. The couple and I stared. She finally fixed the fallen strap of her pinafore. We watched her do this. The guitar stopped plunking. She looked at us. She blinked.

"That's it, y'all."

The word "y'all" coming from those lips broke the spell over us.

I looked at the couple, who looked at each other and then

at me. All three of us clapped awkwardly, not knowing if that was what you did for a "poetic puzzle." Not really knowing what a poetic puzzle was in the first place. All I really knew was that only a few minutes had passed by and I felt like a puzzle in pieces.

After Winnow clumped off the makeshift stage in her heavy boots and stole through the flap behind it, I lumbered to my feet and kicked my legs to get the kinks out.

"Well, that was weird," the boy said.

"What do you want for two bucks?" the girl asked.

*Fair enough.* But somehow, I felt like I'd just gotten a real bargain.

The three of us slipped out the front entrance. The dude who'd taken my money was lying on the grass next to the entrance, staring up at the sky and smoking. I checked my watch: 7:43. *Why do I feel like I was in there for hours?*

I wrapped myself in my backpack and continued wandering. The crowd had thickened and more voices rang through the air. Encouraged by my foray into strangeness and desirous for more, I approached the final tent, but it didn't look open yet. I stood awkwardly outside the entrance, unsure of what to do. You can't really knock on a tent flap. *But what if this tent is even more exciting than the last?* Just as I was about to poke my nose through the opening, two girls who looked like crew members burst out. I stumbled backward, narrowly escaping their sturdy frames.

They stopped to consider me. Like a genius, I tried to lean casually against the tent. I failed. One of the girls caught my arm as I toppled sideways and pulled me upright. This all felt a little too familiar. I battled through these feelings and offered, "Ha-ha . . . first time near a tent."

One of the girls—with arms like a boxer's—smiled widely. The other laughed. This was heartening enough to ask, "Do you know what's happening here?"

Laughing girl answered, "You should definitely come back later to find out. But you have to be eighteen. Which of course you are, right?" She gave me a wink.

"Uh . . . yeah?" It was only about nine months from the truth.

"Perfect. If you like boys in fancy dresses and girls in sharp suits, you won't want to miss it. And who knows whether we'll be here tomorrow." She gave her companion a half smile and an eye roll. The other girl nodded at me as if to say, *It's true.* They traipsed off, boxer girl yelling, "Show starts at ten!" as they did.

*Ten?* I hadn't planned on being here that long, and Charles would absolutely not want to hang out here until then. But I was intrigued and bolstered by recent encounters. *Boys in dresses and girls in suits? The possibility of running into Winnow again?* Something between butterflies and wasps soared about in my belly, and for some reason, that felt . . . okay. Maybe this was what it was like to actually have a life?

I made my way back over to the meeting spot, still tingling

with anticipation. Charles was already there, stuffing popcorn into his mouth.

"Hey, chipmunk cheeks," I called out to him.

He opened nice and wide to give me a good look at a mouthful of pulpy popcorn.

"Nice. Guess you're not into eating a proper dinner?"

He chewed, chewed, swallowed, then said, "This *is* dinner."

"Huh. Okay, well, you enjoy tomorrow's constipation, and I'll grab a plate of barbecue."

He licked his fingers. "I'll walk up with you, but then I think I'm going to head home. Want to watch a movie or something?"

"Nah. I think I'll grab a bite and head home myself."

That was a lie. I had just lied to Charles. It just came out of me, like a miniature mudslide spilling from my mouth. I wasn't even entirely sure why I did it. *Would he understand if I wanted to go back to the festival by myself? Would he want to come? Do I want him to come?*

We exited the Weeds and walked back up to the square. I told Charles a bit about my tent adventures but left out the part where my brain disconnected from the rest of me when I watched Winnow do her thing. Partially because I wasn't sure how to explain what I'd felt. But mostly because I was unsure how he'd react to me moving from one out-of-my-league girl to another.

Since it was later in the evening, the barbecue hut wasn't busy. I got my plate of barbecued chicken, corn, kale, and a biscuit (apparently, punk poetry made me ravenous), and we plunked ourselves down by the community garden.

Charles munched his popcorn thoughtfully. "So, this punk poetry thing—what was the point?"

"You got me. You know how performance art can be—completely befuddling whilst impossible to ignore."

"But the poems were good?"

"Well, I don't know if 'good' is the word I'd use. Kind of . . . 'seductive' is more like it." As soon as I'd said it, my stomach pitched sideways. I stole a quick look at Charles. He'd stopped munching.

"Seductive? Why seductive?"

"Uh . . . I don't know. Just, you know, 'cause she was talking about body parts and stuff. That's all. Maybe seductive's not the right word. Maybe . . . sassy? Or . . . cheeky? Playful? I don't know—" *He'll think you're ludicrous for crushing on this girl, Nima. Chill. Out.*

"Right. Sometimes I wonder how someone as articulate as I am is able to carry on a conversation with someone like you."

I threw a piece of kale at him.

"Yick. Keep your leafy fad-food away from me!"

We finished up and started walking toward Charles's house. He talked the whole way about Tessa and what she was doing right now and whether he'd see her tomorrow if he came back.

I was kind of paying attention. But only between flashes of pinafores and poetry.

# CHAPTER 5

After Charles and I said our goodbyes, I walked back to the Weeds, albeit with some reservations. My weirdness around Charles had made me momentarily rethink my decision to go back for the next show—it'd be so easy to curl up and watch a movie with him, or cozy up in my hammock with a book. I wouldn't need to be weird if there wasn't anything to be weird about. I couldn't make a fool of myself watching a movie with my best friend.

But I told myself if I could just get past my house and hammock without being sucked in by the guaranteed comfort, something else might be waiting for me on the other side. Something that might color me outside the lines and flow into other parts of my life.

The sky had darkened and more lights appeared along the tents and rides inhabiting the Weeds. A few of the standing torches were lit as well, creating vague pathways between one tent and the next.

I checked my watch for what seemed to be the hundredth time since dinner. It was 9:37. *Close enough.*

I wandered over with fake confidence to see whether the last tent was open to the public yet, and to find out what this secret show was all about.

As I rounded a corner, I bumped into the back of an unusually tall woman with very broad, strong shoulders—at least they felt awfully strong when I ran into them with my face—who was standing at the end of a long line.

"Oh my gosh—I'm so sorry."

The woman turned, and I was momentarily stunned by sparkles and sequins.

"Oh, that's okay, sweetheart! People bump into me all the time—only they're usually a little taller and huskier. But you're pretty cute for someone with lady parts." She winked and her eyelashes seemed to wave at me. As far as I could tell, they were false eyelashes (that they were made of silver tinsel gave it away), and they weren't the only things that were add-ons here. Those golden braids were definitely a wig. Enough makeup to sink a small ship. Nails long enough to out-claw a koala. And those boobs were awfully perky.

Pretty sure I was talking to a drag queen.

Not that I knew much about drag queens. I'd read enough books and watched enough movies to know a little about "gay culture." But I was still a small-town girl, an introvert, and completely awkward. And this was definitely my first time meeting a drag queen. Coupled with my punk poetry experience, my eyes were being yanked open tonight.

"Here for the show?" Her eyelashes were shiny, thick daddy longlegs. I guessed her age to be late twenties or early thirties.

"I—I think so. Is this the line?"

"It sure is. They should open up soon, though, don't worry." She gave me a quick up-down. I must have seemed like a Camry next to her Cadillac. "You ever seen a show like this, cutie?"

"Uh . . . I'm not sure, to be entirely honest." *Could I sound any more amateur?*

Her bright purple lips extended across her face into an ecstatic grin, and I could see the dark shine of her gums. She wrapped her arm across my shoulders and pulled me up beside her. "My dear, dear chocolate sister, are you trying to tell me you don't know what kind of show this is?" she whispered loudly in my ear. Her breath was sweet with some sort of liquor and . . . bubblegum?

"No—I mean—well, no. Why? What kind of show is it?"

"Darling. Life is so drastically bereft of exquisite surprises— I wouldn't dare steal this one from you. But do come in as my sugar-filled date!" She gave my shoulders a firm squeeze.

She was gregarious and beautiful, and surprisingly, I was wholly at ease with her. And not only would I avoid attending this mystery event alone, but I suddenly felt something like *cool*. Even if I wasn't. And I wasn't.

"Uh, sure. How could I say no?"

"Oh, sweetheart, you could. And many people have!" She let out a thrilling laugh that soared across the park. A few people in the line ahead of us looked back and chuckled. This only seemed to encourage her further. "Ladies and gents and everyone in between, I would like to introduce you to my date for the evening, the fabulous—what's your name, dear?"

"Nima."

"The fabulous Nima!"

A few people in the line—I noticed now that my date was not the only one in drag—clapped and cheered in delight.

Part of me was ready to bolt, but it was a small part, and every other part of me was growing more and more enticed by the possibilities that might await me if I could just leave bland Nima behind and absorb a little more of this . . . this glittering being in front of me.

"My name's Deidre, by the way, and you may refer to me as a Lady, Banshee, Sorceress, Warrior, and Fairy Queen. And the less interesting Ms., Ma'am, Woman, She, and Her, I suppose. And girl, I have to tell you—you are the cutest date I've had in a while." Another wafting wink.

I could easily call her all those things. "Well, Ms.—uh—Fairy Queen? I should tell *you* that you're the *only* date I've had. Ever." Instantly, I regretted revealing such a pathetic fact about myself. The cool, breezy feelings brought on earlier vanished.

Those eyelashes rose almost to the top of her forehead, and her mouth dropped open. "NO."

I looked away, embarrassed, and nodded in confirmation.

"But you're *adorable*. This is a travesty. A *travesty*, I tell you. It must change, and tonight's the night!"

I laughed uncomfortably. *Good one, Deidre*. But her enthusiasm practically glowed through the sequins on her dress, so I let her think what she wanted to.

The tent flap burst open and a person dressed in a suit, tie, and fedora announced, "Good evening, everyone! Please have your money out. Tonight we welcome you to an evening of gender-bending bliss! Come right in and find a seat, but beware the 'splash zone' up front." The person grinned as she? he? they? pulled back the tent flap and fastened it open.

Gender-bending bliss? Splash zone? My brain tried to register on the scale of "Nima's Naiveté" where this event might situate itself. Above or below pretty punks? On par with gorgeous black drag queens?

The line began shuffling forward and Deidre took my hand, clasping it to her chest while she hoisted a gigantic velvet handbag more securely over her shoulder. I felt underdressed in my jean shorts and tank top—not to mention my backpack—and I wished my fashion sense were more sparkles and less brown paper bag.

By the time we passed through the entrance (I simply ignored the sign stating YOU MUST BE EIGHTEEN YEARS OR OLDER TO ATTEND), few seats remained empty, so Deidre pulled me up a narrow aisle toward the front.

I instantly stiffened and slowed my pace. Surveying the seats populated with colorful, luminous characters, I realized how out of place I was. *Seriously. What am I doing here?*

"Maybe we can sit back there?" I pleaded, indicating an area in the farthest back corner where fewer people would see us.

But Deidre had the opposite inclination. "Oh no, honey—how's anyone going to notice you if you're looking at the backs of their heads? We're going to the splash zone!"

"But I—"

"Not another word." She tugged me forward and found us two seats right smack-dab in the middle of the front-frickin'-row. I assumed they were still empty because everyone else knew something I didn't, and my shoulders quickly slumped.

Both of us lugged off our respective bags and sat down on the rickety folding chairs. The air in the tent weighed heavy with heat and made my skin itchy.

Deidre gave me a long look and asked, "How is it that a lovely little thing like you hasn't had a date yet?"

I pressed my fingers into my knees and stared at the stage. "This is a pretty small town, you know." *Also, I'm a pretty pitiful girl.*

"Honey, don't I know it. You ever make your way up to North Gate? There's a little more action in my neighborhood. Not much, mind you, but enough to keep a girl like me busy." Wink-wink.

"I'm a bit of a homebody, I guess. I don't get out much." Her mouth opened to say something, but I anticipated her words. "*That's* my problem, I know."

Her mouth curled downward into a sympathetic smile.

"It's not a problem that can't be solved, sugar. Stick with me and we'll fix it together."

As we waited for the show to start, I discovered that Deidre had lived in North Gate for about six years. She shared with me about how she got started in drag, and I divulged my dad's muumuu-wearing tendencies. I told her a bit about my drama with Ginny, and she reciprocated with a story about her own unrequited love with an older man she'd longed for as a teenager. The more she spoke, the less hot and heavy the air felt. I could tell already that this was someone to hang on to.

At one point, the hunky-looking guy next to Deidre began chatting her up, and far be it from me to get in the way of that, so I took the opportunity to scan the tent.

About forty to fifty seats filled the space. A makeshift stage occupied the front, five times bigger than the stage in the punk tent. The decor reminded me of one of those old kaleidoscopes—fractured light from a disco ball and a few stage lights panned the room in a circle, coating everything in diamonds of reds and blues and yellows. Twinkle lights lined the edges of the stage, and painted black walls, meant to serve as the wings, I supposed, stood on either end. One wall boasted a mustache painted in pink, while the other presented a set of thick blue lips. Across the bottom of both were the words TUCKED AND PACKED.

*Hmm.* I wondered what Charles would make of all this. I could hear him in my head. *Nima, are you sure you want to do this? It's getting weird.*

He was usually right, and though I still felt like a bland pigeon among a gathering of especially flamboyant peacocks, I *did* find myself wanting to do this. Wanting to see if I *could* do it. The night had already brought me so many enchantments— I adjusted my butt in my seat, leaned back, and tried to absorb all the weirdness like it was meant for me.

Somebody let out a whoop and everyone turned to look. The tent walls at the back ruffled like someone was slapping their hands repeatedly up and down and all around out-side. Then more hands, and music began to play—Beyoncé, maybe? The ruffles outside the tent traveled to the sides and then to the front.

People hooted and hollered, including Deidre. She nudged me and winked for the billionth time this evening. I gave her a confused smile, and she wrapped her sinewy arm around me for a firm squeeze.

The walls of the tent seethed now, and the flapping made its way to just behind the stage. The music rose and morphed into a techno version of "Stayin' Alive," a song I knew well given my dad's loyalty to the sixties and seventies.

The crowd's energy grew into a frenzy, and I wondered where all these people had come from. Looking around, I didn't recognize anyone, and no one I knew would be dressed like any of them, that's for sure. Bow ties, sequins, feathers, leather.

Except that guy standing over there in the corner in plain black baggy jeans and . . . a Rolling Stones shirt. I knew that shirt. Wait, what?

*What the hell is Gordon doing here?*

At the moment, he was staring at the quivering tent, thankfully, and hadn't seen me. I sank into my chair and tried to hide behind the boa of the drag queen to my right. Sneaking glances between fluttering red feathers, I could see it was definitely Gordon, and he looked utterly horrified. He kept glancing at the woman next to him, who wore a full tuxedo and was practically falling over with excitement. His arms crossed his chest, and he hunched down so low that his long hair hung over his eyes. I leaned forward farther to see if he was with anyone, and just as I blew some feathers out of my face, his eyes met mine.

He looked away a split second before I did, but I quickly straightened my spine and faced the stage. A stiffness crept into my neck, and I suddenly found it hard to swallow.

*What the feathery frock?* Gordon was literally the last person I thought I'd see here. Literally. Hadn't he called the festival a shithole and said he was leaving?

I refocused my attention on the stage, and thankfully, it looked like something was about to happen, because the frantic hand-tent-flapping thing stopped. The music continued but kept changing—first a remixed Lady Gaga song, then that screeching sound a record makes when you pull the needle off too quickly (my dad still had a record player, okay?), then some Pink, *screech*, Janelle Monáe, *screech*, some song I didn't know, *screech*, another song I didn't know, *screech*, and then the tinkling piano of Gloria Gaynor's "I Will Survive." With each new song, the crowd's cheering would surge, level out, and resurge—my heart moved back and forth with the energy, and between that motion and Gordon Grant, I felt a little nauseous.

Just as the song broke into its beat, a flap behind the stage burst open and in marched one . . . two . . . six individuals. The crowd erupted.

Each person wore something spectacular. One floated in with delicate fabric wings attached to their back and an enormous, bushy beard growing from their chin. A dark blue wig fell in heaps off the head of another and trailed behind them like a supernatural wedding veil. Two particularly androgynous souls were squeezed side by side into one silver unitard that had been sewn together from two. From each of these two folks' genital area extended a plush, blossoming, tissue-paper flower.

The last two performers were less outrageous but exceedingly attractive. One—an older drag queen—wore a long, lustrous gown engulfed in sequins. She walked haltingly with the aid of two elbow crutches, but the crutches were adorned with dazzling diamonds. Her glamorous hair and dress drew on the classic looks I'd seen in some of the vintage photographs lining the walls at Old Stuff, while the complex tattoos engulfing both her arms rooted her firmly in a more unconventional present. The sick feeling in my stomach eased and I could feel my entire face flush with excitement and awe.

The last performer slipped in stealthily with his back to

the audience. Smartly dressed in lace-up oxfords, fitted black pants, and tight black jacket, this figure somehow saturated the stage with his presence. When he turned, the fedora perched on his head fell low enough to hide his face, but then he looked up, and my heart flopped to one side in my chest.

It was Winnow, the pretty poetic punk from earlier.

A classy suit vest and slender black tie completed her outfit, while a light fringe of facial hair bordered her mouth. Her sideburns had grown lengthier too. If she'd been alluring before, she was even more captivating with this slick, masculine look.

And damned if she didn't look straight at me when she raised her eyes. I may have imagined it once again, but from the way my legs suddenly turned into Jell-O, I didn't think so.

All six figures stood along the edges of the stage, the twins facing left, the winged and wigged looking right, and the stunning queen and Winnow staring straight out front.

The music faded to silence, and the crowd grew quiet as well. Even Deidre seemed to be holding her breath.

Slowly, each performer began to tap their left foot in a methodical beat. The clicking grew loud enough to echo across the tent, and as the reverberations of their beat pulsated through the crowd, my own feet impulsively moved along with theirs.

As the performance continued, my eyes, frantically trying to catch every flick of the wrist, every cocked eyebrow, every toe point, eventually slipped into a blissful stupor and allowed themselves to be mesmerized by the scenes unfolding in front of them, like some fantastical narrative transpiring from the pages of a storybook.

The rest of the show streamed through my vision—alternately hilarious, sexy, poignant, lewd, and ludicrous—and left me with sweaty armpits, a not completely unpleasant swirling sensation in my stomach, and several moments of breathlessness.

With each passing moment, I'd get that feeling you sometimes have the moment you're about to flip the final page of a really good book, when your anticipation for what happens next overwhelms you, but you also know that turning the page means you're closer to an end.

This was a story I didn't want to end.

Amid the blur of images emerging before me, Winnow's performance definitely brought my vision into sharper focus. She performed to George Michael's "Freedom! '90." Between Charles's and my dad's penchant for music from any era other than the present one, I had several decades of music covered.

Winnow held the audience spellbound with a slickly choreographed lip sync to the song and an energy that somehow toyed moment to moment with our sense of her. The sideburns screamed masculine, but her soft, shifting limbs and elegant eyelashes spoke all girl. She emanated stillness and exertion, modesty and brashness. And then none of those things but something in between.

Toward the end of the number, I watched in a haze as she

slowly shed the upper half of her clothing until she wore only shoes, pants, and a thin band of hot-pink flagging tape wound several times around her chest. Every part of my body burned with heat and anticipation as she undressed and prowled the stage on her hands and knees, lyrics unspooling from her mouth like silk ribbons.

My throat clamped shut as she crawled toward me. Leaning over the edge of the stage, her face hovered so close to my own as she lip-synced a few lines and fixed her eyes on mine.

*"I just hope you understand, sometimes the clothes do not make the man."*

This time there was no mistake. The Jell-O in my legs steadily overcame the rest of my body, and I thought I was going to wobble out of my chair. I wanted to hold her gaze, I really did. But I feared she'd see right through me to the quivering mess inside and realize she was wasting her lyrics, so I dropped my eyes to her hands and watched them slip away from the edge of the stage.

When I looked up again, she'd focused her attention on an older woman whose mouth opened into an enormous smile. Winnow stepped down off the stage and sat down just at the edge of the woman's knees. She sang the next few lyrics from there, placing the woman's hands over her own shifting hips. After a few moments, Winnow stood, swiveled smoothly toward her chosen audience member, and placed a kiss on the back of the woman's hand.

That could have been my hand.

My next breath remained trapped in my chest, and my rib cage cracked from the pressure.

Deidre reached over and squeezed my knee, but I scarcely felt it. I could barely do anything except try and get that breath out. When I finally did, a sassy geisha peeked through a gap in the pink tape as Winnow disappeared through the back of the tent. The familiar sense of a missed opportunity swept over me.

One performance followed hers.

I don't remember any of it.

# CHAPTER 6

When the show ended, Deidre wrapped her muscular arm around me once again and gave me a big, lipstick-y kiss on the cheek.

"Girl! You got your money's worth tonight, didn't you?"

"Uh, yeah. That was . . . awesome" was all I could get out. My tongue felt like Jell-O too. Or something mushier. Pudding.

"One number in particular, I think, hmm?"

I sucked in my lips and stared at the ground in front of me.

"Don't be embarrassed, lovely! I'm not one for the female types, but even I can appreciate utter sex appeal when I see it in a woman. And that slick George Michael is simply steaming with it."

*Yeah, that's the problem.*

"Do you want to meet her? I happen to know people who know people—I'm *that* connected."

Before I could answer, she yanked me out of my seat and pulled me toward the exit behind the stage. I'd almost forgotten about Gordon, but I glanced back now. I couldn't see him, and I hoped I wouldn't, but part of me really wanted to know what he was doing there. Another part of me hoped he'd left before seeing me turn into a blob of sticky-sweet gelatin.

We flapped through the tent to the festive world beyond. The night had warped into a whole galaxy of glinting lights, bobbing heads, and bursts of fire. The moment we stepped out, I felt like I'd plunged into a soaring Milky Way of stars and unearthly matter. Luckily, Deidre still had my hand and guided me through the universe and toward the bonfire.

I wasn't sure what time it was, but the party had definitely started. The bonfire raged, its flames leaping high into the night. Crowds of people danced and staggered around the flickering sparks and flares. The rest of the drag-show crowd had also made its way out here—a smattering of feathers and glitz flashed across the scene.

Deidre pulled me into the masses, and we made our way through like salmon swimming upstream. As she tugged me in a zigzag, my hands became hotter and sweatier. What in the world was I going to say to these people? To Winnow? What could I possibly have to say that would be even remotely interesting to someone like her?

*Hey, nice show.*

*That pink tape looks sticky.*

*Does your geisha have a name?*

*Cool sideburns. Is that your real hair?*

*Would you like some Jell-O? My legs are made of it.*

*Good God in glittering gumboots. What am I thinking?*

"Hey, Deidre, I think I should just go home. It's getting pretty late, and I never really let anyone know where I was going, so—"

She stopped dead in her tracks and turned to face me. "Oh hell no, lady friend." Grabbing my face in her hands, which smelled like lilacs, she said, "My darling. You're nervous. I get it." She spoke loudly over the din of the crowd. "But sweetheart, *live a little*."

*Easy for you to say, Queen Deidre. Your "living" probably doesn't involve tripping over yourself and constant rejection.*

Looking me square in the eyes, she added, "Do you really want to wake up tomorrow not having done this?"

*Depends on the "this." What if "this" includes being tongue-tied in front of Winnow? Or being ignored by her entirely?*

But something in Deidre's eyes and sympathetic smile fortified me. I guess she had a point. I might make a fool of myself, but at least I wouldn't regret it tomorrow. Or maybe I would regret it. But at least I'd *know* what I was regretting, instead of regretting not knowing what I would have done. Right?

"Okaaaayyyy. But please don't leave me alone. Please." I didn't mean to sound as whiny as I did.

She gave me a pitying look. "Sugar, I am not that type of girl."

Somehow, I believed her.

She pinched my chin and continued to tow me behind

her, past the bonfire, around to the back of one of the smaller tents, where there appeared to be a separate gathering taking place. Another fire popped and crackled in the middle, with a mix-and-match of chairs gathered around it.

"Come." Deidre hadn't let loose my hand yet, thankfully, and now she guided me toward a group of drag queens who sat in lawn chairs next to a bright red canopy, smoking a variety of substances.

"Well, well, if it isn't the belles of the ball!" Deidre's voice soared, and many extravagant heads turned toward us.

"And if it isn't the balls with bells!"

Cackles.

Just as I started to feel even more awkward, one of the queens stood up, glided over to me in a magnificent fashion, and seized my hand from Deidre.

"*You* are *adorable.* I'm Marsha. What in the world are you doing with this drama queen?"

I tried to focus on her bright blue eye shadow. I'd been called adorable by two drag queens so far tonight and was beginning to wonder if drag queens had something equivalent to beer goggles but, like, drag goggles.

"Hi. I'm—Nima. Deidre and I just met, really."

"Picking up sweet little dykes now, Dee Dee?" Marsha asked.

*Does she mean me?* I'd never really thought of myself using that word either.

Deidre placed one indignant hand on her hip. "Who you

callin' a dyke, you prissy bitch? Nima's just Nima, as far as I
know." She grabbed my hand back and gave it a kiss.

*Getting. More. Awkward.*

Marsha, surprisingly, appeared somewhat abashed. She
looked at me and put a hand on my shoulder. "No offense
intended, cutie. I know better than to assume!"

"Uh, no offense taken . . ." My forehead itched. *What am
I doing here?*

"Girl, you went and made her uncomfortable," Deidre
scolded.

That sent up a chorus of "Oh nooos" and "Girls" and
"Booooos" from the other queens, which culminated in a
cacophonous but somehow soothing fit of laughter.

I couldn't help but laugh as well.

I was offered a beer. I accepted, but nursed it. Not that
Charles and I didn't partake in our fair share of his parents'
wine and spirits now and again, but I wanted my wits about
me this evening. I also thought, though, that a little liquid
courage wouldn't hurt if I did have to face certain pixie punk
types.

The next half an hour involved some of the most surprising conversations I'd ever heard, to say the least.

"Sugar, you will never be-*lieve* the dexterity of the doctor
who gave me these boobs."

"My eighty-seven-year-old grandmother was the first
person to tell me I had a gorgeous figure and should show
it off."

"She just said to 'Trust the Mother Earth Spirit Nipple' and everything would be all right."

"All I have to say is that the worst show I ever did involved a very expensive, purebred, hairless cat. Enough said."

The gathering around us had grown by at least thirty or forty people and the volume had risen too. A couple of other queens joined our group, along with three women dressed as men. All three had BROWN BROTHER POSSE printed across their ball caps, and I learned that they were drag kings. I'd never heard of that before—drag *queens*, yes—but not kings. I guessed that was what Winnow was as well?

This was definitely beyond my research and reading realms. While I'd dabbled online over the past few years, my search history garnering a long list of topics such as *Where do gay girls go?* and *Are straight girls ever gay?* and *Watch lesbian movies free*, my investigations had never revealed anything about drag kings or scenes like the one unfolding in front of me.

As I sipped my beer, I surreptitiously glanced around the crowd, a restlessness brewing in my body. Deidre stayed true to her promise not to leave me alone—and stood beside me, chatting with a couple of boys who weren't dressed in drag. Eventually, I placed my empty can of beer on the ground and touched her elbow. "Hey, Deidre."

"Yeah, baby?"

"Will all the performers from tonight be coming here, you think?"

"Oh, girl, just ask what you really want to ask: Will that sexy George Michael be coming along?"

I tucked a strand of my hair behind my ear and looked into the fire. Trying to keep my voice even, I responded, "Well, I just thought it might be kind of cool to meet her, maybe. . . ."

"Well, I think you've been trying so hard to look like you're *not* looking that you've missed some details. She hasn't missed you, though, from what I gather. Don't look now, but—" She turned herself directly toward me and pointed her finger back over her right shoulder.

I casually leaned over to my left to look behind her. Casting my eyes slowly across the scene, I saw a group of stagehands sitting on some blankets and playing some sort of drinking game. Standing just behind them, holding a can of beer and talking to another girl, was Winnow.

She wasn't in costume anymore. Her hair no longer curved into a peak, nor hid beneath a hat, but instead swept over her right shoulder in an inky, silky-looking waterfall. She wore black jeans and the same heavy boots as before. A green tank top with a photo of Dolly Parton on it hung loosely off her slender frame, and she had a leather bag over her shoulder.

Three times tonight I'd seen her, and each time it was like she'd reincarnated as someone new. All three seemed like people I wanted to know. People who seemed to be causing disruptions to my heartbeat. But also, three people with three possible styles of rejection.

*The punk poet: This girl. You. No, girl.*

*The king: Baby bye bye bye.*

*The girl: \*Blink, blink. Silence.\**

She took a swig of her beer and glanced over to where we were standing. When she caught me looking, I thought she paused mid-sip for a split second. I quickly leaned back in to hide behind Deidre's broad shoulder, but Deidre had already turned back to the boys next to her. I tried to look like I was part of their conversation and laughed a little, awkward as ever. Deidre turned to me.

"Well, did you find her?" she asked.

"Huh? Oh yeah. I think that's her over there by the picnic table."

"And?" Her fake eyelashes blinked demandingly.

"And what?"

"And are you going over there or do I need to drag you?"

"'Drag' me. Ha-ha—good one." Inside my sneakers, my toes curled and uncurled.

"Okay, listen up." She slipped the fingers of both of her hands through my backpack shoulder straps—*oh my God, I'm still wearing a backpack*—and pulled me to her. She had definitely consumed a few drinks by that point, and her breath smelled even sweeter than before, like peaches and medicine.

"Am I going to have to give you pep talks all night? Because you are too lovely to be hiding out here with a bunch of queens and their loyal but delirious fans."

"I can't just walk over there. She's with people. Cool people. What will I say?" Fumbling attempts to profess my

love and Ginny's friendly pats on the back flashed in my
mind.

"That girl has been checking you out since the minute she
got here. Here's what you do: walk over to the Porta-Potties
and stand in line. Just act natural. I promise she'll be right
behind you."

"Mmm, let's meet by the Porta-Potties, sweetheart," I said
with exaggerated breathiness. "How romantic."

"Never mind, smart-ass. Now, I'm gonna say something
completely uninteresting, but you and I are going to laugh like
it's the funniest thing in the world. Then I'm gonna give you a
big old hug, and you're going to walk off to the washroom right
after that. Got it?"

"Uh—"

"Good. Here we go: I really need to get my eyebrows
plucked—they're weighing me down into a frown. Now laugh!"
She let out that spiraling laughter of hers, and just the sound
made me smile. Then I was laughing too. Really laughing.

She wiped a tear from the corner of her eye. "Okay, now
come in for our hug, sugar." She wrapped her lengthy arms
around me. My nose was squished up against one of her plump
boobs, but I didn't mind. I was glad to stretch my arms around
her muscular waist and squeeze tight. This was a good hug,
and it calmed a few of the fluttering wings in my stomach.

As I turned toward the Porta-Potties, Deidre spanked
me on my butt and I let out another loud guffaw. Each laugh
calmed me a little more. Maybe it was just this night in gen-

eral. Everything felt so surreal, so magnificently unusual. Maybe heading to a set of blue Porta-Potties to try and pick up a girl who moonlighted as a drag king made perfect sense on a night like tonight. Maybe I was caught up in some kind of cross-genre, fairy tale–romance–fantasy.

A short line had formed in front of the three weathered Porta-Potties. I stood at the end and dug my hands into my pockets, trying to look as though loitering around portable toilets was totally my thing.

By the time I pulled open the thick plastic door to one of the Porta-Potties, I really did need to pee. I shut and locked the door tightly behind me, muffling the laughter and music of the party. The quiet would have been comforting if the smell wasn't so obscene. I quickly peed, wiped, hand-sanitized, then pushed back out into the noise and fresh air.

My lips released a burst of breath I hadn't even realized I'd been holding.

"That bad, huh? Should I just use a bush?"

Winnow was at the end of the line, but kind of off to the side, like she wasn't really planning on standing in line at all. *Lord in lady pants. Deidre really knew her stuff.*

I wet my lips. *Where's a gallon of water when you need it?* "Uh . . . yeah, it's pretty gross. A bush might be better. Although I can never pee properly when I'm squatting. My legs get tired and then I lose my balance and pee all over myself—"

"Hey, TMI, girly!" someone in the line shouted.

I'm sure all the brown in my cheeks burned red.

"Oh no, I hear you. I always pee all over myself when I try to pee in the woods too," Winnow said. Her hands were in her back pockets, her head tilted a little to the right. She was just trying to make me feel better, but I appreciated it.

Also, that head tilt.

She took a couple of slow steps toward me. "I think I recognize you. Did you come to my shows tonight?" One hand reappeared and played with the pendant around her neck, a tiny crescent moon.

"Uh, yeah." *But I'm not stalking you! I promise!* "I didn't even know what I was seeing, to be honest. Both were just kind of . . . whims."

A couple more steps and she was within arm's reach. "Following a whim is nothing to be ashamed of." She pulled her fingers through her loose hair, combing it down over her shoulder. It could have been actual silk. "What did you think?"

I heard Deidre in my head. *Keep your cool, girl.* "Well, both were . . . surprising. I've never seen anything like them."

"Yeah, the punk poetry thing is just an experiment. Was it too weird? Cheesy?"

For just a moment, her eyes fluttered with worry and a tiny rivulet of relief flowed through me. *Is she nervous too?*

"No, no—not at all. Well, actually, yes—weird and cheesy, but wonderful. Weird, cheesy, *and* wonderful." My cheeks felt splotchy. *Don't give too much away, fool!*

Her face exploded into a grin. My chest exploded with relief. "You're adorable. Come on." She turned and headed back toward the drag crowd.

*Adorable. Again. I need to hang out with these folks more often.*

As we walked, she held her hand upturned toward me and said, "I'm Winnow."

After a confusing moment of deliberating what I was meant to do, I laid my hand on top of hers, our fingers lacing together in a brief squeeze for an odd but wonderful handshake. Her skin felt like it was well used—a bit rough, but comforting. Like well-worn leather.

"Nima," I said, reluctantly letting go of her hand.

"Short for?"

"Pardon?"

"Nima. Short for what?"

"Oh . . . Nimanthi."

"Cool name. Do you ever use it?"

"No."

"Too long?"

*Maybe, but that's not the reason.* "Yeah."

"Where's it from?"

"My mom chose it." *That's part of the reason.*

"Well, it's an awesome name. Can I call you that?"

I wanted her to call me lots of things, but not that. "Sure, but I may not answer."

She laughed and squeezed my shoulder. "Okay, okay. Nima

it is. Nima's cool too." Her fingers slid down my arm before departing.

*Merciful heavens.* I swallowed my heart back into my chest and just focused on placing one foot in front of the other.

She led me back into the party. My bare arm was a mere inch or two away from her bare arm, and my skin tingled at the thought. A shiver ran through me and I involuntarily twitched.

Winnow turned toward me. "Cold?"

"A little, I guess." *But not really.*

"Well, let's get closer to the fire, silly." She said this while rubbing her palm up and down my arm a couple of times.

"Well, okay then." I smiled casually, but my heart played hopscotch around my chest. I tried to temper the feeling with a few breaths. I was still having a hard time trusting any of this—that these people would really like me, that I wouldn't make a complete jackass of myself—and part of me was waiting for the Ball of Doom to drop.

As we strolled over to the fire, Deidre caught my eye, and her teeth took up her entire face at the sight of Winnow and me. I had a hard time not laughing. But Winnow saw me smirk. "What are you smiling at?"

"Just my friend over there—the one in the shiny blue dress. She makes me smile, is all."

"Cute. I've seen her around before. Dee Dee, right? She does a kick-ass show. Introduce me?"

"Sure, no problem." *'Cause I'm cool like that.*

I walked her over to Deidre, whose face was still enveloped by an enormous grin.

"Well, hello, hello, ladies! Aren't you two a welcome sight! All these queens everywhere. We need some diversity around here, people!" she hollered, whipping her head and her tight bronze braids back toward the circle of queens. She had clearly kept on imbibing since I left, although really, she didn't seem that different from her less drunk self.

"Deidre, this is Winnow. Winnow, Deidre."

"I've seen you, girl!" Deidre went straight in for a hug, and Winnow complied gleefully, laughing out loud. Deidre pulled back, holding Winnow at arm's length. "I love a sister who's not afraid to hug a loud, obnoxious stranger!"

"I agree one hundred percent," Winnow said, her eyes on me. I wasn't sure what that look meant. Should I have hugged her by now?

Luckily, Deidre squeezed in between us, turned, grabbed us both by the waist, and guided us toward the fire.

"Ladies and other folks," she announced, "I would like to introduce you to two of the finest people with vaginas I have met today, Miss Nima and Miss Winnow." She turned to Winnow quickly and stage-whispered, "Is it 'Miss'?"

Winnow laughed. "Yes, you can go with 'Miss' at the moment."

"Miss-at-the-Moment Winnow!" Deidre bellowed over the crowd. Then she paused again and whispered to us both,

"And I just assumed you had vaginas . . . sorry!" She giggled.

Winnow and I shared our amusement across Deidre's pronounced boobs.

Giving us both a little push, she said, "Now go on with your bad selves!" and let loose an unruly "Whee!"

Winnow and I trotted a few steps from the force of Deidre's exuberant push and fell into a similar pace toward the fire. My arms welcomed the warmth. I felt even more shy now that we stood still, and alone.

"She's something else," Winnow offered, pulling a couple of cans of beer out of her shoulder bag and handing me one.

Another beer would definitely not hurt right now, so I took it. "Yeah. I feel like I've known her forever, but I only met her a few hours ago."

"Wait—seriously?" Her eyebrows leaped up.

"Yeah. We met in line for your show."

"For the drag show?"

"Yeah."

"I love that."

"What?"

"That you met waiting to see drag. For me, drag is all about community." She pulled open the tab on her beer and slurped up some foam.

"Have you been doing it for very long?" I opened my can and took a sip too, trying to look as cool as her but dribbling a few drops of beer on my shirt instead.

"Officially only a couple of years. But I've been practicing in my bedroom for much longer." She smiled at me—a bit shyly, maybe?

"You mean you pranced around in front of the mirror in boys' clothing, don't you?" I smiled back, wiping the wet spot on my shirt as casually as possible.

"Precisely. You ever done that?"

"Pranced around in men's clothing? No." I thought for a moment. "But I never wear dresses, either. And my dad wears muumuus. Do I get credit for my dad's cross-dressing?"

"Ha-ha, yes. You absolutely get credit for that. And for being adorable."

*Seriously, stop saying that. I might start believing it's true.*

"Do you live here?" she asked.

I had to swallow a few times before I could speak. "Yeah. Just a few blocks from here, actually."

"With your parents?"

"Yeah—well, with my dad."

"So you're in high school?"

*Uh-oh. Should I lie? Probably.* But I didn't. "Yeah, going into senior year. You?"

"Me what?"

"Where are you from, how old are you, et cetera."

She rattled off a half-dozen places she'd lived. I quickly did the mental math and realized she must be at least twenty-one, which gave me a couple of heart palpitations.

"Wow. That's a lot of movement." *Now what?* "Um, how did you get into all of . . . this?" I asked, flicking my hand around me.

"Drag, you mean?"

"Yeah."

"I guess it was just a natural progression out of a bunch of things I enjoyed, like dressing up, dancing, performing. . . ." She downed a few gulps of her beer.

"Taking your clothes off?" I said, before I could control my mouth.

She half choked on her beer and had to cover her mouth with her hand.

I reciprocated by covering my eyes with my own hand. "I have no idea why I said that. I'm so sorry."

She swallowed and laughed easily and loudly. "Don't worry about it. It's true—I do tend to enjoy removing items of clothing." Once I let my hand fall, I could see her eyes glimmering.

*What do I say to that?* Generally, silences didn't bother me. We'd always been good at silences in my family. And Charles and I were comfortable with plenty of quiet. But I felt like silences with Winnow were a sign that I was too boring to carry a conversation. We didn't know each other well enough to hold comfortable silences, right?

"Where do you live now?" I tried.

"Right now? In North Gate. I live in a house with a couple of others and work at a community center up there."

"Nice. Deidre lives there too."

"Yeah, we've performed at a few shows together. I just never got to formally meet her. But now I have, thanks to you."

She leaned in to nudge me with her shoulder, and her arm stayed pressed up against mine.

Another shiver passed through me, but I tried hard not to let her feel it and pressed on. "You travel around doing drag otherwise?"

"Not really. I mostly stay put and do drag once a month at this local bar. There's not a huge, drag king–loving crowd around here, but we manage to pull a decent crowd most nights. This is only the second time I've performed outside of the bar. What about you? What do you get up to when you're not in school?"

I was trying to decipher whether that last question indicated any disdain with "school" and the fact that I was still in it. "I read a lot. Sometimes I garden. I have a part-time job at a gardening shop."

*Good grief.* As I was saying it, I realized how boring it must all sound to her.

"Cool—what do you like to read?"

"You don't really care, do you?" *Nima. Why?*

She cocked her head and looked at me, a slight frown forming on her brow.

*Push through, push through!* "Uh, all kinds of stuff, I guess. But I prefer novels."

"Happy endings or sad?"

"Umm, believable ones, I guess?"

"So what's a believable ending for tonight, you think?" The frown disappeared. More smiling. More looking at lips.

My cheeks burned and I didn't know where to look. To hide my embarrassment, I turned back toward Deidre. "Good question. I'm beginning to wonder if it might end with me hauling Deidre home to sleep on my couch."

Winnow turned to look too. Deidre was now barefoot and in the process of using her four-inch heels to play horseshoes. A stick protruded from the ground, and she was competing with another queen to see who could throw their heels closest to it. They weren't throwing the shoes anywhere near the stick, but they were having an amazing time doing it. A cheering section of queens swung their wigs and handbags around like lassos and hollered out a litany of diva shouts and screams.

"Yeah, I feel you may need some help with that," Winnow sympathized.

"Shall we go hover, in case she can't stand as well in her bare feet as she can in her heels?"

"Let's."

I was thankful for the diversion. We strolled over and stood a little ways from Deidre, watching the commotion and drinking our beer. I snuck a few glances at Winnow as we walked. With her hair swept over one shoulder, her ear and neck lay open toward me, soft and inviting.

I weighed my options here. Was this girl way out of my league? Not only was she wicked awesome and way more interesting than me, but she was also clearly more experienced in a hundred million ways.

But I couldn't ignore this feeling of electricity that moved through me when I stood beside her. And it seemed like that feeling was mutual, maybe?

But maybe not. Maybe I was assuming too much. I could be making up any interest on her part. Why in the world would she be interested in me? She was probably just being friendly. She seemed really friendly.

And then I felt her friendly hand on my back.

She leaned over and shout-whispered into my ear, "You think you'd ever come visit me in North Gate?"

I looked at her. A cheeky smile crept across her face. She looked from my eyes to my lips, back to my eyes.

Swallow. Blink. Breathe. "For sure—I'd love to see one of your regular shows, actually."

"That'd be cool. Maybe I can rope you into performing with me."

I laughed out loud. Loudly. "Nice one."

"You never know."

"Trust me, I know. But I'd definitely be into watching you." *Did that sound weird?*

Deidre's sweaty, hot body crashed into us before I had a chance to second-guess myself some more.

"Babies! I won! I won the drag-queen heel toss! Aren't you proud of me?" She was all arms and wig and lipstick—full of a genuine, contagious excitement.

"We saw. We're impressed!" I took ahold of her arm to lend her some stability. Winnow took the other.

"Yeah, I'm not sure I've ever seen a high-heel toss before. *Very* impressive," Winnow added.

"I know," she drawled, her voice falling an octave. "I can't *help* how talented I am. But now, goddesses, I find myself fatigued and wish to sleep." She rubbed her cheek against mine like a cat. "Your place or mine?"

*My place? To sleep? For real?* The thought of having Deidre spend the night sent an unexpected thrill through my heart, even as it exacerbated the agitation that had set up camp in my stomach. "Uh—I guess that depends on if you have a way home. Do you?" I asked.

"If you're in North Gate, I could give you a ride, if you wanted one," Winnow offered.

Deidre made a pouty face. "Must we drive *all* the way back there tonight?" Then her face lit up and she followed with, "Can't we have a sleepover instead? Girls' night!" She wrapped her arms around us and swayed a little to the left.

The additional thought of a sleepover with Deidre *and* Winnow just about sent every bone in my body flying in different directions. Before losing this opportunity like so many before it, I quickly followed with, "Okay, I guess my place it is." I looked at Winnow, trying to keep my features neutral.

"That sounds amazing," she said, "but I promised a friend I'd give him a ride home tonight. I'll have to take a rain check."

I swallowed the pang of disappointment that rose in my throat.

"But let's get you to a nice, comfortable couch ASAP, gorgeous," Winnow added, taking Deidre's arm and nodding at me to take the other. As I did, I couldn't help letting my mind linger on the thought of a future sleepover with Winnow.

By the time we wobbled our way back to my house, Deidre had managed to give us a whirlwind tour of her early years as a young violin prodigy *and* relay the stories of two separate occasions involving the same feral ferret. Along the way, I found myself wanting to be her best friend forever.

After a tipsy struggle up the three porch steps, we managed to get Deidre in the door, through the living room, and onto the couch. I had to shush Gus as he came bouncing down the stairs to investigate. He instantly flopped onto his back in front of Winnow for a belly rub, which she happily gave him.

The air was warm and so was Deidre, so I just threw a light sheet on top of her. I wrote a brief note for my dad and slipped it under his bedroom door so he wouldn't walk downstairs to a surprise drag queen in the morning. He was pretty chill, but I wasn't entirely sure what his reaction to this whole scenario would be. My usually boring life didn't often test the limits of his easygoing-ness.

"Should I let you sleep now?" Winnow whispered, looking up at me from the floor. Gus had inserted himself onto her lap.

*I'll never sleep again.* "I'm not that tired, actually. Do you want some iced tea or something? It's hot." Pause. "The air, not the iced tea." *Jesus.* "Or, you probably need to get back to your friend—"

"Iced tea would be awesome. I can text my friend and meet him in a bit."

I got two glasses of tea while Winnow texted, and then we sat on the porch steps, our arms touching again.

Determined to start the conversation, I blurted, "I love your back tattoo, by the way."

"Oh, thanks! I love her too. I think people sometimes mistake geishas for these submissive, proper women, but I don't think of them that way. I like to think of her as my alter ego. She's way more badass than I am."

"More badass than you? Doing drag and making up poetry on the spot isn't badass enough?"

"Well, that's kind of what I mean. When I'm performing, I kind of think of myself as this other person. In my real life, I'm pretty shy."

*As if.* "You don't seem that shy to me."

"Well, when I'm properly motivated, I can be more outgoing." She leaned into me a bit, and I had to look away so she couldn't see the goofy smile on my face.

"Okay, let me know if this next question is annoying," she said.

I looked back at her, curious.

"Are you mixed?"

It took me a second to figure out what she was asking.

Before I could find words, she added, "I only ask because I am—my mom's half-Japanese, half-white, and my dad is full

Japanese—and I thought maybe you're mixed too. Sorry if you get asked that a lot."

I smiled at her. "I don't mind when people ask like you just did. Most people are just like, 'What are you?' or 'How come your dad's so white compared to you?'"

"I know—I've actually been asked, 'How come you look so white but have Asian-y eyes?' Seriously? What the eff?"

I laughed at her incredulous face. "To answer your question, yes, I'm mixed too. My dad's white and my mom's brown."

"What kind of brown?"

"Sri Lankan brown. It's a little island off—"

"India!" Winnow exclaimed. When she saw my surprised look, she laughed and added, "My mom used to work for the UN and made sure I learned beyond my own backyard. I have excellent geographical knowledge." She dusted off her shoulder with playful smugness.

*Meanwhile, Nima remains woefully tethered to her own backyard,* my annoying inside voice whispered. Trying to ignore said inside voice, I replied, "Whoa. Your mom worked for the UN? That's amazing."

"Yeah, she's a pretty cool lady, I'll admit."

The next twenty minutes felt like twenty seconds as we talked about our parents' occupations, more pet peeves of being mixed, and what it was like to live in North Gate as opposed to Bridgeton. I discovered that I definitely needed to spend more time in North Gate, for several reasons—namely,

Winnow, Deidre, and a bigger gay scene than I'd imagined.

"So your dad's a mechanic. What about your mom?" Winnow asked after I'd been deliberately skirting the topic of my mother.

I tried to keep things general. "She just worked for my dad, mostly—ran the business side of things."

"Oh, sorry, you said you just live with your dad, right?"

"Yeah." I didn't really know what else to say about that topic.

Winnow was silent for a moment. Then: "Cool. We don't need to talk about that." She took my hand in hers and pulled it into her lap. I wished I didn't have such healthy, sweaty pores.

"Deidre's a real find," Winnow said. "I can't believe she and I have never connected before this."

"Yeah, she's awesome," I said, acutely aware of how each of her fingers laced through each of mine. I stared at the mostly melted ice cubes bobbing up and down in my barely sipped tea. I could feel her looking at me, and I was sure the heat off my face would easily melt the rest of the cubes.

A moment later Winnow dropped my hand, took the tea from me, and put both her glass and mine on the step behind us.

I imagined this was what it was like when someone injected adrenaline into your system.

She placed her hand on my cheek.

*She's going to know I've never kissed anyone before.* I stared at the moon on her chest so hard my eyes burned. Tears welled up.

When she saw this, she hesitated and pulled back a little.

"Are you okay?"

*Oh my God, Nima. Seriously?* "Uh, yeah, sorry." I wiped my eyes. "Sorry, I don't know. . . ." Apologizing just made me want to cry more. It just reminded me how little I had to offer Winnow, how embarrassing this could all so easily become.

"Hey, it's okay. Too soon. I get it."

*No! Not too soon.* "Yeah, maybe. Sorry." Tears rolled down my cheeks. I couldn't look at her and I couldn't wipe them away fast enough.

"Come here." She got to her feet and pulled me into a hug. It felt good. So good the tears came harder and faster. I tried to choke them back, but that just made my chest heave fitfully against her.

"Sorry."

"Stop apologizing." She squeezed me tighter. Then, pulling back to look at me, she wiped my cheeks and said, "Sometimes tears just happen."

*Yeah, at the worst possible times.*

Finally my tears ebbed. I stepped back and lifted my T-shirt to wipe my face.

"Whoa—what's with the six-pack, Miss Universe?" She started to tickle my belly.

"Oh yeah, right." She'd made me laugh, though, which I suspected was her goal.

"Listen, I don't want to go, but I should. My friend's waiting."

*Yeah, I'd want to go if I were you too.* "Okay, sure."

"Can I give you my number, though? Do you have a cell?"

"Really? I mean, yeah, yeah, of course." Surprised she still wanted me to call her after my baffling breakdown, I fumbled for my phone and almost dropped it.

After giving me her number, she squeezed my hand. "Talk soon, I hope," she said, her fingers lingering on mine.

All my words caught in my throat as I watched her walk off into the darkness.

As I lay in bed that night, I played out our almost-kiss over and over again. But this time, our lips reached each other's and I imagined the softness of them, the wet of her tongue, her breath against my face, my hands against her body. This time, there were no tears—just lips and hands and tongues.

It was hours before I fell asleep.

# CHAPTER 7

The next morning I rolled over in my bed to find Gus lying on his side next to me and panting softly. His breath, rank and hot, blew into my face in soft puffs. I drew my hand from beneath the covers and placed it over the side of his face. "Gus. Stop. You stink."

His panting paused for a moment. Then he licked his own nose and resumed as before.

A gentle knock on my bedroom door interrupted this precious moment.

"Nima? It's Dad. You up?"

I rolled over and out of bed, Gus hopping out beside me. My eyes felt like pinpoints, and I tried to blink the sleep out as I opened the door. "Hi, Dad." Then I remembered last night. "Oh, hey—did you get my note?" My voice sounded like sandpaper against wood.

"Yeah, I just thought I'd let you know that your friend is up and making breakfast."

*What.*

After a quick wash, I went into the kitchen, and Deidre was indeed at the stove. Eggs crackled in a pan, coffee dripped from its machine, and sliced mango fanned out across a plate on the table. Deidre still wore her dress from last night, but she was barefoot and wigless. Her short hair was in tight cornrows against her scalp, and she also seemed to have washed most of the makeup off her face. Her skin looked brand-new, and without her lavish wig, she somehow seemed even more womanly. I noticed that her figure still had every curve it had boasted the previous night.

I was in plaid boxer shorts and a tank top, still feeling like a Toyota Tercel next to her Lamborghini.

When she saw me, she said, "Well, well, what is *your* excuse for rolling out of bed so late on this gorgeous morning?" Her smile still shone.

"I have no excuse. I definitely did not think *you* would wake up this side of noon, considering."

"Considering what?" Her lips pursed and smirked all at once. "I'm a pro, girl. That was a quiet night for me! Eggs are almost ready. Where's that handsome father of yours?"

"You met?"

"Oh yes, we've already had coffee and shared stories, and he's told me all kinds of interesting things about his one and only daughter. He made all the pancakes sitting in the oven right now."

Dad and Deidre making breakfast together? And I thought last night was surreal.

"Come, sit," she commanded. "Delford! Breakfast is ready!"

Hearing Deidre call out my dad's first name sent a ripple of surprise and amusement through me.

But there he was. Delford. Instantly at the doorway to the kitchen, ready for breakfast.

"It smells great, Deidre. I'm famished," he said.

"Well, sit on down, sugar. Let's eat."

"You sit. Let me get everything on the table."

Deidre didn't argue. Neither did I. I felt like I could have eaten a dozen eggs and a foot-high stack of pancakes at that point.

As we shoveled food into our mouths like we hadn't eaten in days, my thoughts went back to last night. Had all that really happened? A wave of images rolled through my mind. Then that almost-kiss drifted into view and I wanted to cry all over again. *What is wrong with me?*

After breakfast, Deidre and I ended up on the porch swing, sipping coffee.

"How was last night, sweetheart?"

I thought about it for a moment. "Amazing. Confusing. Awful. Amazing."

She let out a peal of laughter that I'm sure they heard in the next town over.

"I don't even know where to begin," I added.

"Well, let's start with how sweet you two looked together." She put her hand on my thigh. "Honey, do me a favor and don't overanalyze this. You like that amazing girl and she likes you. As my mama used to say, 'You're gonna break that brain a' yours, and then what?'"

I squished my lips over to one side, something I did when I was thinking. Mom used to do it too. Deidre and her mama were right, of course, but I'd never been too good at taking action without overthinking.

"I'll try."

"Good. Try *hard*. That girl is *sublime*."

"She is, isn't she?"

"She is."

"What about you, Deidre? Did you meet anyone special last night?"

"Well, of course, girl—I met you!" She chuckled.

I rolled my eyes. "You know what I mean."

Deidre downed the rest of her coffee, stood up, and stretched. Every inch of her looked strong as hell. Placing her cup on the railing, she said, "I'm taking a break from romance, sugar. Abstaining from drama, if you will."

I contemplated her words. What I'd give for the *need* to abstain from romantic drama. If I had any *less* of either romance or drama in my life, I'd be an absurdist comedy. Maybe I already was.

She dug around in her purse for a moment, wisps of her wig poking out of it, and then pulled out a silver card.

"Here's all my info, sweetheart. I wanna see you. Soon."

I read the card. DEE DEE LA BOUCHE, ROYALTY'S BEST FRIEND. The subhead stated: MAKEOVERS AND MAGIC FOR KINGS AND QUEENS OF ALL SHAPES, SIZES, & PERSUASIONS. I smiled. "I'd love to see you again too, Deidre."

"You're damn right you would."

"Can I walk you somewhere? Or maybe my dad can give you a ride?"

"Oh no, I'm just going to mosey on back to the fairgrounds and pick up my van. That was my B plan—to sleep in my car. But luckily, I ran into your sweet little self instead." She took my face in her hands and gave me two wet kisses on either cheek. She looked right into my eyes and said, "You, my friend, are a gem." And then she strutted away, magically managing to slip her heels on without breaking stride.

Over the next couple of days, I went back to the festival a few more times, hoping to re-experience some of the magic from the first night, but the drag show tent had switched over to a very strange, one-man *Rocky Horror Picture Show*. I left during the intermission. It wasn't terrible, but it was no punk poetry performance or George Michael, that's for sure.

Charles talked me into lingering around the square on Friday and Saturday nights, trying to spot Tessa. The closest we got was on Saturday as we sat on the grass next to the barbecue hut, devouring ribs. I'd warned Charles that ribs were a dangerous choice in case Tessa did show up, but he ignored me at his peril, and then there she was, failing miserably to hide her mild revulsion at Charles's face, which was, of course, smeared with a generous amount of barbecue sauce.

Tessa paused hesitantly as Charles just stared at her. Then, in slow motion, Charles's tongue extended from his mouth as he tried to casually lick the sauce off his left cheek, then above his mouth, then his right cheek, and finally, below his mouth in a perfect, disgusting circle. Tessa and I just watched him, mesmerized and repelled all at once. I finally snapped into action to hand him a napkin, but it was too late. Tessa did this half-wave thing, giggled uneasily, and then practically tripped over herself in her haste to get away.

We sat still until she disappeared around the corner of a stall. Then Charles flopped backward onto the ground and let out a sound that I imagined walruses expressed when they'd had a bad day.

"Sorry, pal," I offered.

He lay there for a few seconds, then replied, "I guess you and I are just destined to live forever in the land of the love forlorn."

"Poetic." I hadn't yet told him all the details about Winnow and my jelly legs or the almost-kiss. I wasn't sure what Charles would think about this new, shimmering world I'd discovered. He wasn't exactly one for sparkles—but neither was I until two days ago. I still wasn't sure I possessed the kind of shine required to fit in, and telling him would make it all too real.

I hadn't even tried to call or text Winnow yet. I really,

really wanted to, but that too would shift the shimmering into the concrete, making failure even more tangible. Besides, I knew enough about dating rules (from TV) to know I was supposed to wait at least a few days. Didn't want to look too eager. Didn't want her to think I was new at this or anything. Ha.

"As poetic as your punk poetry?" Charles was now sitting up, staring at me.

"Huh?"

"Am I as poetic as that punk poetry thing you saw?" He drew his glasses from his face and cleaned the lenses with his shirt, his eyes on me the whole time.

*What is this about?* "Uh, sure. I guess?"

Placing his glasses back over his eyes, he remarked, as though not really interested, "You think you'll see that girl again?"

*Dang. What do I do? Lie? Fake ignorance?* "The poetry girl, you mean?"

"Yeah. Sounds like she was pretty cool, right?"

*Right, but . . .* "Yeah, I guess. That'd be cool. She was cool. I mean . . . she seemed cool." *Good grief.*

Now he was just sitting there, staring at me. Through his nice, shiny glasses. Deliberately lying wasn't exactly my forte.

"Uh, well, actually—I did see her again." His eyebrows raised ever so slightly. "Yeah. After I walked you home Thursday night, I ended up going back to the festival. I guess I got a second wind or something." Half lie.

"Really."

I couldn't read his voice. But the stiffness of his features told me enough.

"And you met the girl?" he asked.

"Yeah, after this other show."

"What kind of show?"

"Um, like, a drag show . . ."

He picked something out of his teeth with his forefinger, computing the information. "Huh. So . . . she was, like, at the show?"

"Yeah. I mean . . . she was *in* the show. As a drag king."

"King?"

"I know. I'd never heard of it either. But apparently, it's a thing."

"Okay, so, you just randomly met her after the show?" he asked, breaking off some cornbread and shoving it into his mouth.

I sighed. There was no turning back now. "No. I met this drag *queen* named Deidre *before* the show, and *she* helped me meet Winnow *after* the show at this drag after-party thing."

"Winnow's the poetry girl."

"Yeah."

"And?" he asked, still munching his cornbread.

"And . . . she was really . . ."

"Seductive?" A hint of something like a challenge gleamed in his eyes now. My fears that he might not be open to sparkle and shimmer crept up again.

"Well, yes, that too, but I was actually going to say mesmerizing. Anyway, Winnow and I got to chatting after the show. . . ." Charles's eyebrow peaked expectantly. Was he waiting for me to say I liked her? I decided that would be a bad idea. "And she was just really cool to talk to is all."

He pushed his glasses up and started inspecting his cornbread—for what, I don't know. It was obvious that I had slipped into tricky territory with him.

"Anyway, you probably would have thought the whole thing was ludicrous. But, like, in an awesome way. It was like they're from a whole other world. I'm *sure* you'd love it." *Not. Sure. At. All.*

"Where is this whole other world they live in?"

"Oh, ha-ha—the other world of North Gate. Otherworldly compared to Bridgeton, I guess." I kept tittering like an ass. "Hopefully we can all get together sometime?"

"Yeah, sounds fun." As fun as a hernia, apparently.

Both of us stared at his cornbread. Then, without looking up, he said, "Will Ginny be invited as well?"

*There it is.*

Not knowing how to respond to this clearly snarky question, I searched for something to say that would get us out of this spiraling disaster of a conversation. "Oh my gosh! I didn't tell you the *weirdest part of all.* Gordon Grant was there!"

He looked up from his crumbles. "What? Where?"

"At the drag show! I couldn't believe it. I looked over at the start and there he was, standing off to the side, looking like he could throw up at any moment."

"Hmm. That *is* really weird." He brushed the remaining crumbs off his hands. "Did he see you?"

He seemed genuinely interested, which was encouraging. "I think so. He was gone by the time I looked over after the show, though."

"What was he doing there?"

"I have no idea." I was glad to get off the subject of Winnow and Deidre. Charles seemed happy to as well, and I could tell I'd have to tread carefully in that area after all. He didn't seem ready for the shimmer, and I didn't think I could handle his rejection of it at the moment. I decided not to bring it up anymore until it was absolutely necessary. And by absolutely necessary, I meant when drag queens flew through Bridgeton on unicorns.

Sunday was the last day of Summer Lovin', but, out of steam, I decided to lie low. I tried to work up the courage to text Winnow, but by seven o'clock, I still hadn't. Charles's hesitancy about the whole thing hadn't helped either, so instead I rode my bike to the Two Suns Café and procrastinated with dessert.

Having consumed my weight in raspberry pie and vanilla ice cream, I came out to the square to get my bike and immediately felt nauseous when I saw Gordon leaning against the bike rack, smoking a cigarette. I hadn't seen him since the drag show, and I didn't know what approach to take. Each of my recent run-ins with him had been confusing and somewhat unsettling.

His smoke floated directly above my bike, forcing me to

wave my arm back and forth in front of my face like a wind-shield wiper as I approached.

He gave me some side-eye. "Get a grip, Clark. It's not even coming near you."

"It is, and it stinks. Aren't you worried about your lungs, dude?"

He blew a slow stream of smoke toward me.

Nice.

"No, but *you* seem awfully worried about my lungs. I'm flattered . . . dude." He grinned through the haze.

I shook my head at him and crouched down to unlock my bike, but the back of my neck prickled. I could feel him look-ing at me.

After a moment, he asked, "What's with you and Charles?"

I looked up at him. He was staring at his shoes, and his profile was all tension and ridges. "What do you mean, what's with me and Charles?"

He looked up for a moment and exhaled into the air, but something in his stiff posture suggested he was trying to look more laid-back than he actually felt. "I mean, what's with you guys? Are you secret lovers? Buddies with benefits? Friends who—"

"What? No!" Did he actually think Charles and I were more than friends, or was he fishing for something? "But you knew that." Everyone at school knew that.

He shrugged. "Just checking if the rumors are true." He smirked.

*Rumors?* "What rumors?"

"I'm just trying to figure out why a chick like you doesn't hang out with more chicks like you, is all."

"Chick like me?"

"Yeah, man. Why do you spend all your time with that guy if you're not into guys?"

I couldn't believe I was having this conversation with Gordon Grant right now. And I didn't *want* to have this conversation with him. I twisted the key back and forth, but the lock wouldn't pop out. Of course. I was frustrated and hot—enough to blurt out, "It's called friendship, Gordon. What about you? What were you doing at the drag show the other night?"

He swallowed and flicked the ash off the end of his cigarette. Coughing like he didn't really need to cough, he muttered, "I was only there for a second. I thought it was gonna be something else."

It was a flimsy excuse, and he knew it. "Whatever you say," I said, wiggling my key a bit more to avoid looking at him in his obvious discomfort.

He coughed again. "What was that, anyway? Why were you there?" Tentative curiosity diluted with fake indifference.

The lock banged against my bike frame as I let it go. I plopped down cross-legged and leaned back on my hands. Peering up at him past the seat, I contemplated how much to tell him. Would he just throw it back in my face at some point? Davis's homophobic crap popped into my brain, and I didn't know what to make of Gordon's presence at the show, or his questions now.

With equal tentativeness diluted with fake confidence, I replied, "It was really cool. There were lots of different kinds of people there. You might have liked it if you stayed."

"Did you? Like it?" Still not looking at me.

A little surprised that he was even remotely interested in what I liked, I answered with complete honesty. "I loved it."

"So, you're . . . what?"

"What?"

"You're like, into that shit or whatever?" More side-eye.

Partly in wonder at Gordon's interest, and partly out of the excitement that rose up as I thought about the show, my words spilled out. "I thought it was awesome, if that's what you're asking. And the people there were really friendly. So real. And hilarious. And kind. Too bad you didn't get to see the whole show. Maybe next time."

A small puff of laughter. "Next time my ass. I told you, it was just a mistake."

Something—the briefest hint of disappointment? frustration?—touched his mouth, his eyes. "Okay. Sure." I watched the ashy end of the cigarette glow as he sucked in.

After blowing out the smoke, he caught me off guard a third time by asking, "Need help?" He nodded toward my lock.

"Uh . . . yeah, sure."

He dropped his cigarette to the ground and pressed the toe of his boot into it. As he knelt to fiddle with the key, I stole a few quick looks at him. His brow had its usual furrow, but some of the tension in his jaw seemed to ease. After a few moments, he managed to pop the lock open, which was both relieving and annoying.

"Thanks," I said, getting up and brushing my jeans off.

"Sure." His eyes still averted, he pulled out his cigarette case from his back pocket, like he wasn't sure what else to do. Then he opened the box and held it out to me, a smirk on his face. "Want one?"

I rolled my eyes and pulled my bike out of the rack without replying.

"No? Your loss. Peace out, asshole." He drew out a cigarette and flicked me a peace sign as he turned to go. As I watched him amble off, I noticed he placed the cigarette between his lips but just let it dangle there, unlit.

The following week I officially started my summer job with Jill—I did odd jobs and she paid me under the table. It was the perfect setup: I only had to work two or three days a week, I got to spend some quality time with Jill (mainly consisting of her bossing me around and grunting amicably when I did something well), I made a little extra cash, and I learned a few things about gardening, clay work, building, etc.

On Monday, I ended up dropping off plants and gnomes that people hadn't wanted to carry home from the festival. Since I didn't have my driver's license (it just seemed like so much *hassle*), I, awesomely, had to pull a wagon around town, gnomes and plants wobbling around like some sort of forest gnome dance party.

I made a loop, and as I progressed back toward Jill's place with one lone gnome left to deliver, I saw Gordon's truck behind the pub. Gordon wasn't in it, though—instead, his dad leaned up against the driver's-side door, smoking a cigarette, dressed in muddy running shoes and dusty jeans. His pale arms hung off him. Everything about him drooped. I couldn't help but think of cheese fondue.

When he caught me looking at him, my rickety wagon trailing behind me, he snapped, "What're you lookin' at?" He'd definitely had a few drinks.

He and Gordon had the same way of pushing out their chins when they were agitated. A twinge of sympathy rose in my chest for Gordon as I thought about what Jill had said. Then another thought arose: *If Gordon's crappy attitude comes from his dad, where does this guy get his issues?*

Trying to remain calm, I said, "Just passing by, Mr. Grant."

"Yeah, yeah." As I continued on, he trudged over and scowled at the superhero gnome inside. "Those things—Jill Walker's crap." Cigarette smoke puffed out of his mouth.

I really did not want to get into a conversation with this guy. I wasn't used to having adults speak to me this way—jerky teenage boys for sure, but not grown men. Whatever his issues, this didn't seem to be the right time to get into them. Instead I said lamely, "I gotta go. I'm late."

"Liar," he sneered. "Just like that Walker woman. You a

dyke too?" he yelled after me as I quickened my pace.

I kept run-walking until I reached Jill's shop. My anxiety that he would follow me kept my brain from working the whole two blocks, but as I shut Jill's gate behind me and found myself in the relative safety of her front yard, my heart and breath finally began to slow.

In my stillness, his words came back to me—"liar" and "dyke" in particular. That was the second time I'd heard "dyke" over the past few days, both times in reference to me, both times making my heart stagger. Only I wasn't sure whether my heart faltered because he was calling me one, as it had the last time, or because he was calling Jill one too.

I wasn't shocked at the idea that Jill might not be straight, but details of her love life had always remained somewhat mysterious. Though we were close in many ways, she wasn't really the type to share personal information. Sure, she'd been married, but I wasn't too small-town to know that being married to the opposite gender didn't necessarily mean you couldn't switch teams at some point. TV teaches you all sorts of things. I think there was an unspoken agreement among all of us— me, Dad, Charles, even Ginny—that Jill was either not interested in anyone or maybe didn't really have a preference. As long as we'd known her, and as far as we knew, she hadn't been in a relationship.

She *was* awfully handy, though. So there was that.

But that man—Gordon's dad—calling her a dyke like it was some sort of disease really ticked me off, whether it was true or not. And why'd he call her a liar? I thought about asking Jill but wasn't sure how she'd react. She'd seemed so reluctant to talk about him earlier. As I removed the leftover gnome from the wagon and placed it on a shelf to be delivered later, I decided that for now, I'd just tuck the information in my back pocket and save it for another day.

As Friday evening rolled around, Charles and I flopped ourselves across the front steps of my porch and read trashy summer novels. We'd reached at least a veneer of harmony between us since our tense, cornbread-infused conversation, mostly because we'd both chosen to ignore it. I realized this may not have been the most mature solution, but it seemed the best (or at least the easiest) one for now.

As I embraced artificiality and turned the page to see which "summer sister" betrayed which, my mind wandered off the predictable story line to lament this equally predictable evening. The last time I'd sat on this porch swing, I'd been engulfed by Deidre's laughter and energy and the world had felt shiny and new. Now the shine seemed to be dulling against my will.

My melancholy thoughts were interrupted as the automatic sprinkler in the yard started its tick-tick-ticking and a spray of water twirled across the lawn.

I sat up. "Oh shit."

Charles glanced up from his book. "What's the matter?"

The sprinkler had reminded me of an unfortunate choice

I'd made at the end of the school year. A groan boiled up from my throat. "I forgot I have to make signs for that annoying car wash tomorrow."

As part of my work for Jill that summer, I had to help her with a project she was doing for the high school. They'd hired her to do some landscaping, but in order to *pay* for the job, the school decided students should help by fund-raising. A group of go-getters (i.e. not me, not Charles) had volunteered back in April to organize a series of events over the summer to raise money. Ginny, full of bubbles and kittens, and also senior class president, *had* volunteered. Which meant that I, obsessed with Ginny, decided to volunteer after all.

Admittedly, even though I was smitten with Winnow, Ginny hadn't completely disappeared from my mind, or my heart. My chest still tightened when I saw her, my nose still craved her smell, my lips still wanted to kiss those freckles. But I could have kicked myself for volunteering to help with bake sales, outdoor movie nights, and car washes all summer. Charles *did* kick me when I told him I had to go to the school (the *school* of all places, in the *summer!*) to make signs. But the fund-raiser was the next morning, so it was now or never.

Like a true friend, Charles said he'd help me if I promised we could make the signs at my house, not at the school. I also had to promise him I'd somehow help manufacture a "chance" meeting with Tessa the following night.

Biking over to the school to grab some supplies, I found

myself wistfully glancing toward the Weeds, which had reverted back to its vacant, abject state. The metaphor had basically been created for me on this one.

The main building of the high school was open on weekdays for summer school, and the doors usually stayed unlocked until much later, when the cleaners were done for the night. I thumped up the stairs to the art room, which was shoved off to one side on the third floor. The metal doors made a heavy *clunk* as I pushed through them, and an aggressive "Fuck!" from the far corner of the room startled me. Standing at the tall counter that lined the back two walls was an unexpected figure.

When Gordon saw me, he slammed his hand down on whatever was in front of him and narrowed his eyes. "What the hell, Nima? Make enough noise?"

Apparently, our semi-pleasant moment at the bike rack had no bearing on the current moment. Irritated, I responded, "My apologies. I didn't realize the art room was for meditation. It's also six o'clock and *summer*. I didn't think anyone would be here."

"Well, don't fucking come near me," he growled, and began gathering together whatever it was he was working on, hunching over protectively. Despite the gravel in his voice, I sensed a tinge of something else, too—something small and tight.

It seemed safer to ignore him, so I did and climbed up to the craft bins. These were nestled into the shelves along the staircase leading to the loft, a half-level area where the pottery wheel was situated.

The loft often doubled as a lunchtime refuge for some of the quirkier kids. Dusty with clay powder, the air up here felt clouded and earthy at the same time. Thin shelves for drying pottery and sculptures lined the walls. These items—in varying stages of completion—were often abandoned. Small model homes and half-painted animals toppled over one another. Plant pots and lop-sided bowls rested next to figurines with legs too long for their bodies, or arms so heavy they'd broken off and now lay, bloodless, next to their torsos.

I could understand why some kids found comfort surrounded by this earthy, broken family.

On the main floor, large windows looked out onto the baseball diamond. At this time of day, a cool, dim light cast the art room in shadows, but a small lamp in front of Gordon spread a low glow around his gangly frame as he continued to collect his materials, his movements angry and faltering.

Arms full of supplies, I leaned over the banister of the staircase and watched him shove sheets of paper and photographs into a notebook. In his agitation, he failed to notice one photograph slip off the counter.

I should have said something, but I didn't. Art wasn't something I'd have paired with Gordon Grant. My curiosity got the better of me and I simply watched as he forced all his supplies into his bag, slung it over his shoulder, and turned to go. Seeing me at the top of the stairs, he set his jaw into its usual steel and glowered at me as he stomped toward the doors and out.

Some Jiffy markers tumbled out of my overstuffed arms

and click-clacked down the stairs. I dumped all the supplies into my backpack and walked across the room to where he'd been working.

I picked up the escaped photo. It was a black-and-white picture of him, facing the camera, in his usual baggy jeans but no shirt. The photo was on high-quality paper—he must have been using the darkroom, which was housed in a cubby beneath the stairs to the loft.

Gordon had drawn over himself with a silver marker, smoothing out the sharper angles of his body with curved, meticulous lines. But he'd blackened out his face entirely.

I didn't know what to make of the image. I found it both beautiful and bleak. I didn't know Gordon had a creative bone in his body, never mind that he'd sit in an empty school by himself to create things. And it wasn't like he was making some violent, dark art either—which was what I would have expected. The hands that had altered this photo had been sensitive, precise . . . thoughtful.

My stomach lurched as I realized I had to return the photo to him.

"Gordon!" I called at his back just as he'd stepped onto the baseball field. He turned, and when he saw me jogging toward him, he looked sick.

I stopped a safe distance from him and held out the photo. Unsure of what to say, I tried the straightforward route. "Here. It was on the floor."

He stared at the picture. His Adam's apple rose and dipped. The steel hadn't left his jaw, and I noticed his hands were tight fists.

Growing increasingly uneasy, I added, "It's really cool."

Nothing.

"I really like it."

Nothing.

Then: "I won't say anything."

His eyes broke from the photo and found me instead. They flashed with fire, but also—something else.

He snatched the photo from my hands and seethed in a low, icy voice, "Say anything about what, Clark?"

"I—"

"HUH?" His face was suddenly an inch from mine.

I staggered back. "Nothing—I don't know. Just—nothing." I turned and speed-walked to my bike, then raced the hell away from Gordon as fast as I could.

I didn't slow down until I was a block away from my house. As I dumped my bike in the front yard and walked up the pathway, I tried to calm my breathing and rearrange my face from flustered to neutral. I couldn't tell Charles about this. I was genuinely terrified of what Gordon might do if he found out I'd said anything, and this didn't feel like something to share anyway. Something was up with that guy—something heavy—and it wasn't my place to tell anyone about it. Not that I even knew where to begin.

When I entered the kitchen, breathing finally under control, Charles had spread the poster board Ginny gave me to use across the kitchen table.

"I got the goods!" I said with fake cheer, dumping my backpack out onto the table as well.

As Charles dragged a fat Jiffy marker across the top of one of the posters to spell out *Car Wash*, I started to draw something that I hoped looked like a car in the bottom corner.

We worked mostly in silence, which was just as well, because my brain was trying to process my recent interactions with Gordon. I'd been terrified by his anger at the baseball diamond, but I couldn't get that photo or the look in his eyes out of my head. By the time we'd finished the posters, a growing bud of sympathy had bloomed in my chest for him, but I had no idea what to do with it.

After a magnificently promoted car wash the next day, most of which I spent trying to ignore all the male attention Ginny was getting in her frayed jean shorts and crop top, Charles and I went back to my place to get ready for an equally magnificent evening of stalking Tessa. After Charles donned what I could only guess was his one pair of non-ratty pants—the gray cords—we scarfed down the burritos Dad left for us, hopped on our bikes, and headed for one of three places Tessa would probably be on a warm Saturday night: the baseball diamond, the square, or one of her giggly friends' houses.

I knew I owed Charles a favor, but the thought of roaming around to all these familiar places and running into a bunch of kids from school led my brain back to its humdrum thoughts again. I was feeling pretty uninspired as we started with the baseball diamond, since that was closest. When we got there, a smattering of tenth and eleventh graders were sitting around, checking their phones. Thrilling. Tessa wasn't there, so we kept riding.

Next stop, the square. We paused our bikes at the edge of the wide lawn area that, just the week before, had been crammed with booths for the festival, but was now business as usual. Surveying the typical summer crowd of picnickers and Frisbee players, we spotted two of Tessa's friends, but no Tessa.

Charles kept scanning, squeezing his brake levers in and out.

"Maybe she's sick?" I offered.

"Maybe." He scratched his nose with special vigor. "Let's just go. I'd rather get ice cream or something anyway."

Seeing his disappointment and also dreading another night on the porch even more than I dreaded this entire excursion, I had a sudden urge to accomplish this mission with as much zeal as humanly possible for someone who was usually more comfortable with reading and hammocks. I channeled a little Dee Dee La Bouche enthusiasm. Maybe if I could inject some adventure into Charles's world, he'd be more likely to accept the sparkle and shine of my potential one. "Where does this girl live?" I asked him.

"Just behind the Laundromat, near Biddy Park. But I really don't want to go, Nima."

"You say that, but I promise you'll regret it if you don't follow through. Come on!" I flicked his shoulder with my fingers.

"And do what? Knock on her door?"

"I have an even better idea," I hinted, pushing off in the direction of Biddy Park.

He sighed emphatically but started pedaling after me.

On the short ride there, I fleshed out the loose idea that had popped into my brain. We needed to show Tessa that Charles could be spontaneous and confident. That he wasn't just an awkward, tongue-tied goofball with poor eating habits.

At her house, lights glowed from a couple of rooms upstairs. We stayed a little off to the side, bordering on actual stalking now. Some voices that sounded like Tessa and her friends arose from behind the house.

We dropped our bikes by the curb and I took Charles by the shoulders, glaring hard into his eyes. "Okay, pal. If you really want this girl to like you, you have to prove to her you're willing to do whatever it takes. Are you? Willing?"

His face did this frown-snarl thing it did when he didn't like what he was hearing. "I don't know, Nima. I'm not sure I'm up to this."

"Charles! Do you like this girl or not?" I squeezed his bony shoulders.

"I do like her. I just—"

"Settled." I pulled some paper and a pen out of my backpack. "Okay, what's Tessa into?"

"Into?"

"Yeah, what is she like? What does she do?"

"Oh, um . . . she plays soccer. And has green eyes. Oh, and I think she teaches guitar?"

"Hm. Okay, I guess that'll have to do." I pressed the paper to my thigh and started scribbling.

"What are you doing?" Charles asked, yanking at his shirt.

"You, my friend, are about to impress Tessa with your poetic prowess. Well, technically *my* poetic prowess, but consider this my gift to you." I handed him the paper, on which I'd written a short but, I have to say, adorable poem.

"What? No way!" he yell-whispered as he looked over the poem.

"Way. You're doing this. Remember—you'll regret it if you don't."

"I'm gonna look like a freak!"

"No, you're going to look like someone willing to take a risk to show a girl you like her. Think about it, Charles—this is your chance to prove to her you're a take-charge kind of guy." I pushed him forward toward the walkway leading around the house to the backyard. "I'll go first and make a quick intro. Then all you have to do is walk back there and read the poem. Just don't mumble!"

I could feel Charles sweating through his shirt, but I knew that he needed to do this—that he had to face his fears in order to make any progress with Tessa.

Just before reaching the backyard, I told Charles to stay put until I called him out. Then, taking a deep breath, I walked out into the yard where Tessa and two of her friends were sitting in plastic lawn chairs, listening to music and giggling about something or other. They stopped when they saw me, and before they could say anything, I announced, "Tessa, Charles has a special message for you. Come on out, Charles!"

Charles poked his head around the corner of the house. I reached over and yanked him out by his arm. Then I nudged him forward a bit and whispered, "Read it!"

After three or four excruciating seconds of Charles staring openmouthed at Tessa and Tessa reflecting a similar expression back at him, I shoved him in the back and he thankfully started to make a sound.

Just as he did, however, the back door swung open and out came Davis McCain and Gordon Grant, each carrying a six-pack of beer.

*Christ in khakis.*

When Davis saw Charles, he bellowed, "No way!" and made a beeline straight for him. Both Charles and I were frozen in place, which made it easy for Davis to snatch the paper out of Charles's hands. Charles immediately looked at me, his eyes full of panic. All I could think to do was place a hand on his shoulder.

"What's this, little Charles?" Davis said, holding the paper out in front of him. "Looks like a love poem! Hey, Tessa, Charlie here wrote you a love poem." Addressing Gordon, who'd walked over to the girls, he added, "Gordo, looks like lover boy here is trying to move in on your territory!"

The panic in Charles's eyes turned to confusion, as did mine. *Tessa and Gordon?*

"Let's see what he's got," Davis continued, placing his six-pack on the grass.

"Come on, Charles, let's go," I said, tugging at his shirt.

"Oh no—you can't leave yet," Davis said, and wrapped his arm around Charles's shoulders.

I looked over at Gordon and we made brief eye contact before he averted his eyes and slumped down in a chair next to Tessa.

Davis dramatically cleared his throat. "For Tessa. A haiku for you." Davis paused to let out a howl of laughter before continuing with an exaggerated lisp. "That girl with green eyeths, in tune with her guitar chordths, kickths at my full heart."

We could barely make out the last few words because Davis was laughing so hard. I found myself wondering if he ever laughed like this when he was alone or if it was reserved only for public displays of shittiness like this one. Tessa's friends were laughing as well, but I noticed Tessa was staring at her knees. Gordon was just sucking back his beer.

"Well, that's adorable, little Charles. I'm sure Tessa will cherish it forever," Davis said, once he'd regained the ability to speak. He dropped the paper to the ground and finally dragged his arm away from Charles's neck. Picking up his beers, he sauntered over to a chair and collapsed into it, as though he'd just done something exhausting. Maybe it *was* exhausting to act like you don't care about anything or anyone.

"Nice, you guys. Really nice," I said, my voice quiet and trembling. Gordon was still avoiding eye contact, but at least the girls had stopped laughing and looked a little subdued. Davis just shrugged and cracked his beer.

I glanced at Charles. His face was slack. He looked like he was about to cry, and I knew he'd hate himself for that, so I took his arm and pulled him back toward the side of the house. He snatched his arm away from me and stalked toward the front yard.

As we left, I could hear Davis repeating some of the words from the poem and forcing out more obnoxious laughter. I was furious for letting myself believe Gordon deserved any of my sympathy.

Charles was marching so fast that I practically had to run to catch up to him. He lifted his bike roughly, climbed on, and booted it back down the street toward his house.

"Hey! Wait for me already." I grabbed my bike and pedaled fast, pulling up beside him in no time.

"Leave me alone. I'm going home. By myself."

"Charles, I'm sorry, okay?" I called out to him. "How was I supposed to know those guys would be there?"

"It was a stupid idea! It was *your* stupid idea," he yelled, scowling at the road in front of him.

"Listen, Charles, I was just trying to help—"

"Yeah, thanks a lot for your 'help.'" He punctuated the last word with a fierce glance my way, and I could see his eyes brimming with tears. "I realize you're all excited about your 'otherworldly' new life or whatever," he said, his voice breaking, "but leave me out of it."

He stood up and pedaled as hard as he could. It wasn't very hard, and I could have easily kept up with him, but I slowed my pace and let him go. He wasn't about to hear anything I said right now, and I couldn't really blame him. I'd pushed him harder than I should have out of some misguided sense that I knew anything about how to impress a girl.

I crawled into bed that night feeling sick. Sick for Charles and his poor little heart, and sick that there were so many things he and I couldn't seem to talk about right now. Real life seemed to be dimming the twinkle and shine of my festival escapade, and I wasn't sure how to revive the glow.

# CHAPTER 8

On Monday morning I schlepped over to Jill's, feeling unmotivated to work. I'd tried calling Charles several times the previous day, but he wouldn't pick up, nor did he return any of my many, many texts. This silent treatment was a new dimension to our friendship. I didn't like it. And it certainly didn't make me any more motivated to reach out to Winnow, either. One set of rejected texts was enough at the moment.

Those complications were nothing compared to the one I was about to find at Jill's, though.

When I entered the side gate into the backyard, Jill was sitting on the wrought-iron bench she'd never been able to sell. Her lanky body drooped over her knees as she stared at an envelope in her hands. She didn't even look up as I approached her.

Not until my shadow crept over the envelope did she finally snap out of her daze.

Then, in her no-nonsense way, she handed me the envelope

and said, "Nima, this is from your mother. I guess she sent it to me so your dad wouldn't see. Want me to leave you alone while you read it?" Her voice sounded steely, forced.

Stunned, I stared at the envelope and noticed that the hand holding it quivered a little. I looked at Jill, my bottom lip beginning its own quiver. Sitting down beside her, I made no move to take the envelope. My eyes grew wet.

"Do you want me to open it, babe?" she offered, a softness seeping in.

Still unable to speak, I just shook my head no. She gently placed the letter in my lap. I didn't move.

I'd tried so hard not to think about my mom's absence, so hard not to piece together her reasons for leaving. The letter had me frozen between a longing for understanding on one hand, and a fear that had slipped into me despite my attempts to ignore it—what if she'd just been bored with us, this life? With me?

"I'm gonna make us a cup of tea." She put her hand on my knee. "You don't need to open it yet if you don't want to."

After she'd gone inside, I willed myself to hold the letter in my hands and inspect the envelope. It was just a regular, plain white envelope with Jill's address on it handwritten in blue ink. No return address, just "Kate Kumara-Clark" in the corner. My mom's writing. Each letter perfectly spaced, tilting forward as if leaning into an oncoming wind. Below the flap on the other side, one simple sentence: *Jill, please make sure Nimanthi gets this.*

Not wanting to tear any of the writing on the envelope, I ripped off a short end and slid out the paper inside. Regular loose-leaf, folded in three.

My own hands shook now as I unfolded the letter. Inside, I found about a third of a page of crisp blue words explaining that she was sorry for leaving, but that things were complicated. That she couldn't come back to Bridgeton to see me or my dad, but that I could meet her somewhere. That Jill and I should come together. That Jill would explain everything along the way. There was an e-mail address at the bottom.

I read it again, this time counting each word to see how many it took for a mother to try and reconnect with her daughter. Ninety-two. Ninety-two words after one and a half years of absence. And not one explained why she left.

Jill must have been watching me from the kitchen and waiting for the right moment to return, because as I finished reading the letter and looked up to stare blankly at a stern gnome scowling at me from across the yard, she appeared at my shoulder with the tea. "Here you go, darlin'," she said. I took the mug and she came to sit back down on the bench. We sat in silence, making eye contact only with gnomes.

Surprise, anger, resentment, yearning, sadness . . . I couldn't tell where one ended and the next began. I was surprised by the letter, of course, but also surprised by the anger I felt toward Jill for—according to the letter—knowing more about my mom than she'd let on. I wasn't surprised by my anger or resentment toward my mom, but the immensity of my yearning did surprise me—as though a secret door in the pit of my belly had suddenly opened to reveal a cavernous, empty space just waiting to be filled with her. Floating beneath all that, a niggling sadness at the tone of the note—the curtness of it, the lack of anything that came close to my longing.

Jill kept glancing over at me and the letter. My words still wouldn't come, so I just passed it to her. She hesitated, but only for a moment, then took it. As she read, I watched her breathe in and out deeply. When she finished, she folded the letter slowly and inserted it back into the envelope, using the time to take a few more careful breaths. Shaking off something I didn't understand, she blinked a couple of times and looked up at me. "Well" was all she said. I couldn't read her tone.

"Yeah" was all I could manage.

"Is that something you'd want? To see her?"

I didn't know what I wanted. Why'd she want to meet anyway? Maybe she wanted to come back. Or apologize. Or maybe she just wanted to say she was never coming back. I'm not sure I wanted to hear any of those things.

"I don't know, Jill." I spat out her name and scowled back at the gnome across the yard. I knew I was doubling up my anger at both Mom and Jill and focusing it solely on Jill, but I couldn't help myself. "What'd she mean? About you explaining everything?"

Jill leaned forward, digging her elbows into her thighs,

and let out a long, whistling breath. She gazed somewhere into the pile of soil bags and gardening equipment laid out in front of her. "Shit, Nima. I'm as surprised by this letter as you are. I'm not entirely sure I know what she means."

A completely unsatisfying answer. "But you must know something," I said, refocusing on the gnome. Then, my voice cool with resentment: "You obviously know more than you've told me."

Breaking our unspoken agreement to avoid looking at one another, she turned to me and slid over a bit. "You're right. I do know more than I've let on, and I'm sorry for that. But it's not my story to tell." She handed me the letter, stood up, and started kicking at the dirt by her feet.

I looked at my mother's name on the envelope. My eyes burned, still threatening tears. But I was mad. Mad at my mom for sending this cold, shitty letter. Mad at Jill for making this more confusing. Mad at myself for sitting here like a fucking lump. My hands suddenly clamped shut, crumpling the letter. And then it was like I couldn't stop them—they started ripping at the envelope, pulling it apart, tearing at the letter inside, finally crushing all the torn pieces together into a ball. Jill just stared at me.

I stood up. Tears hovered but didn't fall. My voice came out like ice—frozen, even, clear. "Fine—you don't want to tell me anything? You're just as bad as she is. You're both liars. I'll figure this shit out on my own."

Jill stepped toward me. "Nima—"

To prevent her from coming any closer, I stuck my hand out and shoved the wadded-up letter at her. She halted and automatically raised her hands to stop my balled-up fist from hitting her in the chest. I pushed the bits of letter into her hands, turned quickly, and walked away, ignoring her calls.

I didn't know what exactly I was doing, or how I'd manage to "figure this shit out on my own," but for this moment at least, I was determined to be pissed off about it all.

I spent the next couple of days holed up in my room, floundering in a rapid river of emotions. With no one else to turn to—Charles in his own spiral of self-pity and Ginny busy fund-raising and flirting with boys—I found myself finally wanting to call Winnow, to hear her calm voice, to ask her advice. We didn't know each other well, and maybe she thought I was an emotional wreck after I'd blubbered away for no good reason the night we met, but I couldn't stop thinking about her, even with all this other shit going on—maybe *because* of all this other shit. It'd been a week since I met her—was it too late to contact her now? Would she be interested in seeing me again anyway?

*Think about it, Nima. Why would she?*

I wanted to kick myself for even thinking she would.

On Thursday around noon, my dad, home for lunch, knocked on my door. He'd always been pretty good about leaving me be if I was experiencing a "teen malaise," as he called them.

And rightfully so. He had his own episodes that I had to contend with too. Every so often, he'd fall into a funk and keep to his room or go for long, long walks. I might not see him until the next morning. We were good at giving each other space, but my episodes didn't usually last more than a day, and neither did his, so I guess he'd decided to check in.

I wasn't ready to have my space invaded, though. And I certainly wasn't ready to tell him about the letter. I still couldn't figure out my feelings about it all, and I didn't want Dad's feelings in the mix yet.

So when he knocked, I responded with, "NO THANK YOU."

He knocked again. "Nima, I'm coming in."

"DAD."

"Sorry—here I am, turning the doorknob, cracking open the door, nudging my toe over the threshold . . ."

I'd been lying flat on the rug by my bed, belly down, cheek squashed into an open book I'd been trying in vain to read earlier. I flipped my face to the other side, away from the door and him, and groaned as emphatically as possible.

I could hear the soft thump of his bare feet across the carpet and then the squeal of my bed springs giving way to his body. Gus had been lying across the small of my back but jumped up when my dad entered, probably excited to see someone who wasn't pathetically moping about their room.

"Nima. This is a lengthy malaise. What's going on?"

I squeezed my eyes shut as hard as I could and turned my

head back toward the door, away from him again. "I don't want to talk about it." My words crept in whispers across the rug.

"Hmm. Fair. However, may I suggest we be silent together, in the kitchen, over lunch? This room is getting a little . . . funky."

I yanked a T-shirt from the floor over my head and said something like, "Mfpmmmfp!"

"Beg your pardon?"

"Uh-uuuhhhhh."

I could feel him get up and step over top of me. His body settled in gently next to mine. Then I felt Gus wiggle in between us and lie down. Dad pulled the T-shirt off my head. "Nima."

I reluctantly opened my eyes. His head rested on his arm, which pushed his glasses crookedly off his nose. "Oh, hello. So nice to see your beautiful face."

I rolled my eyes. "Beautiful face" my ass. I guessed my eyes were red, my lips were dry, and my hair was an unholy mess of frizzy curls straying from my loose ponytail. So . . . the usual.

"Lunch?" he offered again. At the mention of food, Gus shimmied up a bit to make sure he was included in the conversation.

I could see that if I didn't comply, my father would just continue to lie there, making small talk whether I participated or not. "Fiiiine," I moaned.

We did, indeed, eat lunch in silence, save for Gus's persistent whines for treats. I just stared into my plate of macaroni and cheese while Dad read the newspaper. It did feel good to get out of my room and into the kitchen, which was sunny and warm from the midday sun. But the letter—now torn and who knew where—weighed heavily on my heart. Sitting across from my dad, knowing that he had no idea Mom had contacted me, *not* knowing if he knew whatever it was that Jill knew—I felt sorry for him and uncertain about him all at the same time.

We'd barely ever spoken about Mom's leaving. One morning we woke up at the end of November a year and a half ago, and she wasn't there. We'd have worried that something happened to her, but a note on the kitchen table—seemingly written in a hurry, judging from the brevity and unusually sloppy script—announced: *I'm sorry. I need some time away. Love, Mom.*

I always thought that "Love" part to be a little over the top.

I'd found the note first and, not fully comprehending what it meant, had woken my dad up to show it to him.

I remember that even as a fifteen-year-old, something in his reaction to the note had seemed off to me. He hadn't seemed confused, or surprised—just sad. And his sadness had seemed more in response to *my* confusion and questions than anything else. His only attempt at an explanation had been, "I guess she needs some time away, Nima. I won't pretend to know why, or how long she'll need, but I don't think there's much we can do except let her have the space she's asking for."

At the time, his calmness and understanding had infuriated me. I couldn't comprehend how he could just one day wake up without her there and go along with it. I guess I realized now that he was trying to remain calm for me, and that his long walks, which began the very next day after she left, probably allowed him to vent in whatever way he needed to. But part of me remained angry at him for not reacting more—doing more. I'm not sure exactly how I wanted him to react, or what I wanted him to do, but I just wanted him to do *something*.

But then, I hadn't done anything either. We were a perfect pair, avoiding the topic with one another and with ourselves.

And I wasn't ready to change that yet. I needed to get out of the house. I shoveled the rest of the mac and cheese into my mouth and then quickly washed my plate. I could tell my dad was sneaking glances at me as I clattered about the kitchen. Slipping on my flip-flops and grabbing a hat, I said, "Thanks for lunch, Dad. I'm gonna go for a walk."

"Okay. See ya," he replied through a mouthful of pasta, pretending to be more interested in his newspaper.

I didn't want to see anyone I knew, so I walked east, away from Jill's, away from the high school, away from Charles's house.

Eventually finding myself in the playground near the elementary school, I plunked myself down under the shade of a maple tree. Leaning my head against the rough trunk, I watched a group of four younger kids playing soccer on the gravel field close by. As they flailed around, hacking viciously at each other's shins as much as they were at the ball, my brain whirred into metaphor mode.

*Watch as a flock of crows pounces repeatedly at the hapless mouse, who darts from one cruel set of talons to another, narrowly escaping multiple puncture wounds to her soft, exposed skin. What will our vulnerable friend do in the wake of these wicked, dark shadows?*

As if on cue, the children, in a particularly chaotic thrashing, sent the ball floating in a rainbow arc up and away from their small, frantic circle.

*But look! In a miraculous show of determined buoyancy, our furry friend bounces away in a single leap, narrowly escaping the looming swoop of gloom closing in on her from above.*

The ball hopped several times across the field and rolled to a stop a few feet away. It was much closer to me than it was to the kids, and they all stopped to stare at me. I sighed, scrambled to my feet, and plodded over. Maybe this was silly, but even the thought of kicking this damn ball back to some little kids made my heart beat quicker, my stomach wobble—what if I sent the ball in the wrong direction? Or worse, missed it completely, fell on my ass, and had a bunch of turdy little kids laugh at me?

Told you it was silly.

"Are you gonna kick it, or what?" one of the turdy little kids shouted.

Not much choice at this point. I took a funny little hop, hinged my right knee backward, and punched the ball with the toe of my foot. Although my flip-flop went with it, the ball flew directly toward the kids, who cawed their approval and graciously threw my flip-flop back at me.

Feeling disproportionately accomplished, I slipped my foot into the flip-flop and sat back down under the tree. As I watched the kids hammer away at the ball again, a text pinged my phone.

**Hey boo! Just eating pancakes for lunch and thinking bout ya! xx**

Deidre. Another ping followed immediately.

**You texted that amazing girl yet?**

I stared up at the maple's vivid green leaves, smiling at Deidre's simple encouragement. My lips fell a little, though, as my mother's slanted handwriting came back to me. Certainly no pretense of encouragement in *her* words. She'd taken a year and a half to reach out. And she was *my mom.* What if Winnow showed just as little interest in me? What could Winnow possibly see in someone so . . . leavable?

**Not yet,** I texted back, my watery eyes blurring the letters.

**Sugar, she's into you! And should be! Don't wait another minute!** was her swift response.

Her words produced the same sensation I'd had when she

guided me through the festival, through the glowing fires and flickering lights. A warm, firm hand in mine, calming the unease in my stomach.

Things *could* get worse, I thought, but not by much. If Winnow didn't reply, at least I'd know she wasn't interested. There'd be some satisfaction in that, I supposed. I texted Deidre back.

I think you just gave me the push I needed. xo

You know I got you, girl! LURVE YOUUU

Like a friendly slap on the ass, her texts sent a surge of something resembling audacity through my chest.

I scrolled through my contact list and found Winnow's number. If nothing else, waiting a week before texting might make me look ultracool, even if Winnow had no interest in replying. Sound logic, right? Six draft messages later, I finally decided on:

Hey. It's Nima. How are you?

I waited. Nothing. After staring at the screen for several minutes, I got up and started walking home. By the time I climbed up the steps to my front porch, no response. Another girl, another rejection, it seemed.

But finally, around six, I got the ping I'd been craving:

I'm good! Better now that you finally texted me. :) What took you so long???

I sighed. So transparent. I didn't bother waiting an acceptable period to reply this time.

I know, I'm so sorry. I started my summer job.

I paused. *Transparent, Nima.*

Also, I was trying to impress you with my ultracool indifference.

Pause. Send.

I held my breath and stared at the screen.

LOLOLOLOL!!! You brat. You're lucky I like you!

*She likes me!* Ugh. I'm such a dope. I could have been exchanging adorable messages like this with Winnow for the past week. Being cool was definitely not cool. Before I could reply, she texted again.

When do I get to see you again? ;)

*How about right this second?* Instead, I typed: What are you up to this weekend?

Some friends and I are going to this party tomorrow night! Come!

*I'd love to.* However: Foolish Nima doesn't drive and the buses to and from North Gate don't run late. Sounds fun! Not sure about transportation tho. No license. :/

No license! Girl. Ha-ha, no worries.

And then a few seconds later:

If you can get here, maybe you can stay over and take the bus home Sat? *blush*

*Wait—what? Is she inviting me to stay the night?* After about thirty seconds of waiting for my brain to stop melting, Winnow texted again:

Too much? Ha-ha. Whatever works for you. Just thought it might be nice not to rush back or whatever.

Before she thought I was getting cold feet, I quickly typed back: I'd love that. Tomorrow when and where?

Yay! We can meet at my place. 7pm. 7833 Johnson.

Awesome! Just gotta run it by my dad but should be fine.

Cool. :) Ciao, cutie.

This was one of those moments that had me befuddled. How to sign off?

*See ya, sugar!* You're not Deidre, you boob.

*Bye, friend!* Ew.

Bye! Can't wait. ;)

That'll do.

The panic set in instantly. I was going to see Winnow. At her place. And potentially stay the night?

*Christ with cramps. What did I just do?*

# CHAPTER 9

I spent the next hour fitfully imagining all the things that could go wrong.

*See how the still-featherless sparrow takes its first flight directly into the feline's spacious mouth. Notice the tiny guppy whirling down the damp, dark drain. Watch as our newborn lamb's faltering first steps lead her headfirst into a giant pile of cow poop.*

I decided to call Deidre for some advice and encouragement.

"Deidre?"

"Nima, my blossom! How *are* you?"

"I'm okay. How are *you*?"

"Oh sweetheart, I am full of piss and vinegar right now. . . ." She went on to tell me about how a group of eight middle-aged lesbians had hired her the previous night to do a drag tutorial for a couple's bachelorette party. Apparently "those ladies could *drink*," and once they got all "butched up in their menswear, they were full of hijinks. Girl, it was like herding a whole mess of kindergarteners—except with mustaches and beards and a whole lotta whiskey!"

Three minutes into the conversation and I'd almost forgotten every woe I'd ever known. Reluctant to wade back into said woes, I decided to skip the part about my mom's letter and go straight to my most urgent predicament—how to get to Winnow and what the hell to do once I got there.

Deidre's only response: "Well, honey, I'll come get you, of course. And all you have to do in return is cook me some dinner!"

So I had a ride to North Gate. The question was, what should I tell Dad? The truth? I'd never been sure if he knew about my romantic leanings. When I went wild in grade nine over Ginny—suddenly obsessing over basketball and talking about her all through dinner—the only thing he or my mom ever said was "How's that homework coming along?" or "How's the team doing?" I don't think it's that my parents didn't care—more that they both figured it was just an innocent, pubescent girl crush.

And my dad being the hippy-dippy type, he just let things roll along without calling too much attention to them. Aside from muumuu-wearing and his fondness for sixties and seventies music, he practiced yoga (it was a sight to see, my portly father in perfect eagle pose), made his own kombucha, and often welcomed guests into the house to the smell of incense.

Oh, and peace. He was big on peace.

In other words, he was pretty laid-back, but I wasn't sure what he'd make of me—after years of having only two real friends—suddenly catching a ride with someone I'd only met a week ago, to possibly stay the night on the other side of the city with someone else I'd just met.

I guess there was only one way to find out.

When I walked into the kitchen, he was standing at the counter, cutting carrots for dinner.

"Hey," I said, grabbing some juice from the fridge.

"Hello, m'dear. Free from the funk?"

"Yeah, I guess. Can I help with anything?"

He looked over his shoulder at me and exaggeratedly rolled his eyes. "Oh sure, come on in when I'm just about finished!"

I exaggeratedly rolled my eyes back. "I'll set the table."

"'Bout time you earned your keep."

A piece of carrot whacked me in the ear and was swiftly hoovered by Gus as soon as it hit the floor.

Once dinner was on the table and we'd been munching quietly for a few minutes, I threw out a test question. "How would you feel, Father, about me sleeping over at a friend's place in North Gate?"

He looked up and chewed thoughtfully. After swallowing and taking a sip of water, he said, "What friend? When? Why?"

"This girl I met at the festival. Tomorrow. Because it'd be fun?"

"Is it Deidre?"

Ignoring my surprise over the fact that my dad took so easily to accepting Deidre as a girl, I said, "No, not Deidre. I'm fully capable of meeting more than one cool person at a time. Although Deidre said she'd give me a ride."

"That Deidre is something else." He actually looked dreamy when he said it.

"That she is. So . . . can I go?"

"Who is this other cool person?"

"Her name's Winnow—"

"Winnow?" His eyebrows rose. "Delightful name."

"Yes, it is. She's also delightful. We'd be going to a party, and then I could just take the bus home on Saturday. It's only two buses from where she is—I looked it up on the interweb."

Dad usually thought any reference to the "interweb" was hilarious, but I got only the hint of a smile this time. He contemplated his french fry. "Deidre is driving you there, but you're not hanging out with her?"

"Well . . . we might. I don't know. We didn't discuss it." Seizing on his seeming infatuation with Deidre, I added, "But you can ask her yourself if you like—I said if she gave me a ride, we'd make her dinner!"

"Reeeeaaalllly?" He pointed his french fry at me. "And by 'we' do you really mean me?"

"I'll help! We can barbecue. C'mon, Dad—you know you want to." I think he actually did.

"Okay, let's make a deal. Deidre will have dinner here,"

he said, like it was his idea, "and I would also like the number of this Willow—"

"Winnow," I corrected.

"Winnow. *And . . .*" He paused, looked out the window, and cleared his throat.

"And what?"

He brought his eyes back to mine, and I was surprised to find them glistening. "And make sure this Winnow girl treats you like the super cool chick you are." He shoved the fry in his mouth and quickly looked down at his plate to reach for another.

My vocal cords tightened, and all I could squeak out was "Okay." He knew after all. And he was okay with it.

After Ginny and Mom and Charles, this small oasis of acceptance from someone familiar sent a gentle ripple of calm through me.

One quickly followed by a surge of panic and excitement. I had a ride, permission, and an amazing girl wanting to see me. *Shit.*

Fighting back every embarrassing moment I'd ever shared with Ginny, not to mention the niggling image of slanted cursive writing that kept nudging its way into my brain, I tried to focus on the possibility of the moment—a terrifying and thrilling possibility. The kind of possibility that could mean a newer, better Nima.

I texted Winnow immediately after dinner. I told her the

plan, and she texted back about thirty exclamation points—
each of which poked my heart from a different direction.

By Friday afternoon, I had a whole mob of butterflies flapping around in my stomach.

When Deidre arrived in a bright orange, mint-condition
Volkswagen van, Dad came out to the porch and tried to give
her a handshake, which made Deidre giggle before she pulled
him into a giant hug.

Flustered, Dad then complimented her on her van, her
dress, and her hair. It was adorable as hell and I loved him for
it. From the beaming smile across Deidre's face, she seemed
tickled by the attention too. "That beautiful vehicle there is
the Orange Crush, honey, because everyone wants a bit of
this vitamin C!" she exclaimed, snapping twice for emphasis.

Instead of all the glitter and shine of the outfit Deidre
wore the night I met her, tonight she had on a simple white
summer dress and leather sandals. The golden braids had
been replaced by a stylishly relaxed black ponytail. Somehow, even in this casual outfit, she retained the same glow
she'd had in sequins and gleaming makeup.

Having Deidre's arms around me and her lilac smell in
my nose released a wave of cool water through me. During dinner, I still experienced moments of mild hysteria at
the thought of seeing Winnow but managed to curb them
enough to enjoy watching Deidre and my dad banter back

and forth. Dad pulled out all the stops by making his famous beer-can chicken on the barbecue, and Deidre couldn't say enough about it. "I'd go as far as to say it's as good as my mama's barbecue, but you know I can't cheat on my mama like that, y'all."

"Are you close with your family, Deidre?" Dad asked.

"Oh, well, I'll just give you the tasty parts. Mama's still alive and kicking hard a couple towns over, and we're very close. My mama doesn't care 'bout my proclivities—she loves my style!" She flicked her ponytail as she said this. "Daddy is long gone but was a beautiful hunk of a man." She paused, then added, "I'll keep the bitter bits for another time. No use spoiling the flavor of this delicious chicken, am I right?" Chuckle.

I wondered what those bitter bits were and pledged to ask her about them later.

"And you, Delford? Besides your sweet-pea daughter here, who else do you have lovin' you up?"

I thought about the letter and then tried to force it out of my mind. I was still in ignore-at-all-costs mode.

Dad swept a curl out of his face, and his cheeks set into a fixed smile as he cut through his baked potato. "Oh, this sweet pea is all the lovin' I need, Deidre," he said. The smile remained, but his eyes never left his plate.

Deidre must have noticed this too, because she followed with, "Oh, I hear that, sugar! You must be doing something right, 'cause I can tell this girl adores you." She winked at me as Dad continued to cut his potato into a million pieces. I adored them both.

After we'd finished dessert ("Peach pie? Good lord, y'all are gonna have to roll me home!") and helped wash up, I grabbed my backpack, gave Gus a tousle, and kissed Dad on the cheek.

"Remember, you can call me if you need anything at all," he said.

"I know I can." I blew him another kiss and climbed into Deidre's van.

Deidre waved to my dad from behind the steering wheel, then looked at me and said, "Ready, Nima-my-girl?"

"I think so."

On the way there, I let Deidre fill the Orange Crush with her lively music—allowing it to push aside any talk about the letter from my mom. If I brought that up now, I might lose my nerve. I didn't want that moment to ruin the possibilities of this one. And maybe some part of me even thought that I'd be able to change what was possible with my mom if I could change what was possible with me. But I wasn't ready to talk about that, either.

As we crossed over into North Gate, the sun continued its slow descent toward the horizon, and the breeze coming into our windows was heavy with the heat of the day. These neighborhoods lived and breathed in a way my side of town didn't seem to. The streets became wider and busier, and the signs on businesses were less the painted wood type and more the buzzing neon kind.

If you looked at Bridgeton and North Gate from above at night, it would probably look like a bouquet of flowers— North Gate an elaborate explosion of colorful neighborhoods blooming into one another, and Bridgeton its simpler, aligned stems. Our four main streets didn't look like much compared with the curving, interlacing roads of North Gate, and we certainly didn't have the variety of people, places, and entertainment they had, but flowers can't exist without their stems, and North Gate's trendy little cafés and shops wouldn't be so trendy if they didn't have the small-batch ginger beer, organic produce, or one-of-a-kind gnomes made where I lived.

But I can't say I wasn't excited to take a break from Bridgeton and all its quaintness—or that I didn't have all kinds of feelings blossoming inside my body as we rolled into Winnow's driveway around seven.

The small house at the end of the driveway looked like it had seen better days, but several lustrous plants hung along the porch, and a bright red gazebo sat smack-dab in the middle of the front lawn with one of those "give a book, take a book" libraries inside of it. I loved it instantly.

As I grabbed my bag from the back seat, we heard, "Hey there, road warriors!"

I slung my backpack over one shoulder and tried to calm the wiggling creatures in my stomach. Taking a deep breath, I turned to face Winnow, who was hopping down the front steps in black parachute pants and a tank top whose armholes swooped low enough to reveal a very sexy, aqua-colored bra. Not that I was looking. Her hair sat in a messy bun on top of her head and her feet were bare.

Somehow, her ultra-relaxed look served only to magnify my nerves.

Another person (female, I thought, for now) followed Winnow. This other girl's black hair was shaved on both sides, the rest dyed red and slicked back into a thick pompadour. Several piercings decorated her ears and face. She wore a gray tank top, a sleeveless jean jacket, frayed jean shorts, woolly socks, and ankle boots. Her legs were thick and defined, like a rugby player's, and an entire sleeve of tattoos coated one arm. I knew better than to stereotype, but I would have been shocked if she didn't like girls at least a little bit.

"Hey, sugar!" Deidre hollered back at Winnow, and then swooped her up in a powerful hug, lifting her off the lawn in the process. I dawdled near the van.

"It's good to see you, Deidre!" Winnow said, after her feet touched ground again.

"The pleasure is all mine, sweetheart."

Watching them, seeing Winnow and this other friend of hers, a surge of panic moved through me. *This is a huge mistake. Watch as the . . . something . . . gets left out of the, um, something. It's out of its depths and probably drowns . . . and whatnot.*

Winnow looked over my way and met my eyes, which probably conveyed more horror than I wanted them to. Her face grew wide with a sparkling grin and she jogged over to me, pulled the backpack off my shoulder, and dropped it to the ground. Then she wrapped her arms around my torso and gave me probably the most wondrous hug I have ever received in my life. I mean, Deidre's were medicinal, but this one changed my chemistry.

"Hi," she whispered into my ear. Her lips were so close, my earlobes tingled at her breath.

"Hi." I went to pull out of the hug, but she didn't loosen her arms, so I let mine fall back around her shoulders.

One. Two. Three. Four . . . at least five seconds passed before she drew back but left her hands on my waist. "It's really good to see you." I swear she was looking at my lips again. And maybe I was looking at hers, too.

"Same." I had to get ahold of myself. "It's all thanks to this lady, really," I said, stepping back to include Deidre in the conversation.

Deidre drew us both into her arms and said, "That's true! It *is* thanks to Deidre. Ain't she somethin'?"

"Yeah, she's all right," I said, squeezing her waist.

Winnow turned and grabbed her friend by the arm, pulling her into our circle. "This is Devi, by the way—she's one of my amazing roommates." I mentally noted that Winnow used "she."

Devi held out her hand to Deidre and me for a high five. I thought this was a bit bizarre but went along with it anyway. "Hey," she said, nodding at us both.

"Hey," I said.

"Pleasure to make your acquaintance," Deidre added. Then she said, to my dismay, "Unfortunately, y'all, I have to dash."

"You do?" Winnow asked.

*Yeah, you do?*

Winnow added, "You're more than welcome to come with us tonight."

"You're a sweetheart, but I have a gig with a couple of adorable boys in an hour. They want to look like girls," she announced, raising her pointed finger into the air, "and I'm gonna make it happen!" She pecked me on the cheek and whispered, "Just do you, girl," then retreated to her van. To all of us she yelled, "Now you all make sure you do everything I'd do and more!" She climbed in and honked her horn as she drove away.

I watched her van disappear around the corner, a large portion of my courage disappearing with it.

I felt Winnow's hand on my elbow. "Come on in and check out 'La Gazebo.'"

*Deep breath, Nima.* "Wow, sounds fancy," I managed to get out.

"Oh, it is. *Very* fancy."

She picked my backpack up off the ground and flung it over her shoulder. Then she took my hand and led me into the house after Devi. I hoped desperately she didn't notice how sweaty my palm was.

Entering her place was like walking into a temple

devoted to contradictions. Two life-size portraits of fierce-looking drag queens met my eyes as soon as we walked in, as if welcoming us with a *Well, don't just stand there, bitches!* But on either side of the portraits were statues—a sitting Buddha, and a laughing Buddha that made me smile. A gigantic wooden table sat in front of the portraits and statues, like something out of a medieval feast scene. But the chairs around it were a collection of misfits—one wicker, one beat-up wooden chair, a plastic folding chair, and a couple of clunky metal ones.

Multicolored lights bordered the mantelpiece of a brick fireplace. The fireplace looked defunct, but inside it a mountain of candles stood in various stages of their lives. Set around this structure was another grouping of mismatched seating options. A bright red shag rug spread across the very worn hardwood floor, like a sea of flames.

Winnow let go of my hand and spread both arms wide. "Welcome to my abode. What d'ya think?"

"It is unsurprisingly awesome," I uttered.

Winnow beamed at me. Devi looked at her, and something like a smirk contorted her mouth. I wondered what that was about. Had they already talked about me? Was I being too obvious about how much I liked Winnow?

Probably.

I didn't have too much time to wonder, though, because through a doorway at the back corner of the room entered a very large, half-naked man.

"Whoa. Sorry, folks," he said in a deep, gentle voice. "I didn't realize we had company. Just took a shower." He gripped the towel around his waist. His short sandy hair rose from his scalp in spiky tufts.

"Way to make an entrance, my friend," Winnow said. "This, Nima, is Boyd. Boyd, Nima. Now go put on some clothes, Boyd."

Boyd approached me and stuck out his arm. "Hey, Nima." His meaty hand gave my sweaty, hot one a firm shake. He must have been about six feet tall and somewhere in his early twenties too. Many pounds of full but firm-looking white flesh greeted me everywhere I tried not to look.

"Hey, Boyd. Thanks for wearing a towel," I said.

He, Winnow, and Devi laughed, and I felt a little better. I'd said something not too embarrassing, and they'd found it funny. And I hadn't batted an eye about the guy in a towel. Two wins in less than two minutes. *You go, girl.*

"All right, off to find some pants. Back in a jiff." He glided off to a room somewhere to the right.

"Okay. I have some good news and some bad news," Winnow said to me. "The bad news is, we have no extra beds here. The good news is, that couch over there is as comfortable as it looks. But I also have a queen-size bed. So—"

*Oh.*

Winnow looked at me a little bashfully, and her next words flew quickly from her mouth. "You can totally sleep on the couch if you want to, but the bed is an option too.

And I'm a really good sleeper, I promise! No snoring, kicking, sheet stealing, or drooling."

"Uh, well, I do all those things, so—sorry in advance?" My mouth felt full of cotton, but I thought I was doing a pretty good job of faking coolness right now.

Winnow and Devi laughed again. Win number three. Or was it four, given the possible sleeping arrangements?

"Okay, well, let's get your stuff into my room, for now at least." She led me in through the same entryway from where Boyd had made his fleshy entrance, which opened into a spacious kitchen. Past that, a hallway led to three doorways. Winnow's room sat farthest back, a very sultry poster of a 1920s flapper girl plastered across the door.

"Meet Doris," she said, indicating the flapper girl. She opened the door into a small but incredibly inviting bedroom. Setting my backpack on her bed, she continued, "Tiny room, but large bed, as promised. You won't even know I'm here."

*I doubt that. Very much.*

The bed did look massive, though. It was pushed right up against the wall on one side and took up almost the entire width of the room. A closet and several book stacks lined the other side. Twinkle lights packed a massive glass jar at the foot of her bed and crisscrossed the entire ceiling. One more string framed yet another giant, black-and-white portrait of a beautiful woman in a tuxedo. I tried, "Is that Marlene Dietrich?" hoping to impress Winnow by knowing who Marlene Dietrich was.

Winnow laughed. "Wrong skin color. It's Josephine Baker. She's one of my muses," she answered, gazing admiringly at the poster.

*So much for impressing anyone.* I matched her laugh to hide my embarrassment.

When Winnow flicked on the light switch, the ceiling became a constellation of stars and the lighting gave the space a muted but enchanting quality. It reminded me of the first time I saw Winnow—inviting me into the soft glow of the punk tent, looking like she'd just popped out of a flower somewhere.

"I love this room," I said, still standing in the doorframe. I sounded breathier than I'd wanted to.

"What's yours like?"

"Mine? Um, not as cool as this. I have a lot of books too. On shelves. And my bed's just a single. And my closet is way too small." *Wow. Pulitzer-quality description, Nima.*

"Anything you like about it?" Winnow asked, understandably.

"I like . . . the books?" *Jesus.*

"Yeah, books always make a room better." She plunked herself across the bed, propping herself up on an elbow. "You said you liked believable novels, I think?"

*She remembered that from the bonfire? Impressive.* "Yeah— real life ones."

"About?"

Her gaze was so still and self-assured. I couldn't manage

to hold it, so I stared stupidly at her elbow. "Um, lots of things. But . . . I think it's cool when the script flips on you somehow, you know? Like, when you get a completely different side to something you thought you'd already figured out."

"Mm, I see. Like you think you have a character pegged, but then a whole other part of them is revealed?"

"Correct. But it has to be realistic." Feeling foolish still standing by the door, I moved toward her book piles. "What about you? What've you got here?" I knelt down and started scanning the titles.

"I like variety. You'll see lots of female authors there, though. My mom's a serious feminist, and a lot of those books were hers."

"Where is she? Your mom?"

"She's over near Allison Pools."

"Are your parents still together?"

"Yup. And happily, too—can you believe it? In this day and age? I guess no one told them about the divorce rate." She smiled at me, and then her face became serious and she tilted her head a little, which made my heart tilt a little too. "Are your parents divorced, or just . . ."

I ran my finger down the spines of several books. "They're just not together." I guess I should have offered more info, but something in my throat caught, and I thought it best to stop there.

"Sorry."

I coughed a little. "It's okay." My eyes settled on a book

called *Tipping the Velvet*. "I mean, it could be worse. My dad is amazing. An amazing weirdo, too, but a good one." I smiled back at her, beginning to ease into the conversation a bit more.

Unfortunately, Devi's muscly build burst into the doorway and into my ease. "Where's the party at, ladies?"

Winnow laughed. "You can't handle five minutes by yourself, can you?"

"It's just that I can't keep away from you." She bounded onto the bed and tackled Winnow as she did.

"Agh! All your rippling muscles! You're gonna squash me, you brute!" Winnow protested through her laughter.

I sat back on my heels and watched the two of them wrestle. They seemed so comfortable with each other. I wondered if they'd ever dated. I'd read somewhere during my online "research" that lesbians stay friends with all their exes. Maybe it was true.

"I'm just going to use your washroom, if that's okay," I said.

In between gasps, Winnow said, "Of course—second door on the left." She gave Devi a fake elbow drop.

I did actually have to pee, but I also needed a little escape from their familiarity. I wasn't jealous, but I did feel awkward, which was becoming a familiarity of its own.

The washroom was spacious and bright. A purple feather boa lined the mirror, and I wondered who was responsible for the "diva" touches around the house—the portraits in the living room and this plumed accessory.

I did my thing and tried to compose myself. Looking into the mirror, I saw a very young face. A naive face. A face that had never slept in the same bed as a really cute girl before, or hung out with cool lesbians, or really done much of anything.

What would other people do in this situation? Jill always played it cool in any setting. She'd probably jump right onto that bed and wrestle the both of them. Charles would run screaming from the room. Dad would tell some terrible jokes, then go for a walk. My normal "Nima-ness" would not work here, though, I knew that.

But I didn't have a chance to figure anything out, because a heavy knock rattled the washroom door.

"Hi, I'm almost done," I said in an abnormally high pitch.

"Oh, sorry," came Boyd's resonant voice from outside the door. "I just forgot some stuff in there. I'll get it when you're done, though."

I unlocked the door and opened it to his turned back. "Wait, I'm done! Here you go." I squeezed by him into the hallway. He was fully clothed now in a T-shirt and board shorts, fortunately.

"Oh, thanks. My apologies—I didn't mean to rush you." So polite.

"Yeah—no worries. Just trying to figure out who to be, is all." *Inside thoughts, Nima.*

He picked up a pile of clothes from the floor and then stood to face me. "Oh yeah? And who'd you decide on?"

"Ha-ha . . . oh, I didn't say I'd figured it out." He had such a warm smile, and it quieted my nerves a little.

"Who has, really?" He leaned on the doorframe, which I swear curved outward to accommodate his own immense frame. "How do you know Winnow and Devi?"

"Hmm." I leaned my back against the hallway wall across from him. "Well, I met Winnow a couple of weeks ago at this fair she performed at, and I met Devi approximately fifteen minutes ago."

"Nice. And here you are."

"Here I am."

"Well, Nima, I was just about to have a beer. Want one?"

"You trying to steal my date, punk?" This was Winnow, who had appeared in her own doorway, Devi standing behind her. The word "date" caused a small tornado in my brain.

"Hey, I'm just offering our guest a drink. Looks like she might be thirsty, is all."

"Well, shit, let's get her a drink then. A beer sounds good. It's Friday night, after all." She winked at me.

We all moved into the kitchen. Winnow grabbed four beers from the fridge and handed me one, which I gladly accepted. I hadn't really acquired a taste for beer yet, but anything would do at this point. As we settled into the living room—Winnow and me on the couch, Boyd and Devi across the room—Boyd asked, "What's the plan, gang? What time are we heading out?"

"The Pool House doesn't really get going till a bit later, so we have some time to kill," Winnow answered. She looked at me and, registering my confusion, added, "The Pool House is where we're going tonight. It's this weekly party that happens over the summer. It's fun—but you have to see it for yourself." She tapped my bare foot with hers, which just about sent me careening off the couch.

I took a sip of beer and tried hard not to grimace. "Okay, cool. I'll take your word for it."

"What're we gonna do till then?" Devi asked.

"You like card games, Nima?" Boyd asked, his face expanding with excitement.

Winnow leaned over to me and put her hand on my thigh. I died. "Boyd really likes card games," she explained.

Recovering poorly, I stuttered, "I'm, uh, up for anything." But was I?

Two games of hearts and two beers later, I started to feel a bit more relaxed. Maybe a little *too* relaxed. I wasn't used to having more than one or two drinks, and I'd finished the beers a little faster than usual. I guess I'd been trying to keep up with Devi—drinking as fast as her, laughing when she laughed, leaning back in my chair like she did—thinking maybe if I replicated some of her coolness, I'd fit in here a bit more, but I decided to slow down when I mistook the ace of spades for a four and messed up my hand, much to the amusement of the others.

"'Nother beer?" Devi asked, standing at the open fridge,

a cocky smile on her lips. The rest of us were sitting at the kitchen table.

"No, thanks. I think I'll grab some water, though."

"I'll get it for you," Winnow offered.

As Devi and Boyd finished another beer each and played some game I didn't recognize, I joined Winnow at the sink and took the glass of water she'd filled for me.

"Thank you." I smiled at her shyly. Or goofily. Not sure which.

"My pleasure, ma'am." She put her hand on my waist. "Did I mention how glad I am that you're here?"

My neck grew sweaty in a matter of milliseconds. "Me too." In my mind, I moved closer to her and placed my free hand on her hip. In reality, I pretended to pick lint off my shirt.

Winnow's hand dropped from my waist as she got a glass of water for herself. "How was dinner with Deidre and your dad?" she asked.

Happy to talk about someone other than myself, my words rushed out. "Deidre? She's amazing. And hilarious. And beautiful. I think my dad wants to be her BFF."

"Ha-ha, that's awesome." She gave me a crooked smile as she filled her glass from the tap. A few strands of her hair escaped down the back of her neck, and I had a strong urge to run them through my fingers.

"Yeah, it is," I said, and probably blushed a little too.

"Deidre lives around here, doesn't she?"

"Yeah."

"We should all get together sometime—check out a drag show or something. Would you be up for that?"

We were already making plans for a next time, and my face lit on fire. "Yeah, totally."

"Cool."

"Cool," I echoed, and guzzled my water like I'd just crawled out of the desert.

When we arrived at the famed Pool House, it looked an awful lot like a backyard with a bunch of kiddie pools set up across the lawn. The pools varied in size, shape, and pattern, but all were about a foot high and half-filled with water. Some people sprawled across them while others lounged in chairs and soaked their feet. One pool even had a makeshift net arched across it, and two girls sat facing each other in the water, prodding a balloon back and forth over the wobbly apparatus. Red and orange patio lanterns glowed along the wooden fence enclosing the yard, and plucky Hawaiian music floated across the scene from speakers set up on a patio.

We each paid eight dollars to enter and then wove our way through the puffy, jiggling pools to the far corner of the lawn, where a small bar stood. Devi and Boyd waited in line to get some drinks for themselves. I felt a little blurry and figured that the two beers I'd already had were sufficient for now.

I surveyed the yard. "This is hilarious. And brilliant."

"Right?" Winnow responded. "A couple of guys started it a few years ago and it just keeps popping back up each summer. And don't worry, it's superclean, too."

*Why would she say that? Does she think I'm a total neat freak? Because I'm boring? God. She definitely thinks I'm boring.*

I tried to calm my mind, but since leaving Winnow's house, moments like this kept jabbing into my brain, forcing me to reconsider my decision to come here.

As if Winnow could read my mind, she followed with, "I'm super type A, and that was my initial thought when I first saw this place—public pools are pee-filled and gungy. This is going to be even worse. But it's not. I promise." She grabbed my hand as she said this and gave it a squeeze.

Every time she touched me, my chest tightened.

She didn't let go of my hand either. This made it pleasantly difficult to breathe.

We stood there, holding hands, and I racked my brain trying to think of something cool, or funny, or exciting to say. But nothing came. Guess it's hard to generate any of those things when you're none of them.

I could feel her looking at me, and the jabbing in my head continued. My eyes started to moisten. *Oh no. Not this again.* I pulled my hand out of hers and looked away. "Does this place have a washroom? I really need to pee." Fake laugh.

"Yeah, for sure. It's just through that side door of the house over there and to the right. You okay?" She stepped closer.

"Yeah, totally. I just need to break the seal." That was something people said when they were drinking, right?

"Okay. I'll wait for you here."

"Okay, cool." I walked past her toward the house, staring at the ground the whole way. Once in the relative safety of the washroom, I leaned against the wall and tried to quell the tears.

Without Deidre's glitter sprinkled over me, what did I have to offer these people? What if the other night at the festival was a fleeting instance of sorcery concocted by Deidre's enchantments? After all, everything following that night had been anything but magical. It was like I'd found a portal from my unremarkable, everyday existence into a fantastical realm, and now access had been slammed shut. And I had no idea how to reopen it. Not here. Not without some help. If I didn't think of something quick, all these people would realize what a flop I was. *Winnow* would realize.

A cheer arose from outside, and I noticed a small window facing onto the yard. I pulled back the curtain to see what was happening, wiping the wet from my eyes.

Boyd had stripped down to his SpongeBob underpants and was performing an energetic dance in one of the pools while chugging back beer after beer. Every bit of his body shook along with the bouncing music, and his audience couldn't get enough.

*Drinks. Confidence. Fans.*

*Got it.*

I splashed some water on my face and used the too-damp-already hand towel to pat myself as dry as possible. Meeting my eyes squarely in the washroom mirror, I gave myself an inspiring pep talk.

"Nima freaking-Kumara-Clark. Smarten the eff up."

I marched outside with new determination, and while the others gathered around Boyd and his watery moonwalk, I beelined straight to the bar and ordered with as much gusto as possible a double shot of rum. Badass.

"We only have beer and cider," the girl behind the bar said, her eyes full of amusement.

Sheepish, but only momentarily put off, I asked for a can of cider and drank it as fast as I could, watching the crowd. My nose tingled from the fizz and I burped about twelve times, but I managed. Then I ordered another and drank about half of it. I bought a beer for Winnow—'cause that's what badasses do—before sauntering over to the crowd.

I could definitely "feel the fizz" of my ciders, which gave me the idiotic confidence to place the cold beer can against Winnow's bare neck. Smooth like butter.

She squealed and whipped around. When she saw it was me, she looked surprised and exclaimed, "Quite the entrance!"

I held the beer out to her, proud of myself.

"What's this?"

"I got you a beer," I said, carefully articulating each word, which proved somewhat difficult.

"Why, thank you. How gallant. And I see you got yourself

another drink too. I guess they don't ID at this joint," she said, laughing.

Ignoring the references to my age and my beverage count, I gestured to Boyd's exquisite performance and asked, "What exactly is happening over there?"

"Yes, well. You wouldn't know it to look at him, but Boyd happens to be one of the foremost queens in this neck of the woods."

"Like, drag queen?"

"Yeah—why do you think we have queen-ish paraphernalia all over the house?"

"Oh—I wasn't sure—I thought maybe it was yours."

"Because Boyd is so gigantic and manly, you mean?"

I bit my lip. This felt like a faux pas.

She laughed. "Don't worry. It's an honest mistake. Boyd is definitely not your typical drag queen, to be sure."

*Whew.*

"Does Devi do drag too, then?"

"God no, she thinks drag is for peasants. Gay peasants. Her words, not mine."

"Oh." My buzz and accompanying nerve faltered. I felt like such a newbie to all of this.

Winnow put her arm around my shoulders and clinked my can of cider with her can of beer. "Thanks for the drink, lady."

I half smiled at her, but my bravado deflated. I tipped the can to my lips and chugged the rest of my cider, hoping to replenish my liquid courage.

Winnow watched me. "Whoa, *chica*. Careful with that stuff. It can hit you sideways when you're least expecting it." She had her arm around my waist now, and the heat of her hand on my hip filled me with both craving and terror.

My mouth responded to these feelings with, "I'm going to get another. Hey, Devi, you need a drink?" She was in front of us and I tapped her on the shoulder.

She turned toward me. "Hell yes, girl!" Then she looked at Winnow and raised her eyebrows.

Another look. *They thought I couldn't handle myself? Whatever. You guys share your little glances. I can handle myself. Watch me.*

Boyd's dance extravaganza came to an end, and the crowd dispersed to their individual pool parties. I practically jogged to the bar to get there ahead of everyone and ordered three beers and another cider. The bartender passed me the four icy cans, unopened. She'd already anticipated my predicament.

I had four cans and only two hands. I put two cans under my armpits, setting my jaw stiffly against their chill, and carried one in each hand.

Suddenly Winnow was in front of me. "Hey. Let me help you." She took the beer out of my left armpit.

*Ugh.* "Sorry if your beer has my armpit on it," I muttered. *Mother-effing marbles, Nima.*

"Ha-ha . . . no worries. I love me some armpit beer. Of course, I still have the first beer that you bought me two minutes ago." She held up said beer in her other hand.

*Right. Damn.*

"Boyd can drink it, though—he won't complain," she offered.

Her kindness made me feel even more infantile. Badasses don't need anyone to make them feel better. Badasses don't make dumb mistakes. Badasses can handle their own damn selves.

We walked back to a pool around the other side of the house. According to Winnow, this was the VIP pool, and we'd gained access because of Boyd's magical dance routine.

The VIP pool turned out to be an actual hot tub, which I'd normally be super excited about. One problem: I didn't have a bathing suit. I'd had no idea we'd be coming to a pool party, after all. But it didn't seem to be an issue for Winnow. She stripped down to her aqua-blue panties and bra, causing a brief disruption to my already erratic heartbeat. Each curve, every visible inch of her skin drew my eyes in. The muscles in her thighs grew taut as she climbed into the tub. Before lowering herself into the water, she ran her thumbs along the waistband of her panties to adjust them, and my heart fluttered at the thought of touching her there too. I had to divert my attention to the others before my mind completely dissolved into mayhem.

Boyd was, of course, already in his underpants. Devi was in a sports bra and, from what I could tell through the swirling water, boxer shorts. I guess underwear was an acceptable substitute for bathing suits here.

I did a quick check-in with myself, which wasn't easy after four drinks. Which underwear was I wearing? I must have thought of this before I left the house today. Sleeping over at Winnow's equals decent underwear. Right? Right. I just had to trust that while I was sober, I chose the right undergarments. Here goes.

I handed Devi and Boyd their beers and placed my cider on the edge of the tub. Then I yanked off my shirt, revealing the one and only decent, non-sports bra I had: a black Calvin Klein.

Not terrible.

Then I pulled off my jeans to reveal: good old-fashioned Hanes Her Ways. Not exactly sexy, but not entirely embarrassing, either. I got into the hot tub as quickly as possible, which made for a less-than-graceful entrance. Losing my footing on the plastic seating, I fell sideways into Devi.

"Whoa, girl. We barely know each other!" she said, a glimmer in her eye. I couldn't tell if it was a friendly glimmer or not.

"Sorry." Snatching my cider off the tub edge, I slid away from her and took a few more swallows. I wasn't sure whether I was drinking for courage or comfort now.

Winnow moved in closer to me. "Hey, sure you're okay?"

I took another sip, looking as blasé as I could. "Yeah, totally—why?"

"I just want you to feel comfortable. Are you comfortable?"

*Not. At. All.*

"Yeah, for sure. I love this. You okay?" *Smart, Nima. Turn it back on her.*

"Yeah, I'm good. I'm a little thirsty, though. Do you want some water? I can get you some too."

"No, I'm good with this." I held up my cider like a pro. Steam from the bubbling water rose around me.

"Okay." She got out of the tub in all her aqua glory and squeezed my shoulder.

*Whatever. I'm just going to sit here and take in the scene,* I thought, bobbing my head to the music.

"Hey, girl, what's up with you?" Boyd was sitting directly across from me, his elbows propped up on the tub's edge, each hand gripping a beer.

"Me?"

"Yeah, you. All right?"

"Yeah, I'm fine. What's up with you?" I was getting sick of people asking me how I was.

"I'm good. Thanks again for the drinks."

"No worries. That was some show."

"Thanks. You know how it is." He winked at me.

"Not really," I said under my breath. *Say something else, fool.* "How long have you been draggin' it up?" *Draggin' it up?* Now words were just tumbling out of my face.

"Oh, I've been 'draggin' it up' for about two years now." He and Devi shared a laugh.

*Yup, they think I'm ridiculous too.* Trying to ignore the

ever-creeping feeling of humiliation, I asked, "How did you get started?"

"Funny enough, I dated a girl whose brother did drag, and he got me into it. Rad, huh?"

*Wait—Boyd dated girls? Drag queens can date girls?*

Boyd continued, "What about you? Ever thought about getting onstage? Doing a little drag?"

"Me? No way!"

"Why not? You're cute. You'd do well," he said.

*Cute as a baby pug.* "Could you really see me doing drag?" I pictured myself in one of those plastic Groucho masks with the bushy eyebrows and mustache. The drag kings I'd seen were talented, smooth, sexy.

In other words, the opposite of me.

"I could picture it," Devi interjected.

This time, I could tell the glimmer in her eye wasn't a kind one.

"It's obvious you've got a little butch in you just itching to let loose," she continued. "I think you're a perfect fit."

Boyd nudged her and mouthed, "Stop."

But she didn't. "What? I'm not joking. You should try it sometime, Nima. I think you'd love it. You and Winnow could even do a number together. Maybe 'Kiss' by Prince? Or no—how about Usher—'Can U Handle It?' Or 'I Want You to Want Me'?" She smiled over the rim of her beer can and took a sip, then leaned over to whisper something to Boyd, and he laughed.

My eyes instantly watered, so I looked away and gulped my cider. I felt like a twelve-year-old at a big kids' party. I didn't know what to make of all these whispers and glances, side remarks and laughter. What I did know was that everyone here could see what a fake I was.

Winnow appeared at my shoulder with a red plastic cup of water and set it on the ledge next to me. "I know you said you didn't need any, but you can drink it later if you want to." She climbed back into the tub with her own cup. Her geisha peered at me, daring me to look away, then sank into the foaming water.

I downed the rest of my cider. I wanted to go home. Climb into my warm pajamas. Sleep in my own bed. Call Charles. I didn't fit here.

The cider didn't fit either.

In the next moment, it erupted from my mouth in a peachy, frothy cascade. The hot tub's churning water instantly carried the born-again liquor and all remnants of my beer-can chicken from dinner to every single inch of space around me and the others. Boyd, Devi, and Winnow moved so fast that they managed to make only momentary contact with the contaminants. Boyd somehow even managed to keep both his beers upright.

I, however, remained seated, embarrassed into immobility despite my utter revulsion at the bubbling mess around me. My brain conjured an image of a roast, stewing in its own juices. Here I was, again, barfing in front of a girl I liked.

"Nima, get out of there!" Winnow said, as she doused her torso with the water from her cup.

Everything around me seemed slow, blurry. . . . Boyd and Devi spraying themselves with the garden hose, their faces contorted in grossed-out laughter . . . a crowd of people wandering over to see what had happened . . . the two guys who ran the place turning off the jets and dipping a pool net in to catch as many chunks as possible . . . Winnow beckoning, from a safe distance, for me to get out.

The key clicked in the door. The night was a smudge of coal around me, and I had a hard time focusing. Devi and Boyd had escaped after the debacle, offering weak shoulder squeezes and sympathetic half smiles. Winnow had been left to contend with a drunk, pukey seventeen-year-old, and though she'd patiently helped me rinse off as I'd swayed dizzily against the prickling spray of the garden hose, her eyes never once met mine. Not that mine could focus on anything anyway. Our walk back to the house had been quiet, mostly, except for some mundane conversation I could barely remember.

Winnow got me to drink some water, even though my stomach felt like a giant knot, and we leaned against the kitchen counter, sipping in silence. My eyes sagged and time seemed to be hovering around us instead of moving forward.

*Sorry I was such a freak tonight.* The words tried to escape my mouth but sat heavy on my tongue instead.

It was like she heard them anyway, though, because she turned to me and said, "It's okay if you're a little . . . overwhelmed. It makes sense, I mean. We barely know each other, after all, and this must all seem pretty unfamiliar. Is it? Is that what's been on your mind tonight?"

I couldn't look at her, and my tongue felt like mud in my mouth. How to explain to her how terrifying this all was without seeming young, and ridiculous, and pathetic? To explain how much I wanted her to like me, despite my fear there wasn't enough worth liking? Tears formed. *Shit. Please don't.*

She put her water down and placed her hand against my chest. Tilting her head, she added, "Maybe this is all just too new."

"Maybe too new" sounded like an ending of some sort, and a surge of emotion released right through my chest, like her hand was some sort of conductor. My entire body shook, my face crumpled. As the first tears left my eyes, Winnow tried to envelop me in her arms. Hating the thought of her having to absorb my slobbering, pitiful sobs, I pushed her hands away and turned toward the counter, managing to whimper, "Please just leave me alone. I'll sleep on the couch."

"Nima—"

"Please."

After a few moments, Winnow placed her hand briefly on my arm and then slipped away to the washroom.

By the time I'd finally cried myself out, she'd made up the

couch for me and, to my continued mortification, left a metal bowl on the floor. Then she gave me the same delicate squeeze and sympathetic look the others had given me before she left me to curl up on the couch, dizzy, exhausted, and alone.

When I woke up the next morning, a dull ache behind my eyes and a bitter, barfy feeling in my stomach, the first thing I did was peek over the edge of the couch to see whether the metal bowl Winnow had placed on the floor was empty. Thankfully, I could see my blurry reflection in the shiny bottom. The next thing I did was check my phone to see what time it was: 10:22. I couldn't remember the last time I'd slept this late.

I slipped off the couch, still in my jeans and T-shirt from the night before, and pulled my hair back into a ponytail. Then I padded quietly down the hallway to the washroom to brush the sticky, foul taste out of my mouth and douse my face in cold water. I noticed Winnow's bedroom door was open, but I couldn't hear or see any sign of her.

Someone must have just showered, because the air in the washroom was steamy and hot and the cabinet mirror was partially fogged over. Through the fog, my puffy eyes gazed out at me. I splashed water over my face again and again, aggressively rubbing my fingers into my eyes and cheeks. If I could just refresh my face, maybe everything else would feel better too. I wiped my wet hands across my scalp to smooth back some of the escaping curls of my hair as well. I probably could have used a shower, but I didn't want to have to ask for a towel. I was delaying seeing Winnow for as long as I could.

Feeling somewhat refreshed on the outside, but still horribly embarrassed everywhere else, I tiptoed back to the living room to put away my toiletries. The faint smell of toast permeated the air. I stripped the sheets off the couch and folded them neatly, hoping to leave the room as close to its original state as possible—the way it was before I got here and made a mess of everything.

As I replaced the pillows on the couch, I decided to leave right away. Winnow would probably prefer that anyway, and I couldn't imagine passing another minute with her and the others after the act I'd put on last night. Peach cider wasn't the boost I'd been looking for. Unfortunately, my storehouse of strategies for convincing people I was worth their time was near empty.

Bag packed, I took a few deep breaths and looked around. Only then did I notice that the front door stood open a crack. Peeking through, I could see Winnow sitting in the gazebo, reading. Feet propped up on another chair, she had a mug in one hand, a book in the other. I hated to disturb her, she looked so content, but I figured I needed to rip this Band-Aid off at some point.

As I approached the gazebo, she turned her head and smiled at me. A pity smile. She lifted her feet off the chair and shifted toward me. "Morning." I couldn't read her tone. Maybe because it was so neutral. Not particularly a good thing.

Pausing just outside the entrance to the gazebo, I dropped my bag down on the lawn, then shoved my hands into my pockets. "Hey."

"How ya feeling?"

"Like an ass."

"Hey, it happens to the best of us."

*Bullshit.* I looked down at my bag. "You've thrown up in a hot tub too, have you?" I said, like a sullen child.

"Well, not quite, but I've certainly had a few really good barfing sessions."

I hated this conversation. "I'm not feeling great. I think I'm just going to catch the next bus back home."

"Are you sure?"

No protests or pleas to stay, I noticed. "Yeah. But thanks for letting me stay and stuff. I'm really sorry about last night, Winnow." I couldn't look at her. My puffy eyes stung.

"Don't worry about it, Nima. But I get it if you want to head home. Do you want some breakfast or something first? Coffee?"

The thought of consuming anything right now sent my stomach reeling. "No, thanks. I think I'm just going to head out."

"Well, let me give you a ride to the bus stop at least. I can borrow Devi's car. She won't mind."

"No, really, it's okay. I can just call a cab." I went to pull out my cell phone.

"Nima, that's ridiculous. I'm going to grab the keys right now. Put your phone away."

After a mostly silent and thankfully short car ride, Winnow pulled up in front of the bus stop. She put the car in park but didn't turn off the engine. I couldn't blame her for wanting a short goodbye. She did undo her seat belt, though, and to the irritating beeping sound a car makes when someone's seat belt is unfastened, she leaned over to give me a hug. The moment her body touched mine, my chest tightened and my eyes grew moist. Before I got any messier, I cleared my throat, thanked her, and pulled out of her arms. As I opened the car door and got out, I said thanks one more time and "See ya."

"See ya." Winnow waved her hand at me and gave me that same pitying smile.

I shut the car door, and as she drove off, I wondered if we really would see each other again.

# CHAPTER 10

By the time I got home, I'd had plenty of time to replay the events of the previous night over and over again. Each time, I was able to remember some detail that made the whole situation even more horrifying. Winnow's twisted mouth when she realized I'd barfed right next to her. Boyd slipping one of the two guys who ran the place an extra twenty bucks for the trouble of cleaning up. The piece of chicken I found perched in my bra strap as Winnow hosed me off. As I walked in the patio door around noon, I'd compiled a lengthy laundry list of dirty items to wallow in.

Dad wasn't home, which was perfect. I didn't feel like facing questions about my big night out.

I left a note on the kitchen counter saying I wasn't feeling well, and that I'd be upstairs, napping. And then that was exactly where I went to sleep the day away.

The next morning, to add to my misery, I got a curt text from Charles saying, I need my chem notes back for my online course.

When I texted him to ask if he wanted to meet up for some ice cream or something, he never responded. So there was that.

Things just escalated from there.

Dad kept trying to get some dirt on my night at Winnow's, and even though I kept giving him my very best *don't bother me* face, he'd ask something every time we crossed paths.

"So . . . where'd y'all go?"

"Did Deidre go too?"

"What'd you do?"

"Forgot to ask—how old are these folks, anyway?"

It got to the point that I just stopped crossing paths with him—I stayed away from the house almost all day Sunday, and by the time he got home from work Monday and Tuesday, I'd already left to strategically wander around town until he'd gone to bed.

Unfortunately, nowhere was safe. I had another choice run-in with Gordon midweek. This time I'd walked over to the Fast Pick to grab a few items, and he was outside smoking, one indolent arm hanging around Tessa's neck.

It's not like I expected him to bring up Davis's asshole performance at Tessa's house, but I don't think I expected him to be even more of an asshole either. Yet after our run-in at the art room, I guess he'd decided that the best defense was a nasty offense, because he stared right at me, like a dare, and said, "Well, well. Check this out, Tessa—ever seen a queer before?"

Tessa's eyes registered something between confusion and surprise before she aimed them at her feet.

Still reeling from my horrifying night with Winnow, unsure of what to do about Charles or my mom's letter, and exhausted from the lack of sleep all these things caused, I had very little energy left for Gordon Grant, even if I was still curious (and maybe even a little concerned) about him.

But that didn't stop my cheeks from instantly lighting on fire at the word "queer." "Dyke" and "queer" just hadn't been words I'd grown accustomed to yet—maybe I would eventually. But I guess I'd always just considered myself a girl who was into other girls—I hadn't sorted out any labels yet. And I'd never had anyone label me either—certainly not in public in front of practical strangers—until this past couple of weeks. Part of me wanted to respond with, "So what if I am?" and part of me wanted to tell him to eff off for trying to brand me with his own names for whoever he thought I was.

I did neither.

"No snappy answer, Clark? Must mean it's true," he added, glancing at Tessa and laughing a deliberately obnoxious laugh.

Man, it was obvious he was trying so hard to be a jerk. After my own performance the other night, I wondered what kind of deficiencies *his* act was concealing.

I finally found my tongue. "Nothing wrong with a little truth, Gordon." I held his gaze until he sniffed and looked at his cigarette like it had suddenly grown confusing to him.

Curious, I directed at Tessa, "I didn't know you two were a thing."

She leaned into him a little more and shrugged, looking to

him as if for some affirmation that they were, indeed, a thing. When he looked away and placed his cigarette to his lips, she faced me and replied, "Yeah, well, we're just having some fun. You know." Halting titter.

I *wish* I knew what a little fun was like. Maybe being an a-hole was the answer to all my problems. But probably not.

Gordon blew his smoke at my feet, then moved his arm from Tessa's shoulders to her waist and squeezed her in tight. "Come on, babe, let's go have a little fun, like you said." His smarmy smile spread across his face, but it wasn't matched by his eyes. I was beginning to realize that the indecipherable trace of "something else" I'd seen in them before was always there—even when he was being his crappiest self. Was it possible to decode whatever it was? Did I want to?

As if in response, he flicked the butt at my feet and turned to go, bringing Tessa along with him. I heard her ask, "What'd she mean by the truth?" as they walked away, and I wondered how he would answer.

I spent the next day trying to keep myself busy so I wouldn't think about any of the shambles my life was currently in. I *did* text Deidre to see if she could spread a little of her magic sunshine my way, but she said she was swamped with work and would get back to me ASAP.

Staring at my very familiar room and the photo collage above my desk, what I did find myself thinking about after a small hiatus was Ginny. I couldn't really explain why. Maybe it was because—besides the general, ongoing pain she'd caused over the past three years of my life, which was now more like a dull ache than the excruciating humiliation I currently felt over Winnow—things had been relatively normal between us. Relative to all this other nonsense, I mean.

I guess I was just looking for some normal as I walked through the doors of Old Stuff that afternoon, hoping to find an old friend and some old clothes to make me feel better.

I hadn't seen Ginny much since the festival, except at the car wash and once while I'd been running some errands for Jill in town. I must have been a little preoccupied with thoughts of Winnow, because for once, I didn't trip over myself each time I saw Ginny. But I doubt she'd noticed, seeing as she was always surrounded by people wanting her attention.

I did feel a little nervous as the bell above the door announced my entrance, though. Part of me really missed her—and I don't mean just her freckles, either—I missed her cheerfulness, her simple, friendly nature. The only complication about Ginny was how I felt about her—she herself was an open book.

Ginny was standing behind the counter eating a sandwich when I walked in. When she saw me, her whole face smiled and that, along with the tiny dab of mayo at the side of her mouth, made me suddenly feel like crying. My face fell apart, and embarrassed once again by these uncontrollable crying fits, I covered my face with my hands and just stood there, sobbing. *God. When would this effing well run dry?*

I felt Ginny's arms wrap around me and we just stood like that for a minute or so, until I gained control of my face and body. Ginny moved away momentarily to place the BE BACK IN 20 sign on the door and flip the lock. Then she grabbed my hand and led me toward the changing room at the back.

Once hidden behind the curtain, she said, "Hey, you. What's going on? I feel like I haven't seen you in ages."

Not quite ready to look at her yet, I stared at our feet, which were toe to toe between us. "Yeah, things have been . . . weird. I don't even know where to start." Trying to keep it light, I added, "Also, I need some clothes."

She placed the tips of her sandaled feet over the top of my sneakers and tapped them lightly. "Well, I want to hear everything, but I feel like this changing room might not be the best place for a heart-to-heart. I'm off at two. How about we focus on the clothes part, and then chat when I'm done?"

I nodded, wiping my face.

We spent the next half hour rummaging through the store. Once I'd told Ginny that I was looking for comfortable, classic Nima-wear (jeans and T-shirts), she, in classic Ginny form, began choosing the exact opposite of that.

"You need a change, Nima. Something to spice up that mood," she said, handing me a pile of very bright, very furry, very glittery clothing.

Glitter and change. These were complicated things. But she was right. I needed them both. Badly. And wouldn't it be a plot twist if Ginny was the one who helped me get both?

She kept the BE BACK IN 20 sign up the whole time, giving us some privacy, which was nice. But she also forced me to try on every item of clothing she chose in a variety of combinations and perform a little model-walk in each outfit so she could decide what worked and didn't work, which was not so nice. I went along with it, though, since she was doing me a favor, and because I thought maybe a makeover could bring me closer to a Nima exciting enough to spend time with.

But at one point, she had me try on this complicated shirt with more straps and openings than I was used to, and true to form, I managed to get stuck trying it on. Too embarrassed to ask for help, I just made it worse and worse until I had to give in.

"Ginny?"

"Mmm?" she replied from outside the changing room, where she'd been sorting through boxes of donations in between my model walks.

"I think I'm stuck."

I heard her chuckle and then the curtain flew aside. She took one look at me and laughed out loud, then quickly covered her mouth. "Sorry," she said between her fingers, "but this is pretty cute."

I was in my jeans, with bare feet, and the shirt was pulled tightly across my midriff, pinning my left arm to my side. One of the several straps also looped around my neck and my other arm. Ginny moved into the changing room and began gently pulling at various parts of the shirt, unlooping and loosening like she'd unraveled hundreds of people from complicated shirts like this before.

As she carefully untangled me, her hands kept brushing against my stomach, arms, neck. Predictably, these moments of skin-to-skin contact made my heartbeat quicken until I thought she might actually be able to see it through my chest. Finally she managed to get the shirt loose enough that she could pull it off, and I was left standing in a tight space, with only my jeans and a sports bra on, across from Ginny Woodland—the starting point of many, many fantasies I'd had over the years.

She just stood there with the shirt in her hands for a moment, fiddling with a strap but also, I noticed, sneaking glances at my torso. I just stood there awkwardly, not sure what to do. Finally, after what seemed like millennia, she said, "Here" and placed the neckhole of the shirt over my head. I remained still, my face now hidden inside the fabric. "Raise your arms, silly," she instructed. I did. She guided them through the armholes, her hands grazing my arms and armpits as she did, then the sides of my torso and stomach.

When the shirt finally dropped from my face and fell about my body the way it was meant to, Ginny's face was only a few inches from my own and her hands remained on my hips. We looked at each other. She swallowed. My eyebrows rose. She tucked a strand of my ever-escaping hair behind my ear and let her finger glide down my jawbone and come to rest at the side of my neck. I could feel a heart attack coming on.

Her eyes traveled from my neck, to my own eyes, down to my mouth. "You're really beautiful, Nima, you know?"

I blinked. Was this actually happening, or was I about to wake up in my own bed with Gus licking my face? "I'm not," I said.

She leaned in, her mouth a fingertip's distance from mine. "You are," she whispered. The warmth of her breath tickled my lips. Prickling heat rose across my neck as Ginny closed her eyes and pressed her mouth to mine.

No sound, just the silence of two soft things coming together, the heartbeat ceasing for a moment, the stillness of a body suspended in astonishment.

Then: a quiet whoosh of air from our noses as we breathed out. The muted thumping of my heart pumping again. A gentle pop of lips parting for a moment before reconnecting.

Ginny Woodland was kissing me. Her hand remained on my hip and the other was still at my neck and her stomach brushed against my own and her mouth was pressed against mine. After a brief moment where I couldn't get my lips to work, I pushed them back against hers, hoping this was what you were supposed to do.

The past three years of longing for this moment crashed over me like a landslide, and my knees almost buckled under the force. I placed my hands on Ginny's arms just to remain standing. I guess she took that as a sign to keep going, because her lips parted ever so slightly and she leaned into me a little more. I let my lips fall open as well, partly from wanting to feel her tongue against mine and partly from shock, I think. Uncertainly, I nudged my tongue into her mouth and allowed hers to shift and slide against it, a current prodding me this way and that.

The velvety wetness sent a shudder through me and my eyelids fluttered. My tongue pushed into hers. My body, hot and shivery all at once, suddenly took over and my hands pulled her closer. Every single part of me felt like burning-hot liquid and I just wanted to melt over her, consume her, swallow her. I wanted it all, I wanted—

"Wait, wait, wait." She pulled back, and I felt her hands pushing against my hip and chest. "We can't."

I watched the words come out of her mouth, and all I could think of was kissing her again. I leaned forward to try.

"Nima, no. I'm so sorry. I just—I got caught up in the moment. I'm sorry. I didn't mean to—to confuse you . . . or mislead you or anything."

I let my hands fall away from her body and took a step back. Something in my chest ripped open. "But didn't you like it?"

"I did. I mean, it was nice. You're a good kisser." She smiled at me, a consolatory encouragement. "But it's not what I want. We're friends. And I like guys. I just—felt close to you and I guess I was a little . . . curious?"

*Nice. Not what I want. Friends.* My heart plunged into my stomach and shattered into fragments. I couldn't believe I'd let myself think this was going anywhere good. That I'd somehow find consolation or affirmation here. That someone might actually want me the same way I wanted them—least of all Ginny. *That's it, Nima. Keep making the same mistake over and over again. What a champ.*

"Awesome. I'm glad you could satisfy your curiosity." I thought about tearing off the shirt and storming off, but I doubted I could get it off on my own and then Ginny would have to help me, which would ruin the overall effect of my fury. So I whipped open the curtain, squashed my feet into my sneakers, grabbed my own shirt from the floor, and walked across the store, yelling, "I'm keeping this weird shirt and you can suck up the cost yourself!"

"But—Nima! Don't you want to talk? We can still talk, right? Like friends?" she called after me.

I didn't stop. I just shook my head and scoffed as I banged out the front door. I threw my T-shirt over the handlebars and climbed onto my bike, wishing that Ginny would burst out of the store at that moment, run to me, and beg me to come back—tell me she was wrong, that I was too irresistible, that she *did* want to be more than friends—and then kiss me hard and long right in front of the store.

But she didn't.

I pedaled furiously home, threw my bike down to the ground in the front yard, and stomped straight up to my room. Knowing there was no way I'd get this shirt off by myself, and also knowing I'd never be able to wear it again without thinking about that changing room, that moment, that abrupt ending to the very first kiss of my life—I took a pair of scissors from my desk and started cutting the stupid straps, the fabric across my stomach, the sleeves—indiscriminately shredding it to pieces and letting the scraps flutter to the floor.

Fragments. Tatters. Just when I thought a thread of something new and real and wonderful was being woven into my story, rejection stripped it from the seams. Maybe new and wonderful just weren't part of my pattern.

By the time I'd finished, a swirling vortex of fabric lay at my feet, and I felt trapped in the eye of a storm I couldn't escape.

# CHAPTER 11

In the early evening, after I'd spent an hour systematically removing any reminders of Ginny from my walls and letting Gus sniff and trample them on the floor, my stomach let out a hollow growl. I gathered up the photos, wrestling one from Gus's sharp little teeth, and dumped them into the wastepaper basket on the way out of my room.

Feeling no less confused, hurt, or angry, but trying to focus my attention on the simple task of throwing something together for dinner, I swung open the refrigerator door only to have the kitchen door swing open behind me. Expecting it to be Dad, I mumbled, "Hey," and continued to sort through our pathetic fridge contents.

"Well, well, well. There you are, stranger." Jill's voice, way too perky, rose up behind me and instantly my neck prickled. Considering how mad I still was at her, I found her perkiness just plain rude.

At this point, I kind of felt like I'd missed the moment I

should have turned around, so I just kept shuffling jars around in the fridge.

"Come on, Nima, we're going to the Two Suns for dinner tonight."

Normally, I'd be all for dinner at the café. But tonight, all I wanted to do was lock myself up in my room with a grilled cheese sandwich.

"I'm not that hungry," I lied, probably sounding like every ornery teenager who ever lived. *Still not gonna look at you. Still gonna aimlessly search through this fridge, even though I just said I wasn't hungry.*

"Great. You'll be a cheap date then. Get a sweater. It's cool out," Jill said in her no-nonsense voice.

I knew that voice and it would do no good to argue with it. I heaved the heaviest sigh I could into the empty, cold abyss and did as I was told.

Admittedly, the smell of the café's simmering beef stew increased the rumble in my stomach. But that rumble turned into a tight cramp after the server had brought us water and we'd ordered our food. Jill clasped her hands in front of her on the table.

*Here it comes.*

"So, my dear, we gotta deal with this stuff, no?"

I slurped as obnoxiously as I could on my straw. "Nope."

"Nima." Her voice was annoyingly calm. First perky. Now calm. What a jerk.

I started tapping my fork against the table without looking at her. I could be annoying too.

Jill leaned forward. "Doll, we've been friends too long to sit here like this. I know you're mad. You should be. I'd be furious." She reached into her back pocket for something. "I gave you a week to be pissed at me, but now we gotta figure out what to do about this letter."

I looked up and watched as she laid a crinkly piece of paper on the table and smoothed it out with the palm of her hand. She'd roughly taped the letter back together after I'd torn it up. A surprising wave of relief rolled over me.

"You kept it?"

"Of course I kept it, you nugget. It's the only thing we have that will allow us to contact her—if we want to. I mean—if you want to."

I pinned the napkin in front of me to the table with a tine of my fork and twirled the tip around and around, drilling a little hole into the paper. After a moment, Jill gently pushed the letter toward me.

I stared at it, still twirling, twirling, twirling. The few short words on the paper, now shiny with bits of scotch tape, renewed my anger all over again. "Give me one good reason I should see her." My napkin began to fray in the middle.

"Besides the fact that she's your mom?"

I stopped spinning for a moment to glare at her. Then I shifted my eyes back to the fork and continued to twist.

"Okay. Well, *besides* that, don't you think you'll regret it if you don't? Don't you want to hear her side of things?"

I half threw the fork into the middle of the table and the napkin went with it. Leaning back in my seat and folding my arms, I said, "Apparently, *you* can tell me all that, can't you?" Eyeball bullets. *Pew pew pew.*

She leaned back and folded her arms as well, her eyebrows raised, but a typical Jill smirk just beginning to contract the edges of her mouth.

"Don't laugh at me," I said, as gruffly as possible.

"Nima, I'm not laughing at you." She unfolded her arms again and leaned one elbow on the table, then laid her head in her palm. "I just saw a little bit of your mom in you, is all. She could be endearingly stubborn too."

Something about the way she said it—the way her eyes began to glisten—told me that this was part of the story she was refusing to tell me. "This letter says you'll tell me everything. So why won't you?"

Jill sighed. "I don't know why your mother said that. It wasn't fair of her, in my opinion."

"What if I refused to see her? Would you tell me then?"

She peered at me, thinking. Then she sat up straight, back to no-nonsense Jill. "Let's try this. I'll tell you as much as I feel is my story to tell, and you tell me about your new friends."

*Huh?* I sat up straighter. How'd she know about my "new friends"?

*Doesn't matter. Hell if I'm going to make this easy.* "Not much to tell." I grabbed my napkin back and wound it into a tight spiral.

"Oh yeah? Your dad said one of them is pretty fabulous."

*Thanks, Dad.* I shrugged, unraveling my napkin.

"So Deidre's a . . . drag queen? And this other girl you visited? Is she in that business too?" She took a sip of her water.

*Good grief. Great sharing, Dad.* "Yeah, and?" Twist, untwist, twist.

"That's pretty exciting."

"Not really. They're just regular people." Except they weren't at all. But Jill could be like a dog with a bone, so I offered her a tidbit, hoping to appease her. "I met them at the festival. I accidentally found myself at a drag show."

"Accidental drag show? Sounds like a fun accident." She was trying extra hard to look nonchalant, scanning the restaurant, laying her arm across the back of the seat—but I could tell these were deliberate responses.

"Yeah . . ." Thinking on my feet had never been my strong suit. Images of Winnow's sexy performance spun through my mind. "It was fun, I guess." I tore a strip off my now slightly damp napkin.

"So," she murmured just before taking another sip of water, "you gonna see any more of these two 'regular people'?"

I shrugged again. "Maybe." If the Great Hot Tub Barf hadn't completely ruined my chances, that is.

"You know, I've socialized with a few drag queens in my

lifetime as well." Her sentence stopped my busy hands. My napkin lay in limp white ribbons.

"Oh yeah?" I tried to keep my voice calm, even.

"Yup."

I cocked an eyebrow at her.

"Yeah, kings too. Queens and kings. And a few princesses, that's for sure."

*What are you telling me?*

Jill stared at me, her right eyebrow peaked and a glimmer of merriment in her eyes. She was totally enjoying this.

I couldn't remove my tongue from the roof of my mouth.

She lowered her eyebrow and leaned forward, removing the last shreds of napkin from my fingers. Then she took my hands in hers. "Nima, what I'm trying to say in a silly, roundabout way is that I've spent a lot of time in that scene because, well . . . husband or no husband, I'm as gay as the day is long."

I didn't know what to say. The gay part wasn't a huge revelation or anything, though this was the first time she'd confirmed it. The bigger surprise was Jill parading around with the kind of crowd I'd met at the festival. It was a difficult scene to imagine.

My bewilderment must have been obvious, because Jill left her seat and came around to sit next to me. She wrapped an arm across my shoulders. "Looks like we have something in common?"

I looked at her. Something tweaked in my brain. I thought

about Gordon's dad and how he'd called Jill a dyke. Was it just something that crappy people called single adult women who could take care of themselves? Or did he actually *know*? And *how* did he know when I hadn't even really known? When most people in town didn't really know?

In her typical Jill way, she rubbed my back with an intensity that shook my entire body and said, "Listen, babe, it's nothing to be ashamed of, you know that, right?"

I did know that. But something else wasn't sitting right about this conversation.

"I'm not ashamed. But—why didn't you tell me about this before? Does Dad know? Why've you been hiding it if there's nothing to be ashamed of?"

Her arm slipped off my shoulders and she laid her hands flat on the table. "I haven't been hiding it, exactly. I just—I was waiting for a good time, I guess. And your dad does know, kind of."

*What? Kind of?* None of this was making any sense. "Since when do you wait for a good time to talk about anything?" I edged away from her on the seat.

She released an impatient sigh and stared at her hands. "Well, shit, this deal isn't working at all. Somehow we're talking about me again and you haven't told me anything!"

"I didn't have to. Apparently you know everything anyway. Not fair, Jill." I had even more questions now, and that just made me madder.

She pressed her fingers into her eyes, forehead, temples,

cheeks—a signal she was ruminating. Just as our food came, she let out a long breath, twisted in her seat, and told me a story I never would have guessed.

I'd known that my mom and dad first met Jill nine years ago when we'd moved from a tiny house up near Biddy Park to the one we lived in now. Jill had relocated here a few months before and was a Realtor at that time, to help pay the bills while she tried to build her Garden Emporium business. I vaguely remember the move—watching my mom pack up the closet-size room I'd had and throwing a massive hissy fit when she forced me to choose at least half my stuffies and put them in a box for Old Stuff.

What I didn't know was this next part.

Jill looked up at the light hanging above our booth. She inhaled, and with her exhale, allowed her eyes to fall somewhere around my chin. "The first time I shook your mom's hand, outside that shitty little house near Biddy Park, I—" She glanced at me as if she'd stolen something, and her voice dropped. "I had to will myself to let go. Even after I did, it was like I could still feel her fingers in mine as we went through the house—up those shitty stairs, in and out of the shitty bedrooms, into the shitty backyard." She looked down at her hands, as if seeing my mom's and hers intertwined even now. "By the time the tour ended and we had to shake hands good-bye, it was like . . . like we'd been holding hands the entire time."

At this early point in the story, I'm fairly sure my mouth fell open and remained just so for the next several minutes.

Jill said even after she'd miraculously managed to find a buyer for the Biddy house, and Mom and Dad had moved into our present home, the three of them remained friends— my dad and Jill united by their mutual love for tinkering, and my mom and Jill bonded by what Jill described as a powerful yearning for change and excitement.

"I mean, I guess I had other motivations as well, but I wasn't really ready to acknowledge what I was feeling at the time. All I knew was that I loved spending time with both your parents, Nima, and with you. You felt like instant family to me." She gave me a half smile.

As she spoke, the image of the "phantom hand holding" flitted through my mind every so often. Each time it did, I shifted in my seat, trying to alter the confusing mixture of shock, warmth, and bitterness churning in my stomach.

"I guess as time wore on, I started to realize my feelings for your dad differed from my feelings for your mom, but I didn't know if Kate felt the same way. Plus—" Her eyes shot up to mine. "Plus . . . you know I'd never willingly mess with your parents' marriage, right, babe?"

I watched her mouth move around the words but couldn't form my own. My head dipped in something like acknowl-edgment.

"You have to believe me—I tried to stuff my feelings for your mother way down. And I managed to by convincing myself that my feelings were one-sided. I mean, watching your parents work together to build your dad's mechanic business, and to raise you so beautifully—it was easy to believe your mother only had eyes for you two."

Jill's eyes and lips smiled, and I could see in them how much she loved us too. But my lips couldn't find their smile just now, and in the next moment, Jill's flattened out again as well.

"Over the next few years, though, I started to notice some things and realized that maybe, just maybe, Kate had feelings for me too."

A ball of fire formed in my stomach and burst out of my mouth. "Like what?" I said, loudly enough that the people one table over glanced up at us.

She looked up, surprised. "I—well, just little things, I guess. A touch here. A whisper there. Sometimes she'd show up after dinner, on her own, for no reason at all." Jill's brow formed deep creases. "It got harder and harder to push my own feelings down, Nima."

My stomach rumbled, insistent and noisy. I reached across the table to grab my fork, then thrust it into a piece of beef in my stew. As I lifted the fork to my mouth, juices dripped across the table, my jeans, and my shirt, but I didn't care. I clamped down on the mouthful so hard my teeth scraped against the steel fork as I yanked it out. I ground the meat in my jaw, ignoring the juice dribbling down my chin.

Jill's forehead rose a little as she stared at my mouth. She waited until I swallowed, then offered me her napkin, which I ignored.

Dropping her hand to her lap, she went on. "About a year and half ago—November—your mom came over one night."

November. A year and a half ago. My sophomore year. Easy to remember because that was when Mom left. I wiped my chin with the back of my hand.

"We were sitting in the courtyard. The air felt so crisp in my lungs it hurt, and I couldn't understand why your mother wanted to stay outside in the cold." Jill's eyes fixed on a point somewhere between us on the table. "But then she used the chill as an excuse to put her arm through mine, and it all made sense. My thoughts just flew away when she did that. And my hands . . . they got so sweaty in my jacket pockets. I remember thinking how weird that was, since it was freezing out."

In anticipation or nausea—I wasn't sure which—my face grew hot just as a shiver passed through me. My left knee bounced up and down like a jackhammer, the rapid beat matching my heart rate.

Jill didn't seem to notice any of this, though, clearly lost in the moment she was re-creating for me and for herself. "All of a sudden, I felt her lips brush against my neck. I lost all my words, but my shock finally made me look at her, and seeing her—the way she was looking at me—I don't know. I—I shouldn't have, but I couldn't stop myself. . . ."

At that moment, Winnow's lips emerged in my mind and I swear I could feel that piece of beef dissolving in my stomach acid. The last thing I wanted was to think simultaneously of Winnow and this . . . this *thing* Jill was telling me. My arm shot out for my water glass, and I slugged back the entire thing.

Jill stared blankly at me as if in a trance until I'd gulped the last mouthful of water. When I finished, she just continued, thankfully skipping any kissing details.

"I finally got ahold of myself and pulled away, which wasn't easy. I told Kate I couldn't do that. I couldn't hurt your dad or you. I couldn't be that person."

*But you are that person,* I thought, jabbing my fork at various items in my bowl for no other reason than to see the points disappear again and again.

"Kate was furious. She instantly blamed me, saying that I'd been putting out all the signals—which wasn't untrue—and that I couldn't just stop what I'd started."

Jill's next words tumbled from her mouth. She'd remained adamant. She admitted her feelings and apologized, but made it clear that this had been a two-way street. My mother didn't take that too well either, apparently. She shouted at Jill, and when Jill tried to calm my mom down, Mom pushed her off and stormed out of the yard, toward the school.

"I ran after her, of course," Jill continued, now shifting her body and her gaze back to the table. "I followed her all the way into the middle of the baseball field before I could get that woman to pause for a second. She was always so damn quick in everything she did." Jill began pulling at her own napkin. "But when she finally did stop, she just turned and kissed me hard."

*The baseball field is only four or five blocks from our house. Behind my school. Anyone could have seen you.* My fears were confirmed in her next sentence.

"Out of nowhere, we heard a voice. Bill Grant's voice."

Gordon's dad. The acid in my stomach bubbled up into my esophagus.

"He'd been drinking himself silly behind home plate, like he always has, and saw us. Even as drunk as he was, though, he knew exactly who we were and made sure to yell all kinds of trash at us."

*Shit.*

Jill said he'd stumbled into a standing position and started to slump toward them. "I panicked. I pulled away from Kate, who was horrified too but still clinging hard to me." Jill's hands mimicked the damage I'd done to my own napkin, slowly tearing it to pieces. "I could see the hysteria in her eyes—she was already thinking about what would it mean if this got out. I couldn't let that happen—to her or to you or your dad, Nima. But Bill just kept coming and coming, so finally I pushed Kate away from me—hard—and told her to go home. To her family."

She let the napkin shreds fall to the table and dropped her forehead into her hands. The rest of her story she aimed into the torn scraps.

"Bill paused—I guess I'd confused him enough—and was listing so heavily to one side that I thought he'd tip right over. Instead he just sneered and flung his empty beer can at us, then staggered off in the direction of his house."

Jill was hunched over the table and her back rose and fell deeply, as if she was trying to pump the air through her body. Without thinking, I placed my hand against her spine. After a few moments, her breathing slowed enough for her to continue.

"When I turned back to Kate, the look on her face . . . her mouth was all contorted but her eyes were so . . . blank. When I tried to reach for her, she backed away and said that I could keep this boring, predictable life, but she wanted more. That if I wasn't willing to be with her, we had nothing more to say to one another. And then I watched like a fool as she left me standing there."

The words "boring" and "predictable" echoed in my brain. *She wanted more.*

The next morning, my mother was gone.

Jill's story rolled over me like distant thunder—muted rumblings followed by fierce, crackling mountains of sound, then low, deep growls. When she was finished, my back was sweaty and my T-shirt clung to the vinyl seating. I leaned forward and ruffled my shirt to run some air over my damp skin. Jill sat very, very still, remaining bent over the table.

I didn't know whether to scream at her or comfort her. Jill loved my mom. My mom loved Jill. My mom left because Jill wouldn't let her cheat on my dad. *My mom wanted to cheat on my dad and left when she couldn't.* The person I really wanted to scream at, who I would have given anything to scream at, wasn't here.

When I looked over, Jill's eyes were focused on some point

in front of her again. Her jaw was set and she was gulping like someone holding back tears.

We sat like that for a long time, Jill's neck undulating with the pulse of her broken heart, and me, twisting and unraveling, again and again.

Over the next several hours, Jill and I walked in alternating bouts of talk and silence. I hated that I wanted to walk with her, find out more. That I needed to. Wasn't it her fault that my mom left? I just couldn't leave her side, though. I craved every bit of info she had, and Jill allowed me to ask as many questions as I wanted.

"Didn't Gordon's dad tell anyone about you and Mom?"

"Oh, he tried. But he was so hammered that his story must have seemed pretty garbled. If anyone did believe him, they've never said anything that I know of. Thank God." She rubbed both sides of her forehead with her fingers. She looked tired. But I needed more information.

"What about Dad—you said he 'kind of' knew?"

"I thought so at the time. Something happened, months before your mother left, that made me think he knew."

We had ended up at Jill's place, and she was tinkering with her utensil drawer, which hadn't fully closed for over a year. I think the tinkering helped calm her.

"What happened?" I was sitting in a kitchen chair Jill had also made herself, and it creaked with my weight. I pulled my knees up to my chest.

"We were all cooking together in your kitchen, making fried chicken."

The thought of the three of them all trying to make fried chicken together made me think of a Three Stooges scene, given that Jill couldn't cook worth a damn and Dad had barely known how to cook before Mom left.

"Your dad was in charge of the battering and flouring, your mom was in charge of frying, and I was in charge of standing to one side and trying not to hurt myself." She glanced at me and winked. I couldn't help but half smile back.

"But at one point the oil spat and some of it landed on Kate's arm. She yelped and I grabbed her and brought her quickly to the sink to run some cold water over it. As she let the water cool her burn, she absentmindedly said, 'Thanks, my love.' She didn't even realize the words she'd uttered, but I did. And I looked up at your dad, standing there with his hands covered in goopy flour. Even though nothing was going on between your mom and me at that point, my eyes must have revealed the guilt I felt, and he saw it. I know he saw it."

My eyes watered at the thought. "What did he do?"

"Nothing. You know your dad. Your nonconfrontational, peace-loving, generous dad. Maybe he just assumed it was a knee-jerk comment from your mom, but I don't think so. I think, if he didn't know how I felt about her before that, he did after. And he probably knew that she felt something for me, too. But he never said anything to me."

When I heard that, my hand itched and I wanted to slap my dad silly. It was the first time in a very long time that I'd felt anything other than love (or loving embarrassment) for him. He could have at least fought for her a little bit.

Later, both of us seated at Jill's kitchen table, I asked, "Did my mom ever contact you before the letter? Did you ever try to find her?"

"No, she's never tried to contact me before now. But I did look. I waited a few months, thinking if she settled in somewhere, I might be able to track her down using the 'interweb.'" She kicked me beneath the table. I kicked her back and then immediately regretted returning the playful gesture. I was still trying to be mad at her.

"And?"

"And nothing. If she was working, it must have been some low-key job somewhere."

"Some shitty job's more like it. All she's ever done is work for my dad." Jill looked at me, eyebrows raised. I frowned back in reply.

"Your mom has a lot of talents and passions, you know."

*Whatever.* I swiveled in my chair and picked at a piece of splintered wood on the backrest.

"Anyway, I was kind of at a loss after that. I mean, she could be anywhere, really. She's so resourceful, you know? And she loved to change things up. She could've just been living on the road, for all I knew."

I thought of my mom, buying some crappy hatchback and

sputtering her way from town to town, working for room and board or doing odd jobs while she slept in her car. She was resourceful, all right, but was the change and excitement she craved really worth leaving us all behind?

About midnight, Jill and I were both hungry again—I guess emotional turmoil will do that to you—so I rummaged through her cupboards and made us some peanut butter cookies. We ate them by the fire pit in her backyard, our feet meeting in the middle of the bench where we were seated, mugs of tea steaming in our hands. The smoke and crackle of the fire was a comfort.

I stared into the flames. "Why do you think she left, Jill? I mean, why did she *really* leave? *How* could she?"

Jill blew into her mug of tea, thinking. She took a sip and looked at me across the mouth of her cup. I could feel her curling and uncurling her toes next to mine. Finally she said, a sliver of water beneath each eye, "I think she left because she didn't know how to be here after what happened, Nima. Something for her had changed." Her bottom lip trembled— I'd never seen it do that.

*Something had changed.* I wanted to ask her what could possibly change enough to make a mom leave her family, but I was scared the answer might be that she'd realized there was more out there for her than she could ever have with us. As my bottom lip began to quiver as well, I let the rest of my questions dissolve into the darkness.

Later, as I wandered home from Jill's and climbed into bed, I flip-flopped between wanting to go back to talk more, and not wanting to talk at all. I was done talking. I wanted to *do* something. But what that something was remained unclear in my murky mind as I finally drifted off to sleep.

"Show me." Winnow's powdery voice hovers between us—particles glistening like gold dust.

I try to move my feet, to raise my arms, but they remain heavy and still. I wait for the golden dust to settle over me and bring me to life, but it just lingers, bobbing up and down in a slow dance.

"I can't," I murmur.

"Let me show you, then," Winnow offers, her hand moving through the shifting cloud of particles and taking my own. My arms and legs tingle back to life. She leads me through a series of steps and motions while the gold dust swirls around our bodies.

Eventually, the glistening cloud encircles us and contracts, tightening our bodies into one another's. Her thighs press against mine, the palm of her hand finds the small of my back. I grow acutely aware of the softness of her breasts against mine, the curve of her jawline as her lips brush the spot just below my earlobe. Our mouths find each other's, and a deep breath the color of earliest dawn spreads through my chest. Her lips part. I let mine part too. The tips of our tongues meet.

My body surges like rolling waves, crashing, receding, building, over and over.

# CHAPTER 12

In the morning, I awoke exhausted but flushed from a dream now somewhat vague in my mind. I rolled onto my back and stared at the image of two bare feet I'd taped to the ceiling after my mom left. Two bare feet from the side, in motion. The metaphor was fairly obvious and unoriginal, I guess, but I'd wanted to remind myself to just keep moving forward—no fancy footwear or transportation needed—just one foot in front of the other, one step at a time.

I realized that what I really, really wanted to do was see Winnow again. Not my mom, or even Jill to get more of the story—but Winnow. I wanted to see her, ask her how she felt about me, know if we could still spend time together. Maybe Jill's story piqued something in me—something fearful of missing out, or messing up, or not acting when I should. Or maybe I was just captivated by a really amazing person. Either way, I resolved to find Winnow as soon as possible.

I felt weird just texting her, though. I didn't even know

how to enter a conversation—written or not—with her after my barfing debacle. Instead, I started googling "drag shows" in the area and was surprised to find more than one in North Gate. In fact, there were two: one called "Chicks and Chucks" that happened every Saturday night at some bar called Chills, and another called "Tucked and Packed" the third Friday of every month at the Lava Lounge. Remembering that the words "Tucked and Packed" were emblazoned across the stage at the festival drag show, I decided that my best bet was the one at the Lava Lounge, and I took it as a meant-to-be sign that tomorrow just happened to be the third Friday of the month.

As soon as I realized that, my heart began thudding in my chest. It was a good kind of thud, I think. But an unsettling one too. I slapped my laptop shut and started spinning in my desk chair, slowly, to allow for prime percolating conditions.

I needed: (a) a way to get to the bar; (b) a way to get home (assuming I wouldn't be staying the night anywhere there); (c) a way to get my dad to let me go to North Gate two Fridays in a row, without knowing how I was getting there or back; (d) someone to go with?

In the end, a solution to my predicaments presented itself from an unlikely source.

After stopping by Jill's to let her know I needed a break from our chat, I found myself wandering over to Biddy Park. I guess Jill's story about how she'd met my mom at our crappy old house up there spurred a desire to check out the scene of their first spark. If the house was still there, that is. From what I remembered of it, I wouldn't be surprised to see it torn down by now.

But when I circled behind the park, where a few scraggly trees grew farther and farther apart until the ground became a wide expanse of dusty, empty dirt, the misshapen form of a house ready to keel over rose in front of me.

My memories of the place as an eight-year-old were surprisingly accurate compared to what I saw now. Granted, the building seemed to grow out of the dirt itself—so dull and battered and brown were its frame and walls—but the closed-in porch and redbrick chimney somehow managed to hold their shape, even as the rest of the house tilted dangerously to one side. I spent a lot of my first eight years on that porch, just as I've spent a lot of the past nine years on the porch of our current home.

Being on the outside suits me, I guess.

The place didn't look like anyone lived in it, so I decided to take a closer look. An ugly chain-link fence barely stood its ground as I swung open the front gate, and the cement walkway up to the front door was scarcely visible beneath the ever-encroaching desert of dry dust that had taken over the front yard.

Not quite willing to trespass inside, I shrugged off my backpack and sat down on a low cement bench that hadn't been there when we lived in the house. Facing the porch, I shook my flip-flops from my feet and let the fine dust squeeze between my toes. The warmth of the dirt felt comforting, and I pressed my feet farther into it as I stared at the front of the house.

I tried to picture Jill and my mom meeting on the three sad steps up to the screen door to the porch. I could just see my dad standing pleasantly off to the side, completely oblivious to the undercurrents of chemistry taking place right next to him. I still didn't know how to feel about all of this. Of course I was mad. Mad at Mom for being so willing to cheat on Dad, for leaving us. Mad at Jill for getting mixed up in all of this too. Mad at Dad for doltishly standing by as it all happened right beneath his nose.

But under all of that, I think I was also mad at myself— for this confusing feeling of excitement that kept pinging around in my stomach when I thought of my mom loving another woman, being someone who could just take off to find something . . . more. Obviously, that thought made me feel equal parts lousy and excited, because it meant that "more" didn't include me.

Like I said, this shit was confusing.

My brain hurt, and just as I was about to lie back across the bench to rest my eyes for a bit, the screen door slapped open and Gordon stepped out, freezing on the top step when he saw me.

His hair looked even greasier than normal, and a dark purple bruise formed a splotch around his left eye. A bottle of clear liquid dangled from one hand. After wiping his mouth on his shoulder, he thumped down the remaining steps and across the short stretch of dirt between us. Dust puffed up around his legs and caught in my throat, making me cough.

As he got closer, I could see his eyes were red and watery, blurred with whatever was in that bottle, but also with something else—had he been crying?

"What the hell are you doing here?" he breathed over me, each word stumbling over the next.

I was still pissed at him for the whole Davis poetry thing, but I decided that "no sudden movements" was probably a good strategy for now. Finding it difficult to look into his hazy eyes, I stared at my dust-covered feet instead. "I used to live here." I tried to keep my voice as neutral as possible. No sarcasm. No sass. Who knew what he'd do in this condition? "Remember?"

The next thing I knew he'd slumped onto the bench beside me, his elbows on his knees and his head almost low enough to reach them.

*Careful, Nima.* "What . . . are *you* doing here?" I asked, acutely aware of the limited space between us and the stale smell of cigarette smoke.

He didn't say anything. Just shook the bottle in between his legs. The liquid swished around with a wet, metallic sound.

I thought I saw a drop fall from his face.

I tried again. "Do you . . . hang out here?"

In an instant, he straightened his back, inhaled a whole bunch of snot, and spat a huge gob to the side.

I tried not to grimace.

"Sometimes." More silence. He took a couple of deep breaths. The bruise on his face covered his left eye and part of his cheek. I thought it best not to ask about that.

Then he held the bottle out to me, an offer.

I didn't want to say no, in case it set him off, so I took it and raised it to my lips, just barely wetting them with what I assumed was vodka. I handed the bottle back to him and he took a couple of big gulps, his prominent Adam's apple rising and falling as he did. After, he stared at the house and muttered something I couldn't quite make out.

"Sorry?"

Another rise and fall in his throat. "You still garden."

It wasn't a question, so I just offered, "Yeah." And then, "How come you don't?"

He shrugged and took another swallow.

I was getting impatient, and it was overriding my sense of caution. I stretched my back and pointed my toes out in front of me. "What's going on with you?" I finally asked.

His face fell slack. He pulled his legs in tight together and pressed the base of the bottle into his thigh, gripping the neck with both hands and staring, lost, into the opening like he'd find the answer there. He became a little boy in an instant.

I softened. "Gordon?"

He continued to stare. "You know," he whispered.

*Do I?* I wasn't sure. I just stared at him, staring at the bottle.

Finally he looked up at me. "Oh fuck you . . . you *know!*"

He looked away and the bruise on his face seemed to pulse.

"Screw it." Abruptly, he flung the bottle at the ground and started to stagger off.

Something surged in my stomach. "Wait—stop." I leaped after him and touched his arm.

In an instant, he pivoted and loomed over me, fists quivering by his sides. I took a step back. We both stood still for a few moments. Or decades, it seemed. And then his shoulders collapsed. He bent forward, pressed his hands into his knees, and heaved what looked like orange oatmeal at the ground between us.

I hopped back a step. "Whoa, dude."

He spat at the ground. "Just leave me alone." His shoulders convulsed, and I realized he was outright crying.

Okay, now I was really at a loss. But my body acted anyway. I took a step forward and reached out to touch his shoulder. "Hey."

He crouched to the ground, a little too close to the barf for my own liking, so I grabbed his arm and pulled him over a bit. "Careful—come this way."

To my surprise, he allowed me to guide him back to the bench. He leaned over and rested his head in his hands. I dug around in my backpack for a tissue or something, finally resorting to a paper napkin I was pretty sure I'd already used at some point. I handed it to him and he wiped his mouth, then crushed it in his fist.

"Fuck!" he yelled into his lap.

*What the hell is happening?* "Okay, you're scaring me a bit. Can you just . . . tell me what's going on?"

Staring straight out in front of him, he spoke in that same strange voice I'd heard in the art room—thin and faltering. "The photo." He paused.

I wasn't sure whether he wanted me to say something, but I offered, as reassuringly as possible, "Right."

"So?"

"So . . . ?"

"*So?* Don't you get it?"

*Man. This is scary. What if I say the wrong thing?* "I'm not sure I do. But you can tell me. I won't judge . . . I promise."

His eyes closed. Without opening them, he said in a low, careful voice, the slur disappearing, "I think—I think my body feels wrong. Like . . . it's not mine." Tears gathered along his closed eyelids, and I noticed he had the longest eyelashes.

*Wow. Not what I was expecting.* "Um . . . I don't . . . Wow." *Helpful, Nima.*

He opened his eyes, and the tears fell from them. He rubbed them away with his fists and started squeezing his knees. "I don't know what to do," he whispered, his features caving into the middle of his face.

Everything I knew about this guy just sailed out the window. All our interactions over the past few weeks slipped through my mind. The aggression, his presence at the drag show, the photos of him, the "something" in his eyes . . . I wasn't 100 percent sure what he was telling me, but I could see it was huge. And scary as hell for him.

"You feel like walking a bit?" I asked, partly because I didn't know what else to say.

He rubbed his face roughly, even the bruise, which must have hurt. Through a tense, bony jaw, he replied, "Fine."

We walked to the community garden in silence. I think Gordon was trying to process what he'd just done. His shoulders were hunched and stiff. A deep frown creased his forehead.

We sat down among the remnants of July's vegetables and stared into some bags of leftover fertilizer for a while.

Gordon seemed to have fallen into a stupor—his body lay slack against the fence and his long legs were spread out in front of him. I realized I would have to start. And maybe offer a secret of my own.

"Sooo . . . I just found out some confusing stuff about my mom."

Wiping his nose with the back of his hand, he replied in a low, hollow voice. "Yeah?"

"Yeah. Not sure I'm completely ready to talk about it, but . . . it's really messed up."

He dragged his feet into his body, gathering small piles of soil at his heels. His eyes traveled to my lap. "Is she as messed up as me?"

*Oh, sugar,* I heard Deidre say in my head. "It's not that *she's* messed up . . . more like the situation is hard to get my head around." As I said it, I was surprised by my assessment of my mom. *Wasn't* she messed up, though? But if she was, then aren't we all? "You're not messed up either, Gordon. At least, no more than the rest of us."

He frowned, his eyes still blankly gazing into my lap. "Do you feel messed up 'cause you're gay?"

I thought about that for a moment. "No. I don't think so."

His eyebrows popped up and he gave a slight nod. Then, as if assuring himself, "But you *are* gay, though."

It was my turn to raise my eyebrows. "Yeah, you made that clear in front of Tessa the other day."

One side of his mouth tilted downward. He glanced up at me, then shrugged.

*What an ass.*

I pulled out some limp dandelions growing at the base of the fence and started yanking off clumps of the yellow petals.

A barely audible "Sorry" emerged from beside me.

I sighed as loudly as I could and chucked the stems to the side. "Can you *please* tell me what's going on?"

He rubbed his hands against his jeans and looked away. "Fuuuuucckkkk." A few more moments passed. "I don't know. I just . . . I feel weird in my body or something." He took in a deep breath like he was gasping for air. "Like, my body is supposed to be different . . . not so fucking rough and bony and shit." He pressed the heels of his hands into his eyes. Shaking his head, he muttered, more to himself, "Jesus. That's so fucked up, right?"

He said that "Jesus" with such defeat, such sadness, that my chest ached for him.

I tried to choose my next words carefully. "I don't think you're fucked up." Viewing him in my peripheral vision, I tentatively asked, "How long have you felt this way?"

His mouth trembled without making a sound, and then, "A while."

"Have you talked to anyone else about it?"

His head jerked up and the blur in his eyes turned to sharp, focused anger. "No fucking way. And you better not either. I swear to God if you tell anyone—"

"I won't, I promise." His fury made my heart skip.

But then his eyes watered again. "No one can find out about this." A crack in his voice.

"I—I understand." After a few moments of us staring into our own laps, I tried, "Maybe . . . you could also refrain from casually referring to me as a queer in public? 'Nima' will do."

"How 'bout 'raging lesbo' instead?" He smirked.

"Such an a-hole." I threw some grass at him.

His smirk fell away. "I won't. Call you stuff, I mean."

I thought about his arm draped around Tessa's shoulders. "So . . . you and Tessa . . . ?"

"What about it?" Sharpness edged his voice, and his eyes refocused on me.

I searched his face. The set jaw and darkened eyes made me mumble, "Nothing."

His next words plowed through the air. "I'm not a homo, if that's what you're thinking."

My head automatically tilted to the side. "Um . . . hello?"

A very dim light went on in his face. "It's not the same. Two girls going at it is hot. Two guys is sick."

My heart hammered away at my rib cage. "Seriously? You know the same people who say shit like that are the ones who would say stupid shit about you." I felt my face flush with anger.

He picked at a loose flap of rubber on his kicks. "Whatever. I like chicks, all right?"

I could see this was a topic to avoid for the time being. "Fine."

He and I sat for a while, fiddling with rubber soles and ripping up clumps of grass respectively.

"What now?" I asked.

He looked up and stared into the tomato vines. There was that little boy again. "I have no idea."

Not knowing quite what to do with Gordon now that he'd spilled his startling guts to me (literally and otherwise), I shocked the hell out of myself by inviting him back to my place for some lunch. Even more shocking, he agreed.

We walked back to my house in silence, Gordon with his head slung low and hands deep in his pockets, and me glancing sideways every few seconds to try to get a read on him. From what I could tell, he'd gone into sullen mode, and it would take some seriously perceptive moves to keep him from bolting. I wasn't sure I had those kinds of moves, but I was willing to try. Despite my own problems, I couldn't imagine entrusting someone with the kinds of things Gordon had just confided in me.

As we chewed our turkey and cheese sandwiches silently on the porch steps, Gus in front of us, diligently staring at our food, the drama of my own life began to mingle with Gordon's, and a strange plan began to hatch in my admittedly convoluted mind. *What if . . . ?*

I swallowed and cleared my throat. Picking at a wilted piece of lettuce, I asked, "Would you maybe want to see another drag show? Since you missed the last one, I mean?"

"What? When?" Gordon quickly responded, his words muffled through a mouthful of bread and meat.

"Ugh. Chew first. Swallow. Then talk."

"Fuck you," he replied, without chewing or swallowing.

I shook my head. "But seriously. Would you? Come with me? Tomorrow?"

This time he did chew and swallow before speaking. Then he bit at his lips for a while before finally mumbling, "What show? Where?"

"At some bar in North Gate. I think it's the same folks who put on the show we were at before."

"Huh." He took another massive bite of his sandwich and then irritatingly munched it for like, half an hour.

"Come on—we could just check it out, and if it's too much, we can leave."

"It's gonna be a bunch of queers, innit?" His frown was somewhere between concerned and curious.

I sighed. "Yes, Gordon, the crowd will likely be a mix of folks—just like the last show you managed to get yourself into."

"What if some dude hits on me or something?"

"Right, 'cause you're so irresistible?" I took a chance and threw the piece of floppy lettuce at him.

It landed on his shoulder, but he just looked at it.

"Listen," I said, "pretend that piece of lettuce is some guy hitting on you." I wasn't sure where I was going with this particular metaphor, even as I was saying it, but I think my exhaustion was getting the better of me. "Let's say he uses some line, or maybe even puts his hand on your arm. What do you do?"

"Punch him in the face."

"Gordon, *no*. You just brush it off." I flicked the lettuce leaf off his shoulder. "Say no, thanks—not interested—and move on."

"Sick."

Okay, maybe this was a bad idea. "Never mind. I'll go by myself. I don't think you're quite ready for it."

He just ripped a chunk off his sandwich and shoved it into his mouth.

I stared out at the sidewalk and started thinking about alternative plans for tomorrow night, but my thoughts ended abruptly when I saw Charles across the street. He must have stopped in his tracks when he'd seen Gordon sitting on my front porch, because he was just standing there, hands by his sides, staring. I could understand how we might be a jarring sight. I stood up and tentatively waved with my sandwich hand. A piece of turkey fell to the ground and Gus pounced on it.

Even from across the street, I could see the confusion and hurt in Charles's face. He started to march back up the street to his house. We hadn't spoken in almost two weeks, save the crappy text he'd sent me—not since the whole Tessa debacle. I wasn't sure whether he was coming to see me, but I really wanted to explain what he was seeing. "Charles!" I yelled, and ran after him.

Gordon uttered, "Don't you fucking dare tell him anything I told you."

I ignored him and kept running. Charles continued his shuffling, quick walk.

I ran out in front of him and held out my hands to signal *stop*, realizing that I still held the half-eaten sandwich in my hand. I looked at it, then at Charles. Then I held it out to him. "Sandwich?"

He looked at the sandwich, then at me. Nothing.

"Charles, I can explain, but not everything, not yet. Just trust me—there's a good reason Gordon Grant is on my porch eating a sandwich right now."

Even through the sheen of his glasses, the strength of his glare surprised me.

"Please trust me?"

"Trust you?" His voice cracked with the force of his anger. "Trust you to what, Nima? To pressure me into another embarrassing situation? Or to make friends with the biggest jerk around and expect me to tag along? What am I supposed to do? Go on a double date with my gay best friend and the bully who's dating the girl I like? Sounds amazing."

He was right—this must have felt like utter betrayal, and I felt for him. But it wasn't like I hadn't tried to talk to him. He'd ignored all my calls and texts, after all. And I guess I couldn't help comparing his troubles with my own or Gordon's, which made me say this next crummy thing. "Oh, poor you, Charles. I'm so sorry *one girl* doesn't like you and some people laughed at you." I threw my sandwich at his feet. "Try having a mom who basically chose *anything else* over you and then being rejected by *every* girl you like. *Then* we'll talk."

His brow flickered a frown. But now I couldn't stop myself. It's like that moment when you see the dog poop on the sidewalk, and you want to stop your foot from stepping into it, but your foot does its own thing 'cause it's already in motion and it just goes ahead and takes a nice, shitty plunge whether you like it or not.

I lowered my voice so Gordon wouldn't hear. "*Not to mention*, Gordon's got crap to deal with you can't even begin to understand, so . . . *Get. A. Grip.*"

His eyes widened. His chin crinkled. "Are you kidding me? You're defending Gordon Grant?"

*Really? That's all you heard?*

My jaw ached with tension. "You don't know the whole story. I wish I could explain more, but I can't."

"Right. Of course you can't. I'm sure I'm *incapable* of understanding anyway." He pivoted to leave.

"Charles—"

But he just kept walking.

Gordon was still sitting on the porch steps when I came
back. I stopped in front of him.

"So? You and buddy boy make up?" he asked.

"Don't, Gordon. It's partly your fault we're fighting."

"What? Me? Don't blame me for Davis's shit."

"You didn't exactly do anything to stop it!" I could feel my
breathing quicken, but I tried to keep my voice calm as I said,
"Did you know Charles liked Tessa?"

"Nah, man. Besides, I can't help it if she likes me instead."

"Do *you* like *her?*"

He yawned. Actually. Yawned. "Enough."

I made a sound Jill sometimes makes when she's thor-
oughly disgusted by something—halfway between a grunt and
a cough. I guess I knew I was being unfair—it wasn't really
Gordon's fault Tessa liked him instead of Charles—but his
nonchalance right now grated on my already fraying nerves.
The thought of my best friend hating me didn't help. I just
needed a break from all this shit.

"Okay, well, you can leave now," I said, and started up the
steps to go inside.

I had my hand on the doorknob when he piped up with,
"Actually, I was thinking I *would* go to the show with you
tomorrow."

I stopped and turned. "What?"

"Yeah, I thought about it and decided I could handle it." He shrugged. Was that arrogance, or uncertainty?

I studied him for a moment. "Yeah, no thanks." I turned back toward the door.

"Don't be pissy. I'm sorry I'm such a pain in the ass for you and your pal, okay? Let's face it, you don't want to go by yourself tomorrow anyway."

He was right. I didn't. And it would be nice to have a ride. Selfish, but true.

Gus whined at me from the top of the steps. "Ugh. Fine." I yanked at my ponytail with both hands to tighten the band against my scalp. "But you can't be an asshole, all right?"

"Me?" He smirked.

"I mean it."

"Fine, fine . . . whatever. I'll wear my best feather boa and heels."

*Christ up a creek. What did I just get myself into?*

# CHAPTER 13

The Dad situation worked itself out—one of the few things that seemed to work in my favor these days—when he told me Friday morning before work that he'd decided to take a little "bro trip" with his buddy Jack. He'd be away for the weekend, and maybe even until Monday or Tuesday, depending on where their wheels carried them, he had said. He'd already let Jill know, and if I needed anything, she'd be around.

I wondered what that conversation had sounded like, given all the subtext between them and Jill's freshly dug-up feelings about it all. But I didn't wonder too long, because my dad's road trip made it infinitely easier to plan out my weekend. I felt a little guilty about withholding my plans, but not guilty enough to do anything about it.

I texted Jill and told her I'd talked to Dad but was going to hang out with my "new friends" in North Gate tonight, and would she please feed Gus?

She called immediately, and I begrudgingly answered it.

"Nima, I'm not sure it's such a great idea for you to take off while your dad's away. Does he know?"

I contemplated my options and decided to cash in on recent revelations. "No, and I don't want him to. I'm just going to this show. Take my mind off things. I might even stay a night or two. I just need to get away, Jill." Then, plaintively: "Please?"

A deep sigh passed from her end of the line to mine. "You have to promise to answer the phone if I call you. And you have to text me tomorrow to update me on your plans." Pause. "And if you need anything, you *have* to call me."

I couldn't help but smile at her concern. "Okay, I promise."

Gordon's truck looked as grungy inside as it did on the outside. Where Deidre's van smelled like vanilla, his truck smelled like a mix between pot and sweat. Remarkably, however, he seemed to have spruced himself up a bit. Instead of the shabby gray T-shirts he usually wore, a clean black shirt hung over his lanky frame, and he must have broken out his best pair of jeans, because the pair he had on wasn't torn or smudged with any dirt or grease whatsoever. I think he even put mousse or something in his hair, because the long part looked clean and combed.

He tucked it behind one ear as I climbed into the passenger side and buckled my seat belt, which looked like it might actually *help* me die if we did crash. Gordon barely looked at me. In fact, he looked a little nervous. Like he was going to be sick.

"Are you all right?" I asked.

He exaggerated a frown. "What? Yeah. I just ate a shitty burger for dinner."

*Hmm. Right.* But I didn't push it.

Since it was Friday night around eight thirty, traffic up to North Gate was a bit busy, and on the way, Gordon barely said a word. I filled the silence with description after description of each drag performance I'd seen at the festival, which I thought would help—to prepare him and all—but in hindsight, might have just made him more nervous.

When we got close to the Lava Lounge and I told him to pull into any parking spot, he said, "Can we go get a drink somewhere normal first?"

"Somewhere 'normal'? Like where?"

"You know what I mean." He kept his eyes on the road.

"You mean somewhere not gay?" I needled.

"I just need a couple drinks or something first, all right? Gimme a fuckin' break."

I remembered the pool party and softened. Yeah. A couple of drinks can help. Or cause you unending embarrassment. "Okay, okay. But I don't know what's around here."

We found a divey spot a few blocks past the Lava Lounge, and Gordon circled back to park in between the two bars.

The "normal bar" turned out to be a nice match for Gordon's truck. I had the urge to wash my hands as soon as we walked in. The good news was that they certainly weren't picky about their customers, so we didn't get ID'd. I'd been a little wor-

ried about this detail of our adventure. Gordon had, in an unexpected show of initiative, secured me a fake ID just in case. But I
was glad I didn't have to use it, since the girl in the photo looked
at least thirty and was white. I applauded his effort, though.

We sat at a dark table off to one side and Gordon brought
two shots and a beer over.

"Are any of these for me?" I asked, pointing at the three
drinks.

"Yeah, you get a shot."

"Remember you have to drive us home, right?"

"Yeah, yeah. I'll have a few drinks now and by the time we
go home I'll be fine."

I stared at him.

He rolled his eyes. "I *promise*," he said in a whiny voice.
"Cross my heart and all that bullshit. Cheers." He winked at me
and poured the liquid down his throat like he'd been doing it
his whole life. I supposed that might not be far from the truth.

I sipped my shot—the brown liquid burned the crap out of
my throat—and Gordon finished his beer in about three minutes. I let him finish my drink, too.

"One more and I should be good to go." He sauntered
over to the bar and ordered another shot, slinging it back
right there.

"All right, let's hit this fruit stand before I lose my buzz,"
he said, heading toward the door, his chest puffed out.

I could see this was going to be more excitement than I'd
bargained for.

We walked the couple of blocks to the Lava Lounge, which didn't have a line yet since it was still early. In fact, it was so early, the burly woman checking IDs at the door barely glanced at our cards as we passed through. She did, however, give me a once-over and a wink. I thought it best to reciprocate with what I hoped was a flirtatious smile, but which I'm sure looked more like a blend of pre-sneeze and constipation.

Once inside, Gordon lost a bit of his bravado. He went back to his usual slouch and kept pushing his hair behind his ear, even though it was already tucked in nice and tight.

The Lava Lounge was a lot bigger than I'd expected, although I guess I didn't have much to base my expectations on. A glittering bar ran the entire length of the room, and directly in front of it, beyond a vast dance floor, a long but shallow stage rose off the ground with tall, burnt-orange curtains serving as its backdrop. Everything from velvet couches to cramped two-person tables surrounded the dance floor, and a screen along one wall projected distorted images of molten lava. In contrast to the fiery imagery, the air conditioners pumped icy air into the near-empty space. Techno music pulsated from towering speakers around the room.

Despite my nervous stomach, a thrill rolled through my body. Nowhere like this existed in Bridgeton, and though I'd been to North Gate several times over the years with my parents, I'd never ventured into any place like this before.

We found a table near the back. I didn't really want Gordon to drink any more, but I got us another couple of drinks anyway to keep us busy and to give me a little buzz too. We'd never hung out, after all, and maybe this was too big a jump into the unordinary for the two of us.

We stood at the table, awkwardly sipping our drinks, both of us trying to look around without seeming to. A few more folks trickled in, most noticeably a group of five or six younger women, all of whom were extremely attractive. I guess I shouldn't have assumed they were gay from how they looked, but something about their comfortable footwear and variety of short, shaggy haircuts told me they might not be straight.

But really, what did I know?

One girl in particular caught my eye. Two very muscular-looking legs in tight, low-riding jeans and skate shoes rose up to a wide belt with a Wonder Woman buckle. Following after these was a sturdy torso with plentiful breasts and arms that looked like they'd have no trouble performing repeated push-ups on the bar—if, you know, that was your thing. And at the top of all these powerful parts, striking blue eyes and a pretty face framed by short, wavy blond hair. Wonder Woman was weaving through the bar like she owned the place, handing out cards of some sort.

"Woooo . . . Clark is checkin' out the laadddiees!" Gordon jeered. The drinks were clearly doing their thing.

"Please don't be an asshole."

I was surprised to see his eyes drop to his beer. "Sor-RY."

"I just really don't want to draw any attention to us, okay? Let's just watch the show and fade into the background." I also really wanted to see Winnow, but I hadn't told Gordon that.

Gordon just huffed and said, "Yeah, yeah."

As the bar grew busier, I continued to scan the crowd, looking for signs of a beguiling geisha tattoo. Most women were in small groups or couples. Excluding the two girls making out on the dance floor, it was hard to tell whether the rest were gay, straight, or somewhere in between. I wondered how gay I looked. Ginny might have said "Very," but I bet Deidre would say otherwise. I guess perspective was everything.

Gordon had barely said two words in the past thirty minutes. But he was definitely busy examining the crowd, just as I was. Every once in a while, I checked him out in my peripheral vision, and though mostly he looked horrified, once or twice I caught something else in his face—something like wonder or longing. It softened my heart for him a bit.

"Hey," I said, and tapped his arm. "What d'ya think?"

But before he could answer, someone tapped *my* arm.

"Hey there, girly."

It was Wonder Woman.

"Uh, hi." Blink, blink.

She nodded to Gordon, who just stared. Quite the pair, the two of us.

"You look like someone who's *dying* to try something new tonight."

Well, that wasn't completely *un*true, but I dared not say that now. "Um . . ."

She shoved a card into my hand, yelling, "Just think

about it!" and then wandered off to accost other folks.

I stared at the card. Across the top in bold gold writing it announced, ROYALTY FOR A NIGHT! Below that: AMATEUR DRAG NIGHT. TAKE THE STAGE AND EARN DRINKS AND ONE FREE DRAG TUTORIAL WITH DEE DEE LA BOUCHE!

Dee Dee La Bouche? That was Deidre!

Amateur drag night?

Stage?

Horror. Excitement. Panic. Paralysis.

"What's it say?" Gordon asked, leaning over my shoulder.

"Uh, something about an amateur drag show? Tonight?"

He chugged some of his beer. "You gonna do it?"

*No way. No . . . way.*

*Or . . . ?*

As Gordon quickly lost interest and continued to scan the bar, I continued to stare at the card. Glitter and change. Glitter. And. Change. My drink fizzed in my other hand. My conversation with Devi and Boyd bubbled up too. Could I do drag? Devi had been making fun of me, but it had piqued my interest. And now this door swung out in front of me. Like an invitation. Like Winnow's hand. Beckoning.

A drag king can't be boring, right?

*Right?*

When I finally looked up, my eyes caught Wonder Woman, still floating through the crowd, still spreading her terror/thrill.

The next moment I found myself next to her, arm extended, hand gripping the card she'd given me. Blinking. Uncontrollably.

Her face spread into a colossal grin.

I lost my nerve.

She saw this and latched onto my arm.

"You'll be great. Come on, I'll explain everything backstage."

"I—"

"I'm Luce, by the way. You are?"

"Uh, Nima. But I—"

"But nothing. Come on!" She looked back at me and beamed, still pulling me forward by the hand.

The reality of what I'd just done suddenly sent my rib cage exploding into a million pieces to slice sharp, jagged wounds into my heart and lungs, which caused blood and air to leak into my stomach, which was defiantly rejecting said blood and air. At the *exact same moment*, my brain seemed to obsess over the fingers that were linked with my own—strong, confident fingers that didn't show any sign of letting go. I tried to let Luce's confidence flow into my own body and push my feet forward.

The "backstage" area Luce dragged me into turned out to be a stairwell behind the stage. Two other people were already there. One of them clearly *knew* she'd be performing, because she was decked out in some serious platform shoes and a wig so heavy for her tiny frame I thought she'd topple over any second. The other appeared to be more or less in the same boat as me. As far as I could tell, she looked female, and as Luce pulled me into the stairwell, she was wiggling into one of those tuxedo T-shirts. She'd wrapped what looked like a tensor bandage around her bountiful chest. I tried not to look, but obviously failed.

Luce let go of my hand and dug through a duffel bag on the floor. She threw a few clothing items at my feet—a pair of aviator sunglasses, a pleather jacket, and some black pleather pants.

I guessed these were for me.

"Okay, try these on. There're two other pairs of faux leather pants if you need to try another size."

*Of course there are.* I didn't think I'd actually spoken a full sentence to her yet. I tried now. "I'm . . . not sure . . . I'm ready for . . . this." Success!

She raised her eyes from the pair of pants she held out in front of her. I think it was the first time she registered how terrified I looked.

Her face softened a bit, and a pitying smile curved her lips. She dropped the pants and came right up to me. I mean, *right* up to me. Her nose was approximately three inches from mine. Taking both of my hands in hers, she squeezed them firmly and said, "I'll help you, don't worry."

I was still worried. But also flattered by the attention. I won't say I'd forgotten about my whole goal for being here tonight, but I definitely lost track of it in that moment.

"First, let's get you into these clothes. Strip down."

*Sorry?*

"Don't be shy, girl. I've seen it all."

*I'll bet you have.* As if I was a robot controlled by voice command, I slowly removed my jeans. I'd made sure to wear decent underpants tonight, at least. Apparently, stripping down to my undies around attractive women was my thing, in addition to the whole vomiting thing, which I sincerely hoped wouldn't be a thing that happened tonight.

She handed me the faux leather pants, and I struggled to pull them over my legs. "I think these may be a little too tight," I said.

"Oh no, don't worry. They'll get there. And the tighter the better, baby!" Wink.

After some yanking and hopping and sucking gut, we managed to get the pants on and zipped. I'd just slipped my shoes back on when Luce grabbed me by the hips and shuffled me back against the wall. The bass from the music in the bar thumped through to my back.

Luce drew out three tubes of lipstick from her back pocket and inspected each. "Black." She returned the other tubes to her pocket and uncapped the chosen stick.

"You seem like a full-beard kinda king to me."

I noticed a flash of silver on her tongue when she spoke.

"And big-ass sideburns, too."

My eyes must have been golf-ball-size.

She smiled—again, with more pity than humor, I thought. "Hey, just pretend it's Halloween." She hooked a finger over the waistline of my pleather pants.

I took a deep breath, unnerved by the charge her touch sent through my body. I had a hard time saying no to this girl. "Okay. Just . . . do whatever you think is best."

Her smile grew and she immediately flew into action.

As Luce applied a stroke of the black lipstick down my cheek from the base of my sideburns, I felt like a kid at a carnival getting her face painted. But when she held the other side of my face in her hands and moved in so close that her stomach and legs were pressed against me, I definitely did not feel like a kid. I pressed my hands into the wall I was leaning against until my fingertips hurt. The makeup part might be utterly uncomfortable, but this other part was . . . pleasantly unsettling. I tried very hard to keep my body still but had trouble controlling my breath.

In between applications, Luce made a concerted effort to get to know me, which was nice, since I'm sure she was purely doing this as part of some job she had recruiting unsuspecting young gay folks into making fools of themselves onstage for the entertainment of other, more knowing gay folks. We covered the basics—school, jobs, upbringing, etc.—and then—

"You got a girlfriend?" she asked, out of the blue. She finetuned some aspect of my eyebrows with her pinkie finger. The other two "amateurs," I just noticed, had wandered back out to the bar.

This was probably a pretty casual question to ask, but I guess I felt a little sensitive about the whole topic after

Winnow and Ginny, because "No" flew from my mouth like
I was spitting out something bitter.

She paused and moved her face back a bit. "Sounds like a
story there."

I bit my lip and shrugged.

"All right. Girl's gotta have her secrets. I respect that."

She continued working, finishing my eyebrows, then moving back to my cheeks to apply more black makeup to my ever-
growing sideburns. The lipstick she used felt thick and gummy
on my skin.

"Okay, now for the beard and mustache." She leaned back,
and her eyes darted around my face. "Stay still. Don't laugh."

*Don't worry.*

She dotted the skin above my top lip. It tickled. I scrunched
my nose.

"Don't move, I said!"

"It's tingly!"

"Grow some balls, princess!" She laughed at her own joke.

She was annoying and magnetic all at once.

By the time she finished, my armpits were damp and I
really needed to scratch my nose. Luce placed her hands on my
hips and leaned back again, surveying her work. She made a
little head-bobbing motion. "You make a pretty good-looking
dude, Nima."

I shook my head at her. "Yeah, right."

"No, really—you look good." And then she kissed me.
Like, on the mouth. Just like that. *What. The. Hell.*

Before I had a chance to fully register the abrupt feel of her mouth on mine, she said, "Come on," and wiped around her face to make sure none of my makeup ended up on her. "Grab the jacket and sunglasses. Then let's get you a good-luck drink!"

As Luce hauled me past the table where I'd left Gordon, I noticed with some concern that he was gone. *Dear God of everything gay, I really hope he's behaving himself.*

Luce squeezed us between a throng of people at the bar—the place had really filled up while we'd been in the back. She obviously knew the very indifferent-looking bartender, because all she had to do to get his attention was give a short, sharp whistle, which he somehow heard over the pounding music and general din of the place. As Luce ordered us a couple of beers, she wrapped one arm around my waist and squeezed me in tight to her. Something mildly possessive about the gesture bugged me, but in this situation, I mostly just appreciated being looked after.

While we waited for our drinks, someone next to Luce began chatting her up, and not really knowing what to do with myself, I stared down at the steel bar top and tried to look cool and bored. Through the rings of water left by icy glasses and bottles, I could just make out a faint, ill-defined image of myself: a brown blob framed by several black splotches.

Sexy.

"All right, here we go," Luce said as the bartender slid over

two bottles of beer. She grabbed them and flashed another of
her shiny smiles my way. "Follow me, sir." Wink.

As we made our way to a table near the stage, the ever-
growing crowd seemed to suck up all the air-conditioning.
The jacket weighed heavy and hot on my shoulders, and the
pants clung to my skin. We'd done nothing with my hair, so
I was walking around with a ponytail and man-face while the
aviators sat propped on top of my scalp. I couldn't imagine
I looked as svelte as Winnow's George Michael or as comfortable as Luce seemed in her own skin. Luce's whirlwind
of energy had swept me up in its gusts, but now I felt myself
tumbling back to the earth, and the sharp pains in my chest
resumed their assault.

When we got to the table, I touched Luce on the arm.
"Um, I'm . . . freaking out."

She handed me my beer and replied, "Drink some of this."
Then she clinked my bottle with hers and began chugging.
Remembering how well this had gone the last time, I hesitated
for a moment. But picturing myself up on the stage, in this
getup, in front of all these people, I tipped the bottle to my lips
and tried to match her pace. I could only take a few sips before
the fizz overwhelmed my throat, however.

Pausing after she'd downed about half the bottle, she said,
"All right, listen. You get to choose your own song, and you
only do a couple minutes of it. It's basically karaoke but with
lip-syncing. All you have to do is move around a bit. Trust me,
after you've had a couple drinks, you'll be groovy." Wink.

*Song. Karaoke. Lip-syncing. Moves.* I swallowed a few more gulps.

"So? You up for it? Come on . . . you'll be sooooo sad if you don't do it." She put her free hand on my waist and pulled me into her. "Trust me." Then she kissed me. Again. Her lips were firm and full, like the rest of her.

*You'll be so sad if you don't do it. You're sad anyway, Nima.* As her lips left mine, my mouth moved and words came out. "It has to be 'Dancing in the Dark.'"

Luce laughed and kissed me hard again. "Attagirl. You got this!"

I didn't know if I "got" anything, but I guess I was going for it.

While Luce went to tell the DJ my song choice and get us more drinks, I tried to run through the lyrics to "Dancing in the Dark" in my head. It was one of Dad's favorite songs, and he'd play it all the time while he worked on cars. One of my best memories was of us shout-singing along to it while he tried to teach me how to change the oil in our car. Mom came out onto the porch to laugh at us and we'd started singing to her, using a wrench and a dipstick as microphones.

If nothing else, at least I'd had a rehearsal.

"Hey, thanks for ditching me."

I turned to see Gordon standing behind me, leaning against the stage. I noticed he had a beer in his hand too. His eyes were a little glassier than when I'd left him.

"Oh, hey. Yeah, well . . . I'm sure you missed me terribly."
I cocked my head at him.

"Not really," he scoffed.

"Thanks, a-hole." But I couldn't help a half smile at what
felt like a moderately nice moment between us.

"So, like, what? You're supposed to be a dude in this shit?"
He pointed at me with his bottle, spilling some of his beer.

"I guess." I glanced down at my outfit.

He let out a fake-sounding laugh, but his expression held
inklings of that other thing I kept seeing—longing or curiosity or both.

"Wanna get in on some amateur drag with me?" I tried
another smile.

He stuck his finger down his throat in a fake barfing
motion, took a swig of beer, then followed this classiness with,
"Hope you don't choke."

I rolled my eyes. At least he was consistent. "Thanks, I'll
keep that in mind."


At about ten thirty, I found myself standing "backstage" with
the other two "drag performers" getting ready to "entertain."
All of this seemed to belong in air quotes—my life punctuated
with irony and doubt.

When Luce had returned with our drinks, Gordon disappeared again—to "laugh at you from the back," he'd said—and
Luce had given me a few "drag tips" to put me at "ease" while
we drank the rum and Cokes she'd brought us.

"Tip number one: choose some people in the audience to make eye contact with once in a while and throw them a wink or a smile or bounce your eyebrows at them, like this." Her eyebrows bobbed up and down suggestively. "People love that stuff."

"Tip number two: use the stage. Don't just stand there like dead drag-king weight. Three: point, fist-pump, snap, gyrate—anything to jazz up the crowd. And four: any form of naughtiness is always welcome." Eyebrow bob.

*Naughty Nima? What a laugh.*

After this sage advice, my drink tasted decidedly less sweet, but thank God it still added to my buzz.

Now here I was, listening to Luce's muffled voice through the wall as she chatted up the crowd, waiting to make my "drag debut." The other two performers and I had drawn straws and I would perform second, after the girl dressed in the tuxedo shirt. I don't think I'd ever been so nervous in my life, except for maybe the moments before I'd tried to tell Ginny how I felt about her.

No. That was pee-your-pants kind of nervous. This—this was shit-your-pants kind of nervous.

I took a colossal breath and went out to the bar to watch the performances. Tuxedo King and Platform Shoe Queen (all of us had been too nervous to introduce ourselves) were already out there, huddled by the three steps leading up to the stage. Tuxedo King's hair stood coiffed high above her fore-head, and she kept patting the sides with her palms. Platform

Shoes fanned herself with extra-long press-on nails. At least they both looked as nervous as I felt.

Luce appeared born for the stage—she already had the audience laughing and cheering after cracking several jokes about the "baby royals" they were about to see.

Finally she introduced Tuxedo King as "Elvis's favorite cousin, Pelvis," which got another laugh from the crowd.

Pelvis did what I can only call an utterly nerdy, adorable version of "Runaway Baby" by Bruno Mars, complete with air guitar, for the entire two minutes she was up there.

I was minutely relieved to find the audience generous with their applause, hoots, and whistles. But my stomach had taken up residence in my throat, and it was a good thing I didn't have to actually sing.

Tuxedo King (I just couldn't embrace "Pelvis") ran off the stage looking much more elated than she had going onto it. Her smile was enormous. I hoped I looked like that in two minutes.

Luce introduced me as "Bruce Springsteen's lesser known but equally talented sidekick, 'Brute Steenspring,'" and flashed me another wide grin as she bounced down the stage steps and gave me a nudge.

I ascended the stairs and shuffled to center stage. I was already sweating, but the strength of the stage lights flushed me with a surge of heat. The song struck out in its perky, eighties synthesizer and defiant drums. My body, neither perky nor defiant, remained listlessly stuck in some never-ending upbeat.

Standing higher than before, I had a spectacular view of the whole bar. I could see just how many people were out there, waiting for me to do something.

Frozen in place, but face and neck on fire, I completely missed the first few lines of the song. I looked over at the monitor at the right side of the stage, just to get my bearings, and feebly began mouthing the next lines.

> *"Man I'm just tired and bored with myself*
> *Hey there baby, I could use just a little help."*

That little help came in the sudden mental image of the Boss's tight-jeaned thighs and rolled-up shirtsleeves, pumping along to the song in front of his adoring fans. I finally remembered that I had a body and started to bounce my knees and snap the fingers on my right hand, just like Bruce.

Maybe not quite like Bruce. But this was better than nothing, right? *Okay, Nima, now do something else.* I couldn't play air guitar because Tuxedo King had just done that, so I just kept snapping and bouncing, and moving my mouth around. I don't think I was even bouncing to the beat. I tried to look out at the crowd and make eye contact, like Luce said to, but when I did and saw all those faces, I *actually* almost shat my pants and had to look back at the screen. In place of meaningful eye contact, I threw in a few vigorous eyebrow thrusts as I read the lyrics, which, I'm sure, looked super cool.

Maybe it was in my head, but the crowd didn't seem to be

hooting and hollering as much as they had for Tuxedo King. *You're boring them, Nima. Stop. Boring. Everyone.* My breathing quickened. My face felt shiny and wet with sweat, and even with the words right in front of me, my lips couldn't seem to form around them. I looked to the left, where Luce was standing, and she made shooing motions with her hands, encouraging me to move.

I could feel my eyes begin to water and became furious with myself for choking under pressure. This crowd wanted something—someone—naughty and fun and exhilarating. So, in what I can only call a massively desperate attempt to incorporate crowd-pleasing "naughtiness" into my act, I willed my feet into staggering over to Luce and yanked her onto the stage. Pulling her close, I opened my eyes in a question. She responded with that eyebrow thing, and taking a deep breath, I closed my eyes and laid a no-holds-barred, lip-smacking kiss on her. If I couldn't sing, I might as well put these lips to some other use. Thankfully, she grabbed me around the waist and responded enthusiastically.

The crowd loved it. As the music died down just before the synthesizer interlude and our mouths drew apart, all I could hear were whoops and whistles.

Luce grabbed my hand and indicated that I should bow along with her, so I did, and then she pulled me past her body and smacked me on the butt as I walked offstage.

Tuxedo King high-fived me as I skipped down the stairs, and a couple of men close by gave me the thumbs-up sign.

I turned to look at the crowd and some of them were still watching me and smiling broadly—ignoring Luce, who was introducing Platform Shoes as "Lady Blah Blah." My stomach tumbled around in excitement and I felt the urge to run through the crowd, hugging everyone, allowing their admiration to wash over me. I wanted to bob my eyebrows up and down at every girl in the place, to rush right up to people and start serenading them with every eighties song I'd ever known. I wanted to—

Shrivel up and disappear.

At the far end of the stage from me, dressed in a gorgeous three-piece suit and elegant bow tie, was Winnow. Her hair was swept back into a tight, high ponytail, and from where I was standing, I could see hints of a trim mustache and delicate sideburns. My excitement burst into flames and reduced my heart to ashes.

Unlike the others, she wasn't smiling. Instead she kind of bunched up one side of her mouth and gave me a curt wave.

My own smile faded as my brain connected what I'd just done onstage to what she must have thought when she saw it. I raised my hand to at least indicate I'd seen her, but I didn't really know what else to do. Her eyes left mine to watch Lady Blah Blah perform, but my eyes remained fastened to Winnow. In fact, if Luce hadn't bounded over to me and lifted me off the ground in a giant bear hug, I probably would have stood there, staring, all night.

"You nailed it with that kiss, girl!" she yelled over the

music once she'd put me down. Then she leaned in and shout-whispered into my ear, "And don't think that's the last kiss of the night, either!"

But I barely registered her comment because I could see Winnow over Luce's shoulder, looking at us. I wanted to some-how communicate to her that I wasn't interested in Luce—that I still liked *her*. That I came here to find *her*. But I didn't know how to do that from over here, with Luce's hands on my hips and her lips in my ear.

After Lady Blah Blah's performance, which hadn't sunk in through my mortification, Luce hopped back onstage and asked the crowd to give the three amateurs another big round of applause.

"And to show *our* appreciation, the Lava Lounge would like to provide each of you with two drink tickets and one free drag lesson with the one and only Dee Dee La Bouche!"

Luce pulled three envelopes from her back pocket and sig-naled to the three of us to come onstage to get them. We did, and she gave us each high fives as she handed them to us. But when she handed me mine, a few people in the crowd started chanting, "Kiss her! Kiss her! Kiss her!" and then more people joined in, and my face just about melted off my skull from embarrassment. Kissing Luce again wasn't going to help the Winnow situation, but what else could I do with everyone roaring for more? If I ran off, I'd just be dull Nima again—too scared to seize the moment. Luce was grinning and bouncing her eyebrows up and down at me.

Before I lost my nerve, I grabbed her and laid a big, fat kiss on her lips. The crowd erupted in cheers. I thought that would feel pretty good. But all I could think about was the one person who probably wasn't cheering.

Luce led us offstage and someone else took over as emcee. "Thanks, all—you did great! You can leave anything you borrowed backstage. Enjoy those drinks and seriously, call Dee Dee. You'll have a blast." Tuxedo and Heels both said their thanks and wandered off, happily dazed. Luce turned to me and said, "All right, I gotta get ready for my own show. We go on in half an hour. But save me some more of those kisses, girly." Wink.

I thought I'd had enough winks for the night. "Uh, well—" But before I could get any more words out, she'd disappeared into the crowd. I supposed the "professionals" had an *actual* dressing room somewhere.

After changing back into my own clothes and washing off the makeup as best I could, I tried to find Gordon. Even though I was dreading what he'd say, I figured I should at least see if he was all right.

I also may have been avoiding a certain someone else.

I couldn't spot him anywhere in the bar, so I tried outside to see if he'd gone for a smoke and discovered him leaning against the wall next to the bouncer's station. I got a stamp from the bouncer and leaned up against the wall too. "Hey," I offered.

He exhaled a long plume of smoke. I noticed that he blew it away from me, which was an improvement, at least. "Hey," he said, staring at a group of folks in various forms of dress and undress in the line. Then he surprised the hell out of me by adding, "You weren't that good up there, but it was still pretty cool you did it."

I lost my words for a second. He gave me a sideways glance, then asked, "How'd it feel?"

"Um . . . terrifying as hell, but . . . exhilarating."

He nodded slowly. "Would you do it again?"

*Would I?* "Yeah . . . I think I would."

He flicked the ash off his cigarette. "You should probably use those lessons first. And maybe keep your lezzie kisses to yourself."

I looked at him. He smirked at me. That damn smirk. I kicked at his shoes. "Jackass."

We both continued our half smiles, and for a moment, I forgot about the mess waiting for me inside.


While Gordon finished his cigarette, for lack of anything else to talk about I decided to fill him in on why I'd really wanted to come tonight, and about seeing Winnow, and about how I'd probably messed up everything by kissing Luce. Although he didn't offer any helpful advice, and I didn't really expect him to, he *did* seem to be listening, and he didn't seem too pissed that I hadn't told him about my ulterior motive.

The real show was about to begin when we went back

inside, so we fought our way to a high-top table near the dance floor, about midway between the stage and the bar.

The show opened with a fanciful version of Britney Spears as a schoolgirl-turned-school-matron, then a Sonny and Cher number. I silently noted how the Britney Spears queen included a character shift of sorts, and how Sonny and Cher didn't involve a lot of flash—they just sat on stools, lip-syncing into mics—but their lip-syncing was so tight and their facial expressions so in character that they still mesmerized the audience.

By the time Luce strode onto stage, as cocky as ever, I'd really started to enjoy myself, and the floppy feeling in my stomach was dissipating.

Luce had slicked her hair back and painted a bushy mustache across her upper lip. She wore a greaser outfit, and I noticed—admittedly with some childlike wonder—that from the crotch of her tight jeans, a massive bulge protruded. Like, a ridiculously massive bulge. And she definitely made the most of it throughout her act, pushing it out at the people in front of the stage, gyrating, grabbing it, etc. It was a lewd and crude performance, but somehow, she managed to keep it light and fun and not creepy at all—probably because she had an enormous, friendly grin on her face the entire time.

A few other acts stood out—a cheesy but super-fun group performance of "What Makes You Beautiful" by One Direction, a ridiculous Milli Vanilli number, and a Justin Timberlake bit that involved a lot of mingling with the audience. Audience participation definitely increased audience enjoyment, and I put that point in my back pocket as well.

After that, a performer crept on from one side of the stage to staticky electronic music. I realized as the person reached the center and faced out that it was Boyd! He looked androgynous—more androgynous than I thought possible from my limited experience of him. And he could *move*. Seeing Boyd's enormous body shake out each magnificent motion with precision and seeming ease floored me. The dude was fierce.

I yanked at Gordon's T-shirt sleeve and shouted to him, "I know that guy!" Then I added, "And just FYI, he likes girls too."

Gordon rolled his eyes.

But it was the next and final number that really attracted my attention.

Winnow.

Her graceful form—I'd know it anywhere now—drifted onto the mostly darkened stage as if barely touching the ground. When she walked into the light, I could see that her suit jacket had coattails, like the ones on Josephine Baker in her bedroom. She began with her back to the audience in one focused beam of light that shone against the burnt-orange backdrop and then, as the music started, proceeded through a very meticulously lip-synced and beautifully choreographed version of "La Vie en Rose." Lip-syncing in English seemed difficult enough, but lip-syncing in French must've been even more so. Winnow's mouth seemed to form around each word with perfect mastery, however.

Gordon shouted down to me, "I don't get it. Isn't that a girl? How come she's dressed like a guy and singing a chick song?"

I didn't really have an answer for him. It wasn't like I was an expert in drag, but I offered, "I dunno. I guess anything goes?"

He started chewing his bottom lip, and I could see by his rapt gaze that he was thinking hard about the implications of these flexible rules.

The crowd, especially a group of younger women up front, was equally rapt. Some hooting and whistling arose from here and there, but mostly people simply stood, spellbound. As Winnow floated around the stage, bowing to touch someone's hand, or dropping to one knee to focus her attention on some individual, I couldn't help but watch her extra closely, re-familiarizing myself with her features, her smooth movements, her sexy smile.

Crumble, crumble went my heart.

After Winnow brought her piece to a close, and the crowd basically lost their minds with exuberant approval, I swear I let out a breath I'd been holding since Winnow had walked onto the stage.

My eyes followed her as she disappeared through the crowd to wherever the performers dressed. I wanted so badly to pursue her and tell her—what? I wasn't completely sure, but I guess I just hoped I'd know in the moment.

Gordon broke into my daze. "Is that the chick you like?"

"What? Oh . . . yeah."

"Huh." He stared at the empty stage for a moment. "She's pretty hot, I guess."

"Thanks for the approval." Trying to get my mind off her, I asked, "What'd you think? Of the show?"

His hands dug deep into his pockets. He'd remained in his typical hunched position throughout the night so far. Now he shrugged and pulled his right hand out to scratch his chin. "Yeah, it was all right, I guess." But from his fixed look and the way he continued to rub at his chin, I could tell he had more thoughts than he was sharing.

Twenty minutes later Luce sauntered over to us. She had removed her facial hair but still wore the greaser outfit and retained her slick hairdo. The androgynous look definitely suited her.

"Hey, you!" she said, throwing her arm around me. She nodded at Gordon, who nodded back, and to my surprise, volunteered a "Good show."

I quickly piggybacked on his comment. "Yeah, great show. You were really funny."

She said, "Thanks," in between head nods to other admirers as they passed by and cast glowing looks at her. On the one hand, I found myself relishing the attention from this obviously very popular, attractive woman. It wasn't like this was a run-of-the-mill occurrence for me. On the other hand, I was still yearning for Winnow.

I asked Luce, in as airy a voice as possible, "So, do you know Winnow?"

"Winnow? Yeah, totally. Do you?"

"Yeah, a bit."

"How?"

*I practically barfed on her.* "We met at this festival and hung out a little after that."

She bounced her eyebrows up and down like before. "'Hung out'? Or hung out?" she said, drawing out the second set of words.

"Just a normal 'hung out.'" I didn't say I *wanted* it to be the other type.

She narrowed her eyes a smidge but didn't push. "Well, she should be out soon, if you want to say hi."

*God. Do I? Want to say hi?* The scent of other people's sweat around me suddenly became unbearable. "Uh, yeah, maybe. Whatever."

A knowing smile spread across her mouth, and then she grabbed my hand. "In the meantime, let's dance."

Before we could get out to the dance floor, though, I felt a tug at my shirt. It was Gordon, and when I looked at him questioningly, his mouth formed the words, "You're fucked." Then he tipped his head to his left.

Standing a few feet over was, of course, Winnow.

Immediately, my body tensed. Gordon didn't seem to know what to do either. He started chugging his beer. With a quick glance at Winnow, I noticed with apprehension that her eyes were focused on my hand in Luce's. I also noticed she was wearing an alarmingly sheer tank top. Avoiding direct eye contact with her, I chose to gaze somewhere between her and Gordon instead, which I'm sure looked totally normal.

"Hey, Winnow!" Luce exclaimed. "We were just talking about you!"

*Erg.* Not something I wanted her to know.

"Oh yeah?" Winnow replied. I finally forced myself to look her in the face, and her eyes stared directly into mine. "Hey, Nima," she said, a tilting smile on her lips. Her eyes glimmered in the dim lighting, and I tried hard to hold their gaze.

It felt weird *not* to give her a hug, but I was also afraid that if I tried to give her one, she'd shrug it off. Instead I squeezed Luce's hand—some kind of substitute reflex, I guess.

"Sweet performance, Winnow," Luce said.

"Thanks, Luce. You too." Her eyes remained fixed on me. "And you, Nima. That was something else."

*Ugh. And by "something else" you mean utterly pathetic.* "Uh, ha-ha . . . thanks. Not my finest moment, I know." *In fact, no fine moments to speak of . . . in my life . . . ever.*

"Oh, um, this is Gordon, by the way." I used the opportunity to let go of Luce's hand and move closer to him.

"Hi, Gordon," Winnow said.

Gordon replied with a head nod and a clipped "Hey."

Luce looked from Gordon to me to Winnow. "Okay, cool. Well, I'm going to make a round of the bar and say hi to a few people. I'll catch up with you folks in a bit."

"Okay, cool," I called after her, a failed attempt at nonchalance.

I took a quick look at Winnow, who still stood a little ways from our table, watching the lively dance floor. Her throat undulated as she swallowed, and the tiny crescent moon on her neck appeared to glow in the black light. I should say something, but what? It had been a week since I left her place, embarrassed and unsure of where we stood. She hadn't called. Neither had I, but who could blame me? Shouldn't she have made the first move to see if I was okay? If she was interested in seeing me again, that is. But I guess she wasn't. Interested. In me.

The realization sent all the air hissing out of my lungs.

Before I could deflate to the ground in self-pity, Boyd, drunk as ever, crashed into the table and flung his arm around me. "Nimaaaa!" One slobbery kiss on the cheek later, he started babbling about a hundred things I couldn't keep track of. As Boyd continued to prattle on, Winnow shook her head at him with an almost-smile and left in the direction of the washroom. All I wanted to do was follow her, but I didn't. I was pretty sure she wouldn't want a sad puppy escort as she peed.

When Boyd finally paused to take a breath and a slug of his beer, I introduced him to Gordon. "Boyd, this is Gordon. Gordon, Boyd."

Boyd squished in between me and Gordon, which made Gordon curl into himself in utter discomfort, which amused me a great deal.

"Hey, bud," Boyd offered in his disarming way, holding his

beer bottle up to Gordon for a clink. "What's up? You like the show?"

Gordon lifted his beer uncertainly to Boyd's and replied, with equal uncertainty, "Yeah . . . you were cool, man."

*Okay, not bad, Gordon, not bad.*

I chimed in with, "Yeah, Boyd, you were *amazing*. Seriously. So talented."

A lazy smile lengthened Boyd's lips. "Aw, thanks, you guys. I've been working on that one for a while." Then, in a typical drunk about-face, he threw his arm around Gordon and bellowed, "So, Gordo, you playing for my team, or hers?" He fluttered his fingers at me.

Gordon looked a little deer-in-headlights, but managed to get out "Uh . . ."

"Yeah, you know, you like boys or girls, or both or neither or somewhere along the spectrum?" He made air quotes as he said "spectrum."

At that point I elbowed him in the gut and started, "Boyd—"

But Gordon interrupted me. "Girls. Definitely girls."

"Really?" All Boyd's facial features expanded as if by helium. "Sweet! Be my wingman, dude! Come on—let's go find some ladies who like lads." He began to pull Gordon from the table but then stopped abruptly, and his face became serious. "This won't be an easy mission. Are you up for it?" He was totally close-talking right into Gordon's face, and it cracked me up.

Gordon leaned back a little, but I was surprised to hear the words, "Yeah, man—lead the way" come from his mouth. He gave me a wide-eyed look as Boyd tugged him away, but a hint of excitement appeared in his eyes too. I found myself excited for him as well.

Then I realized I was alone at a table in the middle of not only a crowded bar, but also a very confusing situation.

I leaned my back against the table to pretend I was interested in the crowd on the dance floor. I wished I at least had a drink to sip.

As if by telepathy, Luce appeared with two tall glasses brimming with what looked like more rum and Coke. She handed me one and clinked it with hers, then took several long gulps like it was water.

Unsure of what else to do at this point, I matched her gulp for gulp, despite obvious reasons not to. But the main reason I'd come here, at this point, seemed a long shot. And this cute girl in front of me—well, she was in front of me. Buying me drinks. Kissing me. She actually seemed to *want* me. Who was I to pass up being wanted at this point? I could chance it with Winnow and lose out on this, or seize the day and lose what I'd probably already lost.

What better time to drink, am I right?

On cue, Luce shouted, "Drink!" and chugged back the rest of her rum and Coke. I did the same, right to the bottom of my glass, and let out a barbaric burp. Luce laughed, and I yanked her out onto the dance floor. Once situated tightly among the bumping, frenzied bodies, my lips found hers. I shut my eyes tightly and tried to focus on the thumping beat. Her tongue was forceful, strong, deep, and though my brain still whirred in confusion, my body responded quickly and I allowed her to press herself into me. After a lengthy make-out session, she withdrew her mouth from mine and whispered loosely into my ear, "You know Winnow's my ex, right?"

*Wait, what?* I pulled back a bit and looked at her.

She grinned. "Don't worry, I'm totally over it, but I can see you've got a thing for her."

*Whaaaat?*

"Listen, as far as I'm concerned, this is a great way to make her jealous, so just keep kissing me."

*This is messed up.* Finally finding my words, I stuttered, "Are—are *you* trying to make her jealous?"

"Nah. Not really. I mean, if she *is* jealous, it's a bonus, but like I said, I'm over her." But something in her eyes told me that wasn't completely true.

This wasn't happening. If Luce was Winnow's ex, then kissing her was probably ten times worse in Winnow's mind. And Luce probably knew that. Which meant that Luce didn't actually want *me*. She just wanted to use me.

And just like that, I was back in the changing room with Ginny. Reading the letter from my mom. Listening to Jill's story. Wondering who I could trust and if I'd ever be someone's person.

I pushed Luce's hands off my hips and forced my way past the group of girls circle-dancing next to us. Just as I got through that first obstacle, I tripped over someone's bag and in my attempt to regain my balance, reached for the first arm I could find. That arm, coincidentally but predictably given my current luck, belonged to Winnow.

"Whoa. Hey," she said, grabbing me with her other hand and pulling me to a standing position in front of her. "All right?"

I wiped something wet off my arm. "Yeah. Thanks."

She looked at me for a moment, then over at Luce, who had broken her way into the circle of dancing girls, apparently unperturbed by my sudden exit. "When did you and Luce get together?" she asked me.

"What? No—we're not together. I only met her tonight."

Her eyebrows popped up. "Wow. That was quick. I know Luce can be forward, but—"

"It *was* quick!" My next words came out in a desperate tumble. "I don't even really know what happened. I don't know how I got onstage, or where any of those kisses came from, or how I'm even getting home tonight." I searched her face despairingly.

"What's going on with you, Nima?" she asked, concern in her eyes.

*So much.* But I didn't know how to say it, or whether she'd want to hear it. I didn't really know anything, it seemed. Except that I wished I hadn't been such an ass tonight. Instead of answering her question, I simply blurted, "I came here looking for *you*, Winnow." I hadn't really meant to say that, but there it was. Suddenly my feet became sensationally fascinating.

Winnow's hand touched my arm in a distinctly formal manner—fingers cupped in a stiff circle around my bicep. She leaned in and spoke in a voice just barely above the music. "If that's true, Nima, I just wish you hadn't been so easily distracted." Her fingers squeezed my arm lightly. "I hope you're having fun at least." The fingers fell from my arm, and when I looked up, all I could see was the shape of her geisha, hazy and shifting beneath her shirt.

And just like that, in a mass of jumping, sweaty bodies, I felt utterly alone.

I needed to get out of there. I tracked down Gordon and Boyd at the back of the bar, where they were trying to ingratiate themselves with a group of three girls who seemed only mildly interested, and realized very quickly that there was no way Gordon would be driving us home that night. Feeling lost, the only thing I could think to do at that moment was call the one person whose relationship with me didn't feel like a complete mess: Deidre.

After locking myself in a washroom stall, I pulled out my phone and dialed the number, selfishly ignoring the fact that it was way past midnight.

On the fourth ring I almost hung up, but then I heard, "Mmm . . . and just who is callin' me at this ungodly hour?"

Just hearing her voice—even in its sleepy sandpaper whisper—my heart lightened a touch. "Deidre? I'm so, so sorry to call this late. It's Nima. I—I'm so sorry." And then the tears.

## CHAPTER 14

On the other end of the phone, it sounded like Deidre had leaped out of bed and thrown on her clothes as she asked me where I was and assured me she'd be there in less than ten minutes. Through my hiccuping sobs, I managed to get out a few details, including the fact that Gordon was with me.

I told Gordon if he wanted a place to sleep that night, he better finish his damn drink and get his ass in gear. He looked like he was about to argue, but my face seemed to stop him. Boyd offered his place, but that obviously wouldn't work, so I told him no thanks, Deidre was already on her way.

As we stood outside, waiting for Deidre to drive up, Gordon lit a cigarette, which I really wanted to slap out of his hand. I was not in the mood for stanky-ass cigarette smoke.

"Do you *have* to?"

He inhaled and blew out before responding. "Man. What crawled up your ass? Too many chicks to handle in one night?"

Too many chicks. Too many rejections. Too many complications. Too many secrets. Too many fucking questions.

My hands, already tensely gripped into fists, rammed into Gordon's chest. He staggered backward a few steps and lost his cigarette to the ground.

"What the . . . ?" His face looked more shocked than angry. I charged at him again, but just as I got to him, two strong, sinuous arms caught me from behind and held me tight.

"Nima, Nima! Girl! Hold on, sugar!"

Deidre.

Without letting me loose, she said, over my shoulder, "What is happening here, baby? This boy botherin' you?"

"What? Hey—I didn't do anything. She's freaking out and just busting my ass for nothing!" Gordon protested, salvaging his cigarette from the pavement.

"Is that so?" Deidre aimed at him. Then, to me, "This the friend coming home with us?"

Not trusting my voice, I just nodded.

"And do you *still* want him coming home with us?"

In her arms, my heartbeat began to slow its pace. I took a few deep breaths before answering, beginning to realize how this all must look to her.

"Yes. He can come. I'm not mad at him. I'm just . . . mad," I managed, my voice coming out in shudders.

"Well, all right then. Let's get the two of you back to my place and put some food in your stomachs."

After a very quiet ride in Deidre's van, we arrived at a tall, sleek building. Deidre parked in the underground garage, and we traveled by elevator to the eighth floor. Despite my agitated state, I was amused to finally notice Deidre had worn nothing but booty shorts, a tight T-shirt, and flip-flops to come get us. A silk scarf covered her head. I could tell Gordon didn't know where to look as we rode up the elevator.

Walking into Deidre's apartment felt like what I imagined entering a high-end spa might feel like. A subtle scent of lilacs greeted us as soon as we entered. Calming, faint-green hues painted the walls, and natural wood flooring spanned the entire space. The wide living and kitchen area looked like something out of a magazine. This was a soothing paradise, and just what I needed.

When I'd expressed my surprise to Deidre, asking facetiously how much drag queens made these days, she let out that beautiful laugh of hers and revealed that drag and drag "tutelage," as she called it, were her side gigs, and that she was, in fact, an accountant by trade. Another surprise.

Deidre laid out some ingredients on the kitchen island and set Gordon to task. "Make some sandwiches, darlin'. Y'all need to soak up some of that liquor." She then handed me some linens and pillows. "Make up that couch for your friend here, and you can sleep in the spare room, honey. Bathroom's down the hall, and towels are under the sink in there." She also lent us some sweats to sleep in and gave us toothbrushes, since neither Gordon nor I had come prepared to sleep over anywhere.

She placed her hands on her hips and looked around the living room, as if deciding whether there was anything else we needed to know.

"Deidre." I touched her elbow. When she turned to me, I slipped my arms around her waist and pushed my head into her chest. "Thank you. Really. So much."

"Oh, girl, it's no trouble." Her arms pulled me in farther. "I've been there, done that to many, many people in my life. Gotta keep the karma flowin', right?"

I closed my eyes. Snuggled into her like this, I finally felt some of the tension ease from my shoulders and neck. My jaw and brow loosened too.

After a minute or two of this heavenly respite, Gordon's voice broke through, albeit in a gentler tone than I'd heard from him all night. "So, did you guys wanna eat, or . . . ?"

While Gordon and I devoured our sandwiches, Deidre prattled on. I could tell she was trying to give us a chance to settle our minds and bodies, but I couldn't think of anything I'd rather be listening to. We heard about her favorite wig store in town, her obsession with pantsuits, and her first drag show, which was a disaster (and which made me feel a bit better about mine). Then she turned her attention to her career.

"Accounting isn't exactly my *passion*, per se, but you know, it gives me the freedom to do my thing onstage *and* live this life of luxury you see around you."

"How long have you been doing it?" I asked, wiping some mustard from my mouth.

"Oh, about three years now, I guess. It took me a while to get my schooling done. Ain't easy when the only money coming in is from drag, dancing in sketchy bars, and a few other things I won't burden your virgin ears with." Her lips stretched into a cheeky smile over the edge of her mug as she sipped her tea.

Through his full mouth, Gordon mumbled, "How old are you?"

Deidre's eyebrow cocked just a smidge. "Honey, you are cute, but not cute enough to talk at me with your mouth full. You can ask me that question again once you've swallowed."

To my surprise, again, Gordon lowered his head, chewed, swallowed, took a sip of water, then said in a slightly higher voice than before, "I just wondered how old you were, since you're already an accountant and everything."

She gave him a warm smile, and I swear, he blushed.

"Let's just say I've been twenty-nine for about six years now." She batted a beautiful eyelash at us. I swear *I* blushed.

"You said your mama lives close, right?" I asked, thinking back to our conversation at my house.

"She's still in Woodland, where I grew up, and my brothers live on the other side of the country. But I don't speak to them much anymore." She sipped her tea. "They're not big fans of all my fabulousness." She pulled gently at the silver necklace at her throat—two feathery wings—and winked again, but this time, instead of blushing, my heart ached for her. I supposed these were some of the "bitter bits" Deidre had mentioned before.

"So . . . your brothers hate that you're . . . uh . . . ," Gordon started to ask, unsure of how to refer to Deidre, I guess.

"That I'm a woman, that I like boys, that I don't play football . . . all of the above, sweetheart. But I got plenty of love in my world, don't you worry."

Gordon just nodded, staring at his food. My heart ached a bit for him, too.

We munched and sipped in silence for a while, contemplating all the implications of our various identities, I suspected.

But by the time Gordon and I had finished eating, at least my mind was only half-preoccupied with thoughts of Winnow and Luce and the royal jackass I'd made of myself tonight.

I noticed that Gordon, too, had been affected in some way by the words materializing from Deidre's mouth. He'd fallen under her spell as I had that first night Deidre and I met.

Deidre conducted our cleanup from the stool she was sitting on, and when we were done, she said, "All right, snap peas—off to your pods. I wanna hear all about your night, but now's not the time."

I wanted to tell her all about my night too, and hear her thoughts, but she was right—my eyelids drooped and I couldn't wait to feel a pillow beneath my cheek.

♕　♕　♕

Deidre's glorious spare bed brought me a good night's sleep, and in the morning, I felt somewhat human. When I meandered into the kitchen, Deidre was sitting at the island, reading a newspaper with a shimmery silver robe wrapped around her and a pair of black-rimmed glasses perched on her nose.

Looking up over the tops of the frames when I entered, she held open her arms and said in her velvety voice, "Hey, baby. How'd you sleep?"

As if reeled in by her welcome, I floated right into her awaiting arms for another glorious hug.

"Incredibly well, thank you. Your home is so inviting, Deidre."

"Good. It's meant to be. Coffee? Tea?"

"Both?" I looked up at her and smiled sleepily.

She laughed and poured me a coffee from a small metal contraption on the stove. As she watched me scoop sugar into the rich liquid and sip it, she said, "All right, darlin', while that tough cookie is still zonked out over there on my couch, why don't you tell me what's going on?"

I divulged every last piece of drama from my past three weeks—Charles, Ginny, the letter from Mom, Jill and Mom, Winnow, Luce—and Deidre nodded, tut-tutted, patted my hand, and listened to all of it. By the end, I was pretty close to tears, and she just pulled me back into her strong arms and let me weep all over her fancy housecoat.

But she only let me cry for a couple of minutes. Then she held me out at arm's length and said, "That's it. That's all the crying you're allowed for now, because these next couple of days are for replenishing our spirits, girl. I have all kinds of goodies for us to gobble up!"

"But don't you have to work or anything?"

"That's the beauty of having my own businesses—I can do whatever the hell I want, when I want!" she exclaimed, followed by a quiet titter.

"Then . . . you're okay with me staying here another night?" The thought sent my heart leaping around in my chest.

"Sweetheart, you can stay for as long as you need to, under two conditions." She held up one perfectly manicured finger. "One, you trust me and jump feetfirst into whatever Mama Dee Dee throws at you." A second slender finger popped up. "And two, that you don't avoid all this madness in your life for too long." She pointed the two fingers at me. "Ya dig?"

"I dig." Something told me I'd be digging deep this weekend.

We moved out onto the balcony, where the sun had warmed two lounging chairs to a cozy temperature. Deidre took the private moment to ask about Gordon, who was still sound asleep on the couch. Without revealing Gordon's secret, even though I thought Deidre was the perfect person to share it with, I told Deidre about the bumpy nature of Gordon's and my relationship and that he was simply curious about drag. It was difficult to maneuver around why he was here and where his curiosity came from without saying too much, and I'm sure Deidre suspected there was more to the story, but she didn't press.

She did, however, ask, "Do you think your surly friend will want to stay, or . . . ?"

I thought about it. "I don't know. I guess we can ask him. Would it be okay if he did stay?"

"Honey, if you trust him in my home, then I trust him in my home."

*Do I? Trust Gordon?* The jury was out on that one.

When Gordon woke up, groggy as ever and smelling like a combination of smoke machine and cigarette smoke, we asked him over eggs and toast if he'd want to stay and hang out another night. I could tell from his hesitation that he wasn't sure what he wanted. I suspected he was intrigued by Deidre and curious about what we'd get up to, but also that his general distrust of people kept him from wholeheartedly jumping into the situation.

"What're you guys gonna do?" he asked, one eyebrow cocked.

I looked at Deidre. She smiled broadly and tapped Gordon's nose with her finger—something I couldn't imagine anyone else in the world getting away with. "Why don't you just stick around and find out, darlin'?"

The briefest of frowns flitted across his forehead, but then he mumbled, "Uh, sure. I guess I can stay for a bit. But just for a couple of hours, probably."

"Whatever suits your fancy, honey," Deidre said, turning her attention back to her breakfast.

Gordon looked at me, his eyes squinting with suspicion, but I just shrugged and took a bite of my toast.

Before anything else, Gordon wanted to get his truck, so Deidre drove us to pick it up. I think Gordon wanted to be able to escape if he needed to, which was fine by me. We both showered and changed, which made everything infinitely better in my book, and when we'd finished, Deidre appeared from her bedroom in a bright orange cardigan, formfitting blue jeans, and silver flats. A Cleopatra-style black wig cascaded down either side of her face, and a few tasteful pieces of jewelry accented her wrists and neck.

Meanwhile, Gordon and I practically matched in our jeans and T-shirts. I could tell from Gordon's parted lips and lengthened forehead that he was in perfect awe over Deidre.

Deidre didn't seem to mind that we looked like vagabonds next to her. She pulled a humongous purse from a hook on the wall and swung it over her shoulder. "Ready, babies?"

First up on Deidre's agenda: Top Secret. We hopped into her van and drove to a mystery location, which turned out to be a white clapboard building. When I looked up, I saw a light purple cross extending above the double front doors. My questioning eyes slowly traveled from the cross to Deidre.

Her mouth curved downward into a knowing smile. "Don't panic. I'm not taking you to church . . . although this is one fabulous church."

"Okay . . ." *Trust her, trust her, trust her.*

"We're just using the space."

"Uh-huh . . ." *And?*

"Come on, you two." She grabbed my hand and Gordon's and pulled us around to the side of the building. I noticed Gordon shook his hand out of hers right away, but Deidre paid no mind. As we walked, I heard singing from inside. Hymns. But not like the ones I thought they probably sang in other churches.

*"We are stronger together! Women, men, and all between! God's love will sustain us, she is our supreme queen."*

"What the . . . ," Gordon muttered.

"Okay," I said, my hand gripping Deidre's a little tighter, "now I'm starting to have strange thoughts."

She hooted. "I'm sure you are. Just come on."

We continued around the back, where a small yard opened up and another entrance seemed to lead into the basement of the building.

Deidre pulled out a key and opened the door. She flipped a switch and a wide room extended out in front of us under long, cold fluorescent lights. "Sorry about this horrendous lighting. Give me one second." She glided over to the other side of the room, plugged in three strings of lights, then turned on a standing lamp. She then magically produced a lava lamp from somewhere behind an old couch and plugged that in. The lamp turned bright red, but the blob of "lava" sat indignantly at the bottom. "That'll heat up fast, just like me—promise," she said, winking at us and coming back to turn off the fluorescent lights. The room instantly became warm and inviting—groovy, as Dad might say.

She squeezed between us and put her arms around our shoulders, surveying the space. "There. Better, right?"

"Much," I agreed. Gordon just grunted.

She walked out into the middle of the room, kicked off her flats, and spun around slowly with her arms stretched out. "This is my secret rehearsal lair. Like it?"

I nodded as I took the space in.

The room was a large rectangle. On the opposite wall from the doorway we'd entered through was the magical lava lamp couch—a plaid, beastly thing covered loosely with a much more palatable red-and-gold blanket. The longer walls were exposed brick and mostly bare, except for a very large mirror on one side. On the other side sat stacks upon stacks of CDs and a stereo system like the one Jill had—complete with CD slot and *cassette player*. Another doorway at one end of the wall with the mirror on it opened into a staircase, which I guessed led up to wherever the singing had come from. I could barely hear the strange hymns down here, though.

"It's . . . very large . . . and open," I offered.

"That it is. For good reason." She pranced over to us, took both our hands again, and guided us over to the couch. Gordon let her this time. "Sit. Relax."

She pulled off her cardigan and flung it at Gordon, who just looked at it in his lap. I don't think he knew what to do with himself at this point, and I found that amusing. Beneath the cardigan, Deidre wore a fitted sleeveless top. *Great galloping gods. I'd kill for a physique like hers.*

I sat, but the relaxing part was just out of reach. I still wasn't sure where this was all leading. In answer, Deidre pulled something out of her back pocket and handed it to me. It was the coupon for a free drag lesson that Luce had given me last night.

"Found that on the floor this morning. Must've slipped out of your pocket. How come you didn't tell me you'd been granted a lesson with yours truly?" She arched her eyebrow in a mock reprimand and shook her finger at me.

"With all the drama, I guess I forgot about it," I admitted, holding my palms up to the ceiling and shrugging.

She gave me a playful "humph" and skipped over to the stereo. She was clearly excited about something, and it made me smile, even as it caused my stomach to squirm. Crouching, she opened a CD case and slipped the CD into the stereo, searched through a few songs, then landed on one.

Out of a trunk on the floor, she drew a thirties-style felt hat, which she slanted casually on her head, and a feather boa, which she slid around her shoulders. She hit play on the stereo, and an older song I didn't recognize sprang from the speakers.

*"There ain't nothing I can do or nothing I can say . . ."*

Deidre turned coyly from the stereo, her hand on her hip and her eyelashes fluttering at me, then at Gordon. Taking long, slow strides toward the couch, she began mouthing the lyrics in a manner halfway between sensuous and coquettish.

Just in front of us, she launched into a smooth spin, the spar-kliest of sparkles in her eyes.

*"Ain't nobody's business if I do, do, do, do . . ."*

My body sank into the couch, my feet into the floor as I watched, awed by this private performance. Watching her in all her feminine wear was one thing—she was simply a beau-tiful, vibrant woman. But seeing her here, performing, forced the air from my lungs in one colossal burst. It was almost like she transcended her physical self—like I could see her beauti-ful spirit illuminating through her body. From Gordon's utter stillness beside me, I imagined he felt and saw something similar.

As the song came to a close, Deidre moved closer and closer to me. She laughed as she lip-synced, and I couldn't wipe the smile off my face if I'd wanted to. She ended by swinging the boa around my neck, planting the hat on Gordon's head, pull-ing me off the couch into a twirl, then dipping herself (because there was no way I'd be able to hold her up) in an incredible show of acrobatics.

As the music ended, she stepped back and bent forward in a deep, graceful bow. I stood across from her and clapped ecstatically, feeling like I'd just won the lottery.

"Oh, thank you, thank you, my dear," she said. "That was special, just for you two."

"I don't even know . . . what to say, Deidre. That was . . . incredible . . . ," I managed, still breathless.

Before I had a chance to fully express my appreciation,

Gordon bounded from the couch and dropped the hat onto the floor. "I'm out. See ya."

Deidre looked at me questioningly. I frowned and shook my head. Then, to Gordon's back as he stomped toward the door, I called, "What? Why? Where are you going?"

Without looking back, he just muttered, "I gotta go," and made a waving-off motion with one hand. He was out the door before I could say anything else.

"Should I go after him?" I asked Deidre, still staring at the door.

Deidre moved beside me and put her arm through mine. "I don't think so, baby. That little darlin' is overwhelmed. Let him go take a breath."

I trusted Deidre's advice, but I just hoped Gordon wouldn't do anything dangerous. I made a mental note to check in with him a bit later.

Deidre turned back to face me and placed her hands over my cheeks. "You're gonna fill me in on that boy's story later, all right?"

The thought filled me with comfort. "Okay."

She kissed me on my forehead, then clapped her hands together in front of her chest and grinned. Again, she seemed ridiculously excited about something, which released a small butterfly in my stomach.

She put her hands on my shoulders and looked deeply into my eyes. Her face became very serious. "Now, Nima, sugar, sweet, sweet girl—"

*Uh-oh.*

"—you need to trust me, okay? I saw how you watched those queens and kings at the festival, I saw your eyes as you watched me just now, and . . . I think you'd make a stunning drag king—"

*Christ in tights.*

"—so today, I'm bequeathing to you my extra-special, uniquely tailored just for you, drag boot camp!"

My knees quickly liquefied. Another time I may have been excited at this prospect, but after the events of last night, I wasn't so sure.

My face must have conveyed my uncertainty (and probably more than a little horror), because next she said, "Now, now, baby girl—just have some faith and groove with it. No pressure to be amazing, or 'perform,' or whatever—just a rowdy hour or two of something I just *know* you're meant to do. Okay?"

My mouth opened the tiniest bit, but no words came out. Last night I'd thought getting onstage would prove something—that I could be exciting and fun, attention-grabbing and desirable. I'd achieved the attention part, but not the kind I'd hoped for.

Yet here was another invitation from someone I trusted wholeheartedly. Here, I could focus on fun instead of my fears. In Deidre's eyes, I could see myself as I was *and* as who I could be. The thought made the edge of my lips lift ever so slightly.

Deidre saw this hint of affirmation and mouthed the word

"yes" while nodding at me encouragingly and gently squeezing my shoulders.

She looked so expectant, so earnest.

My wobbling legs grew steady.

A "yes" drifted out of my mouth.

And then I was gleefully tackled by what must have been one of the most persuasive drag queens alive.

"Take this . . . and these."

A baseball cap and sunglasses landed in my hands.

"And go change into this shirt and pants."

Deidre produced these items out of a cabinet next to the couch. A ribbed tank top and striped Adidas athletic pants. Apparently, I was the Sporty Spice of drag kings.

"We'll start you off easy—you probably wear this outfit on the weekends, don't you, girl?" Deidre said, playfully tugging my ponytail.

I let out a weak laugh. "Ha . . . yeah, how'd you know?" No part of me was completely on board with this yet.

"Just woman's intuition," she said, sailing toward a wicker basket that had been tucked away under a round table in the corner. From this basket, she pulled a selection of makeup cases and cylinders.

"Makeup? Do I have to?" I whined. Images of my blurry, blobby reflection in the bar last night rose in my mind.

"Yes. Now go get changed." I just stared at the pants and tank top in my hands. "Get going." She gave my arm a loose pinch.

While Deidre fussed over multiple CDs, I undressed and then pulled on each item of clothing in slow motion, trying to moderate my racing heartbeat. The pants sagged comfortably around my bum and crotch, but the tank top hugged me tighter than I was used to. I pulled my ponytail through the opening in the hat and secured the ball cap on my head. For now, I hung the sunglasses from the neck of my shirt.

When Deidre turned to look at me, her face did that thing faces do when they think you're adorable, like a puppy.

"Oh-my-cute-as-a-goddamn-button. Get over here," she said, waving me toward her.

She adjusted my hat a little to the side and tried to push the tank top up a bit to reveal my midriff, which I promptly put a stop to. "Don't push it, Scary Spice," I said.

That set off one of her spectacular cackles, and I felt a tiny bit better.

"Now it's makeup time. Come with me," she said.

She led me up the staircase to a two-stall washroom on the main floor. From what I could tell, this floor housed a large gathering space with rows of foldable chairs and a raised stage. A small kitchen with a cutout counter opened into the bigger space. It was exactly the kind of setting in which I could imagine a church potluck or post-baptism celebration taking place—except with bright purple walls and a billowing rainbow flag strung across the back of the stage.

In the washroom, Deidre placed the makeup containers on

the sink ledge and positioned me in front of the mirror. She stood behind me and we both looked into our reflections.

"What kind of facial hair do you want, sugar?"

*Hmm.* Luce hadn't asked me this last night. She'd just taken charge. "Um. I have no idea?" I said, staring at Deidre through the mirror.

"Long sideburns? Short? Mustache? No mustache? Beard? The sideburns really help sell the boy part."

Besides the blurry bar reflection, I'd seen Luce's work only briefly last night before madly scrubbing the makeup off after the show. I hadn't really felt like looking at myself at the time. I shrugged in mild defeat.

Deidre crouched a significant distance to wrap her arms around my waist and lay her chin on my shoulder. I didn't think I'd ever get tired of having her arms pull me in. "Sweetheart, you are a gorgeous girl and I'm about to make you into a gorgeous boy. Tell me what you want and I'll make it happen, I promise."

I gazed at her face, then at my own. Chewing on my lower lip for a few moments, a collage of facial hair floated through my mind. Leading men from the old movies that put my dad to sleep, Mr. Helm's rough, stubbly layer, all the drag kings I'd seen so far. The image that hovered out front, however, was of the trim mustache and delicate sideburns I'd seen last night across a crowded bar.

I opted for a subtle look. "Maybe . . . shorter sideburns and a modest beard and mustache? Or something like that?"

Deidre's cheek pressed into mine as her mouth spread into a giant grin. "Done and done."

"Now, usually," she said, as she turned me to face her, "we'd use hair clippings and spirit gum, but I'll go easy on you today." She carefully pulled off my ball cap and replaced it on my head backward, then looked at me. "Ready?"

"As ready as I'll ever be."

She began by lightly dipping a soft sponge into a container of dark, creamy makeup, then brushing the sponge gently along the contours of my face—above my eyebrows, down either side of my nose, across my cheekbones, along my jawline. After, she used her finger to blend the makeup into my skin.

"This is just to emphasize your features—make them a little sharper, a little more masculine." She leaned back repeatedly as she worked, checking her craft.

Once she seemed happy with this initial phase, she used a thick brush to apply a powdery substance over the work she'd just completed.

"What's that for?"

"This, my beginner boy, is concealer. It'll keep your new face from falling off." She crossed her eyes at me as she said this, making me smile.

"How do you know what to do for drag kings? Is it the same as what you do for your own face?" I asked.

"Mmm . . . not the same, but there are similarities. The only reason I know what to do with girl faces is I wanted to make sure my side business catered to all types, know what I mean?"

"Who taught you?"

She made a smacking sound with her mouth. "Girl, Dee Dee taught her damn self. Now hush for this next bit."

Deidre picked up a compact with dark eye shadow and a makeup brush that looked like a little fan. Beginning by overlapping the bottom of my natural sideburns, she applied the makeup down along my jaw, to my chin, and then back up along the other side of my face. She added a simple sketch across the top of my lip as well.

Her strokes were firm and swift, and every so often, they sent pleasant shivers across my neck.

Next, she used an eyeliner pencil to make quick, light touches on top of my new beard and sideburns, to mimic hair, I supposed. Clearly there was more to applying your "face" than slapping on some single-tone lipstick.

She continued working, topping up my eyebrows with the pencil, then smudging and lengthening until she was satisfied that my facial hair looked natural enough.

Finally content, she placed the makeup back onto the sink ledge and pressed my chin between her thumb and pointer finger, gently turning my head from side to side to survey her work. "Mm, mm, mm. You are *handsome*, girl."

I shook my head at her. "Do I get to see now?"

She guided my hips around so I faced the mirror. The first thing that lured my eyes was the manicured beard and mustache she'd given me, like a trim, tight frame around my mouth. She'd somehow made it look like real hair, like I could touch it and feel actual bristles. When I automatically raised my arm to do just that, Deidre patted my hand away. "Don't touch. You'll smudge it. What d'you think, lovey?"

She'd been right. The mustache and beard made a significant difference, but the sideburns added a masculinity I would never have imagined possible on my own face. They somehow created an edge to my cheeks, and the edge made me feel kind of . . . sexy.

"I love it."

Over my shoulder, Deidre grinned. She swung me back around to face her. "Come on. This is just the first stage."

"Okay, give me a minute and I'll be right there."

She floated out of the washroom and I turned back to the mirror. Peering closer at Deidre's handiwork, I marveled at the difference, but somehow was equally transfixed by what felt recognizable, if that made any sense. I saw me and a new me—both, together, and somehow more whole. My face, like this, felt familiar.

When I got back downstairs, Deidre was spinning in tight circles, bringing her eyes back to themselves in the mirror on the wall with each and every spin. Something that sounded like disco music bounced off the walls.

Mid-turn, she caught sight of me and her mouth stretched into her trademark smile. She finished her turn and drifted right out of it toward me, then lifted me and swung me around in a circle. "You ready for boot camp, little prince?" She placed me down gracefully and held me at arm's length.

"Probably not. But let's do it anyway."

Deidre let out one of her bursting laughs, which of course made me laugh too.

Once Deidre's voice came back down to earth, she said, "Well, let's get sweaty then, boy!"

The only way to describe the next few hours was as boot camp for sparkly people. Instead of squats we did leaps, instead of chin-ups we pumped our arms up and down. Our version of push-ups were slow wiggling movements across the floor. Where we typically would have sprinted, we swaggered or sashayed. And while I can't say I'd suddenly garnered magnificent athletic abilities that would have made me a superstar on the basketball court, somehow my body moved with an energy and instinct I'd not known I was capable of.

Deidre showed me the delicacies of hand and finger movements, and also how to play masculinity ("or what the world seems to think of as masculinity, child")—taking up space, wearing attitude in my face, my shoulders, my chest. We flowed between femininity and masculinity without restraints or judgment. An elegant twirl unfurled into beefy chest-pounding. Hands slapping against the floor in indignation slid outward into a slow, curvy stretch across the floor.

Only a few moments felt awkward, when I became aware of where I was, what I was doing. Every other moment swept

me into a surprising new version of myself. The instant when
Deidre and I fell into sync as we swept our arms above our
heads. When she picked me up, threw me over her shoulder, and spun me around like I weighed nothing at all. The
moment I closed my eyes to find the beat and opened them to
find Deidre's eyes radiating with pride.

By the time we'd finished, I hadn't thought about my dad or
Jill or Mom or Ginny or Charles or Luce or Winnow or Gordon
once. We lay on the floor, breathing heavily, sweaty and tired
and entirely satisfied. Thinking of my painted face, I suddenly
began laughing hysterically. My diaphragm tightened and my
legs curled into my stomach. I covered my face and bellowed
open, boisterous howls into my palms. My body jerked with the
effort, and I felt as liberated and singular as I had ever felt.

"Deidre," I said, between gasping laughter, "I think I've
lost my mind."

She reached over and tickled my neck. "Looks to me like
you've lost your inhibitions, sweetheart."

My laughter had squeezed tears from my eyes, and I wiped
them away as I sat up. "I can't believe how much fun this was,"
I said, looking at her.

"What do you think? When do we sign you up for the
stage?" Deidre asked, sitting up and reaching her fingers to her
toes in a long, lithe stretch.

My face sobered. "Whoa. Easy, friend," I said, the palm of
my hand flattened toward her. "You said no pressure to perform."

Deidre shimmied over to me on her butt and wrapped herself around me from behind. "But wouldn't that be amazing?" she said, her chin on my shoulder again. "I think if you had a chance to practice, you'd kill it."

"You're joking, right? What makes you think I would ever get in front of people and do this again after last night's catastrophe?"

Deidre playfully dug her chin farther into my shoulder. "What if . . . I helped you? What if you spent some quality training time with Dee Dee La Bouche?"

The thought of making a fool of myself once again made me want to crawl under one of the cushions on the nasty plaid couch, but something in me burned to see if I could be this person outside this room, to share what I'd experienced here with others.

But still.

"I don't know, Deidre. Can I think about it? For like a year or two?"

She chuckled and immediately pulled me a little closer to give me a peck on the cheek. "Of course you can, sugar," she said, as she wiggled her fingers into my sides, sending us both into a tickling, howling mess.

# CHAPTER 15

Back at Deidre's, while she showered, I took out my phone.

There were two texts and one missed call from Jill. Damn. I'd need to check in with her at some point, but not right now. I texted Gordon instead.

**You okay?**

By the time Deidre appeared about half an hour later, wrapped in her silver robe and massaging cream into her hands, he hadn't texted me back.

"Gordon's not responding to my text. Do you think I should be worried?"

Deidre folded her legs beneath her on the couch next to me and placed one hand on my knee. "Tell me why you're so worried about him in the first place, and then I'll answer you as best I can, baby."

I knew what I'd promised Gordon, but I had to trust my gut here, and my gut was telling me that Gordon needed help—more help than I could give him on my own. He'd probably hate me for it, but I decided I was okay with that, if it meant he'd be cared for. And who better to trust with this than Deidre?

I told her everything I knew—going back to my own experience with Gordon's dad, to Gordon's general behavior, to the unexplained bruise on his face, to his artwork, to our conversation the other day. I also told her about Gordon's reaction when I asked if he liked girls.

Deidre listened without interrupting, and once I'd paused long enough to signal a possible ending, she said, "That's a lot."

"Yeah" was my feeble response.

"I don't have all the answers, sugar, but I do think there's some reason to worry. All you can do is make yourself available, though—listen, be there. In my experience, people need time to work through their stuff and good folks around who are willing to let them."

"Should I go find him, you think?"

"You should. And I'll come with you."

Deidre dressed in a matter of minutes. Somehow, even in capri jeans, a collared, sleeveless blouse, and no wig, she still looked glamorous. We hopped into her van and she drove me back to Bridgeton.

I figured the most obvious place to find Gordon would be at his house. I only had a vague sense of where he lived, though, so I asked Deidre to drive south of the high school and hoped we'd catch sight of his truck.

It didn't take us long to spot the blue beast parked outside a small, one-story house whose front yard was really just one giant parking lot for several cars—none of them in any better shape than Gordon's own aging vehicle. Paint curled off the house like someone had taken a carrot peeler to it, and several roof shingles dangled like loose teeth.

Deidre parked across the street. I slid out of the van and trod warily into the yard. The screen door bent outward at an obstinate slant, its top hinge detached from the doorframe, but the front door was closed. I searched from afar the four windows visible from out front, but each had curtains drawn across them. I called out, "Gordon?" in a voice barely above normal speaking volume and listened, half expecting him to appear in the front seat of his truck.

Nothing.

I walked around the side of the house. The back looked much like the front, with two more cars hunkered down on the grass and a tumultuous heap of household fixtures like sinks, toilets, and hot-water heaters piled up against a shed. I tried halfheartedly calling Gordon's name again, but the only reply was a grasshopper's chirrup from across the yard.

No way was I knocking on the door—Bill Grant's leering face loomed in my mind—so I turned to check the shed. As I did, a door slammed. My heart skipped a beat, but I was relieved to find Gordon trudging toward me from the back door.

My relief was short-lived. He made his way through the

maze of derelict cars, the features of his face set in stone. Coming way too close, he grabbed my left arm and snapped, "What the fuck are you doing here?"

I instinctively wrapped my fingers around his wrist. "Ow—Gordon, let go!"

He glared at me for a few moments and then abruptly removed his hand. "What . . . the fuck . . . are you doing here?" he repeated, slowly and quietly, which was scarier than the first time.

Rubbing my arm, I tried to keep Deidre's words in my mind and replied, "I—I was worried about you."

He glanced behind him at the house and then pushed me roughly behind the shed. Once in this relative privacy, he hissed, "You don't need to worry about me."

"Are you sure? You left so abruptly, and—"

"And? I had better things to do."

I gave him an impatient look. "*And* . . . Deidre and I both just wanted to make sure you were okay."

"Deidre?" He looked around in a panic. "Is he here?"

"She."

"What?"

"Is *she* here. And yes, she is. Out front. She's worried about you too."

"*What?*" His eyes turned to fire. He grabbed my arm again. "Why would he—she—be worried about me?"

"I—"

"Hey, y'all." Deidre appeared around the corner of the shed

like a sunrise after two thousand years of darkness. A breath caught in my throat finally escaped my lips.

Gordon dropped his hand from my arm.

"Whatcha all up to back here?" Deidre asked, as though we were playing a game of cards or something equally mundane.

Gordon sniffed and took several deep gulps. Neither of us said a word.

"Come on. This is no place for three fabulous people to be conversing. I'm gonna take y'all for some food. Dee Dee's starving and won't take no for an answer." She ignored the obvious tension thickening the air and cut right through it, encircling us both in her arms and guiding us back to her van. I was shocked that Gordon let her, but he seemed completely stupefied, his arms hanging still at his sides and his face slack.

As we climbed into Deidre's van, the front door of Gordon's house swung open, and his dad staggered onto the porch. The sight prompted a flash of Jill's story in my mind, and my stomach pitched sideways.

But Bill Grant just stood there, swaying slightly and staring. I looked at Gordon, who was frozen, one foot in the van, one on the ground.

Deidre started up the engine and calmly conducted Gordon. "Hop on in, honey."

Gordon blinked twice and lifted his other foot into the van, sliding the heavy door shut after him. I avoided looking back at Bill Grant before climbing into the passenger seat and

slamming the door closed. Deidre pulled away and drove up
to Biddy Park, then past the northern limits of town. Soon we
were on the main road back to North Gate. Gordon must have
noticed too, but neither of us said anything.

Deidre finally came to a stop in front of a restaurant named the
Lotus with a large patio out front. "Come on, babies. Let's eat."

She asked for a table in a corner of the patio, away from
the five or six other people enjoying their meals outside. It was
about four in the afternoon, and the place wasn't busy.

Deidre seemed to know our server, Jeff, and told him to
bring us a large nachos and three iced teas. Once Jeff left, she
looked at Gordon, who hadn't said a word since his backyard,
nor made eye contact with either of us. Since he'd let go of my
arm, his whole demeanor seemed to have switched from furious to . . . subdued? Maybe even willing? I couldn't begin to
imagine what was darting around his mind at this point. But if
anyone could find out, it'd be Deidre.

Gordon's hands lay balled up in his lap, and Deidre
reached under the table to place her hand over one of them.
He let her.

"Sweetheart, Nima's just worried about you, and so am
I. That's the only reason she shared with me a little about
what's going on with you." Gordon lifted his eyes quickly to
hers, then mine. This time, however, they held fear instead
of fury. I could tell his fists grew even tighter, but Deidre's
hand remained firmly in place. She continued, "You can trust

me, sugar. Ain't nobody at this table judging you." She gazed intently at him and waited patiently as Gordon fixed his eyes on the table and remained silent for several more seconds.

I knew Deidre was a miracle, but when Gordon slowly unfurled his fists and grasped Deidre's fingers like they were a lifeline out of deep waters, I had to blink to believe my eyes.

We spent a long time out on that patio—long enough for the sun to set a simmering glow like embers along the skyline. Gordon didn't say a lot, but he shared in his own words the things I'd passed on to Deidre and revealed that the black eye had come from Davis after he'd accidentally seen some more explicit drawings Gordon had drawn. He'd promised in his usual cocky tone that Davis looked much, much worse, though, and wouldn't be telling anyone about the drawings anytime soon. Deidre just nodded and, as promised, didn't judge.

Gordon asked Deidre questions I was completely unequipped to answer, like, "Does this mean I want to be a girl or something?" and "Why the fuck is this happening to me?" Deidre didn't have answers either, but she responded with the kind of fathomless love and understanding that I imagined came only with years of experience and of having similar questions.

Gordon also wanted to know about how Deidre felt growing up, when she knew her body wasn't exactly the way she wanted it to be, and why she sometimes dressed like a "chick" and sometimes somewhere in the middle. For these, Deidre gave her own truths. As she did, I watched Gordon carefully, noticing that even among the uneasy flinches and compulsive hair tucking, his eyes never left her.

The only moment that became a little tense between them was when Deidre asked, as casually as possible, if Gordon preferred to be called anything else besides "he" and "him." His eyes grew wide and he immediately responded with a hard, "No! What? NO." Deidre didn't pay his tone any attention. She just smiled, said, "Okay, sugar," and launched into a story about the first time her mother called Deidre "her" and how Deidre had just about fallen over. Gordon eventually lost his scowl.

I knew I was witnessing something profound and was just grateful to be a part of it, even as a bystander. I found my heart thumping hard, hoping that these moments would help Gordon see there was a place for him in the world, even if he wasn't sure yet how that might look.

As Jeff the server came around to light the candles at each table and the patio lanterns flicked on, Gordon's breathing seemed calmer, and he'd stopped thrusting his hair behind his ear every thirty seconds.

We'd barely touched our nachos—it hadn't seemed appropriate—and the cheese clung cold and hard to the chips. But that didn't stop Gordon from abruptly breaking off a chunk now and shoving the whole thing into his mouth. He looked up into the darkening sky as he chewed, and I noticed with a warm twinge in my chest that his hand remained securely in Deidre's.

We let Gordon stuff himself with the nachos, and Deidre ordered some more food to share. We were all famished—between drag boot camp and all these damn emotions, my stomach was about to consume itself.

After we devoured our food mostly in silence and Deidre insisted on paying the bill, she took one long look at us and said, "I know just what we need, babies."

Deidre drove us back to her place and commanded, "Sit your butts down and don't move." Then she disappeared into her bedroom.

I took a deep breath and turned to Gordon. "I'm sorry if I broke your trust, Gordon."

He slumped back against the puffy cushions strewn across the couch, interlaced his hands on his chest, and stared at the coffee table. "Whatever. I get it."

"You do?"

"Yeah." He perched his feet on the edge of the table, and I resisted the urge to tell him to remove them. "But no one else, Nima." He turned to gaze at me. "Seriously. No one else can know about this." His eyes were puffy and red, even though he hadn't cried once that afternoon.

"I promise," I said, adding, "I'm here, though . . . just . . . so you know."

He sighed and nodded, his attention reverting back to the table.

Deidre emerged from her room, her arms full of clothing.

"Okay, my lovelies, we need to change gears!" She threw a black collared shirt at Gordon and told him to go change into it. He tried to protest, but with one cocked eyebrow, Deidre sent him shuffling off to the spare room.

She then told me to stand up, and before I could even object, she whipped off my shirt and pulled a new one over me.

"This shirt is tight on me but just right on you," she said— if just right meant one shoulder falling loosely to the side and a small portion of my midriff showing. Then she gave me a touch of mascara and eyeliner, some shiny bangles, and a gold necklace with a twisting, spiral pendant on it. "A little gay-girl makeover," she called it. Stepping back to take a look, she exclaimed, "Girl, you know how good you look?"

I didn't. But when Gordon came back in and gave me a slow head nod as he checked out my outfit, I thought that maybe it wasn't completely untrue.

Gordon didn't look half-bad either. The shirt was slim-fitting and short-sleeved, like basically every item of Deidre's clothing I'd seen so far. It was the first time I'd seen him in anything but a T-shirt, and I was impressed with the overall effect. He still looked like casual Gordon, but with a touch of finesse. Trust Deidre to make me use the word "finesse" to describe Gordon Grant.

"All right, sugarplums, I'll be right back." After about twenty minutes, Deidre reemerged in a flowing mint-green blouse, high-waisted black pants, and what looked to be at least three-inch black pumps. Her wrists jangled with gold bangles, and a chunky gold necklace adorned her throat. A sleek black wig angled sharply across her forehead and tucked behind her ear.

Gordon and I had been playing with the mini pool set we'd found in the living room, but when Deidre entered, we both looked up to gape at her. Gordon looked down again swiftly, and I wondered for the first time if his admiration was more of the "crush" variety. I slipped that thought away for now, though—we had enough complications already.

Next thing on the agenda: gay bingo. I, of course, didn't know this was a thing, but it was. Deidre took us to a pub called the Royal about three doors down from the scene of my previous night's embarrassment. I tried to push the snapshots that flashed through my mind of that horror show way down as we entered.

I was worried again that my age would be a problem, and sure enough, the door person wanted to see my ID. But Deidre stepped in and said Gordon and I were with her, and that made us "legit" enough. The door person, clearly as susceptible to Deidre's charms as the rest of us, gave her an awkward, "Aye, aye, ma'am," to which Deidre replied, "Thank you, sweetheart. But ma'am is for my mama," and whooshed us inside.

The pub was small, with a bar and stools on one side, and a low, round stage on the other, separated by several high-top tables. The yeasty scent of beer permeated the air, mixed in with what smelled like pine-tree air freshener. The carpet appeared to have absorbed more than its fair share of both beer spills and stiletto wear and tear—the burgundy material showed a variety of discolorations and bare spots.

"Don't be disenchanted by its appearance, babies. This place is an institution!" Deidre said she used to host gay bingo night here, but "decided to share the red carpet with younger queens."

That night our hostess was named Luscious Galore, and she was luscious all right. She reminded me of the one curvy drag queen on Winnow's wall, full-bodied and proud of it. I tried to ignore the little niggle of sadness that arose in my stomach at the thought of Winnow and just appreciate the scene unfolding in front of me.

Apparently, gay bingo was bingo with a drag queen hostess, lots of off-color jokes, and drag performances at the very end. Prizes consisted of money and drag paraphernalia like feather boas, wigs, and glittery things, plus a few naughtier items that made me blush and made Gordon smirk. Deidre introduced us to a few regulars throughout the night, as well as to a couple of the queens. Just like the night we first met, Deidre remained attentive, funny, and affectionate—and her plan to "change gears" worked. It was impossible to focus on problems with the shenanigans taking place around us.

This world was new to me, and I'd still have these moments when the unfamiliarity caused me confusion, or embarrassment, or apprehension—like when the host cracked jokes about tops and bottoms and bears and twinks, or when the guy at the table next to ours performed an undisclosed act on an undisclosed toy he'd just won.

But I'd have other moments too. Moments when I realized no one here cared that I liked girls, when I was in awe at the artistry of some of the queens' dress and makeup, the ease with which they expressed themselves through their bodies and their performances. Moments when the laughter around me felt free and loose and *real*. I felt like a baby in the big leagues *and* like Alice walking into Wonderland . . . except all the queens were merry entertainers, not despotic murderers.

"Deidre, thanks for bringing us here," I said, as Luscious paused from calling out numbers to gulp back an enormous goblet of her "special medicine."

Deidre nibbled the pickled green bean from her Caesar and smiled. "It ain't your typical bingo scene, is it?" She winked at Gordon, who sniffed and focused his eyes on his bingo card, but whose flushed cheeks betrayed his pleasure. "Sometimes a little gay bingo is just plain good for the soul."

At the table next to ours, an older man wearing a vintage leather cap, studded suspenders, and jean shorts yelled out in a gruff voice, "You got that right, sister!" and reached out his hand for a high five, which Deidre happily reciprocated. They both let loose riotous laughter—the man's a guttural tumble and Deidre's a high-pitched flutter. Gordon looked at them, then glanced at me, his eyebrows questioning but his eyes showing a glint of amusement. His expression made me laugh as well, and then something between a cough and a snort came from his mouth. For the first time in my life, I witnessed Gordon Grant laugh.

By the end of the night, my cheeks ached, and Gordon looked like he'd had some air pumped back into him. We hadn't won any of the bingo games, but it felt like we'd hit the jackpot in other ways.

As Deidre drove us back to her place to crash for another night, we both sank into her buttery leather seats in sleepy bliss.

# CHAPTER 16

The only thing about bliss is that it's sometimes accompanied by ignorance.

I woke up late the next morning, stretched luxuriously in the crisp, clean sheets of Deidre's spare bed, and then quietly went to slip out to use the washroom. On my way, a glow from inside my open backpack caught my attention.

*Shit.* I'd completely forgotten to call or text Jill back.

I pulled the phone from my bag. Six messages, three voice mails.

*Shit in a sock drawer.*

I sat on the bed and read the messages first:

Saturday, 10:22 a.m.: Hey, girlie. Don't forget to check in with me today.

Saturday, 1:17 p.m.: Nima, just shoot me a text to let me know you're alive, okay??

Saturday, 5:10 p.m.: I'm trying not to freak out, but I left you messages and a couple of voice mails. Now I'm freaking out. Call me. ASAP.

The next three messages grew increasingly panicked. I listened to the voice mails.

"Nima, it's Jill. You promised to answer the phone when I called, remember? I texted you too. I'm trying not to worry, but I'm starting to. Call me as soon as you get this!"

The next message was basically the same, but with stronger language.

The third message was left this morning around eight a.m. and almost made me drop the phone.

"Nima, I'm not trying to alarm you into calling back, but I thought you should know . . . I wish I could ease you into this more, but . . . your mom's here. She's here, now, at my house. She wants to see you and here I am, with no clue where you are or what you're doing. I haven't called your dad yet, but you need to call me, please. I'm sorry. But call. Now."

I stared at the screen as the voice-mail lady recited my messaging options, and I wished my real-life options were as simple.

Reply? Forward? Save? Delete?


When I walked in the front door of my own house later that day, much of that feeling of bliss had already seeped away, and I could feel it being replaced by a tightening in my stomach instead, like an angry fist. I resented having to abandon the paradise Deidre had bestowed on me, and Gordon seemed to resent it too.

After I'd texted Jill (I hadn't been able to bring myself to call her at that moment) to let her know I was sorry and that I was fine and that I'd be home soon, and then ignored her immediate call back, I'd had to explain the situation to both Deidre and Gordon. Deidre, of course, went into a mode of calm, deliberate action. She ushered us right into her van to drive us back to Bridgeton, thrusting bananas and yogurt cups into our hands to eat on the way.

She dropped me off first, putting the van into idle and stepping out to give me an enormous hug. She also told me to call as soon as I could and to remember she'd be there no matter what. I believed her, and it helped.

But now, here I was, standing in the middle of my boring old kitchen. Jill must have taken Gus to her place while I was gone, because I didn't even get a welcome-home freak-out from him.

As I listened to the low whir of the refrigerator and saw the still-dirty breakfast dishes on the counter from two days ago when I'd last seen my dad, my backpack seemed to press me down to the linoleum and my knees and hands hit the floor with a thump and slap. I'd barely been alone over the past few days, so I hadn't had to think about all the things Jill told me. And even though not all of the past two days had been positive, the parts that were had instilled in me more joy than I'd felt in a long time. And now, here I was—back in my kitchen, my mother only a few blocks away, and no one around to get me through this. Tears threatened.

I leaned back on my heels and stared at my shadowy shape in the refrigerator door, trying to regulate my breathing, trying to picture the walking feet on my bedroom ceiling, trying to remember the feeling of transporting myself across the church basement, my hand grasped in Deidre's—a fiercer version of myself than I'd ever been.

I slipped my backpack off my shoulders and let it slump to the ground. With one big breath, I raised myself off the floor and walked back out the kitchen door, bound for Jill's house.

When I pushed open Jill's front door, the smell of potting soil filled my nose—usually I'd find this earthy, pleasant. But today, it seemed to remind me only of dirt. Plain, dirty dirt. Hearing murmurs from the kitchen, my stomach plummeted. Was this a mistake? Was I ready to see my mom? Instead of walking through to the back, I pivoted to my right and stared at the shelves of miniature garden statues and baby cacti. Jill had taken the time to alternate the statues with the cacti—a decorative touch that was so unlike her. Tiny earthen fairy, prickly knobbed cactus, tiny clay frog, pudgy round cactus.

There was something mesmerizing about the pattern, and I wasn't sure how long I'd been staring before I heard Jill say, "Nima? What are you doing?" She was standing in the door-frame to the kitchen with her hands on her hips, her head tilted.

"Admiring your surprisingly tidy display, actually."

"Uh . . . that wasn't me."

I frowned at her, puzzled.

"Your mom did that when she got here. I think she's nervous," she continued, glancing behind her.

A cough from the back. A chair scrape across the floor.

My face felt numb. I turned back to the display and stared hard at a gopher statue wearing gardening gloves and gumboots. *Give me strength, little gopher guy.*

An arm was suddenly around me, a hand on my right shoulder. When I glanced at it out of the corner of my eye, the hand was brown, with short, tidy nails and a silver striated ring on the pointer. A shiver ran through me and I resisted the urge to shrug my shoulder to clear the weight. I set my jaw, breathed in, then out, and turned my head to the left.

My mom was staring at the display and didn't turn toward me right away. My eyes traveled down the profile of my own face—short forehead, rounded nose, thick lips, tight chin. I watched her tuck her lips into her mouth and then wet them with her tongue. Her eyelids closed for a moment—a fraction of a second longer than a blink—and then she swiveled her head to face me.

"Hi, Nimanthi."

Hearing this casual greeting along with my full name set a vein in my temple pulsing. *Hi?* That's *your opening line?* I turned my attention back to the statues and cacti. My fingers began to tingle. I lifted my right hand and calmly, deliberately flicked each statue and cactus off the shallow shelving. One by one they toppled to the ground, some bouncing resiliently to the side, some becoming tiny clay explosions.

"Nimanthi?" This was my mother.

"Nima? What are you . . . ?" This was Jill.

What *was* I doing?

Ruining something, I guess. Ruining something Jill created and my mother arranged—taking her careful design and sending it crashing to the floor.

The arm across my shoulders fell away and reached across the front of my body instead to interrupt my petty rebellion. My mother's hand folded over mine and stopped it midair. I let my arm drop to my side but kept staring straight ahead, eyes burning into the empty space left by my innocent victims. *Fuck you, tears. You will not fall.*

Two hands turned me away from the shelves and my eyes came to rest on a silver pendant that Dad let me pick out for her birthday many years ago, when I was only old enough to choose based on what was familiar and shiny. Three gleaming leaves, overlapping one another.

"Nimanthi . . ."

Agitated at hearing my name a third time from her mouth, I yelled, "Is that all you can say?"

She flinched and stepped back, letting her hands fall from my arms. As if for help, she looked back at Jill, and I lost it. "Don't look at Jill! Can't you do this on your own? *Why are you even here?*"

"I—I came to see you, Nima. I missed you. I wanted to explain. . . ." She folded her arms across her chest and her chin crumpled.

*Oh hell no. You do not get to cry either.* "So explain, then!" My arms flung outward. "Explain how you could just leave me and Dad like that! Explain why you haven't contacted us in over a year—how you could write such a shitty little letter like that and expect me to respond. *Please. Explain.*"

She stared at my mouth for a moment, as if examining all the words that I'd just spewed at her. Her eyes closed and her arms fell to her sides again. All the air seemed to leave her body. Finally she opened her eyes and looked at me squarely.

"I don't know if I can explain everything, Nima. I just . . . didn't know how I could stay here and be your mom and Del's wife like before." She looked to the empty shelves. "I needed to sort out my feelings." Turning back to me, she added, "I know I hurt you. And I'm so sorry for that."

I'd thought an apology would help. But it didn't. I didn't want to know she was sorry. I wanted to know she couldn't live without us. Without me.

"Are you moving back?" My fists clenched in anticipation of the answer.

She looked at Jill again, but quickly back to me. "I—not yet. I still need to figure some things out. I'm sorry, Nima . . . it's not that I don't want to, I just . . ."

"Just what? You just have better things to do? Well, that makes two of us!" My face grew hot and my fists ached with tension. Suddenly I wanted her to know how much I'd changed these past few weeks—how different my life was. "You know where I was before you showed up here, unannounced? Having the time of my life—that's where! *Performing*. Onstage! *Dancing*. With a drag queen!"

Her eyebrows rose and her mouth fell open.

"Shocking, huh? Your boring daughter"—my voiced splintered into a whisper—"suddenly not so boring." I wiped away the wet growing in my eyes. "If you moved back, maybe . . . maybe you'd see that." *Maybe you'd love me more. Enough to stay.*

"Oh, Nima . . ." She lifted her arms toward mine again, but I couldn't bear the thought of her touching me at that moment. I stomped away from her, past Jill into the kitchen, and out to the backyard. The screen door thwacked behind me and I found the sound extremely satisfying.

As soon as I stepped foot outside, Gus was at my feet. He must've been snoozing in the sunny grass like he does at home. He nipped at my heels as I marched past him to the back fence and climbed onto the picnic table where Jill displayed her gnomes.

One such gnome—a fireman holding a ladder—toppled from the bench seat as the table shook with my weight. It thudded to the grass below, still intact. I wished it had cracked, but it just stared at me with its glassy eyes instead. *Screw you, gnome.*

I heard the screen door bang shut again and caught Jill's lanky figure approaching from my side view. Gus barked once from where he'd stretched out next to the gnome.

She paused a short distance from me. "Another statue bites the dust, huh?" She crouched to pick up the fireman gnome and soberly declared, "Serves you right, gnome." Then she dumped him off to the side and stood up.

"This isn't funny, Jill."

"I know, hon."

"Why'd she really come? If she's not even staying?" My voice sounded distant.

Jill sighed. "I guess when she didn't hear from either of us, she decided this was the only way to see you."

"Me? Or you?"

"*You*, Nima. Definitely you." But her voice didn't sound definite.

"You mean there's nothing between you two anymore?" I searched her face for an answer before she could make something up. The hand she wiped down her face said it all. "I knew it."

"You don't know, Nima." She stepped closer. "I can't lie and tell you there's nothing there anymore, but I *can* tell you that your mom came here for you. That she's as lost as you are."

"I'm not lost! And I definitely don't need her to find me. And I'm not interested in finding her, either." These were partly untrue, I knew, but I wanted to believe them. I folded my arms in my lap and tucked my head down on top of them. "She left, Jill. She just left."

"I know, babe. But you have to understand—she wasn't

leaving *you*. This wasn't about you. You"—she placed a hand on my shoulder—"are infinitely lovable. Your mom's missing something inside *her*. Something no one else but she can find. But you can't just ignore her. She's your mom, whether you like it or not. And she's here. So come on back inside and let's figure this out. Okay?" Her hand slipped off my shoulder and spread open in front of me.

I stared at it for a while, thinking about Jill's words. The thought of my mom missing something, feeling empty somehow, filled me with sadness for her. I knew that emptiness.

A sigh escaped my lips. Ignoring Jill's unwavering hand, I hopped off the table and walked back toward the house, Gus bounding along next to me. Before I opened the screen door, I took a deep breath. Jill squeezed my shoulder and followed me in. We walked back through the kitchen and into the front room. The carnage of my earlier blitz lay strewn about the floor, as though cacti and statues had engaged in some secret battle while we were gone and stopped just as we entered. Gus dug his nose around in the wreckage.

"Mom?" I breathed into the obviously empty room. Jill checked inside the storage room, but her face revealed it was empty as well.

"Where'd she go?" I asked, more to myself.

"Maybe she just needed some air too," Jill offered, a tremble in her voice. "I'll check if her car is still here." She walked out through the front door and came back in only moments later, her face ashen. "Nima . . ."

The look on my own face stopped her from finishing whatever feeble sentence she was about to attempt.

My eyes didn't know where to go, so I let them land on a collection of shovels resting against the wall. The smell of soil and clay pervading the room reminded me of something, some memory puffing up in my mind like smoke.

I'm digging in the meager garden at the Biddy Park house. My mom is settled in beside me on a piece of old carpet, reading a book while I lift dusty clumps of dirt with my spade and pile them around us, like a small village of dome houses. I stand across from her and look for her approval, proud of this orderly town I've built for us. But she's not looking. She's not reading. She's staring into the forested land beyond our property and fingering the three leaves at her neck. I call her several times, but it's not until I crawl into her lap and start to play with the pendant myself that she breaks out of her reverie and hugs me tight.

Without a word, I walked out of Jill's front door—no clue as to where I was going or what I'd do when I got there.

Sometime later, I found myself in the quad at the high school. Gus had managed to slip out Jill's door behind me and followed as I paced aimlessly. No one hung out in the quad during the summer—somehow, it was okay to spend time in the dugouts and on the baseball field, but only losers hung out in the quad when school was out.

I was in the right place, then.

I perched myself on top of Charles's and my table beneath the cottonwood tree, resting my feet on the bench. It hadn't been our table for a few years now—not since we were in grade nine and doling out nerdy descriptions of our classmates. The tree had never perked up from its original abject state—its branches still drooped, its leaves still provided only sporadic shade at best. But it was still here.

Gus bounded off to chase butterflies, and I was left to flounder in my self-pity and resentment. Did all that really just happen? Part of me was terrified that it had all been the result of my dizzying last few days. That I'd merely imagined it—my mind making me pay for trying to ignore the issue in the first place. Staring down at my sneakers, though, traces of clay dust and soil reminded me that my rampage had been real, and that my mom had only been able to spend a few minutes with me before leaving again.

Soil, dust, clay. Nothing like a few natural elements to remind us that's all we are—lone particles floating through space or laying under foot.

Gus's head popped up next to my feet, his paws scraping at the bench seat, his tongue in full pant.

I tucked my thumbs under his little doggy armpits and yanked him up onto my lap, which wasn't easy with his legs flinging out every which way. Once he was settled into a seated position, I hugged him tight to me and let him lick the bottom of my chin. He licked and licked and I could hear Charles say, *You two are re-PUL-sive*, in fake, drawn-out disgust as he peered down his nose at us.

I missed him. I missed his social awkwardness and his casual contempt of most things. I missed our quiet moments together.

Six minutes later I found myself outside his house.

I crept around to the back and tapped on his bedroom window, not wanting to disturb his parents if they were home. I saw a shadowy movement behind the curtains, and then they slowly drew open. When Charles saw me, he didn't look surprised (who else would it be?). He didn't look anything. His face was best described as perfectly neutral. I noticed he'd buzzed the sides of his Afro into a fade, though. It looked pretty rad. He slid open the window and placed his hands in his pockets. "Yes?" Ice.

"Hi. Sorry. I just . . . I didn't really know where else to go." I could feel my throat closing. I focused squarely on the window frame.

His next words were laced with skepticism. "And you chose here?"

I peered up at him. "Of course I chose here." We held eyes for a second. Then: "I chose someone I trust."

"Where're all your other friends? I'm sure Gordon would love to be your shoulder to lean on."

*Yeesh.* "Charles, I wasn't choosing them over you. It's just—so much happened all at once, and I got caught up in it. I didn't mean to hurt you. But I'm sorry that I did." I could feel my face flush.

"What all happened? Or can't you tell me?" he asked, more uncertain than skeptical now.

I rubbed my eyes. There was so much to say. I didn't even know where to begin.

Seeing my difficulty, he offered, "I guess you can come in . . . if you want."

He walked away from the window and I dragged over the milk crate we used to get in and out of his bedroom in order to sneak out if we needed to. It hadn't been used for a while. I told Gus to stay put and heaved myself up onto the ledge.

Once inside, I just stood aimlessly in front of the window. Charles had flopped onto his bed and was propped on his elbows, staring at his open book, not reading. We stayed like this for a few moments or so.

Finally I tried, "The faucet steadily dripped guilt—plop, plop, plop—until the sink drowned in watery despair. Who would pull the plug and send all wrongdoing where it belonged—into the sewers?"

He turned the page of his book. Then: "And would sewage treatment effectively extricate the organic detritus of human frailty anyway?"

He peered blankly into his book again. I remained a statue at the window.

My knees began to ache, so I finally walked over and knelt by his bed. "Charles, I know that I have no right to unload on you. I just really want you to know that I'm sorry. And I've missed you. So much." I laid my chin on the edge of his bed, trying to replicate the eyes Gus made when he wanted a treat. I threw in a couple of deliberate blinks for good measure.

He scratched his nose. Licked his lips. Glanced sideways.

Finally he closed his book and looked at me. "Don't mistake this for forgiveness, but if you can bring yourself to actually tell me what's going on, I *guess* I could listen and evaluate whether it's truly worth casting your best friend aside like an unloved pair of corduroy pants."

*Ouch. And only moderately fair.* But I let it go. "Okay, but you're gonna need your pants for this story, friend," I said, climbing onto the bed next to him.

After all was said and done, Charles did, indeed, decide there was enough in my story that *most* of my behavior was warranted. I had to give it to him too. Considering the magnitude of my drama—Ginny, Winnow, Gordon (I summed this up as "personal issues I couldn't yet divulge"), Deidre, my dad and Jill and Mom—he remained relatively calm, only crinkling his nose and becoming fidgety once or twice. Mostly, he just nodded and punctuated his listening with a few "Whoas" and "Oh mans." When I finished, he even offered me the rest of the Froot Loops he'd been snacking on, a true peace offering.

I was still reeling from what had just occurred at Jill's place, but sharing everything with Charles in the comfort of this familiar room restored a tiny bit of balance to my dangerously tilting brain.

"Thanks for being so awesome," I said, staring into my hands.

"Thanks for trusting me with all of that . . . finally. And sorry it's all so hard right now." He gave me an awkward but classic "Charles-certified" pat on the back. After a few moments of silence, he said, "But, won't this—us—be too boring for you now? I mean, I don't think I can compete with Deidre and company. You saw what happened when you made me try."

I tapped the back of my hand against his. "You don't have to compete with anyone, pal. I need you as much as I need them. And forcing you to read that poem was a shitty thing for me to do. I thought being someone you weren't—that I wasn't—would help us both. I'm sorry."

He pushed his glasses up his nose for the billionth time.

"You know I'll always love reading on the patio, right?" I said, leaning into him with my shoulder.

Leaning back into me, he replied, "But will you always love buying secondhand underpants, is the real question."

"Always, my friend, always."

"Repulsive, as usual."

"Abrasive—typical." I grinned down at my hands and could feel him doing the same.

"What now?" he asked a moment later.

*Good question.* I thought about the past couple of weeks, and which parts had actually felt good. Which parts had felt like something I wanted more of.

I was surprised at the answer that flickered into view:

boot camp with Deidre, my bearded face in the mirror, two or three brief moments onstage at the Lava Lounge.

I'd told Charles all about my debacle at amateur night and about my stay at Deidre's. "I think I want to try drag for real."

His fidgeting foot stilled. "Even after the 'Dancing in the Dark' fiasco?" he asked.

I nodded.

"Why?"

*Why, indeed.* I tried my best to explain, not comprehending it fully myself. "I guess—I guess it felt different from anything else I've done. Like . . . I had this secret double life, but it was actually my *real* life. And the charge I felt onstage—even though it all went horribly and was probably one of the most embarrassing experiences I've lived through—there was a moment or two when I really just wanted to be there. Like I felt connected . . . with the space, the audience . . . myself." I realized I'd been kneading Charles's bedspread like it was dough while I talked and stopped. I looked at him. "Is that weird?"

His hands, unlike mine, rested flat and still against the quilt. He turned them inward and intertwined his fingers, then rested his head on top of them. "Empirically speaking—absolutely. These are strange things for Nima Kumara-Clark to find motivating. Theoretically, however, I think you always had it in you."

My eyebrows rose. "Really?"

"Yes." He slid off the bed and sat down in front of his

laptop, which was on the floor next to his desk. "Nima, you tried out for the basketball team even though you didn't know the first thing about basketball. You went to a drag show by yourself . . . went after a girl you liked . . . lip-synced on stage at a gay bar. Maybe you weren't completely comfortable doing those things, but you did them anyway. Over and over again."

I scratched my nose. Studied his face. Tried to think of a rebuttal, but couldn't.

Lifting the screen, he asked, "Music?"

"What?"

"What music are you going to use? I think Bruce Springsteen has been done."

The side of my mouth creased into a smile.

We spent the rest of the afternoon lounging on Charles's bedroom floor and searching through his music.

"I feel like the eighties is a good decade to stick with," Charles said, scrolling through his playlist.

I rolled my eyes. "Because I'm a dork, you mean?"

"I just can't see you doing rap"—I laughed out loud at the thought—"or country, or some sort of croony love ballad. And yes, you're also a dork." He paused. "But the kind people could take seriously, if that makes sense."

I frowned. "It doesn't."

"I just think you'd make some kind of fun but smooth eighties tune work. Fortunately, I have a lot of that kind of music, thanks to superior taste." He peered into his laptop, the screen reflecting in his glasses.

"Okay, I'll trust your obvious wisdom in all things drag-related," I said, watching him scrunch up his nose in concentration.

"I may not know much about drag, but I know enough about you."

*True.*

We played song after song by David Bowie, Michael Jackson, Stevie Wonder, and so on. He tested my lip-syncing abilities by playing a song and making me mouth along to it. In the end, Coach Charles seemed satisfied with my performance.

Watching him squinting into his computer, I found myself asking, "Is it okay if Gordon's around a bit? I mean, are you okay with that?"

"Is he still a dick?"

"Yup."

He tapped a few keys. "Things are pretty hard for him, I guess?"

"Yeah."

After a few moments: "I suppose I could give it a go."

We whittled our list down to three songs. Each would require little in the way of coordinated dance moves or complicated costuming, and each also held something appropriate in the lyrics for my current mood and circumstances.

"You know this is all a majorly hypothetical situation we're planning here, right?" I said, closing the laptop.

"Mm-hmm . . . ," he said, nodding his head but clearly not believing me.

Mission complete, we decided to head back to my place. I needed to change my clothes and found myself craving a grilled cheese.

I felt a little bad leaving Gus outside this whole time, but when we rounded the corner to the backyard, he didn't even look up from where he lay baking in the afternoon sun. I had to call him twice and start walking away for him to finally take notice and heave himself after Charles and me.

As we made our way back to my place, an illogical dread of facing the dirty dishes in my empty kitchen again surfaced. I tried to brush the feeling away as I entered my yard.

After the gate completed its customary squeal of indignation, I heard, "Hey, baby girl!" and looked up to see Deidre and Gordon sitting in the porch swing, sipping soda from straws poking out of cans, like two old ladies.

Gordon raised his can at me in a mildly friendly gesture.

"What—where'd you two come from?" I glanced at Charles, who looked like he'd just developed the stomach flu.

"Oh, we've just been driving around, feeling the hot breeze on our faces, and decided to take a cool-drink break on this lovely porch of yours. Hope you don't mind."

Gordon hadn't really been on my list of people I wanted to see right now, but somehow, finding him up there sipping out of a straw with Deidre and seeing Gus bound right up to him—I felt okay about it.

I smiled at them both. "I don't mind."

Deidre rose from the swing seat and leaned over the banister, focusing her attention squarely on Charles, who had slowed to a couple of steps behind me. "And who is this debonair young brother?"

Charles blushed, and I could tell he was trying to hide a smile by sucking in his lips. No one could resist Deidre.

Charles lifted his arm in a floppy, ridiculous wave and I wanted to hug him. "Deidre, this is Charles. Charles, Deidre. And you know Gordon." I tried to keep my voice airy and cheerful for that last part.

Deidre waved Charles over. "Well, get over here and let's have a proper meet, sweetheart!"

Charles looked at me, then at Deidre, and with as much determination as I'd ever seen in his skinny legs, walked straight up the porch steps to meet Deidre, who gathered him up in an enormous hug, leaving Charles to adapt as best he could, not being a hugger and all. After un-smothering him, Deidre looked between Gordon and Charles and said, "You two already know each other, then?"

Gordon gave that annoying head-nod thing he did, like his skull was on a short yo-yo rope, and Charles tried unsuccessfully to mimic it.

"Hmmm, okay . . . ," Deidre murmured, "we'll work on that." She turned away from them and toward me. Using her flattened hand to shield her eyes against the sun, she asked, "How'd things go with your mama, sugar?"

Gordon interrupted, "Uh . . . maybe I should go?" He stood up and started walking down the stairs.

"You don't have to," I said to him, approaching the porch.

"It's cool. I'll go."

"No, really, stay." I touched his arm. He looked at my hand and sat down on the steps. I noticed a smile pass Deidre's lips.

Deidre settled down on the steps as well and patted the space beside her. I sank down between the two of them and stretched my legs out in front of me. Deidre looked up at Charles. "You too, sugar. Plop that butt down over here." He complied, sitting on the top step just behind me and drawing his knees in tight.

I took a deep breath and told Deidre and Gordon all about what had happened that morning at Jill's. Afterward, Deidre gathered me up into her chest, and Gordon even offered a "Sorry, man. That sucks." Funny enough, not one tear dropped from my eyes. Maybe I was all cried out. Or maybe sadness wasn't the central feeling invading my body anymore. I felt loss, but I also felt . . . lighter, a relief *from* loss. My mom leaving definitely sucked. She was gone, again. But the sense of not knowing why was no longer there. I'd maybe never understand exactly what made her leave, even this second time, but I knew that whatever it was, it wasn't about me.

By the time the sprinkler began its skip-and-spray pattern across the yard, I'd moved on from telling them about my mother to sharing my new resolve to get back onstage. After Deidre finished what I could only describe as a very svelte version of a seated hula dance in response to this news, she proceeded to concoct another "big gay agenda" to make it happen.

Part of that agenda included homework. Once Charles and I had shared with Deidre the three song choices we'd picked out, Deidre immediately vetoed two of them. "They just won't do you justice, sugar." Then she tasked Charles with sourcing out an itemized clothing list she made to suit the chosen song.

Deidre instructed Gordon to help Charles, since Gordon had actually seen a drag show, and Charles hadn't. This I knew was a plan devised by Deidre to put these two together, but I thought she was pushing it. Charles's eyes immediately flashed with apprehension. Gordon must have noticed this too, because to my amazement, he offered, "I don't mind helping, if you're cool with that, Charles." Charles considered him for a moment and then shrugged. They made a plan to meet the next day.

Sometimes I wondered if Deidre was secretly an *actual* sorceress.

My job was to listen to the song nonstop until I could lip-sync the lyrics while doing some other activity—"like grating cheese or vacuuming," Deidre said—to prove that the words had "slipped into the nooks and crannies of my brain."

Finally Deidre said I would be expected each night at the church rehearsal space at seven o'clock for practice. Over grilled cheese sandwiches, we began plotting out a loose outline of possible dance moves.

Later that evening, Deidre planted a fervent, wet kiss on each of our cheeks and waved her beautiful hand at us as she zoomed off in her van. Gordon and Charles watched her disappear around the corner, and I wondered if they *both* had a crush on her at this point. After some awkward goodbyes—awkward because this particular grouping of people was an unknown territory for all of us—I walked into my empty kitchen, washed the dirty dishes, changed into my favorite sweats, and tumbled into my own bed for what felt like the first time in weeks, even though it had only been a couple of days. My body sank deep into the mattress, and within minutes, I fell asleep with Gus gently wheezing beside me.

# CHAPTER 17

The next two weeks felt like continuous somersaults: dive headfirst, look up, heave forward, find feet, repeat.

The first plunge I took brought me to Jill's place. I thought about avoiding Jill and my work at the emporium—she'd no doubt let me get away with it. But somehow, it felt like Jill and I were on the same side. She'd been hurt by my mom too, after all, and she *had* tried to encourage a truce between my mom and me, even if it was a complete disaster.

Thus, I found myself in her backyard on Monday morning, staring at her behind as she knelt and dug at some potted plants. She had earbuds in and was poorly singing half sentences of a song I didn't recognize.

"Hey!" I yelled at her butt.

She jumped a little and pulled a bud out of her ear. When she turned to see me, a gigantic smile filled her face and she rose, dusting off her knees. "Hey, doll. I'm so happy to see you." She raised her arms a little, the smile remaining but uncertainty in her eyes.

I shuffled over but paused about a foot away from her. She dropped her arms. I didn't know where to look, so I stared at Jill's work boots, scuffed and dusty with dried soil. A wave of light-headedness crashed over me, and in moments Jill had me in her arms.

Over the next couple of days, Jill and I threw ourselves into work, happy for the distraction. While we lugged slippery plastic bags of soil, watered thirsty plants, and sorted inventory, we said almost nothing to one another, but the silence was an easy one—punctuated with half smiles and slight nods and, every so often, an unanticipated hug in the middle of the storeroom or after loading the truck. They were brief, passing hugs, but they helped us steady one another as we worked through our separate and shared heartaches, and I felt myself slowly regaining some balance.

Dad arrived home on Monday night, in an exhausted, happy stupor from his road trip. Jill and I hadn't talked about whether to tell my dad about the letter or about my mom appearing out of nowhere, but I'd decided for myself that it would only hurt him. Mom hadn't even mentioned my dad at any point. I didn't know where to begin explaining that to him, or to myself, for that matter.

And though a small part of me was still frustrated with

his passivity, and still confused about how much he knew and didn't know, I found myself mostly just yearning to have him home. To have his curly-headed, bighearted self roll his eyes at me and pinch me when I said something sassy.

So when he lumbered through the kitchen door after I'd just arrived home from rehearsing with Deidre, I ignored the niggling in my stomach, gave him an enormous hug, and breathed in—Cheetos, vinyl, sweat. Familiar and comforting.

"What's this?" he asked. "A hug? From my teenage offspring? Has the apocalypse arrived? Is there a new world order?"

I kept my face buried in his thick neck and murmured, "Hush up and be grateful, old man."

One piece of my tumbling, careening life I did share with him the next morning before both of us went to work was that I was helping Deidre with a "project" and would be heading to North Gate each night for a couple of weeks. He seemed curious but remained sensibly nonintrusive. When I told him Gordon Grant would be driving me out there some nights, however, he expressed his surprise.

"Gordon Grant? When did you two become friendly again?"

"Just the past few days. That's what happens when you flit around the countryside with your buddies on irresponsible, middle-aged adventures—you miss all kinds of thrilling stuff." *If you only knew.*

"Yeah, yeah." He filled a glass of water from the faucet. "He's . . . okay to hang out with?"

"Yeah, he's okay. Still a little rough around the edges, but getting there."

"Mmm," he murmured into his glass. "Okay, well, if you need a pickup or drop-off from this old guy . . ."

Watching him sip his drink, his mess of curls pleading for a comb, his toes wriggling at the ends of his Birkenstocks, my chest ached. Despite his own losses, my dad had never made me feel anything but loved.

To his added bewilderment, I kissed him on the cheek and laid my head on his shoulder, my arms wrapping around his waist. "I love you, you old hippie."

My rehearsals with Deidre made our previous boot camp look like a potato-sack race. Her "training" made me feel like I was about to do the Iron Man. Except harder. The Steel Queen. Or Chromium King.

We practiced for an hour each night, Monday to Friday, for two weeks. Deidre used her plentiful connections to secure me a spot at the weekly "Chicks and Chucks" show at Chills bar. Deidre said that Chills attracted a very friendly, mixed crowd, and every show opened with a handful of "virgin sacrifices."

"Don't worry, sugar, 'virgin sacrifices' isn't as sinister as it sounds—all those babies performing will have had a chance to rehearse, like you are, and y'all are a crowd favorite. You'll be loved, I promise."

Though this still put me in a perpetual state of nausea, the thought of sharing myself with a warm audience definitely

sent a thrill up my spine. And the show gave me a finite dead-
line. I was at least confident that in two weeks of rehearsals
with someone like Deidre, things would be . . . no worse than
my last time onstage.

It was easy to see why Deidre was so adored and respected
in the drag community—her patience with my deficiency of
rhythm and coordination impressed me over and over again.
I'm sure with anyone who had an ounce of athleticism or sense
of timing, she could have had them stage-ready in two or three
days. But we spent the first two nights practicing the most
basic of dance moves.

"These here are what I call fillers," Deidre explained,
"steps you can add in whenever needed that still look sharp if
done right."

"Done right," of course, is relative. I discovered that for
Deidre, it meant precise, natural, and fluid—a challenge to my
general way of being. But with Deidre's patience and expertise,
and more importantly, her ability to somehow make all this
sweat and work fun, I slowly managed to acquire some natural
flow for each movement, each step.

Though I'd probably always be a little uncoordinated, and
mostly awkward, this feeling of moving in a way that was new
but also comfortable made me realize I wasn't destined to be
any one way. That was a comfort in itself.

The next day Charles came by to show me the clothes he and
Gordon had found. As I tried on different shirts, I asked him

what he thought of Deidre and Gordon. I hoped he could open himself up to them—especially Gordon—eventually.

He sat on the bed with his back to me. We'd been friends forever, but he'd still never wanted to see me shirtless. After some thought, he ventured, "Deidre is . . . a supernova explosion, *and* the afterglow. Gordon—I don't know. More like . . . dark matter? He managed not to be his usual offensive self when we went searching for clothes yesterday, but he's definitely not charming, either. Or even capable of pleasant, it seems."

"Yeah, he hasn't figured out how to let down his guard yet. I'm hoping Deidre will help with that—if anyone can."

"Agreed."

I wanted to ask him how he felt about the whole Tessa thing too but thought it might still be too fresh in his heart. I tried a general approach. "How are you doing?"

"With what?"

"With . . . whatever."

A few moments of silence. I continued to button my second shirt.

Charles finally spoke. "Well, I'm not sure that costume design is in my future, but at least it's taken my mind off Tessa."

"Yeah?"

"Yeah. I think I'll take up writing poetry full-time instead." He peered over his shoulder and I could see his sly smile.

Throwing a shirt at his back, I said, "Excellent choice." Then: "The right girl will come along, friend. You're a catch."

"That's what I think."

Pushing the last button through its hole, I said, "Okay, you can look. What do you think of this one?" Out of the three shirts he and Gordon had found, this bright tangerine one would best suit my song. The large, sharp collar reminded me of an origami swan, too, and I loved it.

"Snazzy. Gordon said there was a lot of leather at the show the other night. Should we find you a leather jacket or something?"

"Um, no, I don't think so. But I will need a jacket—something bright like this shirt, and fitted. Think you can find one?"

He collapsed dramatically across my bed. "Ugh. More shopping? With Gordon? Please, no."

I laughed. "All right, all right. You've proven your friendship. I'll see if Deidre can find a jacket." I looked down at my raggedy jean shorts. "Okay, what've you got for pants? Please don't say corduroys."

"Okay, sugar, week one was all about the basics, because you know, you gotta learn to walk before you can boogie."

Deidre stood facing the giant mirror in the church basement, her bare feet shoulder-width apart and her arms hanging loosely at her sides. Today she wore tight black exercise pants and a gray sweatshirt with the sleeves and neck cut out. A black durag covered her head, and hoop earrings the size of bangles looped from her ears. She could have been a professional dancer for all I knew.

I was next to her, trying my best to look as relaxed as she did. "Jungle Boogie" bumped and rolled out of the speakers at max volume.

"But now we're done walking—it's time to boogie." Her pelvis began bouncing around in a tight circle to the beat. "It's time to let all the choreography and precision fall away. . . ."

Without warning, she slumped over so her head almost touched the floor, and then she flung her arms out wide. Her arms started rippling as though water moved through them. Pivoting on one foot, she stamped around in a circle, then raised her torso back up, sending waves through her entire body as she did. Before I could close my mouth, she grabbed me and spun me around so many times I almost flopped to the floor from dizziness, but my hand remained firmly gripped in hers and she pulled me back toward her.

Taking my other hand, she raised our arms up and swayed them back and forth. "Here we go, honey! Let the funk move through you!"

She let go of me, closed her eyes, and allowed her body to do whatever it wanted to. Without her guiding me, I felt a little self-conscious, but it was hard not to get drawn in by her energy. I tried closing my eyes too, and then let my whole body go loose, focusing on just the music—dipping with the bass, vibrating with the horns, mouthing the gravelly voice.

When the scat part started, I opened my eyes and they met with Deidre's. We mirrored each other's wide grins and boogied toward one another, singing our own versions of the unrestrained, throaty sounds emanating from the speakers. When the Tarzan yell let loose at the end, we screamed at the top of our lungs too and dissolved into hysterics.

Eventually, I shared more than a clue or two with Jill. I couldn't help it. After her revelation that she'd hung out with a drag crowd herself, I became increasingly curious about her experiences. I broke our comfortable silence one day as we shoveled dirt from the back of her truck into Mr. Karim's garden, my muscles still sore from my "workouts" with Deidre. "So, what was drag like . . . back in the Stone Age?" I asked with a grin.

She paused to lean on her shovel. "You laugh, smart-ass, but those days *do* feel like another lifetime." She gazed into the air in front of her, a smile playing on her lips. "It was fun, though. Those people really knew how to have a good time. It was one of the only places I felt like I could just be a nut."

"So why'd you stop hanging out with them?"

"I moved here to start my business. Not much of a drag scene in Bridgeton, as you know." She crossed her eyes at me.

"No. Not much," I agreed.

"I used to pop over to North Gate once in a while for a show, but I guess I lost a bit of my motivation after—" She looked up at me uncertainly.

"After Mom?"

Jill nodded and kicked at her shovel.

For some reason, Deidre's flailing arms and our Tarzan yells from the night before sprang up in my mind. "Jill, I think it's okay for us to—" *To what?* "To . . . change things up."

She tilted her head and raised her eyebrows. "Oh yeah? And what might that mean?" she asked, leaning her shovel against the truck.

What *did* that mean? "I guess . . . I think it means—we deserve to have a little fun? To let loose?" I grinned at her.

Jill's face perked up in a mixture of confusion and amusement.

"I—I may be doing a drag show on Saturday," I blurted. Saying it out loud made it feel awfully close . . . and real.

Jill's face lit up. "A show? You're doing drag?"

I laughed nervously and nodded.

"Nima! Are you kidding me? Where? Do I get to come? Please?" But then she held her palms out facing me and wagged them side to side. "No, no—never mind. You don't have to tell me anything. I understand if you want this just for yourself." She dug her hands into her pockets and thumped the heel of her boot against the gravel to knock the dirt off.

"Jill, you goof, I'd love you to be there."

"Really?"

"Really."

A grin burst across her face. "Then I'll be there."

Three times in the first week, Gordon drove me to and from rehearsals, and he continued to do so the second week. He would drop me off, awkwardly allow Deidre to give him a Deidre-size hug, then wander off to who-knows-where for an hour while we practiced. He'd appear again a few minutes after eight and awkwardly stand near the door while we finished up.

He definitely acted weird around Deidre, but not in an entirely bad way. He'd blush a lot, then scowl, and sometimes he'd shy away from her touch but other times almost seem to nudge up against her. I could tell he was enamored with her somehow—whether it was in a romantic way or not didn't seem to matter. The fact that Gordon Grant had made friends with a drag queen and treated her with the respect she deserved was the big news.

He and I hadn't spoken about what he'd shared since the night of nachos and drag bingo, but a couple of incidents told me he and Deidre had been communicating outside of our time together—like when Deidre handed him a book as we left rehearsal one day, saying, "That's the one I told you about." Or when Deidre was a couple of minutes late for rehearsal, and Gordon mentioned she had "some appointment" that afternoon, like he'd grown familiar with her schedule.

At one point, Deidre asked him to take some film and photos as we rehearsed, "to get a look at what needs fixin' *and* for posterity, of course." But I think it was her way of getting him to use a camera more—to let him play with his artistic side a bit without having to hide it. We borrowed Charles's fancy camera, and though Gordon was a little reticent at first, by the end of rehearsal, he was even calling out a few directions in his usual tactless style.

I noticed his wardrobe was changing ever so slightly too—

more slim-fit shirts and tighter pants versus ripped, faded T-shirts and drooping jeans. No doubt a touch of Deidre emboldening his closet.

Gordon was still Gordon—moody, sometimes mean, and completely inappropriate at least half the time. But I couldn't be happier for him.

Midway through the final week of rehearsals, I told Deidre I was taking her to dinner—a meager thank-you for all her patience and wisdom.

After cooling down from a frenetic boogie session, we drove to a modest diner Deidre said was a "gem in the rough" and sat at the counter on old-fashioned barstools. Once we'd ordered, Deidre excused herself to the washroom, leaving me to sip my water and twirl aimlessly on my stool. On the third twirl, long, silky hair in one of the booths opposite the counter caught my eye. Her back was to me, but I had no doubt it was Winnow.

I continued my rotation back to the counter and placed my hands flat on its surface. She was with someone, but I hadn't registered who. I hadn't seen her or communicated with her since the Lava Lounge, not that I hadn't thought about her each and every day.

*What to do?*

I took a huge gulp of water, tucked a curl behind my ear, and slid off my seat. Deidre was just exiting the washroom as I crossed the floor to the other side. Catching my eye, she tilted her head in a question. Following my glance to Winnow, she mouthed, "Ahh" my way and blew me a kiss.

I noticed now that Winnow was with Devi, which almost made me turn back to the counter, but Devi saw me, and I mustered up a smile, adding a deep breath on top.

Winnow turned to look at me as I stepped up to their table, her eyebrows relaying surprise, but a not entirely unpleasant look passed over her face.

"Hey," I offered.

"Hey, Nima," Winnow replied, the hint of a question in her greeting.

I looked to Devi. "Hi, Devi. How's it going?"

She glanced at Winnow, then back to me, a slight tug at her lips. "Good, good. You?"

"I'm pretty good." I stared at the food on Devi's plate for a moment. *What now?* With Devi here, things were a bit tricky, and I could tell from her crossed arms that she wasn't about to give me any time alone with Winnow.

*Fuck it.*

I turned away from Devi and leaped. "Winnow, I've been thinking a lot about you and I just want you to know . . . I'm sorry. I've been a bit of a mess, and I didn't know—I *still* don't know—what I'm doing. But I'm starting to figure things out, I think, and . . ." I paused to think through my next words. "And if you could ever forgive me for being such an ass"—her eyes smiled at this, which made me smile—"then I'd love to hang out with you again sometime." I swallowed. Glanced at

Devi. Forced myself to look back at Winnow. Took the next plunge. "Actually, I'm performing at Chills on Saturday night, if you're interested." Laughing in my usual awkward way, I added, "Don't worry . . . I rehearsed this time."

Devi coughed, but Winnow paid her no mind. Her eyes stayed with mine as she nodded and said, "That's really cool, Nima. I'm not sure I can make it, but I'll see."

It wasn't a yes, but it wasn't a no, either, and somehow, I was okay with the uncertainty. I'd said what I needed to say. I couldn't do much else but give her the space to take it in and decide what she wanted to do.

I nodded back. "Cool." I glanced back at Deidre, who was not-so-subtly twirling in *her* seat now, sipping her drink and smiling at me. "I should get back to that lovely lady over there, but it was really good to see you," I said, giving Winnow one more smile.

She waved to Deidre and replied, "You too, Nima."

When I was settled back on my barstool, Deidre reached over and squeezed my hand. "Now, that's the boogie I'm talkin' 'bout, girl."

Thursday. Two more days until show day. I woke up feeling like someone was making scrambled eggs in my stomach. Sleeping wasn't much of an option these last few days, but I didn't feel tired. Nervous, excited, horrified, incredulous . . . but not tired.

Deidre found me the perfect jacket—a shiny, electric-blue piece with fat black buttons and velvet lining. Against one another, the tangerine shirt and blue jacket busted out at you like a 3-D image. Deidre had even taken the time to stitch some sweet crown designs into the lapels—"accents fit for a king."

Charles, like a champ, slogged back to Old Stuff on his own. He was careful to go when Ginny wasn't working, just to avoid any unnecessary tension on my behalf. But to be honest—I was over it. It wasn't Ginny's fault she liked guys, and even if she did kiss me out of curiosity, I can't say I'd take back the moment if I could.

Charles managed to find matching blue pants—the color wasn't exact, but Deidre said it was close enough. With the shoes and sunglasses Deidre found in her secret stash of drag paraphernalia at the church, my ensemble was complete.

For Friday's rehearsal—the last one with Deidre before the show—Deidre made sure I did full dress and makeup so I knew what it would feel like to perform with my boobs flattened by an ultra-tight tensor bandage (it was definitely harder to breathe) and a rolled-up sock down my pants (definitely trickier to dance). As annoying as boobs can be, I'd choose them over a penis any day.

Deidre also made me bring both Gordon and Charles to watch. She said I needed an audience before I stepped in front of the real one on Saturday.

I couldn't think of anything worse than having both Gordon and Charles watch me perform, but as with everything, I trusted Deidre and sucked it up.

After she dimmed the lights in the basement to make me more comfortable, she whispered, "Remember how filthy cute you are, girl," shot Gordon and Charles severe warning looks, and hit play on the stereo.

After an initial resurgence of nausea, I used the mantra Deidre taught me to get into "boogie mode": *Laugh at yourself. Laugh at others. Let them laugh at you. And dance, dance, dance like a goddamn fool.* Then I just let the music move through me.

As the last chords of the song faded out, Deidre squealed and popped up from the couch where she'd been nestled in between Gordon and Charles. She leaped across the floor like I'd seen her do a hundred times and swept me up in her arms. I was hot, sweaty, and out of breath, but my performance felt tight and smooth. I looked over Deidre's shoulder at Gordon and Charles. They both clapped, but in a dazed kind of way— slowly and sporadically.

Deidre released me and twirled to face the couch. "Well, what d'ya all think?"

Gordon stared at his knees. Charles pushed his glasses back up the bridge of his nose. Both suddenly had overactive Adam's apples.

"C'mon, you two, don't be shy!" Deidre encouraged, squeezing my shoulder.

Charles spoke first. "I—I can't believe that's you, Nima." He pushed at his glasses again. "In a good way, I mean. I mean . . . I like the regular you too, but this you is—"

"Fucking rad." Gordon was still staring at his knees, but his smirk had appeared. "Seriously. Fucking. Rad."

Charles looked at him, then back at me. "Yeah. What he said."

Deidre just about choked me with her next squeeze, and I just about suffocated from disbelief.

# CHAPTER 18

Charles, Gordon, and I piled into Gordon's beast around five o'clock. Jill was going to meet us there, since Saturday was her busiest day at the shop. Our plan was to hang out at Deidre's, have some dinner (not that I could eat), and get ready there so I could sort myself out in a comfortable, calm setting.

The reality was this: I was a hot mess.

Sitting between Charles and Gordon on the drive to Deidre's, I insisted on playing my song over and over until Gordon finally yanked my phone from the cord and threw it at Charles's feet. Charles pretended not to notice and just looked out the window. I folded my arms across my chest and sang the words at the top of my lungs for the rest of the trip.

At Deidre's, I locked myself in her bedroom, which had a giant mirror in it, while everyone else ate pizza in the kitchen. I shoved my earbuds in and lip-synced the words to my song over and over in the mirror, making sure each word left my lips perfectly, and then I walked through my steps several times.

Through the music, I heard a knock at the door, then Gordon's voice. "Uh, hey. Deidre says to get out here. She has a surprise or something."

"Okay—be out in a minute."

Sitting on the edge of the bed, facing the mirror, I paused the music and closed my eyes.

I thought of the first drag show I'd seen—the ambiguous conjoined duo, the flowing hair and fairy wings, the elegant queen, and of course, the poetic punk transformed into sultry gentleman.

I hoped I could be as captivating as them. As magical. As sexy. At one of our rehearsals, Deidre shared that for her, the magic in another king's or queen's performance happened when you could see that they only wanted to be right where they were. It was like they were caught up in a story they were telling *and* acting out. The story was unfolding every moment, and the storyteller wanted nothing more than to peel back a page and step onto the next one. And they wanted the audience to come along with them.

I thought about the story I would tell that night. I wondered if people would understand it and want to come along for the ride.

"Okay, lovey, I have one silly surprise and one that I hope you'll love as much as I did when I received it." Deidre stood at the kitchen counter with one hand behind her back. "Silly one first." She danced over until she stood right in front of me and then drew out her hand, which held a shiny purple bag.

I took the bag from her and peeked inside, not entirely sure this wouldn't be incredibly embarrassing and trying to figure out what it was before making it visible to everyone.

But Deidre grew impatient with me and dipped her hand into the opening. She plucked out the cloth contents and snapped her wrist to unfold the item. When she grabbed the other corner and pulled the two ends outward, I could see it was a pair of black underpants, with a silver crown on the crotch area and colorful jewels bedazzling the crown.

I looked from the underpants to Deidre's gigantic smile and couldn't help but let out a loud guffaw.

"Those . . . are going to be the coolest pair of underpants I own."

Deidre held them in front of her own crotch and wiggled her hips back and forth. "You're damn right they are. You have to wear them tonight, of course. They'll be your good-luck undies." She flung them at me and I caught them with my face.

Gordon and Charles were trying really hard to continue eating their pizza like nothing was happening.

"Okay, next!" Deidre hollered. "Now, this is something one of my dear, dear friends gave me when I was just a wee drag queen starting out. It reminds me that when I'm per-forming, I can soar, honey! I'm bigger than that stage, bigger than the room itself." She reached behind her neck and undid the clasp of her chain. Then she reached behind my neck and fastened it again.

"You're giving me your necklace?" I asked, pulling at the silver wings with my fingers so I could see them.

"I am." She placed her hands on my shoulders and crouched to look me in the eyes. "But they come with great responsibility, you hear me?"

That was what I was afraid of. But: "I hear you."

She gave me a hug, then turned to Gordon and Charles. "Well, sugarplums, Miss Nima here and I are retreating to the boudoir to get ready. You two keep yourselves busy. Play some music or something."

Gordon and Charles glanced sideways at each other. Then both reached for another slice of pizza.

Deidre helped me dress, wrapping my chest in the tensor bandage and making sure my shirt and suit sat just so on my body. She also managed, with some sort of Deidre-style wizardry, to work my frizzy curls into a sleek, wavy coif. She let me stuff my own pants, though, which I appreciated.

When she pulled out her makeup kit to do my face, I stretched out my hands in front of me. She looked at my hands, then at me, one eyebrow raising in a question.

"Can I try?" I asked. "I think I want to do it myself. Gotta learn sometime, right?" My shoulders lifted into a shrug.

She smiled. In royal fashion, she leaned forward from her

waist, one toe pointed out to the ground in front of her, and placed the kit in my hands. Then she bestowed a kiss on my forehead and left me alone in the room.

Facing the mirror, I began brushing and contouring, drawing and smudging, just as Deidre had shown me. Abandoning the sponge, I used my fingers to work the makeup into my skin, along my chin, cheekbones, brow. The creamy feel of skin to makeup to skin was somehow soothing, calming. As I applied each layer, I could feel my body relaxing into itself—my forehead smoothed out, my jaw loosened, my shoulders dropped.

And then the details. A small, neat soul patch just beneath my lower lip, a thin mustache that curved over the edges of my mouth, slightly extended sideburns. I filled out my eyebrows a bit and placed a decisive mole on my left cheek. Each stroke, each point a fierce little transformation of its own.

When I was finished, I put the makeup away and peered into the mirror.

There was just no metaphor for it: I looked *good*.

When Deidre came in to check on my progress, she halted in the doorway and placed her hands on her hips, uttering a "Hey nah" and giving me an up-down. Then, her head shifting a little to the right, she let out an emphatic "MMM" and yelled over her shoulder to whoever was listening, "I have a prince in my bedroom, y'all!"

After she gave me a tight but careful hug, she did her own face and dress—"I'm going out and loud for you tonight, girl."

This meant a full black Afro wig and a yellow pantsuit that looked so perfect on her it made me want to die and come back a pantsuit just so I could look like that. Accessorized with chunky black-and-gold jewelry and strappy, gleaming black heels, she was sun, sky, stars, and night all at once.

But for the first time, I didn't feel woefully underdressed next to her.

When we came back out into the living room, where Charles and Gordon had occupied themselves with Deidre's record collection, Charles actually froze and didn't break his gaze for a full minute, while Gordon took one look and immediately diverted his attention to the record in his hands.

"The Orange Crush is now departing, y'all! Time to bring the party to the people!" Deidre threw a feather boa at Gordon and a leather tie to Charles, told them both they had no choice, and ushered us out the door with several wind-mill snaps.

Chills, just around the corner from the Lava Lounge, was a significantly smaller venue, but contrary to its name, much cozier. It consisted of a square room with a small, circular stage in one corner, a four-sided bar in the middle, and a dance floor in between that looked like it could fit about twenty people. Multicolored icicle lights hung from the bar counters and along the darkened windows that made up one side of the room. A massive mirror engulfed another wall, making the space look bigger than it was.

When we arrived, several things lowered my anxiety considerably. One, eighties music blasted from the sound system. Two, the crowd appeared very mixed—a variety of genders and ages and colors, and people dressed in everything from full drag to jeans and T-shirts. Lastly, at least six people turned and smiled at us as we entered. Maybe this was because we were with Deidre, or because of my amazing blue suit and sweet 'do, but whatever the reason, I immediately felt more at ease.

That ease lasted about twelve minutes.

After Deidre took me over to the DJ to give her my music and instructions and we'd returned to the table where we'd left Gordon and Charles, my eyes shifted around the bar to see who made up my audience. When I scanned past the entrance, Chills finally lived up to its name, because my sight line froze and my skin rose into goose bumps.

Winnow.

She stood talking to the bouncer, smiling that sweet smile and gesturing with her hands to emphasize something she said. Dressed simply in a loose green tank top, artfully torn jeans, and Timberland boots, she still managed to detonate a grenade in my chest.

Deidre caught me staring and said, "That's your girl, innit?"

I shook my head. "Not mine, no."

"She could be by the end of tonight."

My heart rose to my throat. "I don't think so."

Deidre leaned in and tugged playfully at my ear. "I think so. She's here, in't she?"

*She's here.*

"I know I invited her! But now what do I *do*?" I pleaded, as Deidre touched up my makeup backstage. Three other "sacrifices" were back there as well—one busy wriggling into their costume, another with earbuds in and lip-syncing to their music, and a third obsessively combing back their bouffant. The space was barely big enough for everyone, but Deidre easily carved out an opening for us in front of an oval mirror on the wall.

"If anything, honey, you should be turning up the heat with her here." She peered into my eyes. "Come on, would you really want her to walk out right now?"

*Fair point.* I was simultaneously anxious and spectacularly gleeful that she was here. I wanted to hide, but I also wanted to impress the hell out of her.

"Nima, you're a hot little drag king, and she'd have to be an ice queen not to fall all over herself when she sees you." Deidre turned to the mirror and added a dab of eyeliner to her own eyes. "Trust me, girl. I see the future, and she's right behind you." She found my eyes in the mirror and nodded slightly to her left. I looked past our reflections and saw Winnow standing behind us, just at the entrance to the backstage area. Our eyes located each other's, and both my real and mirrored self just about cracked in two.

Deidre quickly packed the makeup into her case, patted me on the butt, and bustled out, placing her hand briefly on Winnow's shoulder as they passed each other.

I was still staring at Winnow through the mirror, wondering if objects were really closer than they appeared, because it looked like Winnow was getting pretty close.

"Hey, Nima."

*Deep breath.* "Hey, Winnow." Saying her name out loud felt like some kind of radical act—like by just saying it, I could make the night go any way I wanted it to. I finally turned to face her.

"You look amazing," she offered, reaching out to tug at one of my lapels.

I tried not to think about her fingers touching my clothing. "Thanks. It's all Deidre."

She did that head-tilt thing that knocked my heart over every time. "Not all."

"Are you . . . here with anyone? Boyd? Devi?" I asked, still trying to find words.

"No, just me." That silky hair. Those eyes. The lips.

"Oh." *Come on, Nima, you got this.* "I'm kind of surprised you came."

"Yeah? You thought I wouldn't?" That half smile.

"I wasn't sure. I wouldn't have blamed you if you didn't."

"But I'm here."

"You're here." *Mouth. Move. Lungs. Breathe.* "What made you come?"

TANYA BOTEJU

She placed both hands on my lapels, hanging on this time. "What do you think?"

"Because . . . you missed Deidre?" I smiled.

A laugh. "Yeah. That too." She dropped her hands but remained close. "And . . . because I don't mind people making mistakes if they own up to them. I've made plenty myself."

I hadn't even realized it was there, but a final weight lifted from my heart as I listened to Winnow say those words, allowing me to say, "Well, it would be a mistake not to tell you . . . I'm really happy to see you. And . . . I'd love to see you more."

"Yeah, I'd like that too."

I think we both gulped. I know I did.

"You nervous?" she asked.

No sense pretending. I'd done enough of that already. "Absolutely. Any tips?"

She brushed an invisible piece of fluff off my shoulder. "Just do your thing, girl." I watched her mouth spread into a smile.

Objects were definitely very close.

Unfortunately, I had to cut our reunion short when the emcee came backstage and said it was five minutes to show-time. Winnow—to my utter joy—gave me a soft, slow peck on the cheek, lingered long enough to whisper, "Good luck" in my ear, and disappeared out front.

The emcee had to snap his fingers in front of my face to get my attention again.

"All right, everyone—you ready?"

Was I?

*Laugh at yourself. Laugh at others. Let them laugh at you. And dance, dance, dance like a goddamn fool.*

Over and over I said Deidre's mantra as I made my way onto the stage, took my position, and waited for the music to start. Over, and over, and over.

Standing with my back to the audience, I drew my sunglasses from the inner pocket of my jacket, slipped them over my ears, and let out a long, steady breath.

When the music started—all writhing, tempting groans and the scratchy shriek I could feel coming from the depths of my gut even though I was only lip-syncing it—I didn't even have to think. My body responded to the plucks and grinds of the guitar, Prince's creamy voice, and each whack of the drum like the music was somehow inside of me. Deidre's choreography moved through me the way she'd intended— smooth, natural, simple but sensual.

I mouthed the words like they were my own and toyed with the audience like they were mine too. The stage didn't hold me for long—by the time the second chorus poured from my mouth, I was sashaying past the couples leaning against the wall, pausing to give a few lucky souls a moment of my attention, brushing my hand across an arm or a cheek.

A hip bump with Deidre sent her laughter over the thumping music, and I made sure to lift my shades and throw a couple of winks to Gordon and Charles, enjoying their blushes.

Jill's face appeared behind them—her jaw practically dropping to her chest, her eyes wide and blinking hard. I blew her a kiss. She shook her head and placed her hand over her heart.

As I rounded the mirrored side of the bar and caught my reflection, I mouthed the next few lyrics to myself: *"Do your dance / Why should you wait any longer? / Take a chance / It could only make you stronger."*

The audience loved it—their hoots and whistles sizzled through my body and sent me to a whole new level of daring, just in time for my swagger to find Winnow, and just as the final, breathy words of the song repeated themselves—a plea and an order all at once.

I removed my glasses and let my eyes sink into hers. She watched me, a close-mouthed smile tugging at her lips. As I shimmied in closer, I placed a hand on her hip, exploring the possibilities of the moment. Her hand fell on top of mine. She mouthed, "Body part?" with a peaked eyebrow and sassy smile.

I looked at her lips. Her tongue appeared, wetting them. I let the lyrics fall away. I brought my mouth to hers.

The soft stick of cushiony lips. The honeyed taste of an unsurpassable moment.

We parted slowly, and our eyes opened into one another's.

"Right there," I lip-synced, placing my finger on the smooth indentation between her collarbones and allowing a cheeky grin to follow.

When my fingertip touched her skin, Winnow's lips fell into an easy, open laughter, and I could see the future too.

# ACKNOWLEDGMENTS

I am humbled to live and work on lands belonging to the Musqueam, Squamish, and Tsleil-Waututh First Nations, and I acknowledge their stories and histories that existed long before my own.

So many people contributed to this book, but heartfelt and boisterous applause to my J-Team—my agent Jim McCarthy and editor Jennifer Ung ("Jeditor"). You two have been my hilarious, smart, and enthusiastic supporters throughout, and I feel blessed to have had you on my side. You got from the start what this book meant to me and what I hoped it would mean to others. It's your commitment to diversity in literature (and love for dogs) that brought us together, I'm sure of it.

To the entire magnificent team at Simon Pulse—my experience has felt seamless, and I'm sure it's due to the expertise and enthusiasm of each and every department, from editing to sales to marketing to publicity to production! Thank you also to Emily Hutton for pitching *Kings* for Indies Introduce. And special shout-outs to Sarah Creech and Marina Esmeraldo for their energetic cover illustration and design. You saw the hoped-for joy in the book and managed to put it into color and images!

To the funny and smart Eileen Cook, mentor extraordinaire—thank you for "un-sticking" me when I needed help, offering generously of your time and expertise, and continuing to support me way past the expiry date. And thank you to The Writer's Studio at Simon Fraser University, which provided me with the inspiration, structure, and community to finish this book.

To my "adult" beta-readers (though "adult" might be pushing it)—Christy Dunsmore, Joanne Darrell Herbert, Heather van der Hoop, Ly Hoang, Zosia Dorcey, Jessica Lemes da Silva, Cynthia Huijgens, and Jared Baird—thank you for your insights, suggestions, time, and support. You are everywhere in this book!

And again to Joanne, my Deidre in real life—a magical queen who's there when I need her. Thank you for your excitement and love for this book and for me, my dear friend.

To my "young adult" beta-readers—Anaheed Saatchi (sorry, you'll always be a young adult to me), Alannah Safnuk, Tammy Do, Elise Marchessault, and Emily He—I am so lucky to have taught such wise, thoughtful people. You blew me away with your perceptive, sensitive (and blunt) thoughts on the manuscript. The student definitely becomes the teacher!

To my English 11/12 class for helping me choose between "threw up," "barf," or "vomit." Because: diction!

To the students I've been surrounded by and who I've had

the pleasure of teaching at York House, thank you for continually reminding me how smart and funny, wise and powerful teenagers are. You've taught me more than I've taught you, I'm sure, and I couldn't have written this book without these past sixteen years.

To all my educator peeps who understand how important it is to challenge outdated norms and to continually learn so we don't become those outdated norms—thank you for the work you do. I'm inspired every day by your commitment to young people and to our diverse communities.

To Cafe Deux Soleils and its staff, I wrote most of this book in your booths, eating your food, and drinking your beer. Thanks for remaining Wi-Fi-free. And for staying more Commercial Drive and less . . . those other places.

To the Screaming Weenies, the Brown Brother Posse, and all the other drag folks who made my twenties wild and magical. This book wouldn't exist without you or any of the other kings, queens, and in-betweens who inspire, entertain, and challenge through their art.

To my family—Amma, Thatha, Karen, and Charmaine—for supporting me through this whole process and for your enthusiasm, even though you didn't know what the heck I was writing about. My work ethic grew from this family, and it got this book written!

To so many friends and relatives who have put up with my incessant online posts about this overwhelming and exciting process, who have asked and prodded and applauded and supported—your encouragement has meant the world to me, whether you know it or not.

To you, the readers, for reading books! Keep doing it.

To my Jennifer: you have been my biggest cheerleader—allowing me to read out loud to her and maybe even enjoying it, making me personalized "books" swag, cooking me good food when I just needed to write . . . but most of all for understanding my need to "go into the zone," even though it sometimes means less time for us. You live Deidre's mantra, never afraid to laugh out loud or dance like a fool. Your full, open heart inspires me all the time.

TURN THE PAGE FOR A SNEAK PEEK AT
TANYA BOTEJU'S NEXT NOVEL

Endless stippling spread across my bedroom ceiling, tiny bumps of white pushing back at me like thousands of stubby, pointing fingers.

*Fuck you, stubby bumps.*

Lying faceup on my bed, I glared hard at the ceiling for a few moments before extending my left arm above me and bringing my hand down—hard—against my headboard. The ritual, started a year and a half ago, sent a familiar sting through my palm, a kind of shield against the day ahead. I'd feel the bruising every time I held a mug or grabbed my backpack strap, whenever I pushed open a door, clutched an apple. The pain was something to focus on—like a messed-up stress ball to squeeze whenever I needed it.

I wasn't proud of this thing I'd come to depend on—far from it—but the need to do it was so overwhelming sometimes that knowing I'd feel shitty about it afterward wasn't enough to stop me from doing it. It was protection against other people discovering all the rot in my gut. It was punishment. It was proof I could handle everything on my own.

I forced myself out from the covers and placed my feet on the carpet. Fall air slipped through my open window, crisp and biting.

For a moment, I let the chill lift my skin into goose bumps and stared at my bare thighs spreading across the edge of the mattress. Two quarter-size bruises decorated the middle of my left thigh, and a larger one curved around the outside of my right. I lifted my feet into the air and admired a shin bruise from a week ago. The bruise was barely visible now, its darkness lightening and almost hidden against my brown skin. But I knew it was still there from the painful tenderness when I pressed my fingers into it, which I did now, closing my eyes to let the pain sink in.

"Daya Doo Wop! It's almost eight and you can't be late again! It's still September and you've been in detention once already . . . remember?"

*Jesus.*

My uncle's singsongy voice surged through both my bedroom door and my quiet moment, each sentence rising into a high note. He knew better than to come in, but he still thought these cheerful reminders would help get me going faster.

"I'm up!" I called back, swallowing back the other words constantly threatening to escape from my mouth: *Leave. Me. Alone.*

Handling my uncle and aunt demanded a balancing act: Keep our interactions light and consistent so they didn't worry about me, but discourage excessive interaction in case they mistook it for intimacy. Keep my head above water at school, but not so far above that they got excited about my prospects. Date boys like a "normal teenage girl," but not for too long and not the type my aunt and uncle would approve of. Go to counseling, but only to make them feel better. Get involved, but not too involved.

I listened as Uncle Priam's footsteps receded down the hallway, practically skipping across the hardwood. He and Aunt Vicki were now my official guardians. The paperwork had been finalized recently, after a painful, slow process following my parents' deaths. Priam was my dad's brother, but I'm sure when my parents named him and my aunt my godparents, Priam and Vicki never thought they'd actually have to take me into their home and look after me.

That's just what they've been doing these past many months, though. And they must have learned their version of parenting in theater school, where they met, because I felt like I was in an epic musical most of the time.

P.S. I hate musicals.

If my uncle and aunt weren't singing duets at the dinner table, they were playing dress-up. They were forever trying to get me to watch all these old-timey musicals on TV with them, and a while ago they'd tried to give me singing lessons for my birthday. I pretended to go for six weeks, but in reality I was at the skateboard park.

It was clear we didn't get each other. So my balancing act was as much for them as it was for me—aim for coexistence and not much more. Don't waste their time or mine.

I stood up and stretched, my body aching from an extra-long skateboarding session the day before. Skateboarding kept me muscular, and having more muscle meant experiencing more soreness, which was perfect for me. I lived for that ache. And I liked seeing my body stay thick and strong too. My muscles made me feel like I could defend myself—but also invite pain when I needed to. I pulled on my jeans and hoodie, both protecting and preparing myself for the day ahead.

"Butterfly, you *must* understand!" Vicki implored.

"But honey, it's *Pinter.*" Priam was sitting beside me at the kitchen table, hands out in a plea, face in an impressive sulk.

If it were up to me, mealtimes would look like me eating on the way to somewhere else. But good old Priam and Vicki insisted we eat as many meals together as possible. As part of my balancing act, I relented. But I paid for it.

At breakfast, I usually had to sit through a truncated version of some kind of drama. Sometimes it was real-life drama, sometimes it was an elaborate, fictional kind. Today I was treated to the real-life sort, although it was still hard to believe. Priam had, apparently, booked tickets to see a play that, apparently, was on the same night as Vicki's Glee Girls' Night—a monthly excuse for her and her friends to sit around singing show tunes while drinking wine and cognac.

Currently, Vicki was flapping around the kitchen, banging

cupboards, moving food around for no particular reason, sighing with the weight of a thousand grievances. "That is not the capital *P Point*, Priam! You *know* how deeply I feel about my Glee Girls. How *full* they fill my spirits. You *know*."

"Of course I know, darling." Priam collapsed against the back of his chair, arms falling to his sides. "But it was the only night with tickets still available. What was I to do?" he questioned, his voice gliding upward to its maximal plaintive whine.

Now Vicki swept to the chair beside him, yanking it out and sitting on its edge with a small bounce. She took his hand and held it in both of hers, peering into his face. "Sweetheart. You do what is *right*. What is *needed*. For *you*. For *me*. You buy *one* ticket. You go experience *Pinter*. You share him with me *afterward*. *That* is what you *do*." She punctuated these rousing words with a desperate kiss to Priam's hand.

Leaning my cheek in my palm and working a piece of apple with my jaw, I stared blankly at the scene unfolding in front of me. I wish I could say this was an atypical morning at the Wijesinghe household, but . . . it wasn't.

As the denouement of this particular episode came to a close, they kissed and made up—also typical (and gross)—and once again remembered I was sitting at the same table. I didn't mind their episodes entirely—it limited the amount of time they were focused on me, at least.

Unfortunately, Vicki focused on me now and her face ballooned in excitement. My jaw halted mid-chew, my defensive shield rising. "Daya! Are you free? Next Thursday? *You* could have my ticket!" She turned back to Priam, his hand still in hers. "Wouldn't that be a capital *S* Solution, darling?"

Priam didn't look quite as certain. "Well . . . it's *Pinter*, Vicki. He might be a little . . . highbrow for someone so young, don't you think?"

Priam wasn't really worried about my capacity to understand Pinter. He and Vicki loved forcing me to experience arts and culture. He was freaking out at the thought of being alone with me for three hours. And I got it. I didn't really want to sit around watching some boring play with him for three hours either.

Both Vicki and Priam preferred dealing with me as a tag team. The few occasions I'd had to spend time alone with either of them, we'd filled it awkwardly—trying to find some common ground.

But we'd failed. Every. Time.

I took another bite of my apple and sputtered my reply through a mess of pulp, because I knew it drove them nuts. "I'm busy that night. Sorry." A piece of apple flopped to the table.

Priam's chest rose and fell in relief while Vicki stared at the fallen apple, a hint of repulsion skimming her mouth.

When I made to leave the table, taking the rest of my apple and a piece of toast to go, Vicki shook the mild disgust from her face and thrust out her hand in my direction without actually touching me (she knew better). "Daya, maybe we could spend some time together"—she glanced reassuringly at Priam—"the *three* of us, this weekend? I feel like we never see you!"

*Precisely.* "Uh, maybe. I have lots of homework and some

other stuff, though, so I'll have to see. Can I let you know later?"

They shared a quick look—always a tag team—and Priam said, "Of course, Daya. Of course. We'll just be waiting in the wings for your grand entrance!" He let out a fluttering laugh at his own joke, and Vicki chimed in with her own tinkling chuckle.

I had to will the judgment off my face. "Cool," I replied, and escaped stage left like a pro.

Even before I had to live with them, I'd grown weary of Priam and Vicki. My dad was weary of them, and I took that as a sign that I should be too.

Priam and Dad immigrated here with my mum from Sri Lanka before I was born, and Priam met Vicki shortly after, when he abandoned the path set out for him in engineering to pursue musical theater. Thatha was pissed about Priam's choice, but because they were brothers, my mum had explained, Thatha had helped support Priam through theater school nonetheless. Dad worked extra-long hours at his engineering job to make sure Priam could live out *his* dream.

Lucky you, Priam.

Before the accident, we mostly saw Priam and Vicki for Sunday night dinners, special occasions, and the odd performance one of them found themselves in. And when I say "odd," I don't mean "occasional." I mean rolling-around-on-the-stage-in-spandex-between-inflatable-palm-trees odd. I remember my dad shifting in his seat during the first half of these performances, then dozing off during the second half. He and I would make fun of these ridiculous shows afterward in the car ride home, while Amma sat quietly in the front seat.

Amma had thought more highly of Priam and Vicki than we did, and I remember overhearing one conversation where she tried to convince my dad that Priam did the right thing by following his passion. It was rare for her to speak up like that, and I'd been surprised. Not that she'd convinced my dad or me, though.

I guess Priam and Vicki had seen how much Dad pushed me toward engineering and science, because they constantly sent Amma websites for fine arts classes and kept inviting us out to various performances. Thatha hated that. And I did too, even though part of me was intrigued by the blurbs Amma read out to me—photography workshops, pottery making, taiko drumming. But my contact with Priam and Vicki was limited because my dad made it so.

Once I asked Thatha if he'd be closer to Uncle Priam if Priam was an engineer too, like my dad was. Thatha had laughed. "Priam doesn't have what it takes to be an engineer. Don't talk nonsense." So whenever my mum asked if I was interested in one of the activities Priam and Vicki had suggested for me, I responded with some version of, "Sounds like nonsense to me."

Sitting through Vicki and Priam's morning soap operas—while truly absurd and awkward—could at least be entertaining once in a while. But sitting through classes was just plain excruciating—the kind of pain I *didn't* invite. I had to remind myself, though, to keep my eyes on the prize: graduate and get the hell out of here. I had my sights on a college in Southern California, where it was warm, skateboarding was still rad, and I could figure out what I wanted to do with my life away from here. Away from anyone who knew my "tragic past." Somewhere no one knew me enough to constantly ask how I was feeling.

So though it was painful, I kept my head down and jumped through enough hoops to get where I needed to go. My reward at the end of each day was an afternoon of hurling myself across the skate park. Something to leave me aching, tired, and bruised.

But I had to get through this afternoon English class first. Fucking English. And poetry today to boot.

"Daya, which line did you like the best?" Ms. Leung asked.

*Hmm . . . the last one? 'Cause it was the end?* "I thought 'following the darkness' was interesting."

"What did you find interesting about it?"

*The words. They were made up of letters.* "The word 'darkness' stuck out to me. Like the speaker was really frustrated or something. Like she just wanted to leave."

"Hmm . . . good observation, Daya. Class, where does the speaker want to go, you think?"

*Anywhere but here*, I thought, slumping back in my seat and squeezing my pencil into the palm of my hand as tightly as I could.

"Your arms are spaghetti, Daya!" Dad's lips made that smack-ing sound they always made when he was irritated with some-thing. "Is spaghetti strong?" he asked as he grabbed my boxing gloves and jiggled my arms around.

"Are we talking cooked or raw?"

He didn't smile. Sometimes he did. Not today. Today I'd made too many mistakes. "Don't be a joker, okay? It won't be funny when your opponent thumps you."

He held up his punch mitts in front of me. "Tummy tight, gloves up. Firm, quick jabs. Intensity, Daya!"

We worked like that for hours—Thatha coaching me, building me up so no one could take me down. Boxing had been his "thing" in Sri Lanka when he was younger. An inter-est passed on by his father. He'd been competitive, too—winning small titles here and there. But when he came here, boxing just became another thing he'd had to give up. When

I'd asked him why he'd quit, he'd made that lip-smacking sound and responded, "What? You think we had all the time in the world when we moved here? When would I box? Before work? After night classes? Don't talk nonsense."

Now that he did have time for a few side interests, he spent that time coaching me. I think it was his way of protecting me. Of making sure I knew how to protect myself.

"Mental toughness," he would tell me, "is vital for physical toughness. You can't play sports without both, and you can't succeed here without both either. If you show them weakness, Daya, they win. You *must* be better. Stronger."

I kept his words in mind each boxing session, each match, every obstacle I faced, trying to show him I could be tough enough for whatever life brought me. And he kept pushing me to be stronger. So a layer of toughness had begun to grow along my skin even before my parents died, although I hadn't been sure if I'd ever been strong enough for my dad. And now I knew I hadn't been. I'd failed both of them, eventually.

But I was tough enough now. That layer along my skin had thickened, a full suit of scarred armor that could withstand anything. And I'd keep testing it to make sure it always would.

## ABOUT THE AUTHOR

Tanya Boteju is an English teacher and writer living on unceded territories of the Musqueam, Squamish, and Tsleil-Waututh First Nations (Vancouver, Canada). She believes feminism, committed educators, sassy students, and hot mugs of tea will save the day. She is also grateful for her patient wife, who builds her many bookshelves while also encouraging her to be social. Tanya may have been a drag king in her well-spent youth and knows that the queer community is full of magic and wonder. With this book, she hopes she's brought some of that magic to those who need it most.

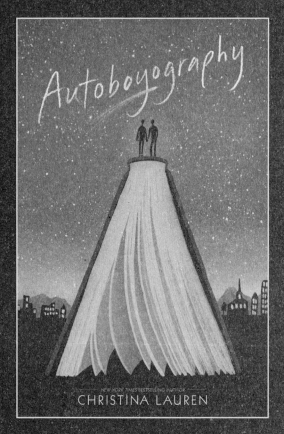

"As sweet and devastating as first love, *Autoboyography* is a masterpiece. . . . I love this book."
—Kiersten White, *New York Times* bestselling author of *And I Darken*

"A hopeful and moving love story."
—*Publishers Weekly*

**W**riting a book in four months sounds simple to Tanner Scott. Four months is an *eternity*.

After all, it only takes Tanner one second to notice Sebastian, his Mormon writing-prodigy class mentor.

And less than a month for Tanner to fall in love with him.

# Transcending stories of life-changing friendship from Benjamin Alire Sáenz

★ "The protagonists and their friends seem so real and earn the audience's loyalty so legitimately that it will be hard for readers to part with them."
—*Publishers Weekly*, starred review, on *He Forgot to Say Goodbye*

★ "Meticulous pacing and finely nuanced characters underpin the author's gift for affecting prose that illuminates the struggles within relationships."
—*Kirkus Reviews*, starred review, on *Aristotle and Dante Discover the Secrets of the Universe*

PRINT AND EBOOK EDITIONS AVAILABLE

From SIMON & SCHUSTER BFYR • TEEN.SimonandSchuster.com